"Romance readers will not be gambling at all in choosing RITA Award–winning Linden's latest as she once again delivers another impeccably executed, witty, and sensual Regency historical."

— BOOKLIST (STARRED REVIEW)

"Intelligently written, strongly characterised and gorgeously romantic . . . Ms. Linden further cements her place as one of the best authors of historical romance writing today."

— ALL ABOUT ROMANCE

"[A] satisfying and romantic ending that won't disappoint fans of this stunning series . . ."

— LIBRARY JOURNAL

ALSO BY CAROLINE LINDEN

DESPERATELY SEEKING DUKE

ABOUT A ROGUE

ABOUT A KISS

A SCOT TO THE HEART

HOW THE SCOT WAS WON

ALL THE DUKE I NEED

THE ULTIMATE EPILOGUE

THE WAGERS OF SIN

MY ONCE AND FUTURE DUKE

AN EARL LIKE YOU

WHEN THE MARQUESS WAS MINE

FORTUNE FAVORS THE VISCOUNT

SCANDALS

LOVE AND OTHER SCANDALS

IT TAKES A SCANDAL

ALL'S FAIR IN LOVE AND SCANDAL

LOVE IN THE TIME OF SCANDAL

A STUDY IN SCANDAL

SIX DEGREES OF SCANDAL

THE SECRET OF MY SEDUCTION

THE TRUTH ABOUT THE DUKE

I LOVE THE EARL

One Night in London

Blame It on Bath

The Way to a Duke's Heart

Reece Trilogy

What a Gentleman Wants

What a Rogue Desires

A Rake's Guide to Seduction

Other Novels

What a Woman Needs

Novellas and Collections

When I Met My Duchess in At the Duke's
Wedding

Map of a Lady's Heart in At the Christmas
Wedding

A Fashionable Affair in Dressed to Kiss

Will You Be My Wi-Fi? in At the Summer
Wedding

Short Stories

A Kiss for Christmas

Like None Other

Written in My Heart

CAROLINE LINDEN

Fortune Favors the Viscount

THE WAGERS OF SIN

This is a work of fiction. Any references to historical events, real people, or real locales are used fictitiously. Other names, characters, places and incidents are the product of the author's imagination, and any resemblance to actual events, locales or persons, living or dead, is entirely coincidental.

FORTUNE FAVORS THE VISCOUNT © 2023 P.F. Belsley

Cover Design © 2023 Erin Dameron-Hill/EDHGraphics

ISBN: 979-8-9862584-3-0

All rights reserved.

*For all the readers who wrote to me, asking for this
story
You are the reason I keep writing*

Fortune Favors the Viscount

CHAPTER ONE

There was little to alarm about the exterior of the Vega Club: an imposing mansion near Piccadilly, seven bays wide and three floors tall of clean gray stone, with pedimented windows and iron railings leading to a broad door painted dark blue. But everyone knew that wickedness and vice raged within.

Emilia Greene peered up at it through the grimy window of the hired hackney, and took another bracing swig from the flask. She replaced the cap with a grimace; no wonder men did stupid things when drinking brandy.

Just the sort of courage you need right now, she reminded herself. She stowed the flask in her reticule and opened the door.

The carriage creaked as the driver turned to look at her stepping down. The sky was overcast, the morning fog muffling the streetlamps that still burned. "Thought you'd changed your mind, miss."

"No." She handed him a coin. "How much for you to wait half an hour?"

He glanced up at the sickly gray sky and sighed heavily. "Three shillings."

Too much. "Never mind, then," she said, pushing aside her misgivings about being marooned at the most notorious gaming hell in London. "Thank you."

He touched his cap as he lifted the reins, and within a minute she was alone.

Emilia faced it again, her own dangerous Rubicon. She considered another sip of brandy, then forced down her nerves and mounted the step.

Early morning, she had been told, was the best time to go. The club closed around dawn, when any lingering patrons had been turned out, and the only people present would be staff, cleaning up after a night of scandal, debauchery, and all manner of cheating and plundering. Or so she assumed; *something* wicked must happen there, to have earned such a reputation.

Once upon a time, her friend Arabella had plotted in excited whispers how they might manage to sneak inside gentlemen's establishments like the Vega Club. They had an air of danger, of licentiousness and tantalizing ruin, of unbearable thrills and excitement. Emilia had played along, more amused than engaged. Of course she'd never sneak into a gaming hell, let alone the most infamous one of all.

No, it turned out she would simply walk up to the door and let herself in.

The entrance hall was as fine as the one at the Willows, with a black and white marble floor and walnut wainscoting. She could see past some towering potted palms into a large salon, where servants swept polished wooden floors and dusted around elegant furnishings. It could have been the aftermath of any society ball. It was much like the great house where she had grown up, and she found that even more disconcerting than if the walls had been covered in black satin and hung with obscene paintings.

How very . . . ordinary. Arabella would be so disappointed.

"Apologies, ma'am, the club is not open." A large burly man appeared from nowhere right in front of her.

Emilia almost leapt out of her skin. "I'm here to see Mr. Dashwood," she said, straightening her shoulders and aiming for a regal, implacable air.

"An appointment is required for that," he said, unperturbed. "Send a note and Mr. Dashwood will fix a time if he wishes to see you."

"Don't be ridiculous." She took a note from her reticule and held it out. The man hesitated, and she fluttered it at him, brows rising. "At once, my good man."

It was the sort of thing Lady Watney would say, imperious and slightly impatient. Emilia had disliked that sharp tone when it was used on her, but she'd always obeyed it. To her relief, this man did the same.

With a frown, he took the note, then hesitated again.

Emilia gave a delicate, slightly exasperated sigh. "Read it if you must, but take it to Mr. Dashwood." She kept her chin up as he unfolded the paper.

The note was a fraud, but a very convincing one. Oliver wouldn't mind that she'd taken liberties with his name; he was the only member of the Vega Club she knew, so she'd had little choice. She only hoped no one would know that Oliver had been rusticating in Aberdeen for the past three months, and couldn't possibly have signed this note.

The large man in front of her shot her an assessing look, as if he weren't fooled, but he merely nodded and said, "Wait here, please," before he disappeared through a concealed door.

Carefully she let out her breath, fighting off any sense of relief. This was only the first hurdle, and the next would be far more difficult. *So make a running start at it*, she told herself. She stepped forward and gently pressed open the door, slipping through it.

It led into a long, narrow antechamber, with three doors. Two were closed but the one at the end was open; the man who'd taken her note leaned in that doorway, arms crossed.

"A right haughty little ladyship," he was saying in disapproval. At the click of the door behind Emilia, he glanced over his shoulder. "If you'll wait, ma'am—"

"I am here to see Mr. Dashwood on an extremely urgent matter," she retorted, still projecting Lady Watney. "And see him I shall."

He turned. He was a big man, tall and broad-chested, and if he meant to throw her over his shoulder and pitch her back into the street, she wouldn't be able to stop him. "No, ma'am. That won't be possible."

"Nonsense," she said crisply. "It will be a very great loss to him if he doesn't hear what I have to tell him."

An even greater loss to her, but she didn't want to think about that, let alone say it.

His face settled into stony lines, and her stomach took a swift drop as she thought he might actually throw her out—until he paused. He glanced into the room behind him, then cast his eyes upward. "As you wish, madam." He stepped to the side, bowing obsequiously and sweeping one arm toward the doorway.

Emilia ignored his tone and hurried into the room before he could change his mind. The big man closed the door behind her with a loud snap.

The room was dominated by a billiard table. Three lamps, suspended above the table, illuminated the green felt surface. A man stood at the far end, his jacket off and shirtsleeves rolled up, holding a cue. His face was impossible to see in the shadows.

"Come in, Miss Greene." His voice was rich and smooth; dry, faintly amused. "Since you insist."

Now Emilia's nerves began to twitch, when she most needed them to remain firm. "Mr. Nicholas Dashwood?"

He bowed his head in acknowledgment. "The very one."

"Thank you for seeing me, sir."

"I wouldn't, normally." He glanced pointedly at the note lying open on the edge of the billiard table, its forged signature just visible. "A delicate and important matter, is it?"

Emilia nodded once. "I have a proposition to make to you."

His shoulders shifted. He leaned down to line up his cue. The light fell across a hard, angular face and cropped hair. His nose had clearly been broken, but his lashes were thick and dark and he was undeniably attractive, if in a dangerous sort of way. "I rarely accept propositions." He took the shot he'd set up, sinking the red ball into the pocket right in front of Emilia.

"You've never received one like this," she told him honestly.

He straightened and began unrolling his sleeves. He was back in shadow, but she still saw his eyes flick downward, moving over her with lightning quickness and hot enough to make her face burn. "Odds are that I have."

She flushed. "It's not *that* sort of proposition. Don't flatter yourself."

He paused, looking at her more keenly. The lamplight caught his face, giving her a good look at him for the first time. His eyes were amber, like a cat's, she thought; glowing golden-brown, vibrant enough to see from across the billiard table. His dark hair was cut short, but not short enough to hide its tendency to curl around his ears. He fastened his cuffs and reached for his jacket, flung over a nearby chair. "Well, that does intrigue. What is it?"

"A business proposition." *Please let this work,* she prayed one last time.

His mouth curled. "No."

She started. "You haven't even heard it!"

"I don't need to." He pulled on his jacket, settling it on his shoulders with a sharp jerk. He smoothed one large hand over his chest, and suddenly looked far more dangerous, in his elegant evening attire, than he had before.

"Please," she said in a rush. "I came here at dawn, specifically to speak to you when the club isn't busy. The least you can do is listen."

"But I don't need any more business dealings." He said it gently, as if speaking to a child. "I don't wish to waste your time."

"It's a cracking good one, my proposition," she

retorted, losing her temper for a moment. "Only an idiot would refuse it."

His face had grown hard as she spoke, but at the last he suddenly grinned. "Indeed? I've been called worse." He regarded her for a moment, then waved one hand toward a door at the back of the room. "Very well. I discuss business in my office."

Head high, heart pounding, she marched through the door and took the seat he indicated. He went around the desk and sat down, leaning back with that trace of amusement still clinging to his face. "Do tell me all about your unrefusable proposition, madam."

She frowned at the way he said the words. "Do you know the name Henry Sidney?"

"He's not a member, if that's what you're asking."

"Of course he's not," she said tartly. "He's been dead for a hundred years."

"Has he really?" He lifted one shoulder. "Then I can hardly know him."

She took a deep breath. This *man*. "With his wife Genevieve, Henry had a son, Thomas, who had a son, and a grandson, and so on and so on."

"How remarkably virile of dear Henry," he said, sounding more than a little derisive. For a moment, Emilia burned to storm out and let the stupid man carry on as he was, a low-class cardsharp.

But she couldn't do that. Damn him. She needed him.

She kept her seat and carried on, her voice growing stern. "But with his *second* wife, Catherine, Henry had another son, William. William of course was a younger son, but he had a son and grandson, too. Do you know the name Samuel Sidney?"

The amusement left his face, snuffed out like a flame. "You'd better go, Miss Greene."

"You do know who *he* is." It was embarrassing how much her confidence soared in that moment. Until that tiny sign that he knew, there had been a sliver of doubt in her mind. If she'd got the wrong man, not only would this interview have been a waste, her entire scheme—desperate as it was— would have turned to dust. "He also called himself Sam Blake and Sidney Blake, I believe."

"He's dead," said her host coldly.

"I know." She rubbed her hands on her knee, her palms damp with sweat inside her gloves. Now her heart was pounding from relief. "It took a devil- ishly long time to sort it all, particularly since he changed his name so many times. But I've got it right, haven't I? He was your father."

"Only," said Mr. Dashwood thinly, after a very long pause that make her think he might deny it after all, "in the most nominal sense."

"That's the only sense that matters." She couldn't stop a smile. "Then you, sir, are the next Viscount Sydenham."

CHAPTER TWO

H e didn't say anything for several minutes. His eyes were hard and opaque, and they gave no clue to his thoughts.

That didn't surprise Emilia. She had expected him to be surprised, shocked, even disbelieving. It had taken a great deal of searching to discover him, and from what she'd learned of his family, Mr. Dashwood probably had no thought of inheriting anything worthwhile. Indeed, she'd had to go all the way back to his three-times-great-grandfather to find his connection to the Sydenham title.

And now she had just told him he would inherit a viscounty. Not just any viscounty, but one nearly three hundred years old with hundreds of acres entailed upon the holder. He likely wouldn't know all that, of course; she would have to explain it to him. She sat quietly, a little giddy in her triumph, waiting for the news to sink in, for him to realize what she'd just told him, for his expression of amazement and gratitude.

His mouth twisted in contempt. "Ballocks."

She started. "I beg your pardon?"

"Rot," he said lazily. "Balderdash. Whatever word you prefer that means *nonsense*."

Emilia bristled. How dare he? Her research was absolutely sound. Perhaps it was fair for him to doubt her, she being a complete stranger, but he didn't have to be so rude about it. She'd just told him he was being elevated to the aristocracy, nothing insulting or demeaning, *how dare he*—

She took a deep breath. It didn't matter if he insulted her. She'd told Arabella that she would strike a bargain with Lucifer himself, and it appeared Fate had been listening. "The last Lord Sydenham died without an heir seven months ago. The title must stay in the family. According to the family records, traced from your great-great-great-grandfather, your lineage makes you the heir presumptive."

He laughed—not in amusement, but in scorn.

She pressed her lips together, clinging tightly to the shreds of her temper. "It's a bewildering process, but I am ready to help you petition the Crown for it. I know the procedure, and can recommend a solicitor who can shepherd your claim through the Committee for Privileges—"

He flicked one hand. "No."

"What?" Her mouth dropped open. "Why wouldn't you want my help?"

"I don't want the title *or* your help." He rose. "We're done, ma'am."

She also jumped to her feet, now in fear. "What do you mean, you don't want it? What sort of fool are you?"

His smile was chilling with indifference. "One who likes his life the way it is. Find another victim,

Miss Greene, and inflict your prim history lessons upon him."

"I can't," she said through her teeth. "There are *rules*. You are the heir with the closest claim. It must be you!"

"You said an heir must petition for the title," he retorted, unmoved. "I refuse to file any such petition. I have a position and a profession that suit me very well, and I see no need to change either."

"All right," she replied, feeling the stirrings of panic—and fury. "But what about the future?"

He shrugged, glancing pointedly at the door.

Emilia rushed on before he could call back his man to drag her out. "Hear me out! You—you may be tolerated by society, at least when they're winning at this club, but that would vanish in the blink of an eye if you should suffer a reverse. Imagine if just one aristocrat lost a fortune at your club and felt he'd been cheated. Imagine if he told everyone in London that you'd rigged the game! Would all your patrons keep playing here?"

He raised his brows in an expression of exaggerated alarm. "Good heavens. Rigged games! Aristocrats losing fortunes! Charges of cheating! How have I never once thought of those things, let alone dealt with them, in all these years of running every sort of card and dice game for the most inveterate gamblers in Europe?" He clapped one hand to his heart in a patently false swoon. "What a marvelous stroke of fortune you've come to inform me about the risks of running a gaming hell. I don't know *how* I've survived without your insightful advice." He dropped the affect and waved one hand at the door. "Go home, Miss Greene."

Why, oh why, must this man be her only hope?

"I am not leaving until you agree to my proposal, Mr. Dashwood."

In the blink of an eye his face changed, becoming still and dangerous. "I have given my answer."

Stubbornly she stayed. "It's not only your position at stake! If there is no viscount, the estates will be put into Holland covers and fall into ruin. The servants have been turned out, even those who've been there for decades and have no place to go. The Sydenham seat in the House of Lords is sitting vacant, when heaven knows Parliament could use a sane, sensible voice—perhaps someone who's seen more of the world than Eton and Cambridge and who might have some care for those less fortunate than himself."

During this he had folded his arms, his expression cynical. "How very noble you make it all sound. Quite unlike the lords who sit in my salons every night, wagering away the fortunes their ancestors built, without regard to servants' wages and Holland covers and certainly not for the less fortunate. What do you want?"

She blinked at the change of subject. "I—I want you to claim your rightful place—"

He snorted. "Ballocks."

Emilia's eyes opened wide in disbelief. That was twice he'd said that. He was being deliberately rude.

Dashwood came around his desk, his sharp gaze never wavering from her. "You didn't mention *your* position, but that's the one you care about most. You think I'm just an uncouth cardsharp—and you're right." To her shock, he gave a roguish wink. "But I didn't get here by being a fool. You haven't come for the sake of the poor servants who will lose their places, nor for the continued glory of the Sydenham family—which does not happen to include you, I notice. No, you said this was a *business* proposal, not a call to moral or patriotic duty." He tilted his head, studying her with a piercing gaze. "You, Miss Emilia Greene, want something, and you've decided I'm your means of getting it. What is it?"

Her throat went dry, and her stomach gave a sickening lurch. "Very well," she said a trifle unsteadily. "I do want something—not for myself but for someone very dear to me." She paused. "The late viscount was not a good steward of his estate."

Mr. Dashwood's lip curled in derision. As if he knew, and had known all along, it would come down to money.

"Lord Sydenham left a daughter, a child of nine. If the estate reverts to the Crown, she will have nothing." And that was the best outcome, compared to the alternatives. It shored up her nerve again. "Yes, Mr. Dashwood," she declared defiantly. "I *do* want you to claim the viscounty of Sydenham. I want you to step into the role and care for the estate and the people who are supported by it, including and most especially this child. There are three entailed properties, from Norfolk to Dorset. You would be master of an impressive domain. It is an old title, with power and respectability that cannot be lost or wagered away."

Unlike the fortune once associated with it. Emilia ignored that and looked him right in the face. "But you need help to get it, and I can supply that. I know where the necessary records are. I have identified a solicitor, practiced and knowledgeable about such things. And finally, I am close to the family. If

I testify to your right to the viscounty, it will persuade people."

"And in return for your inestimable help . . . ?" he prompted, still wearing that mocking smirk.

She took a deep breath. *Persuade him.* She summoned her most appealing smile. "All I ask is for you to help Lucinda. She is your cousin, after all." His brow quirked cynically, and she fought hard to suppress her irritation at that. "Very distantly but still family, and a helpless child to boot."

"How altruistic," he said. "It explains nothing of why *you* are so eager to help me claim something I don't want and don't need."

"I'm her governess. I've been with her for two years now."

His brows went up again. "You must be the most devoted governess in Christendom, to track down a long-lost distant relation and try to bully him into amenability. Ah . . . but you'll lose your place if this child is left with nothing, won't you?"

She would. She could bear that. But Lucy . . . She could not, *would* not abandon Lucy.

At her silence, which he must have mistaken for guilt instead of fierce determination, the dratted man smiled. Not cruelly, but worse—in pity. "Go home, Miss Greene. My answer is no."

Emilia reeled in disbelief. The prestige of the title was supposed to dazzle him. If that failed, she had mentioned the property and power associated with the title. She had tried to prick his conscience about the servants who would be harmed, and the precarious nature of his business. She had even told him of Lucy, whose life depended on him. How could none of those arguments move him, even when she was offering to do all the work and hand him a life of elegance and status? "What about *your* family?" she blurted in desperation.

He stiffened, his expression darkening.

"Being a viscount will make you eminently eligible," she hurried on. She'd done her research; he was not married and had no children. "Almost any woman in Britain would receive you! Your children will have a rank and a preference they never would as commoners, not even with an enormous fortune. Refusing the viscounty may suit *you,* but can you refuse it for all your descendants to come?"

Dashwood said nothing, but Emilia thought it was calculation in his narrowed eyes now.

"You may be accepted by society because this club is popular," she told him, sensing an advantage and pressing it. "It would be nothing to your status as Viscount Sydenham! And while a gaming club could fail and go out of business, a title cannot be taken away. It also casts a halo of sorts over your relations. Before you fling it aside like a cloak you don't want, remember how it can enfold and protect those near you."

At this his jaw tightened. "I've seen that society at close range. They're not eager to welcome an outsider, no matter how gaudy the cloak he wears."

"But when you are a lord, they will have no choice."

He stared at her for a minute, his mouth hard, his eyes shadowed. "There is always a choice."

Emilia realized in horror he was about to reject her proposal once and for all. "Think about it!" She pulled a note from her reticule and held it out to him, then dropped it on his desk when he refused to take it. "Think before you throw away something so rare and valuable. And after you've thought about it"—*when you've come to your senses, stupid man*—"contact me there." Without waiting for his reply, she turned and ran.

NICHOLAS DASHWOOD WATCHED HER GO. Simply dressed, her dark hair in a demure knot and her pelisse primly buttoned, but an attractive woman nonetheless. Her skirt swished very appealingly around her hips as she hurried out the door. If she'd walked past him on the street, his gaze would have followed her—as it did now.

She'd expected him to fall at her feet in gratitude. He'd shocked her, and then deliberately offended her, but she hadn't flinched. She'd argued with him and called him a fool. That one wasn't afraid of anything, he thought, and she was clever, even though she'd clearly been taken off guard by his attitude. She hadn't let it rattle her, but had quickly rallied a stream of logical arguments, and then stormed out before he could turn her down again. Miss Emilia Greene had brass.

He admired that in a woman: intelligence and passion, determination and beauty. He had a noted weakness for that type, in fact, and it had set him horribly off-balance. If she hadn't asked something so outrageous, so *mad,* he might have been charmed enough to give in. When she tilted her head to the side and smiled in that tempting way that brought out a hint of dimple in her cheek, and looked at him as if they were about to become partners in some exhilarating adventure, he'd felt a thrill of true anticipation—which was always dangerous, with a woman.

"Her Mighty Highness is gone." His club manager, Tom Forbes, stood in the doorway again. "Was she trouble?"

Nick's fingers closed around the letter she'd left; he'd unconsciously picked it up. It released a whiff of her scent, and he inhaled before he could stop himself. Something soft and fresh, like spring. "Aren't they all?"

Forbes grunted. "Aye. I'll not allow her in again."

Nick tossed the crumpled paper onto his desk. "No," he said slowly. "That's not necessary. In fact . . ." He hesitated, flattening her note open with one hand. The only thing written in it was *Charles Street, No. 18.*

As the owner of a gaming hell, where large sums of money and property could change hands on the turn of a card, Nick felt it prudent to know his patrons. In a cabinet behind his desk, he kept a file on every member, filled with details of their social positions and fortunes and idiosyncrasies. He paid a small network of servants, merchants, and even a few members of society for the information, and kept it up to date. The more a member wagered, the more attention Nick paid him.

Emilia Greene had just asked him to wager everything he owned—everything he was. And he knew nothing about her.

"Make a file on Emilia Greene," he told Forbes. "She's a friend of Lord Oliver McCorquodale. Start there."

Forbes looked doubtful. "She's applied for membership?"

Nick smiled slightly. Forbes knew he never admitted unmarried women. "No. Do it anyway."

Forbes nodded. "Aye." He closed the door behind him.

Miss Greene presented a conundrum. She offered him—*him*—a viscounty, and claimed she wanted only gratitude in exchange. Nick didn't believe for a moment that she came solely on behalf of a child. She—a governess!—had somehow discovered his father. Old Sam had been a rogue who alienated his own family, but this governess knew three of his aliases. What else had she found out?

Nick hadn't got where he was without learning to sense a trap. There was more to this "business proposal" than she was telling him. Miss Greene might be the bait, luring him in, or she might be trying to spring the trap herself. Either way, he wasn't inclined to fall for it, no matter how fetching or intriguing she was. He ought to have shown her the door—and forcibly bundled her out it—as soon as she said his father's name.

Nick dropped her note into a drawer. In a few days he would know much more about her, and why she was so very keen for him to claim a title. But in the meantime . . .

He wished Emilia Greene to the devil.

CHAPTER THREE

The sky was glowing pale gold when Emilia reached Charles Street. The house was still and quiet, but it had been that way since they came here. Emilia took out her latchkey and let herself in.

"Did you see him?" The eager whisper, so loud in the tomb-like silence, made her jump.

Despite the hour, Lucy sat on the stairs, wearing her dressing gown and slippers. Sir Chester, the large yellow cat, lay beside her, tail flicking lazily. If there had been a full staff, someone would have scolded her and sent her back to bed, but since it was just Emilia, Henry, and Mrs. Watson, here sat Lucy, wriggling with excitement and anticipation.

Emilia mustered a smile. "Lucinda Sidney! Why are you up so early? You'll be falling asleep before dinner."

Lucy grinned. She'd recently lost a front tooth and the gap in her smile made Emilia's heart swell. "I heard you leave. It was still dark out! But then I couldn't go back to sleep. I had to know if you saw him—my cousin."

Emilia's smile faded. She climbed the stairs halfway and sat down next to her charge. "I did."

Lucy's thin face brightened. "You did it! You talked your way into the club and saw him! Oh, Millie, I knew you would do it."

"It wasn't quite like sneaking into Carleton House to see the Prince Regent, you know," she said lightly. "I opened the door and strolled right in. The guards armed with pikestaffs and halberds must have been given the day free."

Lucy giggled. "Will he come to see us? Mr. Dashwood?"

Emilia hesitated, unwilling to disappoint the girl yet. "I don't know, dear. He didn't say."

"I want to be sure to be very clean and neat when he comes," Lucy went on, as if she hadn't spoken. "Papa always said I was grubby, so I shan't take any chances with Mr. Dashwood. Will you help me wash my hair?"

"Of course." Emilia had long since used up her supply of anger and hatred for the late Lord Sydenham. He was dead, and it couldn't happen to a more deserving man.

"And we must ask Mrs. Watson to make cakes again." Lucy's brow furrowed. "May she, Millie? This once, for his visit? I won't eat more than one."

They hadn't had sugar in a fortnight, but Emilia nodded. "The lavender honey cakes, I think."

Those were Lucy's favorite. A dreamy smile settled on her face. "I can't wait to meet him."

"We must be patient," she told the girl, wishing she could be more encouraging. It was her own fault Lucy had pinned all her hopes on Nicholas Dashwood. She ought not to have said anything about him. But the poor child had been so fearful, so anxious about their future, it had been hard not to tell her *something*. Without staff to distract her, she'd clung to Emilia's side until finally Emilia gave in and told the girl what she was doing, searching through all the musty books in her father's study. Now they were joint conspirators in the search for a Sydenham heir. "He's a busy man."

"Yes." Lucy sobered as well. "Will he like me, do you think?"

If he wants to keep his head attached to his neck, thought Emilia. "I'm sure he'll like you much better than he likes me."

"No! Oh, Millie, he couldn't dislike *you*! You're so lovely and clever and kind . . ."

"As are you," Emila returned, wrinkling her nose. "But *you* didn't walk into his club and demand he do this and that, and care for a property in Dorset, where *no one* wants to live—"

Lucy's giggle cut her off. "You wouldn't tell him he has to live in Dorset! That would frighten anyone!"

If they had endured what Lucy had there, it would. "I did not mention Dorset. I thought we'd best wait for that until he's had some of Mrs. Watson's lavender cakes, and is so content he won't care about anything else."

"Of course." Lucy smiled again. It was a miracle she could do that after mention of Dorset.

"But now," said Emilia in mock sternness, "if you're out of bed, you should get dressed, Miss Sidney. And then we must begin anew on French."

Lucy heaved a sigh. "Can't we do dancing? I like dancing so much better."

"Later. After French and sums." Emilia helped her up and they climbed the stairs together.

At the top, Lucy stopped. "Millie," she said hesitantly, "he will come, won't he? And he'll help us?"

"I hope so."

"That's good," said Lucy softly. "Then I will like him." She turned and headed toward her room, the cat trailing along behind her with his tail swishing from side to side. And Emilia could only watch her go, her heart throbbing painfully in her chest.

Mr. Dashwood *would* agree to claim that title, if she had to hound and harass him for the rest of her life.

CHAPTER FOUR

"Here's the report you wanted."

Nick barely glanced at the packet Forbes laid on his desk, focused on rubbing the tight muscles at the back of his neck with both hands. A patron had needed to be escorted out earlier, but he was pickled drunk and in a fighting mood about it. He struck two footmen before Nick could persuade the man to get into a carriage. For his efforts, he'd been thrown against a wall and called a number of rude names, and tomorrow Lord Fitchley would be his usual arrogant self, unapologetic and unashamed. Nick was beginning to regret admitting him to the club.

"Why don't you give him the boot?" asked Forbes, divining Nick's thoughts. "Fitchley's an ass."

"He is," Nick agreed. His shoulder would ache like the devil later. "But he wagers incredible sums of money without blinking an eye."

Forbes grunted. "Is that the new standard for membership?"

"Hardly. It *is* beneficial to our profits, though." Nick cast a weary eye on the packet. "What's this?"

"Miss Emilia Greene." Forbes pronounced her name like a courtier announcing the queen. "The lady who barged in at dawn a week ago bearing a forged note and somehow got an audience on the spot."

"Forged?"

"Lord Oliver McCorquodale has been in Scotland these past two months or more, according to all his household staff."

Nick remembered almost nothing of that note. He wished he could say the same about the woman. "Which means . . . ?"

"The note said it was an urgent matter. Either his lordship wrote that several weeks ago, which doesn't seem very urgent to me, or he didn't write it at all." Forbes smirked. "Miss Greene"—again he pronounced it with airs—"is a friend of his sister, Lady Arabella, though."

Nick glared at his manager. "Close the door behind you."

Forbes grinned. "Aye." He left and closed the door with an impertinent snap that make Nick wince. Fitchley had given him a headache to go with the sore shoulder.

He flipped over the packet and opened it. Forbes's tight handwriting filled three pages, which surprised him. How much was there to report of a governess, even one that bold?

The first page *was* surprising. Miss Greene was actually Miss Greeneborough, niece of the Earl of Harlow. She was the daughter of the earl's deceased younger brother, and around twenty-seven years of age. She'd been educated at a well-respected

academy for young ladies, but through some circumstances Forbes did not illuminate, she'd left her
family and become a governess. Because of her upbringing and education—and despite her attractive-
ness—she was apparently a smashing good one.
She'd been with Lady Helen Fairchild, receiving
some credit for that lady now being Countess Mulworth, and currently had charge of Miss Lucinda
Sidney, aged nine or ten. More or less exactly as she
had told him.

And yet there were two more pages. Nick
flipped to the second with increased interest. What
had Forbes's running boys discovered that required
two additional pages?

Forbes had sensed where the true intrigue lay.
The second page was about the late Viscount
Sydenham, Lucinda's father, dead nearly eight
months now. Arthur Sidney had been a recluse,
surly and rude on the rare occasions he was seen in
society. He had kept mostly to Beaufort Hall in
Dorset, but on his few visits to London, he'd made
quite an impression. He'd been blackballed from
White's and Boodle's clubs. He'd been thrown out
of the Royal Academy summer exhibition after getting into a fistfight with a curator. He'd shoved a
bishop in church, caused a disturbance at the The-
atre Royale, and was widely known to be a hot-tem-
pered, malicious fellow.

In his long history of running card games, Nick
had met every sort of scoundrel and rogue. Each of
them, to a man, had left a trail of unmet promises:
to family, to friends, to neighbors, to superior offi-
cers, to creditors. He knew what was on the third
page before he read it.

Lord Sydenham hadn't just been rude and unlikeable, he'd also been bankrupt. Forbes couldn't learn how deeply in debt he was, but rumors ranged from "skint" to "up the River Tick." His solicitor, Mr. Fitzhugh Bennet, had died suddenly several weeks after the viscount, allegedly leaving his client's affairs in disarray. Servants who'd quit the household complained that they hadn't been paid in two quarters or more. And of course, the man had no direct heir, leaving the estate—whatever there was of it—in limbo.

That explained Miss Greene's desperation to find any cousin at all. Sydenham must have left his daughter in terrible circumstances. It certainly wasn't a unique story, although generally lords were more determined to preserve their estate and fortune than ordinary men. Perhaps Lord Sydenham hadn't cared as much, since he had no son to inherit, and no fortune to leave.

But still: a cracking good governess could find a new post, and the child must have some relations who would take her in. What had made Emilia Greene decide to invade his establishment at dawn and demand that *he* assume the title? Why did she think he'd be any better than the last viscount?

Nick certainly didn't.

With a muttered curse he swept the papers into the file and tossed it into the cabinet. He didn't want to think about Emilia Greene. Not about the way she bobbed up on her toes when she called him an idiot. Not about the way her vivid blue eyes widened in astonishment when he said a rude word. Not about the way her pretty face went pink when he said he'd received many propositions, right before she cut him down to size. He didn't want to think about disappointing her. He didn't want to feel responsible for her.

And yet . . . He couldn't stop thinking about her—and her damned proposal.

Nick didn't like any of it.

He left his office and walked through the club. It was morning now, sunlight streaming through the open windows as the servants cleaned and tidied after another night of profitable gambling. Nick felt the familiar hum of satisfaction in his chest. *This* was his estate, built from a single hazard table in a shabby cellar to the finest club in London. He was someone, a man of means and importance, even without a title.

The thought made him scowl. Never once in his life had he thought about having a title, nor wanted one. Most of the lords who came through his club did not serve to recommend the aristocracy, whether they were pompous winners or sulky losers. But Miss Greene had made him think about other sides of the matter, and he was not pleased by the way it taunted him.

At the back of the dining room he pushed open the baize door and went down to the kitchen. Like the salons upstairs, it was still alive with activity, but on a more relaxed pace than the frenetic rush that began in the afternoon.

The kitchens were one of the Vega Club's prime attractions. While most clubs served dinner, none did it the way Vega's did. Here they served every sort of meal a patron could want, from the time the doors opened until they closed around dawn, and every morsel of it was delicious. The scullery was filled with servants washing dishes, scrubbing pots, and polishing silver from last night's service. The long trestle table in the main kitchen was covered with freshly plucked capons and geese, waiting to be dressed and roasted for hungry diners tonight. Baskets of vegetables and herbs sat on the table under the windows, just delivered. The scent of baking bread perfumed the air. All these signs of industry, prosperity, and luxury filled Nick with fierce pride.

Guillaume, the chef, had his hands in a large mound of dough, but he jerked his head toward a tray on the opposite end of his worktable. "Freshly baked, Monsieur."

He leaned over the plate and inhaled deeply. Guillaume's fresh pastries filled with gooseberry jam, topped with thick clotted cream, were sinfully delicious. Betsy, Guillaume's wife, whisked across the room. "Just a moment, sir, you're early today."

Nick grinned as she laid the pastries in a basket and covered them with a clean cloth. "And hungry. These smell divine."

"'Tis Betsy's gooseberry preserves that make them so." Guillaume winked at his wife.

"I thank you both for the compliments," she said pertly, handing Nick the basket with a curtsy.

He bowed in reply, then went through the narrow corridor outside the kitchen, still cool and dim since the sun hadn't risen high enough to reach the kitchens. He jogged up the stairs in the court-yard and let himself out into the mews, making sure the lock was securely fastened behind him. More than once patrons had tried to sneak into Vega's through the service area, desperate to retrieve something they'd lost at the tables. Nick put a quick end to that, installing tall gates with sturdy locks at every entrance point, and sending imposing employees on frequent tours of the grounds. Gambling might not be an inherently honorable pastime, but when a man lost, he had to pay his debt.

At the end of the mews he turned away from the rumble of Piccadilly Street, toward the quiet, refined heart of Mayfair. He whistled tunelessly as he swung the basket in one hand. This was the best part of his day, every day. Even his headache receded as he walked.

In a quiet little street less than a mile from the club, he turned into a courtyard and let himself in through another gate. The scullery door stood open to admit the fresh morning air, and he walked right in.

The scene was far quieter than at Vega's, although the cook was also kneading bread on the table. At Nick's appearance, she smiled in greeting and curtsied.

"Has breakfast been served already?" he asked, one hand on the swinging door.

"Yes, sir. She's just rung for tea and Nelly took it up," replied Mrs. Barnes, the cook.

Without another word Nick pushed open the door and jogged up the steps, heading for the dining room.

"Nick!"

He laughed as Charlotte ran and flung her arms around his neck. "Good morning to you, too. Have I been neglectful? That was quite an enthusiastic greeting."

She gave him a look of reproach as she resumed her seat and Nick took his, at the head of the table. "You're on time for once. I'm beside myself with astonishment."

"Wait until you see what I've brought." He set his offering on the table. "From Guillaume."

Her dark eyes widened, and Charlotte seized the basket, sticking her nose under the cloth and inhaling deeply. "Guillaume is quite possibly the love of my life."

"I'll tell him you said so."

"Someday I'd like to meet him." Charlotte put a pastry on her plate and handed the basket to Nelly, who busied herself arranging the rest on a platter. "Will you let me come to the club and thank him?"

"No." Nick gave the same answer he always did, but today it came out a little sharply.

"Why not?" she protested. "You allow ladies to be *members*. Why can't I come and see it one day? Don't you think it's one of the best clubs in London?"

"It is the very best, and it's also no place for you." Nick tapped his empty teacup, trying to divert her.

Charlotte frowned at him, but she poured his tea. "What's wrong with me, that I'm not fit to visit the best club in London?"

"Charlotte," he said under his breath, in warning. Every now and then she got her teeth into this subject, and he never liked it. "It is not about you."

Her brows were still drawn together. "Then what is it about?"

"I said no, and that's the end of the matter." He looked at Nelly. "The ham, please."

"You're not being honest with me." Charlotte waved off his offer to serve her a slice of the cold ham on the platter Nelly brought. "And you're in a temper this morning, which spoils all my joy at your punctual arrival."

He gave her an aggrieved look. "You may go," he told Nelly, who curtsied and slipped from the room. "I'm not in a temper." He rotated his sore arm, blatantly soliciting sympathy. "I had to throw out a patron last night and he tossed me against the wall."

She looked at him suspiciously, but her frown softened. "How hard?"

"Violently." He winced—exaggerated for her benefit, but only a little. His shoulder did ache. "I feared it would be out of joint."

"You should put a cold poultice on it."

"I would have been late for breakfast."

Sympathy flooded her face. Charlotte put her hand on his arm. "You silly man. You ought to have gone home and had Pearce look after you."

"But there were fresh pastries," he said, "from Guillaume."

Her lips twitched, then slowly turned into a smile. "You're such a scoundrel, Nicholas Dashwood. Are you even hurt at all?"

"I am!" He started to strip off his jacket. "Let me show you the bruise."

"Stop." She rolled her eyes. "I'm sure it won't keep you from any of your usual habits. And I realize you distracted me from my question, you know."

He only grinned and settled back into his chair.

"Polly invited me to the theater with her family," she said. "May I go?"

The smile froze on his face. "Oh?" He reached for his cup, thinking rapidly. "That was very kind of her."

"Isn't it?" Eagerly she leaned toward him, her

face alight with hope. "Please say yes, Nicky, please."

He looked at her, trying to hide his instinctive response, which was profane and negative. It was such a simple thing, going to the theater. Polly Neale, who lived on the other side of the courtyard, was a good friend to have invited her. Charlotte almost trembled with excitement at the prospect, which made him feel cruel and heartless. Not only had he never taken her to the theater, he didn't want to let her go now.

He let out a sigh, unconsciously shifting his sore shoulder back and forth. Fatigue was catching up to him; he was a creature of the night and it was time for him to go to bed. Instead he had to tell Charlotte *no* again, which would make it difficult to sleep.

Perhaps he should allow it. What could go wrong? "What is the program?" he asked, stalling for time to think.

"Oh! I don't know. Does it matter?"

"Why would you want to see something dreadful?"

Her mouth firmed impatiently. "To see *something, anything* at all, would be lovely! You're going to say no, aren't you?"

"I should." He rubbed his eyes.

Charlotte banged her hands on the table. "Nick! I am not a child anymore. I can't stay locked in this house forever!"

He knew. It was the nagging fear at the back of his mind every day. She was almost fifteen now, and his sister was no longer a child but a lovely girl. Someday all too soon she'd be a beautiful woman, and Nick felt like a doomed man, trying to raise and protect her. God knew he'd seen how vile and evil the world could be, especially to attractive young women of murky history like Charlotte.

Without warning the image of Miss Greene flashed across his mind. If he accepted her offer—mad and far-fetched as it was—he could give his sister the kind of life she wanted and deserved. *Before you fling aside a viscounty, remember how it can enfold and protect those near you . . .*

Bloody hell. He squeezed his eyes shut. He should leave now and get some sleep before he let Charlotte's pleading and Miss Greene's madness lull him into doing something stupid, dangerous, or both.

"Let me speak to Mr. Neale," he said, naming Polly's father.

Charlotte glared at him suspiciously, but her fists uncurled. "Will you do it today? The invitation is for tomorrow evening."

"Yes, I'll do it today."

"Thank you." She beamed at him again, which made Nick feel all the worse. She should not be this excited over a simple trip to the theater.

When he left, he crossed the courtyard and rapped at the Neales' door. The maid showed him into the small front parlor, and a moment later Charles Neale came in, still brushing crumbs from his waistcoat. "Good morning, sir!"

"Neale." Nick nodded in greeting. "I understand you've planned a theater outing."

The man smiled ruefully, obviously knowing exactly what he meant. "Polly wants to, aye. I've told her not to say anything, but she's impulsive—when they get together, those girls do chatter something fierce."

"I know." Nick sighed. He was glad Charlotte had a friend her age, who wanted to invite her shopping and to the theater and probably all sorts of other places. "I'll allow it. Forbes will send James to attend you."

Neale bowed in understanding. "Polly will be so pleased, sir. Thank you, indeed."

Nick nodded once more and left. He saw Charlotte anxiously watching him from her window, so he pasted a wide smile on his face and made a courtly bow in her direction. Her face lit up with joy, and he swore he could hear her little shriek of pleasure.

But the smile faded as he let himself out through the gate. What the devil was he to do now? When he'd brought Charlotte here as a child, it hadn't been hard to keep watch over her. Now she was old enough to go around town without him, and he didn't know how to respond.

Unwillingly he thought once again of Miss Greene. He imagined her blue eyes lighting up with pleasure—and relief?—if he accepted her offer. He imagined himself addressed as *my lord* and admitted to sit in Parliament. That almost made him laugh out loud.

But then he thought of Charlotte, dressed as a viscount's sister, beaming with joy and excitement at being able to attend parties and balls. He pictured her learning all the ladylike manners and skills she so admired. Miss Greene was a governess; she could teach his sister everything she needed to know. Charlotte would adore that. She was as bright and curious as a kitten, but she was growing up very fast . . .

Of course, that made him think of all the terrible things that might happen to her out in London. The way men—like the so-called gentlemen who frequented his club—would look at her. What they would think of her. What some of them might try to do to her. Just thinking about it made his chest tighten and his hands flex. After all Charlotte had been through, he'd kill anyone who tried to hurt her.

Perhaps he *should* take the title, just to avoid being hanged for any future murders he might commit.

Nick exhaled, knowing what he had to do. Letting Charlotte attend the theater with the Neales was only the first step toward admitting he could not guard her every hour of every day for much longer. She deserved better than to be hidden away, safe from harm but also denied a normal, ordinary life.

He reached his own home after a brisk walk. The maid sweeping the front steps moved aside for him, bobbing a curtsy and murmuring, "Good morning, sir."

"Good morning," he answered absently.

He could be a lord.

"Good morning, Mr. Dashwood," his butler greeted him, appearing to take his hat and coat. "Mr. Forbes has sent over the receipts."

He could have a large estate at his command.

"Thank you, Pearce." He took the leather folio that held the accounting from last night at the Vega Club and headed to his study. After his unsettling morning with Charlotte, it would be a relief to escape into the tedium of reconciling ledgers.

And yet. He slumped in the leather chair and rubbed his eyes. *It would be nothing to your status as*

Viscount Sydenham, whispered Emilia Greene's voice in his head. Rubbish—even though she must know, as the granddaughter of an earl. She was from that society. She surely belonged there; she'd be a beauty in silk and jewels . . .

No. He righted his thoughts. He should be thinking of her words, not of *her,* and how her proposed plan would affect Charlotte, not *her.* She was . . . He dropped his head into both hands and groaned. She had intrigued him, and not only with her shocking proposition.

Resigned, he took out a sheet of paper and dashed off a single line. He smiled humorlessly as he sanded and folded it and wrote her direction. The note she'd given him with the information was back at Vega's, tucked into the file of information Forbes had gathered. It was a sign of how doomed he was that he remembered it anyway.

Nick locked away the accounting and rang for Pearce. He was too tired to add up the numbers now; it was better that he get some sleep. When the butler came, Nick gave him the sealed note. "Have this delivered at once."

"Yes, sir. Shall he wait for an answer?"

He knew what the answer would be. "No. Wake me at four."

CHAPTER FIVE

For days Emilia anxiously waited for something from Mr. Dashwood. She tried to hide it from Lucy, because the girl was so convinced he would fall in with the plan that she was already calling him cousin. Emilia certainly had hopes as well, but she also remembered him saying *No* more than once. He might not send word. He might never come. The one man she needed to be avaricious and grasping might turn out to be neither, or perhaps too lazy to be of any use to her, and what would she do then?

But finally his reply arrived. She was dusting the dining room when the rap at the door came, and since Henry was in the kitchen fixing a broken damper and Mrs. Watson was at the market, she answered it herself.

"From Mr. Dashwood, for Miss Greene." The messenger handed over a sealed note.

Her heart leapt into her throat. "Will you wait for a reply?"

"No." He gave her a cocky grin. "Mr. Dashwood says he knows the answer."

He left her gripping the door handle to keep her balance. Dear God. Was he refusing? No, he couldn't . . . he mustn't . . .

She tore open the note. *Call at the Vega Club at half past five this evening to discuss your proposal.* Relief made her knees weak. It wasn't acceptance, but it wasn't refusal, either.

Her first visit to Mr. Dashwood had not gone particularly well. Now she realized she needed every advantage she could scrape, and looking better able to deliver on her promises was one. Her next encounter with him needed to succeed, and to that end, she enlisted Mrs. Watson and Lucy and even Henry.

"The yellow?" She held up the dress over one arm. "Or the blue?"

"The yellow is most fetching," said Mrs. Watson.

"The blue looks best with your eyes," put in Lucy.

"Hmm, yes," said Mrs. Watson doubtfully. "But it's more worn."

"They're both worn." With a sigh she dropped the dresses on her bed and pressed her fingertips to her temples. Which would convey that she knew what she was talking about when it came to the aristocracy?

"What about the black one?" asked Henry from the doorway. "It looks finer."

Emilia flinched. It *was* finer. The black had once been her best and favorite gown, pale pink silk with lace net. When her father died, she'd been persuaded to dye it black for mourning. If she'd known it was the last beautiful dress she'd own for ten years, she wouldn't have done that. "Black! Won't it send the wrong message?"

"Not," said Mrs. Watson thoughtfully, "if you remove the net overdress and add it to the blue. It will add an elegant touch and disguise the worn seams of the blue dress."

Lucy bounced on her chair. "Oh, yes! And I still have that blue silk ribbon that was Mama's, which you may borrow. It would look so lovely in your hair."

Emilia held up the blue gown doubtfully. "That's quite a lot of fuss for one meeting."

"Not if it's an important meeting." Mrs. Watson took the dress from her.

"True." Given how much depended on this meeting, it was foolish to cut any corner. Emilia stifled her qualms and reached for the scissors.

It took hours, but the dress came out better than expected. Mrs. Watson could run a line of stitches faster than anyone Emilia had ever seen, and once sponged and pressed, the blue dress glowed with some of its former luster, even if it was a bit snug. Lucy brushed out her hair as Emilia repaired a hole in her stocking, and by five she was dressed and coiffed, almost as she'd used to do years ago.

"Lovely," said Mrs. Watson with a smile. "How could any fellow refuse you now?"

Emilia smiled grimly. Mr. Dashwood was very much not the usual fellow. "Let us hope."

Henry found her a hackney. They could ill afford it, but Mrs Watson had put her foot down. She'd been aghast when Emilia walked home alone after her first visit to the Vega Club. Henry handed her up, hesitating before closing the door.

"Good luck, miss," he said solemnly.

Emilia gave him a nod more confident than she felt. "Thank you, Henry. I'll do my best."

He grinned, the sunlight glinting on his ginger hair as he bobbed his head. "I know." He closed the door and chirped at the driver, who set off.

She clasped her hands, almost in prayer. Henry, like Mrs. Watson and especially Lucy, was depending on her. She *had* to succeed.

Tonight the Vega Club was lit up like a theater before a performance. The door opened before she could even raise the knocker, in the hand of a young man in footman's livery. Emilia nodded regally to him, trying to act as if she belonged there. The same large fellow who had intercepted her before appeared almost at once. "This way, Miss Greene."

He led her into the large salon beyond the palms and asked her to wait there. She sat on a small sofa and glanced around, interested in spite of herself. How Arabella would marvel at this place. The carpets were thick and luxurious, the walls wainscoted in dark walnut, beneath gleaming chandeliers ablaze with candles. The furniture was light and elegant, and it almost looked like a drawing room, until one noticed the hazard tables and faro boxes. Through a far doorway she spotted white-draped dining tables, and the aroma of roasting beef made her inhale longingly.

It took her a moment to realize Mr. Dashwood was there at the end of the room, deep in conversation with another man in evening clothes, but from the attentive way he listened and nodded, she sensed he was an employee, not a patron.

Mr. Dashwood himself was dressed like a gentleman. His coat and trousers were dark, exquisitely cut and perfectly fitted; his waistcoat was a sultry saffron. As she watched, a quick smile slashed across his face, turning the hard planes of his face dangerously attractive.

Emilia's stomach took a hard lurch. He still looked ruthless, but nonetheless she felt a pull, a visceral sense of fascination. Who was this man?

She was still reeling from it when he turned her way. His smile was gone but those otherworldly eyes were fixed on her, rather like Chester's when he was stalking some prey. She jumped to her feet and groped for her scattered wits, desperate not to be wrong-footed this time.

"So this is what a gaming club looks like," she said as he reached her. She turned her head as if in earnest study, when it was also partly an attempt to dodge his gaze. "I've long wondered."

"Have you?" He was amused, his dark brows arching. "Good evening, Miss Greene."

"Good evening, sir." She bobbed a curtsy. "Thank you for seeing me again. I've brought some notes—"

"Let's have a tour first." Without waiting for her reply, he turned and took a step.

"What?" Her heart leapt into her throat. "No!" Walk through the most notorious club in London? She didn't dare. She had expected to speak to him in his office again.

"No, no, allow me to satisfy your curiosity about the Vega Club. Don't worry, no one will see you," he said over his shoulder, correctly divining the reason for her alarm. Emilia was forced to hustle after him.

"I've come to discuss my proposition, not see the club," she said breathlessly as he led the way through the high-ceilinged salon into a dining room, where perhaps a dozen tables were covered with white linen, silver candlesticks gleaming. The scent here of roast beef and fresh bread was almost aphrodisiacal; she couldn't stop herself from inhaling deeply.

"We serve dinner from six o'clock until four o'clock in the morning," he said. "Not quite anything you want, but close." He took a decanter from a nearby table and poured two glasses of wine. "And we keep an excellent cellar."

She took the glass he held out without thinking, then blushed as his fingers touched hers on the glass. "I didn't come for wine."

"But you might as well have some, now you're here." He sipped his wine and waited until she took a reluctant sip herself.

Oh merciful heavens. It had been an age since she'd had good wine. Her eyes half closed as she took another sip, this time slower, savoring.

Mr. Dashwood was watching, his expression intent. Emilia lowered the glass with a twinge of regret. She wasn't used to drinking, and needed to keep her head clear. "I would like to know your thoughts, sir."

He nodded. "First the tour. This way."

He led her through the dining room and very briefly through the kitchen, which was a whirl of activity and delicious smells. He showed her into what looked like a library, with dark paneling and leather chairs and ranks of freshly ironed newspapers. Upstairs were elegant salons that held tables with bowls set into the center for markers, and rooms that resembled a gentleman's study, scented of pipe tobacco, with shelves full of leather-bound books. He took one out and showed her; it was a listing of private wagers between members.

Emilia tried to hide how impressed she was. The club was elegant and refined, nothing tawdry about it. No wonder it was popular.

He opened yet another door and Emilia stepped into a room of unquestionable luxury. The table was polished mahogany, the chairs upholstered in deep blue damask silk that matched the thick drapes covering the window. No fire burned in the small hearth but the room was still pleasantly warm. Fine crystal sat on the small sideboard. A bucolic landscape in a heavy gold frame was opposite the mirror over the fireplace, lending a genteel air to the room. The only hint this wasn't a lord's private closet was the faro box and stack of dice on the mantel.

He closed the door behind him. "Now," he said, "we can discuss."

CHAPTER SIX

Emilia nodded, her heart racing again. "We could have done that half an hour ago."

"No," he said thoughtfully. "I wanted you to see the Vega Club. So you know what I'd be risking if I fell in with your mad scheme."

Her mouth dropped open in outrage. His mouth curled but he only pulled out a chair courteously.

Emilia sat, trying to gather herself. *Calm, confident, and persistent,* she told herself.

"My scheme is not mad," she said.

"Brandy?"

"Indeed not," she said, sounding like the stuffiest dowager she'd ever heard. She still held her glass of wine. This was not going well. He had put her off-balance and kept her there, when she had plotted so carefully to be more prepared this time.

He poured a glass and set it down in front of her anyway, and took the chair opposite. "Your scheme is delusional."

She breathed deeply. "No, it is very rational. I've brought a summary of the documents I found."

She took them out of her reticule and began spreading the papers on the table. Six months of work, condensed into three short pages. It had taken her hours to decide what to include. "If you would call on me, I can show you the comprehensive records, which demonstrate your right to the title . . ."

"Put it away. I don't care to see your notes."

Emilia closed her mouth, murder burning in her heart. He had a deck of cards in his hands, expertly flipping them from hand to hand as if he hadn't a care in the world. She was half dead from anxiety about this, and he didn't care. He wasn't going to help her, or Lucy. What else could she do? She had wagered *everything* on him . . .

"What do you play?" he asked.

"Whist," she said after a moment. "But only penny stakes."

That curious, seductive half smile crossed his face. "We're far past penny stakes, Miss Greene." The cards jumped between his hands as if they were living creatures performing at his command.

"Believe me, I know," she muttered. And then, before her brain could stop her mouth, she blurted out, "I'll wager I can prove your claim to the title."

Dashwood's brows went up. "Would you?"

Emilia nodded, her face stony. She wished fervently she had any other option besides this man.

"What is your stake?"

She frowned.

"Every wager requires a stake, Miss Greene," he said in a low, taunting voice. "What will you risk?"

She gave a disbelieving laugh. "If I prove it, you'll be a viscount. Isn't that enough for you to win?"

He shook his head, his gaze never straying from her. "I already told you, I don't want that. Here's my wager. If I win, you'll burn every scrap of your evidence. And in exchange," he added at her horrified expression, "I'll give you five thousand pounds for the keeping of the little girl."

Emilia was frozen, mouth open in the beginnings of a furious protest. "What?" was all she managed to croak.

He was mocking her again, damn him, his eyes glittering and his mouth crooked in that devilish smile. "I'm not a monster. If she is indeed my cousin of some degree, I wouldn't like to see her suffer."

Her thoughts were whirling, at once too fast to organize and too slow to instruct her words. "That is deranged," she finally said.

He laughed.

"You would rather give me five thousand pounds than inherit an estate and title." She had to say it aloud before she could believe that's what he truly meant. He was nothing like she had anticipated.

"Far rather."

Emilia pressed one hand to her forehead, dazed. "You're a very odd man, Mr. Dashwood."

He grinned and shuffled the deck, the cards a blur in his fingers.

"If I win," she said slowly, thinking hard, "you'll agree to pursue your claim to the title."

He made a quiet noise of assent. "But I shall need something from you."

She blinked at him. "What could you want from me?"

Too late she realized what she'd said. He realized

at once, of course, and his tawny gaze flashed over her, hot and all-seeing.

"If you win," he said, each word careful and precise, "I'll examine your proof and give strong consideration to pursuing a claim to the title. That is all I can promise, without seeing the documentation," he added as she drew breath. "If it's as sound as you say, you've nothing to worry about."

Suspicious, but unable to argue, she nodded slowly.

"And in return for the monumental inconvenience and disruption to the life I have chosen and built, you will do me . . . a favor."

Her skin flushed hot all over. "What?"

He leaned forward. "It's not *that* sort of favor," he said, softly mocking. "Don't flatter yourself, Miss Greene."

Emilia knew herself to be a terrible, wicked person—not because she had flushed at his request for a favor, but because it had been more from arousal than alarm. Mr. Dashwood was a magnetically attractive man, especially when he was tilting toward her like this, his eyes glowing and his wicked little smile suggesting he knew exactly what sort of wicked things had burst into her mind at the word *favor*—and worse: that she didn't find them repulsive.

Stop it, she told herself frantically. He could have half the women in London, dangerous, gorgeous, and rich as he was. He probably already had. A governess with empty pockets was fooling herself if she thought this man cared a whit about her.

"Thank goodness," she said as stridently as she could. "I'd hate to have to slap your face just as we become allies."

"I daresay there will be more opportunities in the future." He sat back.

"If there are more provocations," she returned. "What is the favor?"

Still smiling in that lazy, confident way, he shook his head. "It's something within your power to grant, and it involves only decent, respectable behavior."

She flexed her fingers in her lap. Her hands had grown stiff from being clenched. "Very well. How shall we decide the wager? We haven't enough players for whist."

"Simple tricks. Aces high, no trumps. Black over red." He sent the cards through one more flying shuffle, then set the deck before her. "Deal," he prompted as she gaped at him. "So you trust that it's fair."

Dear heavens. Was Lucy's life to be decided by a rash wager and Emilia's skill at cards? It had been a long time since she'd played with any care. But perhaps she shouldn't be surprised that a gaming hell owner would leave the direction of his own life to a hand of cards.

Heart thudding, Emilia picked up the cards and dealt them.

"You may lead," he said courteously.

"Do you make all your decisions based on cards?" She played the ten of clubs.

"No." He tossed the queen on top of her card and swept the pair to his side of the table. "Some I leave to the dice."

"Of course," she said dryly, taking his king of diamonds with the king of spades.

"Everything in life is a gamble. I merely embrace it instead of fighting it."

She looked up. "What rubbish. Life is what you choose to make it."

"What is a choice, other than a gamble on a certain course of action?" He tossed his card on top of hers, winning another trick. "You, for example, took a gamble that you could persuade me to fall in with your mad plan."

"It's not mad," she said under her breath.

"It was a risky play. Who knew what sort of man you might have found here, in this den of iniquity and vice?"

Her jaw ached from being clenched so tightly. "I did consider that." She played the jack of spades to win his nine.

"Sorry to disappoint."

"You didn't," she said, laying down the ace of clubs.

He tossed out a two of diamonds. "Thank God. My soul is at peace once more."

Emilia looked up from her cards. They were tied at a pair of tricks each, but she could tell he was toying with her. He'd probably been gambling since before she could count. "What sort of man did I expect?"

"I know my own reputation."

She regarded him. "I didn't."

"Your good friend Lord Oliver McCorquodale must have told you something, before he gave you such a moving introduction." He spoke somberly, seriously, but his eyes gleamed with amusement.

Emilia froze. He knew she'd lied to get in to see him. Slowly she laid down her cards, and picked up the wineglass, still nearly full, and took a sip.

Everything in life is a gamble.

Well, she knew that. She didn't like to call it

gambling—she preferred to think of it as thoughtful, considered decision-making—but she'd taken any number of chances in her life. Some had been forced upon her, but others . . . others she'd deliberately taken. To avoid something worse, to spite someone who deserved it, to follow what her heart told her to do instead of what her head knew was wiser.

The larger the wager, the larger the winnings, she thought, remembering one of her father's favorite phrases, and drank more wine to avoid thinking of the other possible outcome.

"I forged that note," she said. "Oliver is indeed my friend, but he's in Scotland and has no idea I'm here. I wish he *had* been in town, because I would have welcomed his help."

Dashwood said nothing, but one brow quirked slightly as if to say *How unfortunate for me.*

She took another drink. "I suppose you could call that a gamble. Fortunately, it paid off."

"Did it?" His voice was low and even. Faintly threatening, she supposed, but she wasn't unnerved by it now. The wine must be helping.

"Obviously, since it gained me an interview." She gave him a slight smile, the glass swinging easily in her hand. "That turned out to be very important, because it taught me a great deal about you."

"Did it?"

Emilia nodded, feeling rash and reckless. "You say you like your life as it is, but you're intrigued by what might be. You don't want to give in too easily, not to a mere governess—or perhaps you don't wish to be thought a snob like the rest of the aristocracy—but you're asking yourself . . . what if I *were* a lord? What if all these pompous people *did* have to bow to me, and say *yes, my lord* when I speak to them, and allow me into their hallowed halls of power and even—some of them—let me court their daughters? Because a single viscount in possession of a large fortune will be a matrimonial prize, and more than one family will covet his wealth and title enough to disregard any undesirable traits of the man himself. Not flattering, I admit, which is perhaps why you're trying to disdain it." She selected a card from her hand at random and wagged it at him. "But if you hide behind a wager, you can say to the world, 'why, it isn't that I *wanted* the title, it was just how the cards fell. Fate decided for me!'" She tossed the card on the table and drained her wine. By God, that was excellent stuff. "You *want* me to win this wager."

He watched her with glittering eyes. "Is that so?"

Emilia shrugged. "What have you to gain by winning? It would cost you five thousand pounds and, worse, any chance of knowing what I discovered. I *would* burn it all," she added as his mouth flattened. "I'm a woman of my word. But then, you'd never know what I found. I think that would bother you."

"You're wrong," he said.

"Oh, well. Then I'd be wrong." She raised her arms in a dramatic shrug. "*I* know what I found. I suppose if I, a lowly governess with only some stubbornness to her credit, was able to discover it, someone else could, too, but if you truly wish to remain as you are, I would respect your wishes and not tell a soul." She pursed her lips and pressed one fingertip to them as if to silence herself.

He stared at her with such an expression, it

would have made her nervous—if she hadn't been frustrated and desperate and, it must be admitted, a little tipsy. She hadn't eaten in hours and the wine was going rapidly to her head.

"Why do you want so badly for me to be the next viscount?" he finally asked.

She waved one hand and picked up the other glass. Brandy; liquid courage. "It doesn't matter to me who the next viscount is. I don't care a fig for you or for the Sydenham title." She raised the glass in mock salute and drank, before thumping it back on the table. "What I care for, is Lucy. She's almost ten. She loves drawing, and lavender cakes with honey, and a fat yellow cat called Sir Chester Cheddar, and I will never leave her because she has no one else in the world to care for her. It's not her fault her mother died when she was a babe, nor that her father was a monster who didn't die soon enough. She deserves to be safe and loved, and I can't give her that without help.

"So *yes*, Mr. Dashwood. I want you to be the next viscount, because you are the best chance I have to ensure she's provided for. I'd be happy to take your money for the same purpose, but I wouldn't have a legal right to keep her, being a mere governess, and I would forever live in fear that someone would challenge me for her." She jabbed a scolding finger at him. "An orphan child with five thousand pounds would be prey to a great many charlatans and villains. *You* could take custody of her, though, as head of her family. *You* could ensure that she has a safe home, warm clothes, and good food until she's old enough to make a respectable marriage. But only, of course, if luck should lead you that way," she finished a bit bitterly.

His face had gone hard again, and his gaze was blistering. "No such thing as luck," he said thinly. He tossed out a card and Emilia blinked, realized the trick was hers, and took it.

They played the rest of the game in silence, a rapid smack of cards on the table. Emilia didn't even look at her cards until the trick was played; she stared defiantly at the man across from her, whose posture remained lax and easy even though she could tell he was as angry at her as she was at him.

At the end, she looked down and realized with a start that she'd won. Because of the wine, she had to count twice to be certain. As she absorbed that, he got to his feet.

"Oh dear," he said sardonically. "Look how the cards have fallen. I have lost our wager. Fate has decided for me." He went to the door, where he paused. "I'll call on you tomorrow to examine your papers. Early. Mornings are the end of my day, not the beginning."

"Of—of course," she stammered.

Without another word he walked out, leaving her wide-eyed and speechless.

What had she done? She skimmed her fingertips lightly over the cards, hardly daring to believe she'd beaten him, but no—the cards said she had.

She'd won.

Emilia regarded the empty wine and brandy glasses, her head beginning to swim. He was coming tomorrow to see the proof that he was the next Lord Sydenham. It was what she'd wanted, and yet she felt a tremor—partly apprehension, partly anticipation, partly an incipient headache from drinking so much.

And what on earth was the favor he wanted from her?

NICK STALKED THROUGH THE CLUB, his hands clenched and his heart bumping erratically in his chest. That had not gone to plan.

She'd thrown him off from the start, turning up in a form-fitted dress that reflected her eyes, a silver locket shining at her plump décolletage that lured his eye like a beacon. He'd tried to regain the upper hand, only to be upended again by her expression as he showed off his life's work.

He'd thought it would give her some pause in her crusade to make him change his life. She would realize how unsuitable he was for her purposes, beyond all hope of reform. Perhaps she would simply be offended and leap on his offer of five thousand pounds.

Instead Emilia Greene was impressed—even intrigued. Nick saw it, and it sent a thrill through him.

That led him astray in the card game. He couldn't simply tell her no, not when she looked at him with those lightning-blue eyes, her barely-contained breasts swelling above her bodice with every indignant breath she took, so he bargained with himself: show her what a callous cardsharp he really was. She only played whist for penny stakes. She would lose, and retreat in a huff.

Instead she gulped down a glass of his best Madeira, followed by a generous dram of French brandy, and started telling him off directly, so unerringly that he'd lost his mind yet again. There was something dangerous about Emilia Greene in a passion, flushed and reckless as she snatched up the gauntlet he'd tossed down.

Now he was going to call on her tomorrow morning and spend an hour with her leaning over his shoulder, her face next to his, her beautiful bosom almost near enough to taste. She was going to show him what she'd done. She had promised him a favor.

Nick had told Forbes to wait nearby, and his manager materialized within five steps of leaving the private room. "Send her home," he said curtly. "Discreetly. Pay the hackney driver double to keep silent."

Forbes raised a brow but nodded. "You're done with her, then?" Forbes had given him a suspicious look when Nick told him to keep an eye out for the plucky governess. Nick supposed the man questioned his motives, what with Miss Greene having lied to gain her first interview. Or perhaps it was her aristocratic connection. Or the fact that she kept coming back, and that Nick couldn't stop himself from seeing her.

Forbes was probably right to worry about that.

"Dis aliter visum," he said. *The gods decided otherwise.*

Forbes's eyes narrowed; he hated when Nick used Latin.

"For now," he growled, and strode away.

CHAPTER SEVEN

His night did not improve from there.
Louis found him at the hazard tables around midnight. "A word, sir?"

"Go on."

Louis lowered his voice. "A member is questioning the odds. What ought I to tell him?"

Nick took his time answering. Louis was one of his newer employees, a tall, handsome young man with a charming manner. He'd applied for a post as a croupier, but had proved himself so knowledgeable about horses and racing that Nick had put him in charge of the turf book, where members could place their bets on the races. "What does he want?"

"It's not so much that he wants better odds, sir, as that he's scoffing at the ones set."

Nick's brow rose. "He wants worse odds?"

Louis hesitated. "Seems so."

"He's got some hedge in mind, I suppose."

"Likely, though he's not tipping it to me. But many of the members look to him about the races, and I suspect he's stirring up discontent with how the odds are fixed."

Nick's mouth thinned. Those odds were set after advice from a closely-held network of jockeys and stable masters at the racetracks. Members were free to make bets between themselves at any odds they liked, but if they wanted to wager against Vega's, they had to accept Vega's odds. "Who?"

"Baron Fitchley, sir."

He sighed. That blighter again. "Is he correct?"

"Not a bit," said Louis promptly. "Though he is uncanny at the races."

"Oh?"

"He's up nearly eight thousand this year, after some brilliant luck at Newmarket."

Nick nodded. "Invite him to take his wagers elsewhere, if he finds the odds at Vega's not to his liking—*all* his wagers, mind you." Vega's had two rules for members: hold your tongue, and pay your debts. The latter covered any wager entered in the turf book, and violating it would see a member expelled.

Louis grinned. "Right, sir."

Forbes came up as Louis strode away. "Trouble?"

Nick's gaze swept across the room again. "A baron with a taste for the turf disagrees with our odds, and believes that is enough to make us change them."

The manager grunted as they began walking. "All the intelligence gets bred out of these swells."

Once upon a time Forbes had been head footman in an earl's household, primed to become a butler. He knew every intricate rule and nicety valued by the aristocracy. But then he'd been dismissed from his post—unjustly, from what Nick could see—and it had soured his mind against the whole class. He didn't like them, but he knew them, and that was why Nick had hired him.

For a moment Nick wondered how Forbes would react if he knew Emilia Greene's true mission. If he knew that she'd dangled not herself, as Forbes clearly suspected, but a title in front of Nick. Would Forbes stand by him still, or turn on him?

"They would be the last to admit it," was all he said. "But keep an eye on Fitchley, will you? I believe he's testing Louis, and Vega's, to see what he can get away with."

"Right. Anything else?"

Nick paused in the doorway of the main salon. The hazard tables were behind him now. Card tables were arranged through the rest of the room, just far enough apart to permit some pretense of privacy. Strategically placed potted trees offered a bit more. But from this vantage point, one could in fact see the whole room. This was his world, his kingdom, where he was lord and master and no one could ever tell him he didn't belong. He had worked for over fifteen years to be standing here surveying it.

For the first time he wondered if he wanted more.

"That's all," he said, and resumed his rounds.

A dispute broke out over one of the faro tables, and Nick had to suggest the two gentlemen take their quarrel elsewhere if they wished to retain their memberships. Someone drank too much wine after losing a large sum and cast up his dinner along with all the wine on the hearth in the dining room. Two young bucks got impertinent with Lady Rotherwood, and Nick had to send them away, and then listen to Her Ladyship's indignant tirade on what crass good-for-nothings the men of Britain were becoming.

By morning he should have been exhausted. Normally he would take breakfast with Charlotte, then get some sleep and have a soak in a hot bath, or an invigorating ride on Primrose Hill, before another evening at the club. But today he had promised to call upon Miss Greene and see her alleged proof, and he wasn't remotely tired.

He went to the kitchens, where Guillaume had just set out a tray of strawberry tarts. Impulsively he took one and bit into it, still warm from the oven and sticky with jam.

"I'll wrap these in a trice, sir," said Betsy, spreading a fresh cloth in a basket.

"Divide them," he told her. "Have Rudy take half to Queen's Court. I'll take the other half."

"Very well," she said with a flicker of surprise, reaching for another basket.

He took his basket and left. There would be speculation about where he was going, if not to Queen's Court. Nick told no one about his personal life, but Forbes had once told him people believed he kept a mistress in Queen's Court. Nick did nothing to discourage this rumor. He didn't care what people thought, and it kept Charlotte shielded from his world.

It was a much longer walk to Charles Street. The house was narrower than its neighbors and its brickwork was in sore need of repair. He climbed the single step and rapped at the knocker. The door flew open almost immediately. "Good morning, sir!"

In the morning light Miss Greene was fresh and lovely, wearing a yellow dress that made her eyes brighter. A wisp of dark hair fell loose beside her cheek, tantalizing. Arm still upraised, Nick felt that premonition of alarm again, louder this time. There was an air of determination about her that hadn't been there the previous evening. Miss Greene's confidence was up.

"Please come in," she added with a bright smile. "We've been expecting you."

We? Silently he stepped into the house.

"I hope you don't mind joining us for breakfast," she said as Nick took off his hat and gloves. "I meant to get up early but there was so much to do. This way." Beckoning him to follow, she led the way down a corridor so narrow, he didn't think two people could pass in it. The dining room was similarly small, and dark to boot. But the girl standing beside the table caught his attention.

"Good morning, sir." She gave a careful curtsy.

"Good morning." He bowed.

A gap-toothed grin flashed across her face for a moment before she assumed a more reserved expression. She was small for her age; Nick would have guessed she was seven or eight, but Miss Greene had said she was nearly ten. She was pale and thin, with a dull red birthmark on her left cheek. Her light brown hair was neatly combed and braided, and her large brown eyes shone at him with interest.

"May I present Miss Lucinda Sidney," said Miss Greene. "Lucy, this is Mr. Dashwood."

"A pleasure to make your acquaintance," said Nick gravely.

"Welcome, sir." The girl gave him a very proper nod and pulled out a chair. Miss Greene followed suit, and with a small start Nick realized they meant for him to take the chair at the table's head.

He cleared his throat. "How kind to invite me to take breakfast with you. I've brought a contribution." He set his basket of pastries on the table.

"How thoughtful! Thank you, sir. Let me fetch a plate." Miss Greene was out the door before he could stop her.

"What did you bring?" asked Lucinda softly. Her wide eyes hadn't strayed from the basket on the table.

"Tarts with strawberry jam."

She inhaled so loudly, he thought she must be trying to inhale them. "Thank you, sir, *thank* you."

Miss Greene whisked back in with a chipped platter in hand. "Here we are," she said breathlessly, laying aside the cloth. Nick caught the brief blaze of pleasure in her face as she set the tarts on the plate. "What a fine breakfast we shall have today!"

Grimly Nick took his seat. He'd known they were in straitened circumstances, and now he was faced with the evidence: the sparsely set table, the mended tablecloth, no servants, the small, dark house. Miss Greene poured them both coffee, but from the way she breathed in the aroma from her own cup, he suspected the coffee was for his benefit, a luxury in a household without many of them.

But it was hunger in the little girl's eyes, and he didn't like that. It reminded him too much of Charlotte's face when he'd finally found her.

He expected Miss Greene to defer the serious conversation until later, when Lucinda was out of the room, but he was wrong. Within minutes, she brought up that very topic.

"I've gathered all the documents in the drawing room," she said. "There are quite a few. I hope you've the whole morning free."

Free, if he didn't need sleep. Nick felt strangely alert at the moment, but knew it would fade. "I don't intend to query every word of them, Miss Greene. If I'm satisfied with my initial review, I'll send them to my solicitor to investigate."

Her spine stiffened. "I've not agreed to that!"

Nick just sipped his coffee and watched her.

She flushed and lowered her gaze. "Naturally, I understand you will want a solicitor's opinion."

"Our proof is un—unpeachable, isn't it, Millie?" piped up Lucinda. She was eating her tart in tiny bites and had scarlet jam on her chin. "Miss Greene," she quickly corrected.

Millie. Emilia. He rolled the name around in his mind, liking it too much.

"Of course it is." All pique vanished from her voice as she smiled at the child. "You know how carefully we gathered it."

Lucinda's smile was wide with relief. "Of course it is," she echoed quietly. She gave Nick a little nod that again put him in mind of Charlotte as a girl, which unsettled him. He did not want to see his sister in this child.

"How do you like London?" he asked, striving for a neutral topic.

Her gaze darted anxiously to Miss Greene. "Tolerably, sir."

"Oh? Do you prefer the country?"

This time her glance at Miss Greene was almost frightened. "Not much," she whispered.

"Have you lived here all your life, Mr. Dashwood?" broke in Miss Greene, determinedly pleasant.

Nick's lip curled. "No. I thought you would know that."

"Another few days and I might have discovered it," was her smart reply. "We have only discovered your origins thus far."

And not even the full truth about those, thanks be to God, Nick thought. "Have you," he said mildly.

"Yes, sir," said Lucinda—surprising Nick yet again. "Your father came from Liverpool. He was a ship captain. You own a gentleman's club in London. You haven't got a wife or children . . ." She hesitated. "As far as anyone knows."

He couldn't resist a startled laugh as Miss Greene gasped. "Nor have I got a secret wife or children."

"Lucinda," said her governess. "That was impertinent."

The girl turned pleading eyes on her. "He's my cousin. May I not hope to know him a little?"

Nick's brows went up. Miss Greene seemed nonplussed. She shot a hesitant look at him, then glanced away the moment their eyes met.

After that they ate in silence. Lucinda seemed absorbed in not missing a single crumb of her tart, and Nick saw how she furtively took a second when Miss Greene wasn't looking.

When breakfast was over, Miss Greene rose. "I know you're a busy man, Mr. Dashwood, so shall we get to business?"

"Yes." He followed, not surprised when Lucinda slid from her chair and came as well.

The drawing room was above the dining room, just as small but with better light. The sofa was threadbare, the chairs mismatched, but it was the tables that caught his attention. Four—no, five, Nick counted, arranged at angles near the front windows that overlooked Charles Street. One looked to be a lady's dressing table. Every inch of their surfaces was covered with books and neatly stacked papers.

"Where would you like to start?" She laid her hand on the back of a chair pulled up to the center table.

He stared. She hadn't been lying when she called it voluminous. He'd pictured a bundle of papers, when she had enough to fill a hay-wain. For the first time he wondered if she really did have proof. Until this moment, he would have wagered it would come to nothing in the end.

"At the beginning." He took the chair she indicated. She pulled up one next to his, and Lucinda stationed herself on her far side.

CHAPTER EIGHT

Emilia had been striving toward this moment for months, and yet her hands shook with nerves as Mr. Dashwood sat down. What if she'd gone wrong somewhere? What if she'd missed something? She had this one chance to persuade him, and if she failed—

Beside her, Lucy whispered, "Start with the Bible, Millie," and it jarred her out of her panic.

"Of course," she whispered back. "Thank you."

The Sidney family Bible was rather large. Mrs. Gregson, Lucy's former nursemaid at Beaufort Hall, had once told her it was over two hundred years old, and had recorded the family since the first viscount received his coronet. That helpful bit of information had aided her search tremendously, when the crisis came.

She opened the cover gently, the aged leather giving a creak. "This is the family record of the Sidney family back to the time of King James," she said. "Here is the first viscount, William Sidney." She pointed to the spidery writing, barely legible on the thick old paper. "It's difficult to read but you can make out his marriage record here, and his children here."

She turned the pages. "Here we have the fourth viscount, Henry Sidney. His first marriage was to Genevieve Robart. The parish register from Dorset confirms it. Here is their son, Thomas. But here—" She moved her finger. "Here is his second marriage, to Catherine Clement after Genevieve died."

"Would that he'd remained a widower," he muttered.

Emilia's mouth firmed. "His five-year-old son needed a mother." She was very conscious of Lucy standing silently beside her. "There are three unnamed infants from this time buried in the family plot. I suppose Genevieve died doing her duty."

He merely grunted.

She went on, pointing out Henry Sidney's son by Catherine: William Henry. His birth, marriage, and death were recorded in the Bible as well, but nothing else. It was Thomas Sidney's lineage the Bible enshrined, all the way down to Arthur Sidney and his only child, Lucinda Mary.

"William remained in Dorset near the family home." She put aside the Bible and reached for the parish register she'd covertly borrowed when the elderly rector left her alone with it. This was another reason she wasn't anxious to hand over her research. It was probably a sin to take the register from a church, even though she had every intention of giving it back. "He went into the church, and had a very prosperous living near Bournemouth. He had a large family, several daughters and one son, George. George went into the navy and became a captain." She glanced at him. "Perhaps that's how your father chose his vocation."

He scowled at the register. "I didn't come to hear speculation."

"All right," she said in a mingled surprise and offense. She was only trying to make this more interesting, since he looked grim and displeased. She and Lucy had whiled away long, tense hours wondering about the people they uncovered in the records and making up exciting histories for them.

"I located records at the Naval Office listing his postings. I was able to discover him in the parish register at Plymouth, where his marriage was recorded." She spread out the letters from the vicar there, attesting to it. "By a stroke of good fortune, his first two children were also baptized there, a son named Percy and a daughter, Martha. Percy Sidney also went into the navy, rising as high as lieutenant. He wed Mary Blake, daughter of a Liverpool merchant. And their son Samuel—"

"Yes," he said shortly. "I know the rest."

She hesitated. There was more proof, reams of it, painstakingly coaxed out of elderly servants and parish vicars and former sailors and gossipy relations. She hadn't wanted anything left to chance. "Then do you believe you're the heir?" she asked cautiously.

Mr. Dashwood leaned back in his chair and ran one hand over his face. "I allow that it's possible."

"It's more than possible, it is the truth!" she exclaimed. "There is no male heir from the main Sidney line. From William Henry on, there is a scarcity of sons, yielding fewer branches of the family to investigate. You are next in line."

For a moment he sat in silence. "Miss Sidney," he said abruptly, "might I have a moment alone with Miss Greene?"

Lucy's eyes grew anxious, and she looked at Emilia. "Go on, dear," she said, trying to be as comforting as possible. "I'm sure it's some very tedious question that would put you to sleep."

"It absolutely is," put in Mr. Dashwood. "Horridly tedious."

A hesitant smile flickered across the girl's face. "Yes, Miss Greene. May I come back later?"

Emilia had no idea what he was about to say. "If I send for you. For now, you have your sampler to stitch."

The girl's sour expression almost made her smile. Lucy left, dragging her feet, and closed the door behind her. "I'm sorry," she said before she could stop herself. "I know I ought not to allow her such impertinence—"

"I don't mind." He gave an absent flick of one hand, staring moodily at the paperwork.

"Are you persuaded?" she asked tentatively.

He turned his brooding gaze on her. He still wore his elegant evening clothes. Now she could see fine copper embroidery on his saffron waistcoat, which suited his tanned skin. His face was all sculpted angles, his brows thick black slashes above his eyes. "Why did you come to me?"

She flushed, realizing she'd been staring. "Birth, marriage, and death records led me," she replied. "As you see."

He made a doubting sound in his throat. "Why was it left to you to scour birth, marriage, and death records in the first place?"

"I told you. Lord Sydenham died without an heir, which left Lucinda with nothing."

"No provision in her father's will?"

Oh no. The will. Emilia took a deep breath.

"When we located his will, it stated she would have seven thousand pounds from her mother's dowry, but the funds were missing. Somehow Lord Sydenham found a way to get at them, and he spent it—with, I suspect, the help of his corrupt attorney, who skimmed off a piece for himself."

"Her own father stole her inheritance?" His brows drew together.

Emilia nodded. "He was that sort of man."

"Fitzhugh Bennet died very soon after Sydenham," remarked Mr. Dashwood.

She looked at him in surprise. How did he know about the attorney? "He did. I—I believe he took his own life. There was a large sum missing from the estate accounts, which were in a shambles. Lord Sydenham was . . . not a careful steward. I suspect he either didn't know or didn't care that Mr. Bennet was stealing from him, so long as Mr. Bennet helped him get at Lucy's money."

"Thieves don't usually like to be stolen from."

Emilia gave a bitter sigh. "I don't know what went on. Mr. Bennet was the one who related the terms of the will to us. He smiled so kindly at Lucy, when he'd been stealing her inheritance—" She stopped, choking with anger again. *Everyone* had failed Lucy. Emilia was determined not to do the same.

"Why do you believe he killed himself?"

Emilia flushed. "Henry, our manservant, heard he'd died of a bullet to his brain, alone in his office."

His eyebrows shot up. "Well. That is persuasive."

She moved to the edge of her seat, ready to plead. "The estate has been mismanaged, but it's large, and could be made productive again. The title

is old and respectable, despite the late Lord Sydenham's . . . eccentricities. Without an heir, everything
will revert to the Crown. But it is rightfully yours."

He rested his elbows on his knees, hanging his
head. His long fingers dug into the back of his neck.
"How did you find me? I know I'm not in any
Sidney records," he said without looking up, as
Emilia drew breath. "There must be a dozen other
twigs off the family tree who would make more acceptable heirs."

"No," she said firmly. "There are not. No other
male cousins. I looked. All I found was your
father."

"My father," he muttered. "He wasn't the sort
anyone would leave an estate to."

"That doesn't matter!" she burst out. "The
rules don't demand an heir be respectable or sensible or even sane. It only matters that he's legitimate."

"And how did you leap from the Sidney family
Bible to me?"

"I didn't find much of your father," she said honestly. "I located a man who'd sailed with him, and he
told me your father had married in the West Indies. He
remembered a son who had sailed with Captain
Sidney as a boy before going to live with family in England. So I looked for his siblings and found Heloise,
who married a man named Josiah Dashwood. One of
her former servants said Mrs. Dashwood had taken in
her nephew, a boy called Nicholas." She stopped, remembering what else the servant had said about
Nicholas Dashwood: that even as a boy he'd been im-
pervious to all his aunt's gentle teachings. She ought to
have given that more attention.

His shoulders tensed. "There must be someone else."

"No one nearer than you."

Now he looked up, expression hard. "So there *is* someone who might lodge a competing claim?"

"That's not the point," she said in frustration. "It's not a lottery where anyone who purchases a ticket could be chosen. There are strict rules dictating the matter!"

"That's not what I asked." He was out of his chair, looming over her, his voice ominously low. "I have some idea what would be required to pursue this. I also know that my appearance as heir will not be welcomed by many people in London, if any. They will try, mightily, to reject it. Don't pretend otherwise," he added as Emilia drew breath to respond. "You of all people should know how coldly they can shut out someone who doesn't fit their mold."

Her mouth fell open. He knew about *her*—her family, her history. How? "Have you got some terrible secret in your past?"

"I have no stomach for a public brawl over this title," he said, ignoring her question. "I've already told you, I don't even want it. Is there any other possible heir?"

"No!" she exclaimed, jumping to her feet. "I *looked*. Assiduously!"

His eyes narrowed. He leaned toward her, his chest rising as if he would speak. Emilia stood straighter and folded her arms, meeting his gaze defiantly. They were almost nose to nose. She could smell his soap and see the flecks of dark brown in his eyes.

And the way his mouth eased from a hard line to a more sensuous one.

And the way his throat worked.

Emilia blinked rapidly, trying to keep her eyes fixed on some uninteresting part of him. Her gaze skipped over broad shoulders, strong hands, crisp dark hair, square jaw . . . She closed her eyes in defeat and thought of Lucy. She was doing this for Lucy, and no one else.

"You knew I wasn't a gentleman," he said at last. "You would have preferred someone else. You don't even care who holds the title."

"No, I don't," she said stubbornly. "You're as suitable as anyone. All I want—"

"Is someone to provide for Lucinda, yes," he finished for her. Then he frowned. "Surely her father chose a guardian for her."

Emilia tried to hide it, but she was sure he saw her flinch.

"He did. Who is it?"

Oh no. She'd hoped he wouldn't think of that.

"You mentioned the will," he went on as she stood, paralyzed and mute. "If her father left a will and made a bequest to her, he must also have named a guardian for her."

She swallowed hard and tried to calm her breathing. "Well—he did—but not a suitable person—"

"Miss Greene." If she'd thought he was annoyed at her before, now he was angry. Furiously angry, and all the more intimidating for being icily calm. "If your sole desire is to see Lucinda provided for, that is the man you should seek. It is his right, and his obligation, to care for her."

Emilia cracked first. She looked away, gripping

her elbows so hard her fingernails dug into her arms. "I cannot appeal to him," she said stiffly.

"Why not?"

She set her jaw. "I don't think he even remembers he *is* her guardian. He hasn't contacted us once since Sydenham's death."

Thank the merciful heavens, she added silently.

For a moment he stared at her. "And because of that, you decided to badger a complete stranger into becoming her new guardian. Are you mad?" He exhaled and turned toward the door. "We're done, Miss Greene."

Emilia clenched her jaw and squeezed her eyes shut, but the sound of his footsteps, loud on the uncarpeted floor, jarred her out of it. "Wait. Wait!" she cried, swinging around and running after him. Dashwood stopped, his hand on the door.

"Her guardian doesn't care for her," she said, breathing hard. "He doesn't even know her."

"That doesn't matter," he replied, flinging back her own words. "The rules don't demand that a guardian be loving or kind or that he have your approval. Her father named that man, and that is whom the courts will favor, over me or anyone else who petitions for her custody. You must know it."

"He's unfit," she pleaded, trying to keep her voice down. She wouldn't put it past Lucy to linger outside the room and listen at the door. "If it were merely my pride at stake, I would have set it aside and gone to him at once, I swear to you. If I thought him a reasonable man, I would have applied to him, or even taken her to him. But . . ." She took a deep breath. "He's not."

"Who is he?"

Her hands were clenched so tightly she was shaking. "Baron Fitchley."

She didn't doubt he would know the name. Fitchley was notorious in most of London. Arabella said the baron was barely received, to which Oliver always muttered that there was good reason for that. And Emilia had her own reasons for hating the baron. There was no way she was letting that terrible man have Lucy.

Mr. Dashwood stared at her. "Emmett Fitchley?"

"Yes."

"Fitchley is her guardian?" he repeated in disbelief. He pushed his fingers into his hair, ruffling the crisp waves. *"Fitchley."*

Emilia's heart boomed in terror. Oh, this might go from bad to dreadful if he were somehow a friend of Fitchley's, after she had just called Fitchley unreasonable and unfit. And even worse—he might alert Fitchley about Lucy. "Do—do you know him?"

Against her will, Emilia pictured Fitchley walking through the door downstairs, a vindictive smile on his face, his cold eyes settling on Lucy. She pictured him taking Lucy away—not out of friendship for Lucy's father, not because he cared for Lucy, but because he could. She couldn't even imagine how frightened Lucy would be if that happened. And Emilia would be powerless to stop him, because Fitchley had every right to do it under the law.

Mr. Dashwood pinched the bridge of his nose and said nothing for a long moment. "I'll send my solicitor to examine these papers."

Emilia's hands spasmed around folds of her

skirt as a fearsome thrill of hope shot through her. "Of course." She wet her lips. "Have we a bargain, then? The one you proposed last night?"

He looked at her for a long moment. There was no longer anger or impatience in it. He looked . . . resigned. Weary. But then, he'd been awake all night. Morning was the end of his day. "You agree to honor those terms?"

Slowly she nodded. "What is the favor you want of me?" she asked hesitantly.

A humorless smile flickered over his face. "I'll explain that soon."

"Then you believe me?" She hardly dared breathe. Who cared what the favor was, if he would save Lucy from Fitchley? "You find my evidence persuasive?"

He opened the door, then paused. His golden gaze fastened on her once more. "Damnably so. You may expect my solicitor, Thomas Grantham. Good day, Miss Greene."

He was out of the room and down the stairs before she recovered enough to go after him. There was no response to her hastily called thanks, just the firm thud of the front door closing below. Still dazed, Emilia braced her hands against the drawing room doorway.

Footsteps on the stairs made her look up. Lucy was creeping down, wary but eager. "Did you answer his question, Millie?" she whispered.

This time her smile was real. "Yes, Lucy, I did," she said softly. "And I believe he's beginning to agree that we're right."

CHAPTER NINE

Against his better judgment, Nick began to set things in motion.

He sent for Grantham, who turned up at the Vega Club that evening. Even explaining it aloud made Nick feel foolish; who did he think he was, expecting to become a viscount? Grantham listened in silence, nodding once or twice and asking a few questions, but never once bursting into laughter or casting doubt on the whole idea.

Finally Nick had to ask. "Could this actually be true?"

"It sounds perfectly possible. You're a legitimate descendant of the family. There may be others, but Miss Greene claims to have done her diligence on that score." Grantham raised one brow. "Don't you want it to be true?"

"It's too incredible," he muttered.

"Not really," countered his solicitor. "The rules of descent are fairly rigid. If the heir turns out to be an illiterate cobbler from Wapping, he has the right to be invested."

"No one in Parliament will want me sitting beside him."

Grantham folded his arms and rested one hip against the billiard table. "I suppose someone could lodge a protest and try to persuade the Crown not to confer the title. But if Miss Greene is correct, and there's no more direct heir, that would be difficult. The estate would fall into abeyance. It couldn't be granted until someone else filed a better, more substantiated claim. You could file a suit in that event—"

"God, no." Nick dropped his cue stick on the billiard table and paced restlessly. "If I do this, the initial petition must be so convincing, so solid, there won't be half an inch of ground left to contest it. She says she's got proof, but she's blinded by her devotion to the little girl."

"Did it not look reliable to you?"

"It did," Nick had to admit. Everything she'd showed him had the ring of truth. It didn't account for the chance that she'd missed something, though.

"I assure you, I shall investigate everything in minute detail."

"Everything, including any unintended consequences or unforeseen complications. And I don't want one word of this getting out," Nick went on. "I expect more than your usual discretion, Grantham."

The other man nodded. "Of course. I'll apprise you of my progress."

"Do that."

Grantham left and Nick went to make his rounds. He spotted Forbes at the back of the salon, where the tables were larger and the stakes higher, and headed there.

"Lord Fitchley is stirring up trouble again," Forbes told him. "He made a very rude insinuation about Lady Alleyn and almost came to blows with one of the lady's companions."

Nick said a curse on that man's name. "Offer Lady Alleyn and her companions the use of a private room and send Mr. Carter to attend them." The baroness was one of his favorite members, an older widowed lady with immense sangfroid. She had a ribald sense of humor and a keen eye for the ridiculous, and she never caviled at losing. Would that more men were like her. "Lord Fitchley cannot seem to remember his manners."

Forbes sighed. "No. Louis deterred him, but he's gone to the dining room and ordered a great quantity of drink. He's restive tonight."

Nick stifled the thought that his patience with Fitchley had ebbed significantly since hearing Miss Greene say his name. The thought of her having to beg Fitchley for anything roused all manner of dark thoughts in his head, none of which he wanted to examine closely.

"I'll speak to him," he said. "By the bye, I shall be late coming in tomorrow night."

He sensed Forbes's start of surprise. "Very good," was all the man said, though.

Nick had missed nights before, but not many. He'd been at the Vega Club when he was ill, when he was broke, even on the night he'd finally got word of Charlotte. The club was his everything, the precious jewel he guarded like a jealous dragon. He trusted Forbes and his other employees, but Vega's was not theirs. Nobody cared for it like he did, nor needed it like he did. Just the thought of walking away from it, even for one night, made him irritable.

The perfect mood to confront Lord Fitchley.

"Carry on," he told Forbes, and went to the dining room.

There he found, as expected, a rowdy group. Emmett, Baron Fitchley was the worst of the lot, but not because his mates weren't trying their hardest to match him. Thomas Adams and Geoffrey Parker-Lloyd were arrogant asses, possessed of large fortunes despite rumors that they weren't made in legal ways. Edmund LeMont was an inveterate gambler, although he didn't dare cheat in Vega's. Lord Julius Castor and Lord Bricklemore were the dissolute sons of wealthy noblemen, whose fathers had paid their losses thus far, although Nick didn't expect that to continue indefinitely. He'd already had to revoke the membership of another of Fitchley's circle, after the man lost almost four thousand pounds at the faro table and refused to pay it.

Tonight the six of them lounged around a table that already held several bottles. As Nick approached, Castor's elbow hit one, sending it to the floor with a splash of burgundy on the carpet. Nick waited until a waiter swooped in and carried off the empty bottle.

"Good evening, gentlemen."

Adams glanced up blearily. "Our benevolent overlord!"

"Mind your manners, lads," put in LeMont. Nick gazed at him, expressionless, until his eyes veered away. LeMont knew he was closely watched every moment he was in Vega's.

"This club would be immeasurably improved

with some whores." Fitchley took a cigar case from his pocket. Nick felt a spike of fury. There was no smoking in the dining room; it was permitted in the private rooms and the smoking room, but out of deference to female members, it was prohibited in the dining room, and everyone knew it. "Get some tasty bits of skirt, Dashwood. Other hells have them."

"Then you know where to find them," said Nick evenly. "Might I have a word, Lord Fitchley?"

Trimming his cigar, the man squinted up at him. Fitchley's face was narrow, with eyes set close to his nose, and his thin-lipped mouth turned down at the corners. He put one in mind of a shrew, even when he was in good temper. "Not now," he replied in a patronizing drawl.

Nick said nothing. He had learned that argument was pointless, force was messy, and even polite request merely emboldened his quarry. Silent and immovable, he simply stood beside Fitchley's chair and waited.

It took only a few minutes. Despite turning his back, Fitchley was unquestionably aware of him. Parker-Lloyd gazed boldly at Nick, a slight smirk on his face, but said nothing. No one said a word. Finally Fitchley stabbed his unlit cigar into his case and barked, "Oh, very well. As you wish." He lurched out of his seat, though his dramatic storming off was somewhat spoilt by the way he collided with LeMont's chair on the way and almost fell on his arse.

"Good evening, gentlemen," Nick murmured again, bowing his head to the table and walking off after the baron.

"What?" snarled Fitchley as they walked. He

had to steady himself from time to time on a nearby pillar or chair. A fellow sitting in one of those chairs exclaimed indignantly at the jolt, but sank back down as he saw Nick.

"This way." Nick directed him to a small room near the front hall. Most members he saw in his office, but this room was built for the others: the ones who might turn nasty. It was furnished with nothing but a pair of leather chairs, both heavy enough that they could not be wielded or smashed into weapons. When the Vega Club had been a home, it had been an antechamber where guests would await the master of the house. Now the windows were covered by stout shutters, firmly barred, the small fireplace had been bricked up, and the thick oak door had a lock that wouldn't be out of place in Newgate.

Fitchley brushed hard against him as he entered, even though Nick had stepped back to make way. In spite of himself his temper began to spark.

"What?" growled Fitchley, prowling the room with his hands twitching.

"You've been spoken to three times about acceptable behavior, sir. There shan't be a fourth time."

Fitchley scowled. "Three times! Over nothing."

"Twice for fighting and tonight for harassing Lady Alleyn."

"Fighting!" He made a face and waved it away. "Disputes happen, over cards."

"Disputes that end with one man bleeding and threatening to summon the constables are properly called fights."

"And that old biddy ought not to be here,"

Fitchley went on with contempt. "Can't play, never quiet, ugly as bear-bait—"

"Lady Alleyn is a member," Nick interrupted him. "You will be civil to other members within this club, be they royal dukes or fishwives, as well as to every member of my staff. There are no exceptions to this rule. Do you understand?"

Fitchley glared at him. "Or what?"

"If you find it unacceptable, or cannot abide by it, I will accept the return of your membership token and bid you farewell. Once that happens, you will never be welcome in the Vega Club again, not even as a guest."

The baron's mouth turned down sullenly. Again Nick thought of Emilia Greene. Just thinking of her made him want to eject Fitchley. "That's damned unsporting, Dashwood."

"Do you agree to abide by this and every other rule of the Vega Club?" Nick asked in the same emotionless tone. "At all times?"

Fitchley scowled and took a threatening step forward. He was nearly as tall as Nick, but sturdier, especially around his middle. Nick arched one brow in warning. He wasn't going to be pushed around by Fitchley. It must have shown in his face, for the baron lowered his hands. "Yes," he muttered.

"Very good, sir. Remember it."

He stepped aside and let Fitchley slouch past him, no doubt returning to his companions in the dining room to complain bitterly of his treatment. He closed the door behind him with a bang, and Nick exhaled.

This part of owning a club had no appeal for him. In the early days, when he'd been running card games in dimly lit tenements and back rooms, there had been no policy; any man with money in his pockets was permitted. All disagreements were settled swiftly and brutally with fists, sometimes by Nick himself, often occasioning more betting by the onlookers.

The moment he took premises, though, Nick cracked down on fighting. No one was going to break *his* furniture or windows, no matter how much they paid in membership fees. If members wanted to fight, they could so in the street like common brawlers.

He let himself out of the Cold Hold, as the staff called it, and closed the door behind him. Perhaps he did need some time away from the Vega Club.

NICK WAS LATE ARRIVING in Queen's Court. Charlotte had finished breakfast already and was stitching half-heartedly at a handkerchief, which she tossed aside the moment he came into the room. "Nicky!" she cried at his appearance. "Where have you been? I thought you weren't coming today."

"I'm moved to tears by your concern." He pinched her chin when she rolled her eyes. "I had some business to deal with, but of course I haven't forgotten you."

Reluctantly she smiled, and sat beside him on the sofa. She pulled her feet up under her skirts and folded her arms around her shins. "What business?"

"It ought to be the business of teaching you how to sit like a lady," he said with a pointed glance at her posture.

Charlotte made a face. "A lady! As if I know anything about that. Besides, you and Polly are the only people who ever come to see me, so I don't see why it matters how I sit."

Nick drummed his fingers on his knee. He did not want to have this conversation. Of course, it was partly—mostly—for Charlotte's benefit he was contemplating this mad scheme to claim a viscount's coronet, and even if he decided against that, he would still have to face the fact that his sister's behavior was becoming inappropriate to her age. "How was the theater?"

"Oh, it was divine!" Her eyes lit up. "Nicky, it was so splendid! Not dull at all, and terribly droll and witty at times!" She sighed in delight. "I wish I could go every week. May I? Please?"

"We'll see." It was pure joy to see her so happy, and pure terror to imagine her going out every week, let alone every evening. "I've come about that, in fact. I've been thinking it's time you learned more ladylike arts." Was that the right way to say it? God, Nick had no idea. "Do you want to?" he added quickly, with a swift prayer that he wouldn't make a total hash of this.

Charlotte scoffed loudly. "I do! But it won't make any difference if I'm never allowed to go anywhere." Her brow wrinkled up in pleading. "The theater was so marvelous! I want to go again. Polly asked if I could go to Astley's, and she said her mother is taking her to a dressmaker for the first time, to get a proper gown. She invited me to go with her. May I go? Just to the dressmaker? Oh, how I long to see the shop and help choose the cloth and color of her dress. I won't ask for anything else for at least a month if you say I may!"

"An entire month?" He gave a low whistle. "How will I endure the silence?"

Her mouth firmed. "*Please.* I don't need a dress myself—not that I have any occasion to wear a fine new dress—please?"

Moments like this reminded him of the time he'd fallen overboard from his father's ship. First the unalloyed terror of the fall, then the shock of the water closing in on him, seeming to want to squeeze the breath from his lungs and suck him down to the bottom of the ocean. Now would come the mad scramble to swim back to the ship and haul himself up the rope, dripping and red-faced, to face the laughter of the crew.

"Perhaps," he said, ignoring the way her face brightened with hope. "I've come to talk to you about that. About being a lady, and needing new gowns and going to the theater more often."

"Nick!" She flung herself forward, throwing her arms around his neck. He barely kept the two of them on the sofa. "Do you really mean it? When? How?" Her elation darkened in an instant to suspicion. "Are you teasing me? Did you say that just to put me off wanting to go to Astley's?"

He set her back on her side of the sofa. "Am I really so cruel, to dangle that before you only to pull it away?"

She pursed her lips.

He raised a brow.

Charlotte exhaled loudly. "No, likely not. But explain!" She bounced on the cushion, but stayed in her seat this time.

"I would like to bring someone to meet you," he said, choosing each word with care. "Someone who could instruct you in all the ladylike ways you seem rather . . . indifferent toward."

She rolled her eyes again, but they shone with eagerness now. "Who?"

"She's a lady who's helped other young ladies." He paused, then committed himself. "She's a governess, and I think she can prepare you to go into society."

Charlotte fairly vibrated with joy. "Society! Oh, *Nick*."

"I won't let you go out until you can behave properly," he told her firmly. "It's not your fault you don't know how—it's mine. God knows I haven't the first idea how a young lady should behave. But I believe this lady can help you, and then . . ."

"Then?" Charlotte prompted eagerly when he hesitated. "Then we shall go to the theater, and to Astley's, and to shop in Bond Street?"

Miss Greene would know how to chaperone those outings. Nick quieted his misgivings and nodded. "Yes."

Charlotte whooped so loudly he winced. "Yes! Yes, of course! When shall I meet her? Shall we go to her? Can I—?"

"I'll bring her to you." He rose. "If by chance you don't like her, you must tell me honestly—but not in front of her. To her, I expect you will be gracious and polite."

She glared at him in scorn. "Of course I will! You think I'm a true heathen, don't you?" She leapt off the sofa. "I'm not. I can be a proper lady." In demonstration she swept a very respectable curtsy. "When will you bring her?"

"Tomorrow, if she's amenable."

"What's her name? Is she clever? Is she good-humored? Is she fashionable? Oh, I cannot wait to meet her!" She clapped her hands together, and looked like she might dance in pure excitement. "How did you find her? Is she a member of your club?"

Charlotte, Nick reflected grimly, had a lot to learn. "Her name is Miss Greene, and I met her by chance. She isn't a member of the Vega Club."

"Is she fashionable?"

He hesitated. The gown she'd worn to the Vega Club had been years out of fashion, with signs of wear. Who could expect a woman on governess's wages—which likely hadn't been paid at all in recent months—to be stylishly dressed? On the other hand, she had looked delectable in that old, too-snug dress. "I believe so," was his cautious answer.

Charlotte seized his hand. "Then I'm sure I'll like her. Oh, thank you, Nick! Bring her as soon as you can."

He couldn't help smiling. "I will."

CHAPTER TEN

Emilia had been thinking about her argument with Mr. Dashwood since the moment he left. Was there another heir? *Could* there be one? After Lucy went to bed every night, she feverishly combed the family tree she'd drawn up, double-checking every note until she satisfied herself that it was extremely unlikely, if not strictly impossible.

Still, she worried. And as the days went by with no word, she worried more. When the solicitor's note arrived at last, she almost wept with relief.

Thomas Grantham arrived early in the morning, before she and Lucy had finished breakfast, with two clerks in tow. He was a tall, rangy man with untidy blond hair and round spectacles, and a sharp-edged smile. "Mr. Dashwood has asked me to tend to this matter as swiftly as possible, so I hope you'll forgive me for asking so directly for your materials, Miss Greene," he said as he removed his coat and handed it to Henry.

"Of course, sir," Emilia said brightly. Lucy was peeking wide-eyed around the dining room door, and Emilia didn't want to worry her. "This way."

She led the solicitor and his clerks to the sitting room.

Grantham looked at the neat stacks of papers and books she'd arranged on the tables. "Very good, Miss Greene. Thank you." And he maneuvered her out of the room, closing the door in her face.

Well. Naturally he wanted privacy to do his first examination. She went back to Lucy, who was bursting with excitement at the arrival of so many people and the prospect of progress. They talked in excited whispers, Lucy's growing wild and irrational until both dissolved into laughter. When the meal was done and everything cleaned away, Emilia decided they should do lessons as usual, even though she had no real expectation Lucy would retain a word.

When they had finished history, arithmetic, and geography, she went back to the sitting room. A clerk stopped her at the door, assuring her they needed nothing. Nonplussed, she went back to Lucy, dragging her charge through French before venturing back to the sitting room.

The same clerk stopped her again. When she asked if she could help, he asked if she could send a tea tray. Disgruntled, she went and helped Mrs. Watson prepare one, then took Lucy for a walk in the park to distract them both.

By late afternoon, when Mr. Grantham and his clerks had been working for several hours and yet had told her nothing, curiosity and temper overwhelmed her. This time she didn't knock, but walked right into the sitting room.

The sight that met her eyes when she opened the door made her gasp aloud. Her papers, so painstakingly organized and sorted, were now spread all over the room, not only on the tables but on the floor and even pinned up on the walls. Mr. Grantham stood in the center of the room directing a clerk who was scribbling rapidly in a book. The other clerk was on his hands and knees, sorting papers and calling out information in response to terse queries from the solicitor.

"What are you doing?" Emilia exclaimed, clutching the door.

Grantham looked up. "Creating a record, Miss Greene. Every word will have to be verified."

"I know that. I verified them myself." She frowned in annoyance. Why did everyone doubt her work?

He smiled patiently. "I understand. However, Mr. Dashwood charged me with doing it again, to be certain nothing was missed. Any fault in the petition can cause it to be denied."

Yes, she knew that. She reminded herself he was only doing as Mr. Dashwood had instructed, and tamped down her temper at being told things she already knew. "How can I help?"

"It would be better if you did not," he said. "I must do this independently. It will make the case more reliable."

Emilia nodded, seeing that rationale. "I thought I had everything organized, but it seems not to your liking."

He coughed. "Part of the process, madam. I don't demean what you've done, but I hope you understand that I must do things my way now."

He looked at the door in a clear hint for her to leave. She ignored it. "How will you prove everything, independently and thoroughly? I have the ledgers and registers here . . ."

"Those will be returned." He gave her a stern look. "Stealing a register from a parish church is against the law, Miss Greene."

Her face burned. "I needed proof!"

"And by taking it, some might suggest you forged the proof you cite." He raised a brow. "The registers will be returned, and my men will collect sworn statements from the vicars and rectors involved."

Emilia snapped her mouth closed. "Of course." She came into the room and sank onto an empty chair, despite Mr. Grantham's unmistakable air of dismissal. "How long will it take?"

"A fortnight, perhaps a month," he said absently, his attention back on his clerk's work. "It *is* easier with a trail to follow."

"You're welcome," said Emilia under her breath. He shot a sharp glance at her, and she flushed again. "I suppose Mr. Dashwood can hire several investigators to travel around collecting information."

Grantham nodded. "They left two days ago."

She jolted. Mr. Dashwood had told her he wouldn't proceed at all unless he believed the claim was utterly solid, with no other heir to be found. But perhaps he'd believed that all along. He might have planned this from the moment she told him he was the heir. Had he pretended reluctance because he didn't want to help Lucy? Her hands curled into fists. Why couldn't the Sydenham heir have been a more gentlemanly sort?

She looked at the solicitor, who was ignoring her again. She'd thought it would be a relief to hand over her research to the heir; she'd thought it would be the end of her battle to see Lucy provided for.

But now it was clear that things had begun to shift out of her control, and she had the sense it was only the end of the beginning. She would have to be more vigilant than ever to protect Lucy's interests.

As if hearing her apprehensions, Lucy pushed open the door with a creak. Her wide eyes skipped around the scene in the room.

Emilia leapt up and hurried to her. "What is it, dear?"

Lucy turned solemn eyes on her. "He's here, Millie. Mr. Dashwood."

She started. "Now?"

The girl nodded. "Downstairs. Waiting for you. He came in a very handsome carriage, which is waiting in the street outside. Henry told me to fetch you because he was nervous about interrupting *them*." She looked at the clerks.

"All right," said Emilia over the sudden pounding of her heart. "We'd better go see him." She ushered Lucy out and closed the door behind her, aware that the solicitor and his clerks were pleased to see her go. "Did he say anything?" she whispered to Lucy, hesitating at the tiny landing.

Lucy shook his head. "Only that he needed to see you."

Emilia squared her shoulders and marched down the stairs.

He was standing with hands clasped behind his back and staring out the window. Even though it was only half past four o'clock, he wore evening dress, today with a waistcoat in shimmering blue-green silk. Emilia's favorite shade of blue, in fact.

He turned at her entrance, and her lungs seized. Heaven above, he was devastatingly handsome. His eyes were like liquid gold in the afternoon light.

"Good day, Miss Greene." He bowed slightly.

"Sir." She bobbed a curtsy, relieved when she didn't topple over. He had a knack of putting her dreadfully off-balance. "Mr. Grantham is here. Have you come to see him?"

"No." There was no flicker of surprise, no spark of interest. "I've come to take you for a drive."

She tensed. "Now?" she asked stupidly.

"If it wouldn't be inconvenient."

Emilia pressed her hands to her worn skirt, trying to ground herself. "May I ask why?"

Finally he looked away from her, pulling a pocket watch from his waistcoat and flicking it open for a second before replacing it. "The favor I asked of you."

In exchange for his pursuit of the Sydenham viscounty. In spite of herself, Emilia was desperately curious about that. "Oh?"

He nodded. "I want to show you."

Now her brows shot up. "Show me?"

He cleared his throat. "After a fashion."

Emilia stared at him. "Mr. Dashwood, would you please simply tell me what it is? There's no need to be coy."

He just looked at her. "Will you come?"

She bit her lip in frustration. "Why won't you tell me what you want? I have bared all to you."

He went still, amber eyes fixed on her with sudden heat. Emilia flushed crimson as she heard her own words, hanging in the air between them. She had a true genius for embarrassing herself in front of him.

But he looked away before she could stammer an apology. "I beg your pardon." He ran one hand over his head and gazed out the window again. "I'm not playing coy. My request involves . . . a delicate subject, which is very dear to me. I am not accustomed to speaking of it." A rueful smile flashed across his face as he glanced at her, making her sway slightly.

"F-Forgive me," she stammered. "I've been very nervous about it, and I tend to ask too many questions in that state."

"You've no need to be nervous." He frowned, clasping his hands behind his back again. "If you find it objectionable, you may decline."

Emilia wasn't so certain she believed that. He'd gone to some effort to extort that promise from her, and she needed something to make him keep his word to her, about Lucy. Unless he was about to ask her to murder someone, she didn't know how she'd say no.

"But if you decline," he was saying, "I must insist that you keep the request in strictest confidence. Not even telling Lucinda."

"I—Very well," she said after a startled pause. "If I decline."

"Yes."

"If I accept," she continued cautiously, "will I also be bound to secrecy?"

"No." He sighed, his chest rising and falling heavily. "If you accept, it will become public knowledge."

She had to know what it was—to distract her from whatever the solicitor was doing, if for no other reason. "All right. I'll come."

NICK COULDN'T SAY when he began to regret making any sort of bargain with Emilia Greene, but he did not appreciate the unaccustomed lash of his conscience.

What he wanted was utterly respectable, he argued to himself. Charlotte needed a governess, and Miss Greene was a highly regarded one. Miss Greene wanted something from him, which made it fair to ask something in return. He was only seeking her professional skills, and he meant to offer her a proper salary for them.

But by the time she put on a green pelisse, with dark curls escaping her straw bonnet to fall around her neck and her eyes bright with wary curiosity, he regretted it. Perhaps because he'd spent far too much time thinking about her in that tight blue bodice getting tipsy on Madeira and daring him to refuse her. Perhaps because he'd remembered, a bit too late, that he liked women like her too much for his own good. Perhaps because it had dawned on him that if she accepted this proposal, she would end up living in his house, where he would be unable *not* to think of her and see her and talk to her and—likely—provoke her into arguing with him, and then he might lose his mind.

And now she was climbing into his carriage, leaving the little girl watching anxiously from the window, and Nick told himself it was time to show his cards. He said a word to his driver and swung into the seat facing her, pulling the door shut behind him.

It wasn't the first time he'd been alone with Emilia Greene, but something was different now. Perhaps because he was about to—as she had put it —bare all to her.

God. He needed to stop thinking about her bare.

"You are a well-educated woman," he said abruptly. "Raised as a lady."

She visibly stiffened. "What of it?"

"You have been employed as a governess for several years, teaching elegant manners and ladylike accomplishments to other young ladies. You helped launch Lady Helen Fairchild, who made an excellent match with Lord Mulworth."

Miss Greene's eyes narrowed. "Yes."

Nick nodded. "You've demonstrated a remarkable resilience in the face of obstacles with your current post. Most governesses would have looked for a new position upon the death of an employer. Instead, you've become Lucinda's erstwhile guardian, not only seeing to her care and education but doggedly investigating her family for a relation who could not only become the new viscount but take responsibility—at least financially—for Lucinda."

He had a sense of how she'd done it now. The day after their card game, he'd sent Forbes out for more information about her. It appeared she had pillaged every portable valuable from the Sydenham estate that might plausibly be considered Lucinda's inheritance and sold them. She'd managed to get the embezzling attorney to pay six months' lease on a London house before he shot himself. In town they lived frugally, even meanly; one of Forbes's boys had followed their servant, a young man called Henry, to the market and shops, and watched what he bought. No sugar, no beef, half rations of tea, tallow candles. They had only Henry and a cook left, although Forbes's man thought it was an emotional bond keeping the two servants, not because Miss Greene had any money to pay salaries.

She said nothing to his statement. Nick nodded

again. "I prize that combination of cleverness and determination in my employees."

"In your— What?" She blinked. "Are you offering me a position?"

"I am."

"As—as a governess?" she asked in disbelief.

"Yes."

"To whom?" she blurted. "You haven't got a child, you said the other day you hadn't . . ."

"I have," he said carefully, "a ward."

She almost fell off the seat. "Who?"

"A girl of fourteen. Her upbringing has been . . . unconventional, but she is bright and eager to learn more ladylike behavior."

Miss Greene gazed at him, her lips parted in astonishment. Her whole expression was so unguarded and open, Nick had to look away. He was unpardonably pleased to have surprised her so completely.

"Tell me about her." She was still flustered, but quick to gather herself. This time Nick did smile. He liked that about her, too.

"She is nearly fifteen," he said again. "Her name is Charlotte."

"Whose daughter is she?"

"None of your concern," he said before she'd even finished the question.

She gave him a fulminating stare, jaw tight and eyes glittering like lightning. Emilia Greene in a fury was a sight to behold. "If you mean for her to go out in society, people will wonder. If you don't tell them who she is, they will gladly invent all manner of histories for her, and I assure you, none of them will please you."

"I'll deal with that when I must."

He could see the struggle in her face. She wanted to argue. But at last, she said, grudgingly, "As you wish. But this means we must discuss Lucinda again."

"Oh? How so?" He leaned back, draping one arm across the seat cushion as the tension in his shoulders eased. The carriage was rolling through Westminster, taking an idle tour of the city until he rapped on the wall and told the driver to take them to Queen's Court.

"I am responsible for Lucinda, who has no one else. I am her governess, too, and it will be very difficult to instruct two young ladies and still have time to shepherd your petition through the committee."

Grantham was going to attend to the petition. Nick shrugged, deciding not to argue that point now. "Can you not manage two pupils?"

She gave a little huff. "Of course I can, though it won't be easy. Why didn't you tell me this before? From your air of mystery, I'd no idea it would be something so mundane that you wanted from me. I imagined all manner of scandalous requests."

Oh Lord. For a moment an image blazed through his mind, in vivid, erotic sound and color. Nick breathed slowly, willing his pulse to steady itself. He had to remind himself that he *did* only want this one, mundane, decidedly-not-scandalous thing from her. "It is not mundane to me," he said gravely. "Charlotte is exceptionally dear to me."

Her eyes widened. "Oh! Oh, no—I didn't mean to suggest any slight—"

Nick waved one hand. "Never mind. Will you take the position?"

She caught her lower lip between her teeth. "I should meet her first. At her age, young ladies often wish to have some say in their governess. If she doesn't like me, it won't matter how carefully or diligently I teach her, the entire attempt will be a disaster."

He raised one brow. "You wish to meet her?"

"It's madness not to," she said bluntly. "Presuming you wish it to succeed."

"I do," Nick assured her. He raised his arm and knocked firmly on the carriage panel. "We're almost there."

CHAPTER ELEVEN

They turned into a small cobbled courtyard, with a pair of neat red brick houses on each side and a wall at the end. It was neatly kept, clean and bright, with urns of flowers or herbs by each door. The carriage circled around and stopped, and Mr. Dashwood jumped down. He gave her his hand, and Emilia tried not to shiver at how his fingers enveloped hers. It had been years since a gentleman offered her his hand like that, or handed her down from a carriage so solicitously. Or done so with such a large, strong hand. Or looked back at her with a searing glance that made her heart leap into her throat—

He released her and turned away, heading toward the house on the left. Emilia followed, blushing with embarrassment. He might become her employer, for heaven's sake.

A flutter of curtain at a window overhead made Emilia think they were expected, and indeed a maid opened the door just as they reached it. She deliberately lagged a few steps as they went up the stairs to the drawing room, hoping to have a moment to assess the young lady, but Mr. Dashwood blocked her view, striding forward to greet the girl and whisper a word in her ear. Emilia could only see her skirts until the man stepped out of the way and gave a slight bow.

"Miss Greene," he said, "may I present to you my ward? Charlotte, this is Miss Emilia Greene, the lady I mentioned to you."

A beaming, nervous smile on her face, Charlotte curtsied. She was as tall as Emilia but as slender as a child still, with a golden complexion and curly black hair neatly tied up with a pale blue ribbon. Her eyes were dark and bright with interest under long eyelashes. Her dress was simple but high quality, deep rose pink. "It is a pleasure to make your acquaintance, Miss Greene."

Emilia bobbed in turn. "And I yours, Miss Charlotte."

"Won't you sit down?" The girl glanced anxiously at Mr. Dashwood. "And . . . would you care for tea? I shall send for some."

Why on earth had Mr. Dashwood been so secretive? He'd acted as though his ward was a terror, wild and rude, when she actually appeared rather charming. Reminding herself that Charlotte wasn't to blame for her guardian's actions, Emilia smiled. "Thank you. Tea would be lovely."

Charlotte rang the bell and perched on the edge of the sofa, her eager gaze fixed on Emilia. Mr. Dashwood sank into an armchair opposite them, watching with subtle tension.

Emilia cleared her throat. "Such a lovely drawing room. It's so light and airy."

"Isn't it?" cried Charlotte in delight. "I do like it. If only—" She stopped short, her eyes flicking toward her guardian. "That is, I am delighted you approve, Miss Greene."

If only what? Emilia wondered. "Very much so. It's as fine as anything by Robert Adam."

Charlotte beamed. "Of course it is! Nick only wants the best—" She stopped again, biting her lip. "Thank you, ma'am."

She was trying so hard to be proper and dignified, when it was obvious she was dying of curiosity and excitement. It had been a long time since Emilia had felt that, but she did remember. Instinctively she liked this girl.

After tea had come, and Charlotte had very carefully poured three cups, adding three lumps of sugar to her own and only milk to Emilia's and Mr. Dashwood's, and no one had said anything beyond a few desultory comments about the weather, Emilia decided to take command. It was obvious neither Mr. Dashwood nor Charlotte knew what to say, and at least she had done this before. She set down her tea.

"Mr. Dashwood believes I might suit you as a governess, Charlotte. I'm certain you know you're a bit older than most girls are when they first have a governess, and I wonder if you have any questions for me, about what we might do together."

Charlotte's eyes rounded in alarm. "Oh—Oh, I did not know I would need to ask . . . I don't really know, Miss Greene."

She nodded in sympathy. "All right. Shall I tell you the usual things I would begin with, instructing a young lady new to me?" Charlotte nodded, rapt. Emilia glanced at Mr. Dashwood, now sprawled in his chair, chin propped in one hand, but no less attentive. It struck her that there was a striking similarity to their alert gazes.

"We would start with manners," Emilia said. "You will never do wrong by treating others graciously and behaving with dignity. One can tell a true lady by the way she conducts herself both in company and in private. I would also advise you on your dress, and all that is proper for a young lady to wear."

"Jewels?" asked Charlotte hopefully.

Emilia shook her head with a smile. "Perhaps a locket. Flowers in your hair. Young ladies don't wear much jewelry. That's the mark of an older woman, be she married or not."

The girl's face fell but she nodded.

"Musical instruction," Emilia went on. "Have you had any?" Charlotte bit her lip and shook her head. "I find most young ladies are able to acquit themselves tolerably well on the pianoforte, with some practice. Mr. Dashwood, will there be a pianoforte?"

"If one is required," he said, shooting a glance at Charlotte.

"Do you like the pianoforte?" Emilia prompted. "If you don't like to listen to it, you will hate playing it."

Her face eased. "Yes, I do. I will happily try to learn."

Emilia nodded once in approval. "Do you dance?"

"A little," said Charlotte, looking anxious again.

She smiled. "If you can count, you can dance. Once again, practice is all most ladies require to become proficient. Perhaps Mr. Dashwood will lend himself as a regular dance partner."

Charlotte whirled on her guardian. "Oh, will you, Nick? I do long to dance!"

Looking tense, he nodded.

Emilia noted the use of his Christian name as she smiled. "I'm sure you'll learn quickly, then." She chose her next words with care. "How much education have you had?"

"Plenty," said Charlotte, to her intense relief. "I adore geography. Mathematics, not as much."

"Any languages?"

Charlotte made a face. "I speak tolerable French, but I detest reading it. Must I learn that, too?"

"That will be up to you," replied Emilia, "and Mr. Dashwood."

"What languages do you speak?" the girl wanted to know.

"French, Italian, although not as well as French, and enough German to be polite."

Charlotte's eyes rounded in admiration. "So many!"

Emilia laughed. "It's important for a governess to know more than her pupils."

"What about artwork?" asked Charlotte. "Or embroidery?"

"Every girl should be proficient in embroidery and sewing, for practical reasons if no other, but I don't consider it worth torturing a girl with embroidery if she despises it. If you want to learn painting, I'm afraid you must find another instructor," said Emilia ruefully. "I've absolutely no talent for it, but I can instruct you a bit in drawing."

"At last," cried Charlotte with a peal of laughter. "Something you're not brilliant at!"

Emilia's smile faded. She was all too aware of

her many shortcomings. "There are a great many things that might be described that way," she murmured before rallying. "But I do prize diligent effort and close attention. I will happily answer any questions you have about why you must do something a certain way, but I shan't have any patience at all with someone who doesn't wish to learn." She clasped her hands again. "I will take your preferences into account when designing lessons. If I cannot teach you a subject adequately, I will inform Mr. Dashwood, so that he might locate a better qualified teacher. It is your education, and you should have some say in the direction of it. But if you willfully ignore what I *do* teach you, I'll resign the post." She raised her brows as Charlotte stared at her. "It would be a waste of my time and yours, don't you think?"

The girl smiled nervously, glancing at her guardian again. "Yes. I do want to learn, Miss Greene."

Emilia smiled back to put her at ease. "Then we should get on famously."

BY THE TIME THEY LEFT, Charlotte beaming as she bade them farewell, Nick felt almost ebullient.

Charlotte had laughed and nodded throughout the visit. She had liked Emilia Greene, and Emilia Greene had liked her; he could tell. He'd been more nervous than he'd thought, he realized, and now felt as though he'd just drawn an inside straight to win the pot. He gave his hand again to help Miss Greene into the carriage and tried not to think that he would be doing that much more in the future.

"You, Mr. Dashwood, are a man of secrets," remarked his new governess as the carriage started off.

"I'm relying on you to keep them," he replied.

"But why?" She tilted her head, a tiny frown on her brow. "She's lovely and charming. Why should she remain mysterious?"

He sighed and ran one hand over his face. Now that the visit was concluded, he felt a nip of fatigue. He'd risen earlier than usual to make time for this. "A man of my reputation isn't the most suitable association for a girl her age. I know our relationship will need to be explained, but . . . for now, teach her the usual things."

Her brows went up. "The usual things?"

Nick nodded. "Yes. Manners and pianoforte and how to dress. As you said."

Her lips pursed. "That's all a governess does, is it?"

"I've no bloody idea what a governess does," he admitted. "I only know that I cannot teach her what a lady, or a woman, ought to know. That's what I want you to do. Start with the basic information and . . ." He made a vague gesture. "I'm sure whatever you teach her will be fine."

"How demanding," she said under her breath.

"I will be reasonable," he answered with dignity.

This time she couldn't quite stop the incredulous laugh. "Virtually nothing you've done so far has been reasonable."

He shrugged. "You're one to talk, Miss Greene. Barging into a gaming hell after hours with a forged note and telling a complete stranger he would be an idiot to reject your proposal."

Her face colored and she looked abashed. "Did I really say that?"

"Emphatically." Nick grinned, forgetting that he ought to be businesslike and reserved with her now. "I quaked in my boots."

She gasped. "You did not!"

"I would have, if I'd not been so astonished by what you said."

She shook her head. Her blush was a beautiful shade of pink. "Astonished! Vexed, I would say."

"Perhaps somewhat," he agreed.

"Somewhat!" She was smiling, and Nick reveled in that. "I should hate to see you truly vexed, then."

He laughed. "I must confess, Miss Greene, in my world, most proposals are transactional in nature. Nothing is free, and everyone has an ulterior motive."

Her amusement faded. "I certainly did."

He leaned back and regarded her thoughtfully. "Yes. But not for your own benefit. That was unusual."

She looked away, nibbling her lip again. Nick stared at her teeth against her plump flesh and imagined her biting *his* skin, her lips moving over him . . .

"We haven't discussed terms," she said, still staring out the window.

Name them, he thought. *Anything.* "What do you want?"

She shot him a sideways look from beneath her lashes, and God help him, he thought for a second that she had understood him too well. That she could feel the desire burning through his veins, that she knew he wanted her enough to agree to anything. "Terms of my employment."

Employment. She, his employee. He, in control of her living. The most unequal relationship. Breathing hard and trying to conceal it, Nick nodded curtly, forcing his mind back to that footing. Employee. Employer. A contract for services not to include anything of an intimate nature.

Nick was used to women wanting something from him. Running an exclusive gambling club appeared to confer an aura of danger and excitement on a man that women found attractive. He'd been flirted with, teased, and outright propositioned, and sometimes he found the offers tempting enough to accept.

But that wasn't what Miss Greene wanted from him. Mixing pleasure with business only ruined both. Whatever his failings, Nick never neglected business.

"Right." He cleared his throat. "I propose to engage you as a governess for my ward, Charlotte. I agree and understand that you will also continue to care for Lucinda as you see fit, and I agree to compensate you for her instruction as well. Would one hundred pounds per annum be sufficient salary for instructing two young ladies?"

Her eyes popped in astonishment at the amount. "Yes, indeed!"

"To achieve this, I propose that you and Lucinda move into my house in Portland Place. Charlotte will also reside there as soon as the petition is filed for the Sydenham viscounty. It's a large house, mostly empty, but it will provide ample and comfortable accommodation for everyone. I am rarely there, but I have a superb staff. You may bring your own servants as well, if you wish," he added as she opened her mouth.

She closed her mouth, nonplussed.

Nick tilted back his head. "In return, you shall surrender all your research regarding the Sydenham title and allow my attorney to conduct the petition through the appropriate channels. I don't question your knowledge, your abilities, or your determination in assembling it," he said as she colored up again, her eyes flashing. "It is not to snub you, only to put the matter into the hands of a well-qualified solicitor who has experience and connections to speed the process along. Because"—he leaned forward, his voice becoming coldly serious—"it will not be filed, nor spoken of, nor even mentioned in public, until there is no scintilla of doubt that it will succeed, and I choose Grantham to accomplish that." He paused. "Do we have an understanding, Miss Greene?"

She sat stiffly, tensed as if about to lunge forward and slap him. Her hands were fists in her lap, one white knuckle showing through a small rip in her glove. Her bosom rose and fell rapidly, fluttering one of the ribbons from her bonnet where it caught on a button of her pelisse. If he weren't so focused on her eyes, which blazed furiously at him, Nick would have enjoyed the sight.

"Nearly," she bit out. "Lucy needs something."

He smiled cynically. "Ah, yes. I'll put five hundred pounds in trust for her."

"Five thousand."

"I offered five thousand," he said precisely, "in exchange for you burning your gathered evidence. Are you offering that bargain again?"

Her expression murderous, she said nothing.

"One thousand pounds," he allowed. "Since I

shall be housing and feeding her for some indeterminate period, I trust that will suffice."

"She deserves more!"

"And I deserve to live my wicked, debauched life free of your interference, yet here we are." The carriage had stopped. Davis, the driver, would wait as long as need be. Nick held out one hand, cajoling this time. "Come now, Miss Greene," he said softly. "We shall be partners. After all, we want the same thing—an excellent education and secure home for our respective charges. I shall leave you a free hand in all matters of . . . governessing. Can we not agree?"

"But *you* shall end this bargain a viscount, while I could be dismissed at any moment," she said acidly. Pointedly she folded her arms, tucking her hands beneath her elbows. "It is an *unequal* partnership, to say the least."

"I cannot change your profession, but I grasp your concern. If I dismiss you for anything other than proven theft, it shall be with a parting sum of five hundred pounds."

"Write it down and sign it."

He shrugged. "As you wish."

"And I shall sign it when the trust for Lucy is arranged, with myself named as trustee," she added. "Until then, we do *not* have an understanding."

Nick felt a surge of triumph. "As you wish."

Her throat worked, and she nodded, a savage jerk of her chin. "I also want my own chamber. A *private* chamber. I want approval of Lucy's living quarters as well, which shall be near mine. I will make all decisions regarding her well-being and instruction, including an allowance of thirty pounds per annum for her care, solely under my control, separate from the trust and my salary."

"Yes, Miss Greene, I understand my role will be to pay the bills and stay out of your way," Nick said dryly. "You may see to the rearing of Lucinda."

"I am not pleased by this, Mr. Dashwood," she warned him. "It is far beyond what I originally asked, and I do not like being coerced and manipulated."

"A feeling I know well," he drawled. "Perhaps you should decline the position, and we each go our separate ways."

She huffed. "As much as I wish to, I won't."

"Then we have an understanding?"

Glaring, she nodded and clasped his hand, just long enough for his heart to surge against his ribs and his nerves to draw tight.

Nick leaned back. "You won't take out your pique at me on Charlotte, will you?"

"I have absolutely no objection to her, sir," she said tartly as she gathered up her skirts. "Only to *you*." She flung open the door herself and stormed out of the carriage.

Nick was still grinning as he told Davis to drive on. She'd said yes. He should not find that exhilarating.

But he did.

CHAPTER TWELVE

F or a fortnight Nick waited, half in hope, half
in dread, for Grantham's report on the
progress of his investigations.

Hope, because Charlotte was ecstatic about her
new governess. Every morning when Nick arrived
for breakfast, she peppered him with questions
about Miss Greene and when they would begin and
how on earth did Nick expect her to wait patiently
when she might already be learning dancing and
pianoforte? She asked about attending the theater
again, and Astley's, and if Miss Greene would take
her to a modiste in Bond Street. It was hard not to
feel buoyed by her enthusiasm.

But also dread, because it was hard not to
wonder if claiming the Sydenham title would be a
Pyrrhic victory. When he strolled the rooms at the
Vega Club, or reviewed the club's receipts with
Forbes, or visited the little haven that was Queen's
Court, it was difficult not to think that Dame Fortune had already smiled on him rather kindly, and
daring to grasp for more would probably only
tempt her to dash it all away. He had built the life

he wanted; upsetting it for the chance of gaining another was a rum bet, and he knew it.

Finally, when Nick had nearly convinced himself that Miss Greene's sleuthing couldn't possibly hold up under scrutiny, Grantham turned up.

"Well?" he demanded as soon as the door was safely closed behind his solicitor. He found he was tense, his heart thudding. No matter how much he told himself he wasn't cut out to be a viscount, the thought had inarguably taken root in his mind. Or perhaps he just didn't like to lose. "Is it all a myth?"

Grantham set down the large case he carried. "No. It is not." He paused. "My lord."

Good God. Nick's knees gave out and he sat heavily in his chair. "She's correct? The claim is sound?"

"It is." Grantham took his own seat. "Quite impressive, really, that she was able to parse out that much history and detail, given what she had."

He raised his head from his hands. "What do you mean?"

"Apparently she had only the Sidney family Bible to start, and the recollections of an elderly nursemaid. With that she wrote dozens of letters, and then began visiting vicars and rectors across southern England via the mail coaches." A dry smile flickered over the solicitor's face. "I believe she thoroughly charmed them. Most are getting on in years, and to a man they spoke fondly of her concern for Miss Lucinda and her delightful manners. Even the rectors whose registries she stole."

"Stole?"

"Walked right out with them under her shawl." Grantham looked mildly impressed. "One fellow, Mr. Fisher, made any number of excuses for her. We returned it, of course, and secured his statement that the relevant pages were exactly as he remembered them when she visited him."

"Very good." Nick plowed his hands into his hair. "But what might she have missed?"

"We were able to verify the deaths of several branches of the family tree, rendering them devoid of heirs. She anticipated us there as well. She wrote to every former servant, neighbor, great-aunt, or second cousin thrice removed who might have known any of them. If there's someone out there, they're well hidden."

Nick said nothing. A family Bible and an elderly nursemaid. Stolen parish registers. Letters to former servants. His Miss Greene was a marvel.

No. Not *his* Miss Greene. Just . . . Miss Greene, who charmed elderly vicars and stormed gaming hells in pursuit of what she wanted. Clever, bold, indomitable . . . beautiful and tempting . . .

Grantham went on speaking. "The only aspect of her information that was thin and lacking was that of your immediate family."

Nick tensed, all pleasurable thoughts of Miss Greene vanishing. "I suppose you have no choice but to include that in the petition."

Grantham nodded. "Enough to satisfy the committee."

That would be bad enough. Nick scrubbed his hands over his face. "I have it."

He had a good sense of what people would say when his petition was filed. He was accepted now for what he was—the owner of a gambling hell, wealthy as sin and powerful in his own way, but still as common and crass as one might expect such a person to be. When he set his sights on a higher status, it would not be received well. The gossip would be ugly and it would be everywhere: that he ought to slither back into the gutter where he'd come from, and stay there. He was sure every filthy detail of his life would be dragged out and maliciously dissected in the drawing rooms of London.

But in the end, he was going to win. Miss Greene was correct: a title, paired with wealth, would outlast the rumors and open almost any door in the kingdom.

Nick didn't mind taking risks, but he hated to lose.

He rose and unlocked one of the cabinets behind his desk and took out a green dispatch box, the aged leather worn shiny in spots and cracked in others. It had belonged to his Aunt Heloise, who had kept her correspondence in it. She gave it to him shortly before her death, when she lay wheezing for breath in her austere home. "Do not lose sight of whence thou came," she'd rasped at him, clutching a handkerchief to her mouth. "I charge thee not to make my efforts in vain."

Nick had laughed at that. He'd considered burning it all, and had settled for locking it away and never touching it.

Opening the lid released the scent of dust and lavender. Heloise had believed lavender warded off illness, and the smell still made him think of a sickroom. Gingerly Nick sifted through the pile of papers. He remembered the long letters his aunt would write: to her acquaintances, to her father, to her brother, to her husband, who was often away. She herself was kept at home by, she claimed, a weak constitution, although in the end she outlived all of the supposedly heartier men in her family.

His aunt's handwriting, rigidly precise, covered many of the pages; one letter was prominently addressed to him and still sealed with her crest in crumbling red wax. She'd said he should read it when she was gone, her last exhortation to him. Rebelliously, Nick had stuffed it into the green case and left it there.

He put it aside now. Grantham needed documents establishing his lineage and legitimacy, not Heloise's dying lament over Nick's wicked soul.

"My aunt took me in as a boy," he said for Grantham's benefit. "She changed my name and made me her heir, as she had no children." He drew out a thin sheaf of paper, then another. "A copy of her will, and of her husband's."

He dug deeper, and produced the legal document when Heloise changed his name. Nick handed it to Grantham with a fresh burst of bitterness in his chest. He hadn't wanted to live with Heloise or become her son, but she'd ignored him; she always knew better than anyone else and never let anyone change her mind, certainly not a ten-year-old boy.

Of course, Nick's father was the one who'd allowed it to happen by giving away his son. Well—not quite *giving*. After Heloise's death, Nick discovered that Sam Sidney had sold his firstborn child to his sister for four hundred pounds. That was only one of the reasons why Nick hated his father.

Near the bottom of the box he located the certificate of his baptism and then the most important paper of all: the copy of his parents' marriage lines.

"Antigua," read Grantham, his brows twitching upward.

"My father was a sea captain. You'll see I was

baptized in England." Another of Heloise's maneuvers, Nick was sure, since he remembered no trace of piety in his father. But it would have been unthinkable to Heloise that her nephew not be properly baptized, and as usual, she'd got her way. He closed the green case. "Will it suffice?"

"It should."

"Perhaps Miss Greene could steal the register from Antigua. I doubt an ocean voyage or two would deter her."

Grantham smiled at his dry remark. "We'll leave that as a last resort."

Nick smiled back, grimly. He'd come too far to quibble over anything. Now all his markers were in the pot, and he had no choice but to play.

Vincere est totum. Winning was everything.

CHAPTER THIRTEEN

Emilia was not prepared for the speed at which Mr. Dashwood proceeded, once he decided to proceed.

He gave her barely a day's warning before a wagon arrived in Charles Street to transport them to his home. Lucy was agog, running from room to room, scattering her few belongings around the house in a frenzy of certainty that she would forget something.

Emilia herself scarcely knew where to begin. Mr. Grantham had taken all her papers, and her wardrobe was pitiably small, but somehow a day and a night seemed impossibly short a time to uproot herself.

"Such a hurry, I'm sure I don't understand it," said Mrs. Watson under her breath as she bustled into the room. "There's your pelisse, dear, I mended it for you."

"Thank you." Emilia smiled as she folded it into her trunk. "You didn't have to do that."

The housekeeper patted her arm. "I didn't mind a bit, not when you've done so much to keep

us all fed and under a sturdy roof! I hope Mr. Dashwood can do half as well."

"The new Lord Sydenham," Emilia reminded
her. "And I expect he can do a great deal better."

The woman pursed her lips. "We'll see." She
and Henry were going with them, although Emilia
didn't know what to tell them about their future
employment. Not for lack of trying to discover it;
she'd sent Mr. Dashwood no less than three letters
before realizing he was ignoring her.

Emilia had seen his house. Despite his lack of
communication, she'd asked around until someone
gave her the direction, and she and Lucy walked
across London to examine it. It was impressive,
gleaming pale stone and freshly washed windows
overlooking the wide boulevard. In the morning
sun it shone like a church. They'd stood on the
pavement and contemplated it, Lucy wide-eyed and
silent, Emilia wondering what she'd got herself into
with the owner.

"Oh, Millie! They're ready for our trunks!"
Lucy ran into the room, her cheeks flushed and her
braid coming undone. "I'm not finished packing,
what shall I do?"

"Finish packing." Emilia stowed her hairbrush
and the small wooden box of keepsakes in the trunk
and shut the lid. Her spare bonnet was already in
the hatbox next to the trunk.

"I can't!" Lucy gulped for air, looking frantic.
"Are we really to take up residence in Mr. Dashwood's home?"

Emilia sat on the bed and opened her arms.
Without hesitation Lucy dived into her embrace,
her thin arms going around Emilia's neck as if she
were still a child.

"We are," she reminded the girl gently. "He's now the head of your family, and he wishes to have you close. We saw for ourselves that his home is much nicer than this one."

Lucy's head was on her shoulder. "And Dorset?" she asked in a small voice. "Will he make us go there, too?"

"No," Emilia answered at once. She would scratch out the man's eyes before she let him send Lucy back to Dorset. "I told you, no one wants to go to Dorset, and Mr. Dashwood has never even been."

"Are you certain?"

"Absolutely," Emilia lied.

Lucy was silent for a moment. "Will I like it there, Millie?"

Emilia took a deep breath for courage. "I hope so—I hope you will try very hard to like it, and to be gracious to Mr. Dashwood. He's your cousin, after all." She hesitated. "I've been meaning to tell you, there will be another young lady in the household."

Lucy's head came up. "Who? Has he a daughter? Oh, who is she, Millie?"

"She's his ward," said Emilia, choosing her words carefully. She suspected Charlotte had a closer link to Mr. Dashwood, but didn't want to say it aloud.

The girl bit her lip. "Will I like her? Will she like me?"

"That depends on how you comport yourself, I believe," she replied in amusement. "I have met her, and she struck me as a very amiable young lady. Mr. Dashwood has engaged me to be her governess, too."

Lucy brightened. "That will make lessons more pleasant!"

Emilia still had no idea how much their lessons would overlap. Somehow she would have to balance the education of two girls. "That's the reason Mr. Dashwood requested we move to his home. It will be much easier for me to instruct you both there."

"Is this young lady kind?" Lucy wanted to know. "Is she fashionable, and witty, and will she find me dull?"

Emilia thought of Charlotte's bright, eager face. "I expect she'll be just as curious about you as you are about her. She's about five years older than you. I don't think she's been out much in town."

"I think I will like her," said Lucy more confidently. "And Mr. Dashwood will want us to be friends, won't he?"

He hadn't said any such thing, but even he couldn't be so oblivious as not to consider it. "I'm sure he does," said Emilia, pushing aside the flicker of irritation at the man's silence. "I hope you'll remember the manners I've taught you."

"I will try," Lucy promised. "I always try!"

"Lucy." Emilia took the girl's hands. "You must do better than try. I have great confidence in you," she added firmly as Lucy's fingers twitched and her face went pale. "I know you can do it. But our fate is now in Mr. Dashwood's hands, and we must remember that at all times."

"But he'll be kind, won't he?" she asked anxiously.

"I believe so, but we neither of us know him yet. As we come to know him, it will become clearer how to behave, if he is excessively formal or restrained, or a more relaxed gentleman." Emilia didn't add any of her own concerns—about who Dashwood's associates were, what sort of employer he was, and what freedom they might expect as members of his household. She didn't have much choice, so she would have to learn quickly.

Lucy nodded vigorously. "Of course! Do you know, now I'm looking forward to it!" She slid off Emilia's lap and ran from the room, calling to Henry that she was almost ready for him to take her trunk.

Emilia stood and looked around her small room. Here in Charles Street, she'd put Lucy in the best room and then rebelliously taken the room next to it for her own. There had been no one to tell her otherwise, when she was the de facto head of the household. Emilia knew she was a servant, but she'd hardly acted like one for the last several months. Just as she'd reminded Lucy to mind her manners, she would have to remember her true place now.

When they arrived in Portland Place, the butler greeted them with a bow. "Welcome, Miss Sidney. Miss Greene. I am Mr. Pearce."

Lucy's eyes were like saucers as she looked around. The house was as bright and elegant inside as it appeared from the outside. "Thank you, sir," she whispered, staying close to Emilia's side.

"Allow me to show you to your rooms." Mr. Pearce led the way up the stairs, Henry bringing up the rear with Lucy's trunk on his shoulder and a footman carrying Emilia's. Another footman took Mrs. Watson and her things to the kitchen.

"Oh my!" Lucy's eyes rounded in astonishment as he showed them into a large bright schoolroom on the top floor with several windows overlooking the street and two small bedrooms off it. Together the space seemed larger than an entire house in Charles Street.

Lucy wandered through the rooms, her head swiveling from side to side as she took it all in. Emilia started toward the bedrooms, expecting one of them to be hers, but the butler stopped her. "This way, Miss Greene." He opened a concealed door in one wall and led her down a narrow flight of stairs into a beautiful room directly below.

Emilia stopped in the doorway. "Is this the chamber for the lady of the house?"

"I suppose it was," said the butler, unruffled. "There's been no lady of the house since I arrived, ma'am."

Her gaze narrowed on a door in the opposite wall. "Is that Mr. Dashwood's chamber?"

He coughed. "Ah—no, ma'am. That leads to Mr. Dashwood's private study. A locksmith came yesterday to disable this door. No one can go in or out through it." In illustration he crossed the room and turned the knob, demonstrating its uselessness.

That was better than being next to his bedroom, but still not right. "I prefer to have the room upstairs."

"I beg your pardon, but Mr. Dashwood gave instructions that Miss Charlotte was to have that room. He assigned you this chamber since it gives you convenient access to both young ladies, and they to you, while still affording you some measure of privacy."

Emilia suffered a qualm of conscience. That sounded very reasonable—considerate, even—but he had to know it was improper. She ought to be in the servants' quarters, not installed near his bedroom.

"If you are displeased with the arrangements, perhaps you wish to discuss it with Mr. Dash-wood," suggested Mr. Pearce.

"Thank you. When do you expect him?"

"Mr. Dashwood normally rises at four o'clock. If you wish, I will inform him that you would like to speak to him."

That was a few hours away. She resolved not to unpack just yet. "Yes, please."

Mr. Pearce showed them the rest of the house, from the elegant drawing room on the first floor, with a gleaming new pianoforte, to the empty dining room on the ground floor. When Emilia asked why there was no furniture, Mr. Pearce said Mr. Dashwood did not entertain and saw no pur-pose in it.

"It's a very large house, Millie," whispered Lucy, gripping Emilia's hand.

Thank goodness, she thought. Less chance of crossing paths with the owner. "But handsome," she replied, determined not to let her dark thoughts and worries frighten Lucy. "When is Miss Charlotte expected?" she asked the butler. The arrival of an-other girl would divert Lucy.

"In the morning, ma'am."

"Very good. Thank you, Mr. Pearce." That gave her one night to pin him down, once and for all, about what he intended to do—with Lucy, with the viscounty, with her.

NICK SENSED the change in the house almost from the moment he woke.

Normally it was quiet and calm. As much as possible his staff had inverted the daily schedule—he rose at four in the afternoon, giving himself time for a ride or a visit to the boxing saloon for exercise, then a hearty meal before washing and dressing. By six every evening he was at the Vega Club. In the morning he would return to a house with closed draperies, a light meal ready, and his bed, obscenely comfortable after being on his feet most of the night.

Today, however, servants were coming and going on the stairs. As he started down the stairs, tugging on his gloves, the tinkling sound of the new pianoforte, delivered just two days ago, greeted him. He had planned to slip out for a ride, avoiding contact with his new governess. Practically the first sentence out of Pearce's mouth today had been that Miss Greene wanted a word, and that it didn't promise to be a soft, grateful word. But somehow he found himself at the drawing room door anyway.

Miss Greene sat next to Lucinda, their heads together above the keys. It could have been a mother teaching her daughter, gently guiding her hands on the keys, an encouraging word on her lips despite the stumbling notes. It was a scene of utter domesticity, and entirely alien to Nick. He'd never thought to see the like in his house.

"Like this," said Miss Greene, and played a scale.

Lucinda began to play. The notes came haltingly and badly, a nervous banging on the keys compared to Miss Greene's smooth playing.

But oh, Miss Greene. Her dark hair was pinned up, and one tendril had escaped the pins to lie in a sensual S on her bare nape, an almost palpable lure.

Her dress was yellow, like fresh lemon curd. She swayed very slightly as she played another scale, almost as if she were moving in the arms of a lover. A flush went through Nick's body like a spring fever, scalding and fast.

"Good afternoon," he said to banish that thought.

She looked up. Lucinda twisted in her seat to face him as well, but Nick's gaze was on the governess. Who looked good enough to eat in slow, savored, lemony bites. Who was his employee now, and therefore would not be licked, tasted, or even touched by him, no matter what her hair tempted him to imagine.

"Good afternoon, Mr. Dashwood." She murmured something to Lucinda as she rose. The girl's expression drooped, and she turned back to the keys and began hammering out the scale again, each note loud with pique.

Miss Greene crossed the room to him. "I wished to speak to you," she said quietly, beautifully pink in the face. "About my bedchamber."

Again that flush ran through him, hotter than the fires in the sugaring houses of Antigua. "What about it?" asked Nick, ignoring the flush.

"I would prefer to be lodged in the nursery with Lucy," she whispered. "Give the finer room to Charlotte."

He smiled briefly. Pearce had hinted she was displeased about that, so he was ready to refute it. "It's more appropriate for you to have that room and Charlotte to be upstairs."

Her eyes widened. "It is next to your bedroom!"

"Through a door that no longer opens," he said. "If it comforts you, Pearce will see that you have the only keys to your room. Charlotte isn't the lady of the house," he added, guessing her next argument and having the pleasure of seeing her blush deepen.

"Nor am I!"

"No," he agreed. "But you requested a private apartment in close proximity to Lucinda's. That room fits the bill, and no one else is using it. I've only tried to give you what you asked for." He nodded at her and continued on his way instead of watching her breast swell with indignation again.

"Wait!" She followed him, biting her pretty lower lip. "Mr. Dashwood, you can't do things like this—I am a governess, not the lady of the house, and it is wrong to put me in that room."

He stopped on the stairs and looked up at her. "Miss Greene," he said lightly, "I do things the way I think they ought to be done, not according to some rule thought up by mysterious and nebulous 'people' whose opinions mean nothing to me. That room is the most convenient for your situation, therefore it is yours."

"Mr. Dashwood—"

"If we are arguing about which room you shall sleep in, it doesn't bode well for the future, when we must agree on other more challenging points concerning Charlotte and Lucinda." He couldn't completely check his temper. Not only was he missing his one chance to get some fresh air and exercise in the daylight, it was a stupid argument to have. What did it matter where she slept? He wouldn't be here while she was sleeping anyway, which he supposed to be the root of her resistance. He didn't think he could stand that, lying alone in his own bed thinking of her doing the same, less than twenty feet away.

But her expression—frustrated and embarrassed—made him relent. "You're welcome to dine with me when I return in an hour. I won't change my mind, but I'm willing to explain my reasoning at greater length."

She stared at him a moment, then looked down. Her fingers whitened where she gripped the balustrade. "Thank you, sir," she murmured.

Damn it. For all that he kept reminding himself she was now his employee, he found he didn't like it when *she* remembered it as well. He much preferred her brash and unafraid, challenging him to a wager, demanding a contract for her services, insisting she was right and he was wrong about who could become a viscount.

"No need to thank me," he said bracingly. "It's what we agreed, isn't it?" She glanced sideways at him, wary. Nick leaned closer, training his gaze on her face and not on her bosom, which was right at eye level. "Partners," he whispered, and strode off.

CHAPTER FOURTEEN

Emilia lost the battle.

She had marshaled every argument about suitability, propriety, and even convenience she could think of, as well as some that weren't quite true. She was prepared to say she talked in her sleep, and snored very loudly, and would be a terrible nuisance to him if her bedchamber were within range of his. She had been ready, calm and logical once more, when Mr. Dashwood returned from his ride.

But when he did, there was someone waiting from his club. He listened to the man in silence, changed his clothing, and left immediately. Emilia and Lucy sat down in the morning room to a delicious meal—a lavish combination of breakfast and dinner — without him.

"Mr. Dashwood is at his club every night," Pearce answered her query when she asked.

"When does he return?"

"In the morning, ma'am, usually around seven o'clock." The butler paused as Emilia absorbed that. "If you ever have anything urgent to communicate to him, it's best to send a note to the club."

"Would he come?" she asked in surprise.

Pearce's eyebrows arched slightly, which she supposed passed for shock on his part. "Of course. If the matter were truly urgent, that is. I would never disturb him for something less."

"No," she murmured, and turned back to Lucy, who was swinging her feet under the table as she enjoyed a second lavender-honey cake. Mrs. Watson had gone straight to the kitchen and become fast friends with the cook. Lucy was in heaven.

"Shall we even see him, Millie?" she asked. "If he's at his gentlemen's club all night, and sleeps all day, I don't think we shall ever cross paths."

She sank into her seat. Perhaps that was why he'd been so dismissive of her concerns about the bedroom. It still wasn't proper, but if he were never home, it did seem less important. "We saw him this afternoon. If he hadn't been called away, we would have dined with him." Albeit very early for dinner in town. "He's a busy man, Lucy."

Her charge shrugged. "I don't mind. It's so lovely that this house is near Regent's Park. May we go, Millie? Mrs. Watson says there's a canal with ducks."

Emilia smiled wryly. "Yes, we shall visit the park."

It seemed they would have plenty of freedom to do so.

GRANTHAM HAD SUBMITTED his petition for the viscounty of Sydenham that morning, quietly and without fanfare, but by the time Nick reached the club that afternoon, the news had already got around.

Forbes met him at the door, an ominous aura about him. "Is it true, sir?" he asked point-blank. "You're a lord?"

Nick kept walking, jerking his head to indicate Forbes should follow.

Once the office door was closed behind them, Forbes folded his arms. "Are you?" he asked again, his expression mulish.

Nick tossed his hat and gloves onto the desk. "What if I were?"

The other man's mouth flattened. "Why would you even want to be?"

"If I were, it would change nothing about who I am."

His manager shook his head. "You tell yourself that, but it would. It will." He glanced around the room. "What about this club? What would happen to it if . . . ?" He grimaced, as if he couldn't even bring himself to say it aloud.

"Nothing," said Nick in mild surprise. "You can't think I would give it up."

Forbes scoffed. "Lords don't run gaming clubs. They might own one, and they'd certainly gamble in one, but they don't dirty their hands with anything like work."

Nick leaned against his desk and folded his arms. "Why is that?"

"They're lazy," said Forbes immediately. "Arrogant. Think they're better than the lot of us. Accustomed to people pampering them, giving way to them, always bowing and scraping. Can't even dress themselves."

"Hmm. So much like me," mused Nick.

Forbes flushed. He was one of the few who knew a little about Nick's upbringing. A very little, but enough to end that line of argument. "Dash—trust me in this. I saw 'em up close for near twenty years. That sort of privilege and arrogance roots deep and grows fast. They're useless without an army of servants, none of whom mean the slightest thing to them. And when they *do* own something worthwhile and prosperous, it's nothing but an income to them. Work it harder, squeeze the profits, lower the wages, never mind what happens to anyone else." He frowned at the floor. "You've seen 'em, here at Vega's. You know I'm right."

"You're not wrong," Nick agreed. "But Tommy . . ." The man looked up skeptically. "I wasn't raised thinking I was too good to clean my own arse. I never ate off silver plate. This is more of a . . . business decision."

"Business!" Forbes's scowl turned ferocious.

"Family business," amended Nick. "Presumptuous though it may be, this title is worth something."

"Ah," said the other man, disillusionment spreading cynically over his face. "An estate. Comes with some good acreage, aye?"

Nick gave a bark of bitter laughter. "Every inch of it neglected and run into debt, with an uninhabitable house. The previous viscount left everything in shambles, and his attorney may well have embezzled it into penury." The picture Grantham had painted of Nick's future domain was not rosy.

Forbes's anger melted into bemusement. "Beggin' your pardon, but why do you want it, then?"

Nick studied his shoes. He couldn't say that the title came with an orphaned little girl who would go hungry without an heir stepping in to bring some order to the estate. He wasn't about to mention the blue-eyed governess who had single-mindedly tracked him down and forced the title into his hands. Those were not the reasons he had petitioned the Crown for the viscounty.

"I have a sister," he said quietly.

Forbes inhaled in astonishment.

"A younger sister," Nick went on, "who will benefit immeasurably from being elevated to the sister of a viscount, instead of the sister of a gaming hell owner. I may not deserve to be a lord—nor want to be one, if you want the truth—but she deserves to be a lady."

"I'd no idea . . ." Forbes's voice trailed off. "Ah," he breathed. "Queen's Court."

Nick shot him a look of warning. "This was all in complete confidence. *Nothing* will change at the Vega Club. I certainly won't be selling it." Not only was it his lifeblood, he couldn't afford to. It would take a monstrous sum of money to restore prosperity to the Sydenham properties. The Vega Club had made him a rich man, but Nick remembered too well what it was like to be poor to surrender his golden goose.

Forbes was not persuaded. "Things'll change," he said morosely. "You just see if they won't."

"Things always change." Nick stood up. "But you can set your mind at ease. This won't change me."

Forbes was not the only one who had heard. When Louis saw him, the man gave a big grin and bowed with an ostentatious flourish. "My lord," he murmured as Nick strode past him. Nick stopped and stared him down, until Louis cleared his throat and ducked his head with a murmured apology.

The trouble that had brought him to the club

hours earlier than planned had begun in the kitchens. Betsy had caught her husband Guillaume in the butler's pantry with Clara Birtwhistle, who advised Nick on the decoration and menus of the club. They had been discussing turbot à la crême in a manner Betsy found suspicious, and she'd thrown a large jar of preserves at Guillaume's head.

Fortunately, she'd missed—but the jar had shattered and covered Clara, Guillaume, and half the plate in the pantry with gooseberry preserves, sparking a blazing row that eventually encompassed virtually all the kitchen staff on one side or the other.

Forbes had separated the main parties before sending for Nick. He went first to see Clara, who was mortally offended anyone could think she would dally with a chef, even a handsome one who made ethereal pâte feuilletée; then to Betsy, who cried her way through three handkerchiefs and declared she was going home to Hertfordshire, that she'd had enough of sly, charming Frenchmen even if they were good cooks and better lovers; and then finally to Guillaume, who adamantly maintained that he was not having an affair with Clara, and it was naught but a bit of idle flirting, nothing for Betsy to fret about.

The only good news was that none of them knew about Sydenham—yet. He sorted everyone out, promising the incensed Clara a new dress to replace the one spattered with gooseberry, sending the teary-eyed Betsy home with a fresh handkerchief, and threatening Guillaume with sacking if he stirred up such trouble again with his wandering eye and casual flirting.

By then it was past six o'clock. Nick thought of

his missed meal with a pang. Not only did he savor that leisurely dinner in his own house, this time he'd missed it with Miss Greene. It hadn't promised to be a friendly, intimate dinner, with her fuming at him about her bedroom, but after today, there would likely be no chance he'd have her alone again. That was good, he told himself firmly, and collected a plate of cold meats and vegetables from the kitchen before he went back to work.

That evening the club was packed. It wasn't his imagination; Frank came to ask where he should store guests' coats and hats, because the cloakroom was full to bursting. Nick tried to stay more aloof than usual. Every circuit he took, people put their heads together behind their cards and hands as they watched him pass. Tomorrow someone would ask about it to his face, Nick judged. He wasn't looking forward to it, but it was going to happen sooner or later.

When the club closed in the morning, he bypassed the kitchen—still divided into uneasy factions after the skirmish between Betsy and Guillaume—and went straight to Queen's Court. Another pang hit him as he let himself in through the gate. Charlotte was not expecting him for breakfast today; he was taking her to Portland Place.

She was dressed and waiting, her hat in her hands and her trunk sitting by the door. Her excitement eased some of the doubt Nick felt. Charlotte's one moment of pause, when Polly Neale flew out of her house and flung her arms around Charlotte, passed quickly. Within minutes the two girls were chattering about the adventure Charlotte was beginning—it turned out Polly was wildly jealous of the lovely and clever new governess—and there was a smile on his sister's face as she climbed into the carriage with him.

"Good-bye!" she called to her friend, waving her whole arm so hard out the window, the carriage swayed. "Write to me!"

"Polly can visit, you know," said Nick mildly. "You won't be but a mile away."

Charlotte bounced back onto the seat. "I know! She will. I invited her to come as soon as she can."

"Ought you inquire with Miss Greene before you do that?"

Her mouth opened in alarm. "Oh! I didn't think . . ." She trailed off, her brows knit in worry.

He smiled. "It will be easier to remember when you're with her every day."

"I'll remember," she promised, her delight reviving. "I shall be the best pupil Miss Greene has ever had!"

When they reached Portland Place, Charlotte's eyes went wide. She'd never been here. "Is this yours, Nicky?" she whispered.

"Yes."

"Such a large house?" she demanded. "For one man?"

"Now one man, two girls, one governess, and several other servants." Nick nodded at the maid who'd left off sweeping the steps and sprung to one side.

Charlotte was craning her neck to see the façade of the house. He had to call her to follow him inside. He handed over his hat to Pearce and motioned for Charlotte to remove her bonnet. With a startled chirp, she did, blushing furiously.

"Pearce," said Nick, "this is my ward. Charlotte, this is Pearce, our butler."

He wasn't sure who was more startled, his sister or his butler. He was a little surprised himself, that the word *our* had come to his tongue so easily. The butler recovered first, bowing deeply. "Welcome."

Charlotte goggled at him, but gave one of her better curtsies in return. "Thank you, sir."

"Take her things up to the schoolroom, next to Miss Sidney's room," Nick told the footman waiting behind Pearce. "Where is Miss Greene?" It was early still. The governess and Lucinda might be abed for all he knew.

"In the morning room, sir, at breakfast."

A thrill shot through him. Of danger, he told himself, not anticipation. It was breakfast, with two observers.

It didn't matter. His nerves tingled and his heart thudded hard. He led the way to the morning room, Charlotte trailing behind him.

Miss Greene rose at his entrance. "Good morning, Mr. Dashwood," she said politely. The window was behind her, giving her a halo of light that outlined every curve of her figure so brightly his eyes burned.

Ah Lord. He was in deep trouble.

Lucinda slid off her chair and made a wobbly curtsy. "Good morning, sir." She barely looked at him, her eyes flying to regard Charlotte with hopeful curiosity.

Nick swept out one arm. "Miss Sidney, may I present to you my ward, Charlotte. Charlotte, this is Miss Lucinda Sidney. You know Miss Greene already."

Lucinda bobbed again. "Pleased to make your acquaintance, Charlotte." She glanced sideways at her governess.

"And I yours, Miss Sidney." Charlotte looked more cowed than Nick had seen her in years. The two girls did not seem to know what to make of each other.

"How lovely to see you again, Charlotte," said Miss Greene warmly. "I beg your pardon, we did not know when you would arrive, and had already sat down to breakfast."

"Of course." Nick took his seat at the head of the table, which suddenly seemed rather small. He couldn't remember the last time he'd dined at home with anyone else. He ate alone, or at the Vega Club, or with Charlotte.

They sat in silence. Starving, Nick loaded his plate and waved the footman forward with the pot of coffee. Lucinda kept peeping at Charlotte, who gave a tentative smile in reply. Miss Greene buttered another slice of toast.

They ate in silence, though everyone seemed to be stealing glances at everyone else. Nick caught Miss Greene eyeing Charlotte, then Lucinda. Charlotte was looking from him to the governess and back again. At one point he caught Miss Greene's eye on him, and he winked, inwardly pleased to see her eyes widen before she looked away.

After the uproar in the Vega kitchen, Nick had been braced for more tumult at home. He was pleasantly surprised that there was none. Perhaps he'd been wrong about the upheaval this would cause in his life. It was lovely to be home already, he acknowledged, but still have Charlotte's company. Lucinda was exquisitely behaved, and if he didn't look directly at her, he could even imagine he and Miss Greene were in perfect harmony as well.

The governess cleared her throat. "I thought we

might walk in the park this morning. It's very near, and it promises to be a lovely day."

"No," said Nick without thinking.

Charlotte's and Lucinda's heads came up in dismayed, mirror images of each other. Miss Greene looked at him in astonishment. "May I ask why not, sir?"

He already knew he'd made a mistake. His instinct to protect Charlotte and keep her sheltered ran too deep, and had been too long held. But something made him dig in his heels instead of backing down. "Why should you go out so soon?" he asked in reply.

Her chin set. Her eyes sparked with something dangerous, and dangerously alluring. "Well," she said in a tone that put him on guard even as his heart thumped in anticipation. "Exercise is very beneficial to young people—to all people, really— and a long stroll in the park is eminently proper exercise for young ladies. The park is also near, yet removed from the dirt and traffic in the streets, making it safer than parading up and down Portland Place. I believe it was built for the very purpose of allowing Londoners a pleasant place to walk, and therefore it seems ridiculous not to make use of it when the weather is so fine. In addition, it will leave the house quiet, which I have learned from Mr. Pearce suits you. And lastly," she finished, "there is your agreement that you would not interfere in matters of *governessing*, which I certainly consider this to be."

At the last, she widened her big blue eyes as if to say *that's why, you damned idiot*, like the final flourish of a swordsman who had just disarmed and impaled her opponent. Charlotte's mouth was hanging open. She and Lucinda were watching with a mixture of alarm and glee.

Nick was enthralled. In fairness, he was distracted from her meaning by the way her ripe pink lips formed each skewering syllable.

"Millie," whispered Lucinda, "is *governessing* a word?"

"Yes," she said firmly, the determined smile glued to her face. That smile pulled out small dimples right beside her mouth. They were magnificently appealing.

"I've never heard it," whispered Charlotte, stealing a glance at Nick.

"Now you have," said Miss Greene.

Lucinda glanced at Nick again. "And what is he doing? If you are . . . governessing."

"Thinking," said Nick. "She is governessing, and I am thinking."

"It's taking a very long time," said Charlotte under her breath. Naturally, she would recover her spirit in time to tweak him.

Nick took a sip of coffee. "It's an important question."

Miss Greene stared at him, her expression halfway between stubborn and perplexed. "Apparently so." With a little shake she tore her gaze from his. "Perhaps we won't walk in the park today. We shall have a lesson right here in the house. On how to defend ourselves from villains."

In unison, Nick, Charlotte, and Lucinda jerked upright in their chairs.

"We will?" gasped Lucinda

"With what?" asked Charlotte eagerly.

Miss Greene patted her lips with the napkin. "Parasols and hat pins—any pins, really. A swift, well-aimed kick is always beneficial. And of course, our wits, a lady's most useful defense against men who wish us ill."

Nick shot to his feet, almost knocking over his chair. "Come," he told his infuriating governess, and stalked from the room.

She marched past him through the dining room door he held open. "This is governessing? Talking of swift kicks and hat pins?" He closed the door, aware that it was just the two of them, the exact dangerous circumstance he had told himself to avoid but couldn't stop thinking of. The only way to survive it was to argue.

Her cheeks were flushed. "I suggested a simple, ordinary thing. *You* argued, and I proposed an alternative."

"How to stab people?"

She widened her eyes innocently. "It's important for a lady to be able to protect herself."

Nick flung up one hand. "They are girls!"

"It's never too early to learn," she insisted. "You've no idea what ladies face in this world."

"You didn't mention this when we discussed duties," he charged, incredulous.

"You didn't mention that you would prohibit respectable strolls in the park!"

No. It was beginning to sound deranged, even to him. He took a deep breath and slowly exhaled it. "I'm not accustomed to being told what to do."

"I never told you to do anything," she retorted.

"You didn't ask my permission first."

Oh Lord. Another mistake. Nick acknowledged it inside his head as Miss Greene's bosom swelled temptingly in indignation. "You promised I would have free rein!"

"With Lucinda." She paused, her lips already parted for another argument. "I agreed you would have a free hand in the rearing of *Lucinda,* not of Charlotte."

Her expression blanked with astonishment. "You prefer that I leave Charlotte at home while I take Lucinda to the park?"

Yes, he did, but Nick knew it was wrong. Not only would it provoke a storm of protest from his sister, the entire point of hiring a governess was for Charlotte to go out. He cleared his throat. "Speak with me first before proposing outings."

Her face wrinkled in confusion. "Of course I would, before most outings. But the park? It's perfectly respectable for young ladies to walk in the park with a chaperone. At this time of day it will be full of children with their nursemaids."

"Will it?"

"Of course," she said in surprise. "Surely you've seen them."

"I've never been in Regent's Park."

The admission seemed to astound her. Her eyes widened further, and her mouth stayed open in a perfectly mesmerizing O. "Never?"

He shook his head, trying not to look at her mouth.

"But why not? It's a beautiful park, and it's so nearby . . ." She paused. "Did you mean, not in the morning?"

"I said never, and I meant never." When he'd had the time to do things like wander through parks, he'd been a scruffy lad, escaping his strict aunt's household to seek out gamblers in the rough part of Birmingham. When he'd become more established and the gamblers were coming to him, he'd had no time for things like parks.

But Charlotte did, and it was why he'd brought her here, after all. No need to prevaricate and dither like an old man; he'd already committed himself by filing that petition.

He cleared his throat. "I'm not familiar with the park, but I will allow it. James will go with you."

"I don't need a footman to chaperone two girls in Regent's Park."

"Nonetheless," Nick said firmly, "James will go along wherever Charlotte goes. Every time. Do we understand each other?"

"Is there something I don't know?" Her brows creased in a worried little frown. "About Charlotte?"

Nick opened his mouth, then closed it. He turned toward the windows, overlooking Portland Place. It was a wide, elegant street, despite the building work being done up and down the length of it. He'd bought the house because it was new, it was convenient, it was *safe*. He sighed. "It's a complicated story, Miss Greene. Must we do battle over it now?"

"No," she said after a longer pause. "It's been a long time since I had to deal with an employer who wished to oversee my work so closely. I apologize."

"Accepted." He turned and put out his hand. After a moment she took it, her hand smooth and warm in his. A perfect fit. A perfectly ominous glow seemed to warm his hand from the contact. "James will be at your disposal any time you wish to go out. He'll be ready to go to the park when the girls and you are."

"Thank you," she murmured. She wet her lips

—Nick closed his eyes against the sight—and added, "Perhaps you would like to accompany us?"

He thought of walking in the park with her on his arm, the sun catching her eyes. He pictured her turning her face to the sun, smiling at its warmth, smiling at *him*, and— He released her hand. "You'll enjoy it more without me."

She blinked. Nick headed for the door, so tired now he thought he'd just go up to bed. Food could wait.

"Mr. Dashwood . . ."

He paused, hand on the latch.

She stood in the center of the room, twisting her hands. She looked genuinely contrite, and somehow even more lovely, biting her lip and gazing at him with soft eyes. Nick began to weaken. He ought to apologize, to assure her he wasn't usually so abrupt and irrational. Perhaps he ought to go to the damn park—just to assure himself it was safe for Charlotte, not to see the governess's face flushed with exercise . . .

"Have you no plans to furnish this room?" she asked.

Nick blinked, then looked around. The estate agent who'd shown him the house had extolled the handsomeness of the spacious dining room: the excellent light from the large windows with their finely molded architraves, and the elegant fittings, from the laurel-wreath frieze of the cornice to the ornate Carrera marble mantlepiece to the intricate parquet floor. Nick had agreed, and then only entered the room a handful of times in the seven years he'd owned the house. There wasn't a stick of furniture in it, nor even a carpet. "I'm never here, Miss Greene. What would be the point?"

"Yes, so said Mr. Pearce. In that case, would you mind terribly if we used it for dancing lessons? It would avoid moving the furniture in the drawing room, if we could put the pianoforte in here." She wet her lips again. "And it would be less likely to disturb you."

He stared, mesmerized by the slide of her tongue along her lips. He was losing his mind, watching a governess's mouth while she took over his house, his sister, and his life. "Yes," he murmured. "Whatever you want."

He was far beyond disturbed.

CHAPTER FIFTEEN

As puzzling—and unsettling—as that first morning conversation was, Emilia vowed to learn from it. What was she thinking, to argue with Mr. Dashwood? Any other employer would have sacked her on the spot. Losing her post would mean losing Lucy, and Emilia wasn't about to let that happen.

It helped greatly that she hardly saw him during the next fortnight. By the time they'd returned from walking in the park, there was no sign of the man—but the pianoforte had already been moved to the dining room. From then on, Mr. Dashwood was always at his club, out somewhere else, or sleeping. He did often take breakfast with them, but it was obvious his mind was elsewhere. Charlotte could make him smile, even laugh at times, but Lucy was still quiet and shy around him. Emilia kept her voice quiet and her eyes lowered, and in return Mr. Dashwood barely glanced her way.

Her apprehension about lessons faded as well. She tried to leave word with Mr. Pearce about her plans, but the reply was always the same: *As you think best.* Even the matter of her bedroom seemed moot. At times it felt as though she and the young ladies had the house entirely to themselves, and in that circumstance it didn't matter that she had the mistress's bedroom. She wasn't immune to the luxury of having such a room, large and quiet and comfortably furnished. And when Lucy had a nightmare, she heard the screams at once and it took her only seconds to sprint up the stairs.

"There, dear, there," she crooned, hugging the girl fiercely. "It's only a dream."

"It was dreadful," Lucy sobbed against her neck. She clutched Emilia's shoulders so tightly, Emilia could feel her fingernails. "Papa found me here, in the drawing room. He-he-he shook me, Millie, and called me filthy and I-I-I couldn't get away."

"He shan't hurt you, ever again," Emilia vowed, finding that she could, in fact, still hate the late Lord Sydenham.

"He took me to the bathhouse and pushed me in and I fell so deep and couldn't get out," Lucy went on, her voice choked and shaking. "I couldn't breathe, Millie, I couldn't, and the whole time he was watching me . . ."

"He's gone, Lucy," she whispered, over and over, until the girl's trembling subsided and her sobs had died to whimpers. "No one shall hurt you," she murmured, smoothing Lucy's damp hair. "No one, do you understand? They would have to battle me first, and I would never let them."

"Truly?" Lucy hiccuped against her shoulder.

"Truly," Emilia promised. "I'm quite fierce with an umbrella, and as for my skills with a hatpin— well! I can draw blood at three paces."

Her reward was a thin, weak smile. "Will you always, Millie?"

"Always." She found a handkerchief in a drawer of the wardrobe and handed it to Lucy, who obediently scrubbed her face. "Can you go to sleep now?" Lucy nodded, and settled back into her pillows. Emilia tucked the covers around her before cupping her hands around Lucy's thin face. "You are a strong, brave girl," she whispered. "That doesn't mean you won't ever be frightened, but it does mean you will survive and triumph. Do you hear me?"

Lucy nodded. In the moonlight her face was pale, her eyes puffy. "Where is Chester?" she whispered.

"In the kitchen." Emilia made a snap judgment. "Would you like me to fetch him?"

"Yes, please."

When he was drunk, Lucy's father would go rambling through the house in destructive rages: he threw things through windows, took a sword to the woodwork in his late wife's sitting room, and burned family portraits in the dining room fireplace. One night Sydenham had dragged his five-year-old daughter from bed and told her to get out of his house and not come back, terrifying the child and her nursemaid. After that Chester slept on Lucy's bed. Once the cat had scratched the viscount's face when he tried to wake Lucy, and been banished from the house.

Well—Sydenham had bellowed for someone to drown the damned cat, sending Lucy into a paralyzed terror. Mrs. Watson had conspired with Emilia to hide the animal in the stables until the viscount forgot.

After Sydenham died, Lucy hadn't needed Chester on her bed nearly as often, but she still loved him. When they arrived in Portland Place, Mr. Pearce had looked down his nose at Chester and had a footman whisk him off to the kitchens. Tonight, though, Emilia resolved to fetch the cat. She and Lucy could return him in the morning before Mr. Dashwood came home.

As Emilia let herself out of the room, she realized Charlotte had also woken. The girl stood, silent as a wraith, just outside Lucy's door.

"Is she ill?" Charlotte's voice was a bare whisper.

"No." Emilia hesitated. "Her father was unkind. Sometimes she has nightmares about him."

Charlotte's eyes flicked to the door. Her face was still and unreadable in the dim light. "She must have been terrified of him."

"He was terrible," said Emilia. "I'm sorry we woke you."

Charlotte shook her head slowly. "No, it's no trouble." She twisted a fold of her nightgown between her fingers for a moment, still gazing at Lucy's door. "I know what it feels like," she added, her voice almost too low to hear.

About to suggest the girl return to her own bed, Emilia paused. "She wants me to fetch the cat," she said instead. "Would you like to come with me?"

Charlotte nodded. Emilia waited as she fetched her slippers and dressing gown, and together they went down the stairs.

"It feels rather daring," Charlotte whispered as they moved through the darkened house, "creeping about in the dark."

Emilia smiled. "Does it? I hope I don't catch any trouble for it."

"No," said Charlotte immediately. "Nick would never say a word of reproach, if he knew why."

Emilia said nothing. They had reached the kitchen door. Mindful of the servants who slept off the kitchen, she tiptoed through, relieved to spot Sir Chester sleeping on a table under the window. She handed Charlotte her lamp and scooped up the sleepy cat, scratching his head when he meowed indignantly. They retraced their steps back up to the nursery, and when Emilia opened Lucy's door, the cat darted in and leapt onto the bed, eager to reclaim his rightful place. As she closed the door, Emilia heard Lucy's weary sigh of happiness: "Oh, Chester . . ."

She turned to find Charlotte watching her. Worry made her look much older than her fourteen years. "Will she be all right, Miss Greene?"

"Yes." *As right as anyone could be, after such a childhood,* Emilia thought. "You should go back to sleep, too," she added quietly.

Charlotte handed back the lamp, but didn't go into her room. She ran her hands up and down her arms as if suddenly chilled. "I don't think I can," she whispered, "not yet."

"Nor can I," murmured Emilia, making another quick decision. "Come sit with me."

This time they took the small winding stair to Emilia's room. Abandoning sleep, Emilia lit two more lamps as Charlotte made a circuit of the room, studying everything with interest.

"Is this the mother's room?" she asked.

"Yes, I think it would be."

Charlotte's head bobbed slowly. "It's lovely. I'm glad Nick gave it to you."

Emilia stirred uneasily. "It's only temporary . . ."

Charlotte glanced at her with a flash of impish humor. "You think he'll give it to me when I'm grown?" She shook her head. "I'd rather stay upstairs. Being able to see over the trees and rooftops is wonderful."

"You won't need a governess when you're grown," said Emilia.

"But Lucy still will."

Emilia folded her arms. "Perhaps."

Charlotte ran her fingers through the thick folds of the drape at one window. "She'll want you by her for a long time. It takes years for nightmares to fade."

"Do you have nightmares, too?" Emilia asked quietly.

A fine shiver ran through Charlotte, but she gave a firm shake of her head. "Not anymore. Years ago I did. Nick gave me a pistol to keep by my bed."

Emilia's jaw dropped. "What?"

"It wasn't real," cried Charlotte hastily, covering a smile with one hand. "I should have said that! It looked quite real, and I thought it was, but later Nicky showed me—it never was." She laughed a little. "I should have known. He never showed me how to load it, or shoot it, or anything. He simply laid it on the table and said it would scare away anyone who tried to hurt me."

Who would try to hurt you as you slept? Emilia wondered. "I suppose if it was a comfort, and could cause no harm, it wasn't a bad thing to do."

Charlotte's smile faded. "I doubt he knew what else to do. He must have thought having a pistol by the bed was a perfectly normal way of sleeping. I'm so much younger than he, how could he know what else to say? And we were almost strangers to each other."

Emilia had been wondering about the relationship between guardian and ward, but now she thought she had it. There was less than twenty years' difference in their ages, which made it unlikely Mr. Dashwood was her father. But the name *Nicky* made her believe her second guess was right: brother and sister. Why would siblings be strangers? And why would he keep it secret?

"He did the best he could, and I shall never fault him for that," Charlotte was saying. "Just as Lucy will always love you, for how you've cared for her."

That only reminded Emilia of how much she couldn't do for Lucy. "Mr. Dashwood has done a great deal of good for her, too."

"He likes to help people, no matter what he might tell you. When my friend Polly's father lost his position in a factory, Nick got him a new one, and helped her family find a place to live. It was directly across from my house, which was ever so lovely, as there were no other girls nearby." Charlotte came and plopped down on the small settee. "He despises injustice, no matter how small."

Emilia took the chair. "Very admirable."

She nodded eagerly. "He's very admirable!" Then she made a face. "Sometimes too admirable. He's very strict at times."

"Because of James?" guessed Emilia. She'd seen Charlotte roll her eyes at the footman hovering behind her.

Charlotte twisted the ribbon of her dressing

gown around her fingers. "I ought not to complain about him. It's lovely to be allowed to go out at all."

"Were you not allowed out before?" asked Emilia in astonishment, before she could stop herself.

The girl looked startled. "Oh—Er, well, not often." She looked away but her cheeks were scarlet. "Nick is much too busy to take me around, you know."

And Charlotte had had no governess. Emilia's thoughts raced in different directions. "So you never went anywhere?"

"Not much. I was permitted out in the court, particularly if Polly and her brothers were out. We raced hoops and skipped rope. Still, I wished we could venture out more, to Astley's or the Tower, or to Bond Street . . ." She went quiet suddenly, then jumped off the sofa again, as if she couldn't hold still any longer. "This room must have a brilliant view of the park. Does it?" She pulled back one drape and stared into the night.

Emilia came to stand beside her, trying to hide her seething interest. Charlotte was charming, with an open, eager curiosity about everything around her. But she'd slept with a pistol beside her bed, given by a guardian—brother?—who was a stranger to her, and she wasn't permitted out without a personal attendant. And she knew what nightmares were.

"It does," she said with a smile, in answer to the girl's question. "I hope the future lady of the house has a fondness for views, for this one is splendid."

"Lady of the house? You mean . . . his wife?"

Emilia nodded.

Charlotte let the drape fall. "I—I doubt it."

Emilia turned in surprise. "Why not?"

"Nick says he'll never get married."

Emilia looked down to hide her wry smile. "He will be a viscount, Charlotte. He will need a legitimate heir—"

"No," repeated Charlotte. "He doesn't care about that." She saw Emilia's confusion. "Because of our father. I don't think Nick has a high opinion of marriage."

Ah, so she was right: brother and sister. "How so?"

But Charlotte seemed to have decided she'd said too much. She fluttered her hands and made a face. "He didn't tell me! But I should go back to bed, so you might do the same. Good night, Miss Greene." She made an uneven curtsy and crossed the room to the nursery stair. "Sleep well," she said with a small smile.

"Sleep well," echoed Emilia as the door closed behind Charlotte, her mind awhirl with questions that had no answers.

NICK HAD FORESEEN TROUBLE, but not this much.

"Three more," reported Forbes. He set the membership tokens on the desk.

"How many is that?"

"Twenty-seven, with eight more rumbling about it."

Grimly Nick surveyed the tokens, specially struck silver ovals with stars on one side and the script V of Vega's on the other. Twenty-seven tokens returned, twenty-seven members resigned. That was almost two a day since the petition. It wasn't the number that bothered him, it was the rate.

"I also received four inquiries," Forbes offered. "There's some blokes who don't mind wagering at a lord's club."

Nick swept up the tokens. "I daresay there will be more, for the notoriety if nothing else."

"Right."

He unlocked an iron strongbox from the cabinet, put the tokens in, and relocked it. "More importantly, how are receipts?"

Forbes hesitated. "Up two percent."

Nick looked at him. "We're making more money, with twenty-seven fewer members. Is that correct?"

The manager nodded. "Record numbers of guests."

"Very good." Guests were only permitted four evenings per month. Nick counted on that taste to persuade them to apply for membership, and so far he'd not been wrong. In a few weeks, this furor would have died down, replaced by some other scandal, and the gamblers of London would remember how superior Vega's was to every other club.

Or so he hoped.

There was a tap at the door, and Forbes opened it to reveal Jimmy, one of the boys Nick employed for errands. "Mr. Carter would like a word, Mr. Forbes, sir," he said.

Forbes disappeared to go see the head croupier, and Nick waved Jimmy to come in. The boy slipped through the door, clutching his wool cap and waiting alertly. "What's the latest chatter about me, Jim?"

The boy's face scrunched up. "You, sir?"

Nick nodded.

Jimmy looked thoughtful. "A lot o' flutter about you aimin' to be a lord. It makes 'em nervous, to think you might 'spect to speak to 'em in Parliament or some'ere. One bloke were swearin' that he'd tell all his lady acquaintances to keep their distance."

Nick smiled humorlessly at that. "That all?"

Jimmy shrugged. "All I've heard."

"Very good." Nick flipped him a shilling and the boy grinned before slipping back out the door.

He leaned back in his chair and scrubbed both hands over his face. Members were quitting his club because they didn't want to speak to him in Parliament or let him court their daughters. If only Miss Greene could hear that, after she had held those very things out as temptation.

Miss Greene.

He inhaled deeply, then let it out. No matter how he tried to avoid her—even the thought of her —she was everywhere. He'd spent less and less time at home to avoid meeting her, and still he could smell her scent in the air and hear the murmur of her voice even from two floors and several closed doors away. At least, he imagined he could, lying exhausted but awake in his bed, picturing her leaning over Lucinda's stitching, that lone curl brushing her bare neck, or teaching Charlotte how to sweep a grand curtsy, her bosom swelling over the neckline of her gown.

Being at the club was scant reprieve, though. Not only were members leaving, word had spread through Vega's, and he'd had to address the full staff to repeat the assurances he'd already given Forbes that the Sydenham title would change nothing about the club. Guillaume, still smarting from the dressing-down over Clara, had remarked rather snidely that a lord ought to pay lordly wages. Forbes, still smarting from having to quell the battle royale, had retorted that, in his experience, lords paid lower wages and often not even those, and then Nick had had to promise that no one would be sacked or have their wages cut.

As if all that weren't enough indignity, Grantham arrived the next morning with more.

"This was at my offices this morning." The solicitor handed him a letter.

Nick set down his billiard cue and read it. It took him a moment to decipher the meaning, couched as it was in vague and flowery words. He glanced at Grantham. "Someone wants me to sell this club?"

"For your own good," he replied dryly.

Nick handed back the letter and took up his cue again to conceal his fury. Between the lines of that letter was a threat: Nick knew too much about too many people. His pursuit of the Sydenham title would be complicated—even outright opposed—if he maintained control of the Vega Club. The letter writer, who hadn't deigned to sign his own name, had suggested Nick either relinquish his claim, or unburden himself of the club, and proposed an insultingly low sum.

Nick was coming to agree with Forbes about aristocratic gentlemen: arrogant, ignorant, and useless. A plague on all of them.

"Twice someone's come 'round to query my clerks," Grantham went on. "Sniffing for any fault in the petition. They claimed to be from the Committee for Privileges, but they weren't."

"I presume they found no faults." Nick lined up his shot. Billiards helped him keep his temper under control, and soothed his mind after a difficult night. He was playing a lot recently.

"Of course not." His solicitor was affronted. "Nor will they. Miss Greene did the work of five investigators."

Nick's shot veered wide of its target, and he swore in frustration. "Never underestimate a woman on a mission." He moved around the table and sighted another shot along his cue. "Although I still fully expect someone to emerge from the wilds of Dorset, a distant eccentric cousin who lives in an isolated cottage on a moor and takes no newspapers or letters, to lodge a competing petition."

Grantham waved it away. "They'd better come bearing proof of an unknown marriage to some hapless Sidney never known to anyone else. Miss Greene searched diligently."

Nick missed his shot again and rose to glare at his solicitor in irritation for saying her name over and over. "It sounds as though I ought to be paying Miss Greene rather than you. Apparently she put in all the effort."

Grantham laughed. He'd drawn up the agreements the governess had demanded for her salary and Lucinda's trust. "You *are* paying her. Very handsomely."

Nick gave up. He stowed his cue in the cabinet. Billiards weren't helping.

"The newspapers have got hold of it, too," Grantham went on. "I did my best to quell the worst rumors, but some things are irresistible to gossipmongers. You ought to put your servants on guard not to speak to anyone about you."

Nick shrugged. He'd been in the scandal pages for years, and only expected it to get worse. But he'd also never been one to sit back and take abuse. He'd recently invested in a newspaper, and the grateful owner had been eager to offer advice about how best to preserve one's reputation among the fourth estate. "My people are tight-lipped, and have been for years. As for the newspapers, I've made plans."

"Oh? Anything I should know about?"

"Not really," murmured Nick, spinning a billiard ball across the felt. "If that's all, I'm going home."

Grantham bowed his head. "Certainly. Until next week."

The solicitor left and Nick stood motionless for a moment. Why weren't billiards helping? They required concentration, calculation, a perfect stillness in body and mind before a decisive strike. He played them to clear his mind and forget other cares. Normally a few games left him calm and quieted, but today he had been playing for over an hour and still felt restless and unsettled.

It must be exhaustion. He hadn't slept more than five hours a day in weeks—not since Emilia Greene took up residence in his house. It was almost ten o'clock in the morning; perhaps the gods would smile on him, and she would be out walking through all the parks in London when he returned home, and he could collapse into oblivion without seeing her and being shocked alive all over again.

He inhaled deeply. Not *alive*. He was perfectly, normally alive already. The crackle of lightning that seemed to course through him every time he caught her looking at him or overheard her laugh . . . that was probably illness, he told himself. He was neglecting his health. A good day's sleep, and he would be his usual self.

He put on his coat and headed for home.

CHAPTER SIXTEEN

Pearce swept open the door as he strode up the front steps. "Good morning, sir. Mr. Forbes has sent over the receipts, and they are in your study."

Nick nodded and shrugged out of his coat. The house was not quiet and still. Someone was playing the pianoforte, but far too well to be Charlotte or Lucinda. "Very good. What . . . ?"

"Dancing lessons, sir," said the butler. "The dance master arrived half an hour ago."

"Ah."

Pearce waited another minute, but Nick just stood there, listening to the music emanating from the dining room. Charlotte had mentioned dancing; she was eager to begin. The music was a sprightly piece. Almost in a daze, he walked to the door and gently pushed it open.

A slender young man was playing the pianoforte. Miss Greene was turning pages of the music, and a dark, elegant fellow of about forty was holding Charlotte's hand in dancing posture and pointing out the steps, marked in chalk on the floor. His sister had her skirts pinned up a few inches so she could see her feet, and a fierce frown of concentration puckered her brow. In a chair by the window sat Lucinda, a book open in her hands but her attention on the dancers.

Lucinda saw him first. She whipped up the book in front of her face, which caught Miss Greene's attention. She turned toward him, eyes wide, lips parting in surprise. Nick gripped the doorknob to keep from striding across the room and taking her in his arms. For a moment, happiness flashed in her eyes, a smile blooming on her lips, as if she'd been waiting for him to walk in and was delighted that he finally had . . .

The music stopped. Miss Greene turned away. The dancing master had noticed Nick as well, and now he came forward, one hand over his heart. "Good morning, sir," he said in accented English, with a courtly bow. "Mr. Dashwood, I presume."

Miss Greene hurried over, beautifully flushed. "Mr. Dashwood, this is Signor Giacomo, the dancing master we discussed."

Nick had no memory of that discussion. "Welcome, Signor."

The man beamed. "Grazie."

Charlotte hurried over. "We're learning a quadrille," she said breathlessly. "Do you know it?"

"I do," he said in amusement.

Her eyes grew wide and she whirled to clasp Miss Greene's hand. "I cannot picture how it should look from Signor Giacomo's description. Will you dance it with Nick so I can see it?"

The room went stone silent—or so it seemed to Nick, as he met Emilia Greene's shocked gaze and thought, deep inside himself, *God yes.*

"I—I could dance it with Signor Giacomo while you watch," stammered the governess.

"Oh, please dance it with Nick," begged Charlotte. "It's so difficult to learn a quadrille with only one couple. I shall watch you, and it will be so helpful, say you will, please, Nick?"

His gaze hadn't left Miss Greene, who snapped her mouth shut and raised her chin. "I have no objection. Miss Greene?"

Her smile returned, a bit brittle. "Of course not."

They took their places. The young man at the pianoforte, waiting for Signor Giacomo's signal, began playing.

Nick faced her. She wore the yellow dress again. She curtsied, he bowed, and his mouth went dry at the splendid view of her bosom. The dress was demure, but a hint of white ruffle peeked out at one side, a tantalizing glimpse of her undergarments. No lace, for a woman in service, but still a little touch of delicate luxury. Beauty. Sensuality. Temptation.

They clasped hands and took the first few steps. Dimly he heard the dancing master instructing Charlotte, but he had no idea what his sister was doing. All he saw was the curve of Emilia Greene's cheek, the slope of her shoulder, the swell of her breasts. All he felt was her hand in his. All he thought about was pulling her closer, tasting her skin, breathing in her gasps of pleasure . . .

She held herself gracefully, holding up her skirts, never faltering. For a few mad moments, Nick allowed himself to think her hand clung to his a moment longer than necessary, that she swung herself toward him eagerly, though she never met his eyes. Even when he took Charlotte's hands, all he could see was the flash of the governess's ankles as she turned with the dance master. The exercise brought a luscious color to her cheeks, loosening tendrils of hair to drift down her nape, and jarring more of that tantalizing ruffle into view.

His Miss Greene was mesmerizing.

"The promenade," called Signor Giacomo. Miss Greene stepped beside him, arms extended. Nick took her hands: left in left, right in right. His forearm brushed her waist; the back of his right hand pressed against her belly. Her hip brushed his, and something stirred inside him. They moved in the promenade, side by side, and finally she looked up at him.

Her eyes were deep, deep blue, turbulent with dismay, a whiff of embarrassment . . . and helpless awareness.

It almost made him miss a step. She felt it, too —this powerful but inconvenient pull between them. It should have alarmed him, this warning that the precipice was even closer than he'd thought, but instead it made him ache to take the plunge all the more.

He couldn't have this woman. He *would* not. But God above, how he wanted her. And now he knew she wanted him, too.

"Beautiful," declared Signor Giacomo. "Very good." The music had ended. Charlotte was watching them with a curious expression. With a soft gasp, Miss Greene jerked her hands free and re-coiled a step.

"You dance splendidly, Nick," said Charlotte. "And you, Miss Greene. You make such a handsome couple."

The governess's face turned scarlet. "Thank you," she said in a strangled tone. "Perhaps you should dance the next one with your brother, Charlotte, while Signor Giacomo instructs." She all but ran back to the pianoforte and seized the music.

Charlotte whirled toward the dancing master. "May we learn a waltz?" she asked eagerly.

The Italian clicked his tongue. "No, Signorina, not today. First we conquer the quadrille. Next week, perhaps."

Nick cleared his throat. "I'll mark it in my diary. If you want me back," he added as his sister turned to him, beaming with hope.

"I do! It was ever so helpful, truly it was, watching you and Miss Greene. Thank you for agreeing to do it again."

His hands still tingled. Emilia Greene kept her back to him, paging furiously through the sheet music as if in search of the secrets of immortality. Wisps of hair trailed down her neck, practically begging him to brush them aside and press his lips there, where her shoulder met her neck in a curve of satiny skin. He wondered how many of her undergarments had ruffles, and where they were.

"My pleasure," he said.

WHEN THE DANCE lesson finally ended, Emilia surprised her pupils by declaring they would rest.

"I'm not tired," protested Charlotte.

"I didn't even get to dance," cried Lucy.

Emilia felt as though she'd run to Richmond and back. Her pulse still raced, and her cheeks still burned. She wasn't sure her legs would support her much longer. "*I'm* tired," she declared. "If you are still energetic, perhaps you could begin copying your French lesson, Lucy, and you may review your history lesson, Charlotte."

Lucy made a face of agony, which Charlotte mimicked to a lesser degree. "Couldn't we go to the park instead? It's sunny out today, and it's not even noon."

"No."

"James could walk with us, if you're tired—"

"No!"

Such denial was unlike her. Charlotte pushed out her lower lip and Lucy screwed up her face to argue and plead.

"Do your lessons. I'm going to my room to rest," announced Emilia, to head off all of it, and marched out the door.

Too late she realized that Mr. Dashwood was upstairs, in his bedchamber. Very near to hers. Likely stripping off his clothes for bed right this moment. Unbidden her mind fastened on that thought. She'd seen him in shirtsleeves, his forearms bare. Did he sleep in a nightshirt with a woolen cap on his head? She doubted it. Arabella had told her once that Oliver slept naked, which she'd learned the night his chimney began to smoke and he'd fled into the corridor with only a blanket clutched around his waist. Arabella had laughed and made sport of her then-nineteen-year-old brother's thin arms and hairless chest, but that was not what Emilia pictured under Mr. Dashwood's clothes. His arms weren't thin at all. His hands were large and strong. His shoulders were broad and his chest was solid. And his eyes—

She was nearly running by the time she reached her room and closed the door hard, leaning against it as if she'd escaped something terrible.

If only she could. *She* was what she was trying to escape, her own primal reaction to a man—the worst possible man. Worse still, he knew it, because she hadn't been able to conceal the longing humming inside her when they danced.

Emilia had long ago given up expecting to fall in love and marry. That had all been tossed out the window when her father betrothed her to one of his own friends. He'd told her it was for her own good, and that she would be glad of it one day, but when Papa died, Emilia broke the engagement the next day. Her uncle had roared in fury, but by then she'd been old enough to defy him and stubborn enough to take herself off to seek employment, rather than submit to what the men in her family chose for her.

Her first position had been as companion to an elderly countess, a friend of Arabella's grandmother. Lady Watney had been demanding and imperious, but also liberal-minded about many things. She was the one who'd taught Emilia the primary rule of females in service: keep a chary eye on the men of the household, especially the master. *A man who pays a woman's wages,* the countess would say, *always overestimates what he has purchased.*

After a year, Lady Watney told her she was too young and sprightly to be a companion, and suggested she work with children. She'd given Emilia a letter of recommendation to the wife of an admiral, who needed help with her four children while her husband was away at sea for months at a time. Emilia had loved those children, three young ladies and a boy who wrote poems about his father's ships. Her next charge had been Lady Helen, just

making her come-out at age eighteen and in woeful
need of guidance, since her mother was preoccupied
with six other children and her father, an absent-
minded earl, was lost in his botanical studies most
of the time.

With Lady Helen's marriage to Lord Mulworth, Emilia had developed something of a reputation among governesses. She had three offers of
employment, but somehow the inquiry from Mr.
Bennet, Lord Sydenham's solicitor, had tugged at
her heart. He wrote of a widower seeking a responsible woman to care for his poor, motherless daughter, only seven years old, and he'd named a lovely
high salary. Mr. Bennet had brought Lucy to the
interview at an inn, and Emilia had lost her heart to
the thin, quiet child with big, yearning eyes.

It had seemed entirely respectable. Lady
Fairchild, Lady Helen's mother, had known the late
Lady Sydenham and assured Emilia her child must
be lovely. Only later did Emilia realize that she'd
said nothing of the viscount himself.

She hadn't even met her employer for two
months. Sydenham had turned out to be cruel and
petty, and the lovely high salary turned out to be a
lie, but by then Emilia had fallen completely in love
with Lucy, and she'd waged a pitched battle to keep
both of them out of Sydenham's sight.

And now . . . Nicholas Dashwood.

After so many years of keeping her distance
from men, of being on guard against their attentions and intentions, she'd thought she had grown
immune to them.

She'd been wrong.

Slowly she crossed the room to the other door.
It led to his private study, Pearce had told her.

Emilia rested her cheek against the polished wood, but heard nothing. Lightly she rested her hand on the knob. It didn't turn—she'd tried it the first day to be certain—but for a moment she wondered what would happen if she could open it.

If she *did* open it.

If she walked through the door.

If it were just the two of them.

Would he be there, leaning one hip against a desk like the one in his office at the Vega Club? Perhaps with his jacket off and his sleeves rolled up, as the first night she met him. Perhaps with his neckcloth loosened—discarded. Perhaps he would look at her as he'd done while dancing, with his amber eyes burning with hunger that made her want to throw herself at him. Perhaps he would smile the wicked smile he'd given her when he'd said he was an uncouth cardsharp. She felt his hand around hers, the brush of his body against hers, and inhaled a deep shuddering breath.

With a start she backed away from the door.

She'd known she would have to protect Lucy. She hadn't considered that she would have to protect herself.

CHAPTER SEVENTEEN

Emilia was ashamed to admit herself a coward, but after that she began actively avoiding Mr. Dashwood.

He was away so much, it wasn't difficult, but now she took care to ask Mr. Pearce when he was expected home. Every day she planned something that would occupy her and her students during those times: French lessons, pianoforte practice, visits to a museum, walks in the park. Dancing lessons were put off until midday. And whenever an excuse offered itself to get away from the house, Emilia seized it.

Mr. Dashwood had explicitly told her to acquire a proper wardrobe for Charlotte. Emilia decided to enlist help, in the form of Lady Arabella McCorquodale. Not only had Arabella been her steadfast friend since childhood, she was the daughter of an earl who possessed an impeccable sense of fashion, as well as the funds to afford it.

Arabella swept in with a whiff of perfume and a flutter of paisley shawl. "Em," she cried, taking

Emilia's hands and pressing her cheek to Emilia's. "It's been an eternity since I saw you!"

"*You* went to Scotland," Emilia reminded her with a grin. "I've been here all the while."

Arabella made a face as they sat on the sofa. "Oliver's mad idea! He's still there, you know, poor man. I wish you hadn't broken his heart. We would have made such wonderful sisters."

"And that's why I could never marry him," returned Emilia with a laugh. "Because I already *am* like a sister to you—and to dear Oliver." Oliver didn't love her, let alone want to marry her. He was a marvelous fellow, loyal and good-natured, but he was hardly ever serious about anything. He'd been laughing when he proposed, and he'd laughed when Emilia had said *"Don't be silly, Ollie."*

Arabella made a face. "Well, I *do* blame him for not being persuasive enough, but I still wish you had said yes. Now, tell me what you're up to," she said, switching topics with her usual rapidity. "Nicholas Dashwood! The very last person in London who would need a governess, if you ask anyone in society."

Emilia pleated her handkerchief and smiled. She had to handle this delicately; Arabella did love a good gossipy story. "Yes, well, you must have heard the news by now." She hadn't told anyone save Lucy, Mrs. Watson, and Henry about her search for the Sydenham heir, but now he was common knowledge. It had even been printed in the newspapers, which she knew because she'd asked Mr. Pearce to save them for her. Such a luxury, getting the newspapers again, even if what they printed about her employer verged on libelous.

"Viscount Sydenham!" Arabella smiled and fluttered her eyelashes. "Is His Lordship home?"

Emilia laughed. "He's not the viscount yet, and no, he's not at home."

She didn't know why, as it was late morning. Normally he would be here by now, albeit asleep. But today he hadn't appeared.

"I shall meet him sooner or later," said Arabella breezily, unconcerned. "He cannot keep to this cloistered nocturnal existence as a peer."

"I wouldn't know what he plans," Emilia murmured. "But today I need your help, Arabella. I hope it's not an imposition—"

"For you? Never!" Arabella sat up straighter, wiggling her shoulders in eager determination. "What shall we attempt? A siege of White's, or Boodles? Are we bent on stealing back an indiscreet letter to a former paramour?"

Emilia snorted with laughter. "Of course not! On second thought, perhaps I shouldn't ask this of you. It may require too much diplomacy, tact, and sensibility."

Her friend made a face at her. "I can feign all those things when I wish to. What is our mission?"

Emilia shook her head, still grinning. "I need to outfit a young lady on Bond Street, and it's been so long . . . Well, I would like a friend to remind me how elegant people shop."

Arabella reached out for her hand. "You never have to beg for my help. It will always be freely given. Your father—" She stopped at Emilia's warning look. "And your uncle—"

"Arabella . . ."

"And Fitchley—!"

"Arabella!" Emilia glared at her. "They are dead to me."

"Would that they truly were, all in miserable and painful ways," muttered her friend. "I shall never forgive them. But who is the young lady?"

"Mr. Dashwood's ward."

Arabella's eyebrows climbed up her forehead. "A ward! How old is she?"

"Nearly fifteen."

"And he wants her dressed in Bond Street?" Arabella raised her brows even further. "She's a bit young for it."

Emilia lifted her hands helplessly. "I think the young lady wishes it more than he does, but he told me to take her." He'd left a note with Pearce containing instruction about where to send the bills.

"If I have one indisputable genius," said Arabella, recovering from her surprise, "it is shopping in Bond Street. Shall we go now? I'm glad Oliver and Papa stayed in Scotland, it will be a month before they see the bills I run up . . ."

Emilia rang for Pearce and asked him to fetch Charlotte. She hurried into the room, her face bright with excitement. She made a very proper curtsy when Emilia introduced her, and even kept her poise when told they were going to Bond Street with Lady Arabella.

"Are we still to meet my friend, Polly Neale?" she asked.

Emilia nodded. "Of course. I thought Lady Arabella would offer more fashionable advice than I can." She saw Arabella's startled glance, and ignored it. "If you fetch your shawl, we shall go. Pearce has sent for the carriage."

Charlotte beamed, curtsied, then finally lost control and fairly skipped out of the room.

"She's only fifteen?" asked Arabella.

Emilia smiled wryly. "Nearly." Charlotte might be a girl who giggled at rabbits cavorting in the park and laughed over her musical mistakes with Lucy, but she was going to be a beautiful woman. With her hair no longer in braids, clad in stylish dresses instead of girlish frocks, Charlotte would look far older than her years.

Perhaps that was what made Mr. Dashwood uneasy about her going out; the few times they were in the same room, she'd caught him looking at Charlotte with a mixture of trepidation and delight.

"My, my. What about your other pupil?" Arabella asked as they went into the corridor. "Have you resolved the troubles there?"

"Well, I—" Emilia stopped short.

Lucy sat on the stairs, clutching Chester in her arms. Her thin face looked tragically woebegone, and at the sight of Emilia and Arabella, a fat tear rolled down her cheek.

So far she and Charlotte had done everything together, and Lucy's shyness around the older girl was almost gone. But Lucy was only nine, and Emilia wasn't taking her to Bond Street. She'd explained this to Lucy already.

"I shall meet you downstairs," she murmured. With a curious glance at Lucy, Arabella nodded and went down the stairs.

Emilia stopped in front of Lucy. "Lucinda, have you completed the row on your sampler?"

"No," she whispered.

"Have you finished copying the French verbs into your book?"

"No," said Lucy again. Another tear wet her cheek and splashed onto Chester's head. The cat began wriggling, and Lucy's arms tightened.

"Then you must go back to the schoolroom and work on those," said Emilia gently. "You should be finished when we return, and—"

"I want to go to Bond Street!" Lucy wailed, and burst into tears, burying her face in the cat's fur. Chester writhed at this confinement, meowing loudly.

Emilia stepped forward and took the cat, releasing him to streak up the stairs. Lucy put her face in her hands and sobbed harder.

"Lucy," said Emilia when the tempest seemed to be lessening, "you know why you may not come."

The girl swiped at her wet, blotchy face. "B-b-but I want to, so desperately, Millie! Charlotte says it will be splendid, with beautiful dresses and jewels and then you're to g-go for ices, and I want to have ices, too!"

"We will not buy any jewels, and there will be other trips to have ices. Compose yourself, Lucy. When you are fifteen—"

"That's ages away!" choked the girl.

Emilia smiled in sympathy. "But it will come, and when it does, I shall take you to Bond Street for new dresses as well—"

"No, you won't," went on Lucy, lost in misery. "You'll have launched Charlotte as a beautiful lady, and it won't be the same with a plain, misshapen girl like me—"

"Lucy!" Emilia sat down beside her and framed her charge's face in her hands. "You are beautiful and perfect as you are," she said fiercely.

"B-but I haven't got anyone to look after me,

like Mr. D-Dashwood does for Charlotte," hiccuped Lucy. "No one will care what I wear."

Emilia's heart twisted painfully. "You've got me," she declared. "And Mr. Dashwood looks after you, too."

"Oh, Millie." Lucy swabbed her face with her skirt, and Emilia let it go. "He doesn't care about me. What if you're not still here when I'm fifteen?"

And just like that her heart cracked. "I will never forget you or desert you. I expect you'll have many friends who are more amusing and fashionable than I when you're fifteen, but if you ever wish me to take you shopping in Bond Street, I will," she vowed recklessly.

"Promise?" whimpered Lucy. Tears clung to her pale lashes, making her look like a sea creature.

Emilia nodded, her gaze unwavering on Lucy. "I promise."

The girl wilted. "All right."

"And we'll go for ices another time," Emilia added. "Soon. Charlotte would like to see her friend, but it's not as though Gunter's will close forever after today."

At last, a weak smile lifted Lucy's drooping mouth. "Tomorrow?"

"Perhaps. We'll see what state your sampler is in." Emilia got to her feet and offered her hand to Lucy, who dragged herself up from the step. "Go on, now. We'll be back before you know it."

"Because it takes forever to stitch a sampler row," muttered Lucy, plodding up the stairs.

The cat sauntered across the top stair, and Emilia added in a conspiratorial whisper, "Perhaps Sir Chester will help you." Lucy's head came up, and she sped up, catching the cat in her arms when she reached the landing.

Emilia took a deep breath. She ought to have expected that. Naturally Mr. Dashwood would take a greater interest in his own sister, who was older and in more pressing need of things like gowns and dancing lessons. It wasn't his fault Lucy had been so neglected her entire life that an outing to get ices seemed imbued with unspeakable excitement.

It wasn't her fault, either, but Emilia felt the weight of Lucy's disappointment.

She straightened her shoulders and summoned a smile as she went down the stairs. Charlotte peered anxiously around the brim of her bonnet. "Shan't Lucy come?"

"No," said Emilia, taking her own bonnet from Pearce. "There will be a time for her to come, but today we are outfitting you! Lucy would grow bored sitting and waiting, and you'll wish to spend time with Miss Neale."

Charlotte hesitated, but finally smiled a little and nodded.

Arabella led the way to the carriage, chattering brightly about which modistes were in fashion this Season and which had grown *de trop*. Charlotte revived with the talk of the new dresses she would soon have, and Emilia let James help her into the carriage. He sprang up on the seat with the driver and they were off.

It had been quite a while since Emilia visited Bond Street, and she couldn't deny a thrill of delight as they turned into the fashionable street. Unlike Arabella, she had never had carte blanche to shop here as a matter of course, but she'd been able to afford a few select items. A bonnet from Mme.

Roche's shop. Gloves from Dewey's. Her best gown, a gift from her grandfather years ago, from Madame Follette's.

"Where shall we begin?" asked Charlotte. She was doing an admirable job of keeping her composure, although she was gripping her reticule in a stranglehold of eager excitement.

"What do you need most?" Arabella smiled at her.

"Oh . . ." Charlotte looked uncertainly at Emilia. "A dress?"

"We shall start with some day dresses and a dinner dress," said Emilia. "With shoes, bonnet, gloves and the like."

Charlotte's face lit with joy. "Oh, yes," she breathed.

Arabella nodded in satisfaction. "Very good. Brissotte's, I think."

The dressmaker's shop was bright and clean, with elegantly dressed dolls in the two front windows. Madame Brissotte, an older Frenchwoman, came forward with a smile, and soon the three were ensconced in a small, neat room with delicate furniture. There Arabella took charge, laying out the array of clothing they wanted, with specifics of colors and styles that made Charlotte's eyes grow wide.

"Very good, my lady," Madame Brissotte said approvingly. "Françoise will know precisely what to do." She rang a bell and a moment later a young woman came into the room, sketchpad and pencil in hand.

For over an hour, Emilia and Arabella sorted through sketches, ignoring Charlotte's gasps of delight to cast aside several. The young assistant nodded almost constantly, her pencil flying across the pages as she revised the sketches to Arabella's demands.

Once they had five approved sketches, the cloth was presented, unfurled from soft, shining bolts that evoked another pang of envy in Emilia's heart. There was a rich sea-green silk that made her gasp softly, and before she could stop herself, she put out her hand and touched the glowing cloth.

Arabella shot a keen glance at her. "It would look stunning on you," she murmured.

Emilia withdrew her hand with a sigh. "I have no reason to own a dress made of that."

"There is always a reason, sooner or later," put in the dressmaker. She held up a bit of the silk near Emilia's face. "It *would* be very striking."

"Oh, you would look so beautiful in that, Miss Greene!" gushed Charlotte.

Emilia laughed. "Beautiful, to supervise French verb conjugation and outings to the duck pond!" She shook her head at Madame Brissotte, who put away the silk without further comment. Arabella, bless her, immediately asked for paler colors, suiting Charlotte's age, and no one else said anything about Emilia ordering a new dress.

Still, she thought about it, while Charlotte undressed to her stays and petticoat and stepped up on the stool to be measured. It would be so lovely to have one fine dress—nothing as fine as that aquamarine silk, but something pretty. Something that fit, that wasn't years out of date. Mr. Dashwood had paid her first quarter's wages. Emilia did have money. And she couldn't stop thinking, in a dark and secret corner of her heart, about the searing way

Mr. Dashwood had looked at her when they danced . . .

"Let me buy it for you."

Arabella's whisper made her jump guiltily. "Oh, goodness, don't be silly."

"Don't *you* be silly and refuse a friend's gift." Her friend touched her arm. "It would make me so happy, to give it to you. I have accepted that you won't have Oliver, the hopeless wretch, but I still think of you as my sister." She paused as Emilia bit her lip. "I've missed you, Em."

She caught Arabella's hand and squeezed. "And I you, Bella. Thank you so much for coming today."

The other woman laughed. "Of course! I haven't forgotten the pleasures of shopping for someone else." They both glanced at Charlotte, who was currently pinned into a long swath of sprigged muslin and admiring herself from every angle. "You will have your hands full."

"Nonsense," said Emilia stoutly. "She's a charming girl with good sense."

"Hmm. And her guardian?"

Without warning Emilia's memory conjured up another moment during the quadrille, when her hands had clasped his, pulling them close together, when they'd been moving together as one. He'd looked down at her with such focused attention, as if he wanted to see right to the bottom of her soul . . .

"He trusts me to guide her properly," she said repressively, before leaping from her chair and heading for the door. "I need a breath of air." She grabbed her bonnet and bolted.

On the pavement of Bond Street, she inhaled

deeply and flexed her fingers. She couldn't be so big a fool to fancy her employer. That would be mad. He had behaved honorably, scorching glances aside. She, on the other hand, had all but blackmailed him into supporting Lucy, made a fool of herself arguing with him, and nearly drooled at him when dancing. She had far more to lose by forgetting herself.

"Why, bless my soul," exclaimed a man behind her. "Can it really be Miss Emilia Greeneborough?"

Emilia froze. All worries about Nicholas Dashwood vanished in one painful lurch of her heart.

He strolled around to face her. "It is, indeed!" Geoffrey Parker-Lloyd said in a tone of false delight. "How *do* you do, Miss Greeneborough?"

Spine like steel, she raised her chin. "Perfectly well, thank you."

His smirk grew broader as she said nothing else. "What a delightful surprise to cross your path. It's been an age, hasn't it?"

Emilia said nothing.

"Yes," he mused, resting both hands on the head of his cane and tipping back his head as if in deep thought. "It must be . . . a dozen years? No, it cannot be so long. Eight? Ten?"

Emilia stayed silent.

"Ah, yes, I do recall now," said the man in triumph. He was toying with her. "I've not seen you since you broke poor Fitchley's heart."

CHAPTER EIGHTEEN

Emilia cursed herself for not being more alert. She was standing on Bond Street in broad daylight, too distracted by scandalous thoughts about her employer to pay attention to her surroundings, and now she was paying for it.

Parker-Lloyd bent forward, over his cane. He was a little taller than she, and lean, posing to show his elegantly tailored burgundy coat to perfection. Emilia had always thought he looked like a fox, with thick auburn hair slicked back from his pale face, and nothing about him had changed in the intervening years. His long, narrow nose practically twitched with the prospect of mischief.

"What a treat, running into you. And looking so . . ." His gaze ran down her figure, one brow rising in frank disdain for her simple dress and pelisse. "So like yourself," he finished. "Fitchley will be delighted to hear you're in town again."

Was that a threat? It sounded like one.

She gave him a stony look. "I doubt Lord Fitchley remembers me after all this time."

He laughed. "You're wrong! He remembers you very well. Exceptionally well, I daresay."

Emilia cursed silently at the way he said those last words. "Your pardon, sir. I must rejoin my friends." She turned back toward the dress shop, only to see with horror Arabella heading right toward her. Her head was turned as she spoke to Charlotte, so she didn't catch Emilia's frantic look.

"Allow me," drawled Parker-Lloyd, reaching out to hold the door. He bowed as they stepped out. "Lady Arabella! What a pleasure."

Arabella stopped short, looking him up and down with all the distaste Emilia felt. Arabella's brother, Oliver, had once accused Parker-Lloyd of cheating at cards, and the men had nearly dueled over it. All the McCorquodales despised him. "Oh. You."

He smiled at that, showing his teeth like a predator. But then he caught sight of Charlotte, who was peering curiously at him, and Emilia's heart almost stopped. "Good day," he murmured salaciously, eying the girl with open calculation. "Won't you introduce me to your young friend?"

"Indeed not," said Emilia forcefully. "I only introduce her to decent people."

Parker-Lloyd's face darkened. Arabella pushed past him. "James! Is the carriage here?"

"Yes, m'lady," said a voice at Emilia's shoulder, making her start. James had materialized without a sound, and he was watching Parker-Lloyd with a dangerously calm expression.

"Excellent. Stand aside, please," said Arabella with regal hauteur. She linked her arm through Charlotte's and towed her toward the carriage.

James fell in behind them, purposely blocking Parker-Lloyd's view.

Emilia started after them, but the wretched man snared her arm. "Who is that girl?"

"Let me go." She gave him a freezing look and ignored his question as she tugged against his hold.

His grip tightened. "How dare you dismiss me."

"I wonder that you care," she said coolly. From the corner of her eye, she saw James returning. "Insignificant little nobody that I am."

Parker-Lloyd was still for a moment, then released her, smiling his flat smile again. James was back, looking large and threatening.

"Are you?" Parker-Lloyd murmured. "I confess I did think so once . . . but now, I wonder."

She ignored him and walked away, James at her side. "Did he hurt you?" murmured the so-called footman.

"No." She hesitated at the carriage step. "James . . . I expect you'll tell Mr. Dashwood about this, but I should tell him first. There are things I must explain."

His face didn't change. "As you wish, ma'am. But he'll want my report this evening."

She gave a nod. "Understood." She climbed into the carriage and sat next to Arabella, gripping her hands together tightly to hide their trembling. She would have to find Mr. Dashwood as soon as they returned home. For now, she tried to shake it off, and mustered a smile for Charlotte. "A first lesson in London gentlemen, my dear. Not all of them are gentlemen, and some are to be outright avoided."

"He's a foul man," put in Arabella. "He tried to cheat my brother at cards."

Charlotte's wary expression eased at that explanation. "The bloody sharper!"

Emilia closed her eyes as Arabella laughed. "Yes, he is," Emilia conceded. "Even if I cannot condone that language."

The girl giggled. "I know far worse! Are we still to go for ices?"

"Yes," said Emilia firmly. She didn't want Charlotte to dwell upon Parker-Lloyd or his comments.

Thankfully there were no other disruptions at Gunter's. Polly Neale and her mother were waiting, and the two girls seized each other's hands and began chattering at a speed that repelled any other participant. The conversation veered from fashion to pets to flavors of ice and then back to fashion, with Polly hanging on Charlotte's every word about the dresses just ordered.

By the time they returned to Portland Place, Arabella and Charlotte were fast friends, debating the best number of buttons on a pair of gloves and whether one needed a parasol if the bonnet had a broad enough brim. Emilia was in a state of quiet anxiety.

"Would you please tell Mr. Dashwood I must have a word with him when he wakes?" she asked Pearce once they'd said farewell to Arabella and Charlotte had hurried upstairs to tell Lucy all about the outing.

The butler bowed his head. "He is not here, Miss Greene."

She blinked. "Not here?" It was three in the afternoon. When did the man sleep?

"He returned briefly, but has gone back to the Vega Club."

Damn.

She delayed until after dinner, hoping he might turn up. When that didn't happen, she debated sending a note, as Pearce had once suggested. This was urgent, wasn't it? Parker-Lloyd wasn't the type to keep gossip to himself. But she gave up that idea after trying to compose the note in her mind, and realized it would sound either hysterical or deranged.

She bundled Lucy off to bed. The girl looked recovered from her earlier upset, with Chester on her lap all evening. Charlotte was trying to hide a yawn as Emilia left Lucy's room.

"I'm going out," Emilia told her charge. "Will you be all right?"

Charlotte nodded. "Where are you going?"

"To have a word with Mr. Dashwood at his club."

Charlotte perked up. "Oh! May I go see it?"

Emilia imagined her employer's reaction if she brought his sister to his gambling club. He was going to be furious enough when she turned up there, even before he heard what she had to say. "Are you trying to get me sacked? Of course not."

Charlotte rolled her eyes with a smile, and Emilia went downstairs.

Pearce offered to call for the carriage, but she shook her head. She needed some time and fresh air to organize her thoughts. A walk was just what she needed, even with James beside her.

It didn't take long to reach the club, whose windows were brightly lit again. She eyed it with trepidation as she climbed the front steps; the last time she'd come here, she'd drunk too much wine and behaved rashly. James stepped forward and rapped the knocker. "They keep the door bolted now," he told her.

"Why?"

"Couldn't say, Miss Greene."

Should have had some wine, she thought. Her nerves were only getting worse.

The young man who opened the door spotted James first. He opened the door wider, his expression friendly, and then he saw her. "Madam," he began.

"I must see Mr. Dashwood," she interrupted. "Urgently." From the corner of her eye, Emilia saw James give a slight nod of confirmation, which apparently held more weight with the fellow.

"This way." He let them in, then bolted the door and led the way down the same corridor Emilia had traveled once before. At the end, he opened a familiar door. "Wait here, Miss." He left her alone in the room. James had gone his own way at the front.

It was the billiard room. Emilia took off her cloak and circled the table, pulling off her gloves as she studied the balls. She'd played billiards, long ago. Her grandfather had been fond of the game and had a table at his country estate. He'd taught her, laughing as she crawled atop the table because she was too short to reach.

Mr. Dashwood's table was magnificent, made of polished oak with the green baize pressed perfectly flat. The balls were ivory, one cue ball marked with an ornate V. On a whim Emilia lifted a cue from the stand. She took off her bonnet and put it aside. "Left corner," she whispered to herself, leaning over the table and lining up the angles. She drew back the cue and took the shot.

It missed.

"Try again," said a voice directly behind her, and Emilia startled so badly she dropped the cue and almost fell as she leapt away from the table.

Mr. Dashwood had come in as silently as a ghost. He stood behind her, hands clasped behind his back, golden gaze on her.

It had been a few days since she'd seen him, and even longer since she'd been this close. He was barely two feet away, tall and dark and lethally attractive in evening clothes. The lamps caught the sharp angles of his face, giving him a brooding, dangerous look.

"I beg your pardon," she said quickly, though it came out in a husky whisper. "Forgive me . . ."

He peeled off his jacket. "Try it again."

The old Lord Sydenham would have sacked her on the spot for daring to touch his billiards table. Emilia didn't know what this Lord Sydenham would do. "Oh, no, I shouldn't . . ."

"No, no. You look like you know what you're about." He went around the table and took his own cue from the rack.

Emilia couldn't keep her eyes from his shirtsleeves. Just like the first time she'd met him, right here in this room, when she'd told him she had a proposition and he'd looked her up and down with hot, knowing eyes. "I needed to speak to you, sir, or else I wouldn't have come."

He shrugged, undoing his cuffs and rolling up his sleeves. The muscles of his forearm stood out as he swooped one hand to gather the balls. "Billiards, I find, help quiet my mind. Is anyone at home ill? Injured? Is the house ablaze?" Emilia shook her head after each query. "Then there's no need to pelter along. Play the shot again."

In spite of everything, Emilia's nerves began to settle at his calm demeanor. She took up the cue again and made her shot, managing a glancing tap on the red ball.

"Better." He circled the room, eying the ivory balls before leaning down to line up his own shot. He lowered himself to the table unhurriedly, those bare forearms flexing in the light of the oil lamps burning above him.

Emilia looked away, fixing her gaze on the cabinet at the far end of the room. It was *wrong* to find her employer so attractive. She'd mostly avoided thinking about it by avoiding him, but now she found that tactic had weakened her resistance, not bolstered it. "Something happened today," she began, telling herself that the sooner she got this over with, the better. "In Bond Street."

Silence, then the soft tap of his cue against ivory. The unmarked white ball streaked into the pocket by her hip.

"Two," he said.

Emilia nodded, fishing out the ball and getting ready for her own shot.

"Rest more of your weight on the table," he said. Emilia glanced up in surprise. "You're standing stiffly away from it," he explained. "Let your shoulders relax."

"Oh." She smiled awkwardly and adjusted. "It's been a very long time since I played."

"Who taught you?"

"My grandfather." She squinted one eye, peering along the length of the cue. "He had a footstool for me to stand on so I could reach the table.

That's how long ago it was." Carefully she took the shot, just barely missing.

"I find billiards peaceful." He circled the table, lining up his next shot. "No one to antagonize, nothing to argue, merely a test of your ability to calculate angles and forces. It requires a clear, calm mind."

"My grandfather liked the solitude of it. I fancy it was his retreat from . . . disagreeable things."

Dashwood glanced up. His pose was languid, angled toward the table, the cue very still in his hands. "What sort of disagreeable things?" He took his shot, and again the ball found the pocket.

Our family, she thought. "My grandmother was from a prominent family, and preferred London society. My grandfather preferred the country. He was a great sportsman, very fond of the outdoors. There were . . . disagreements."

She didn't add that the disagreements had crossed generations; her father and her uncle had taken after their mother and become rakish bucks of the *ton*. She didn't mention that when her own mother died, her father had deposited her in Kent with her grandfather and gone back to those carousing ways. And she certainly didn't mention the appalling scheme Papa and Uncle John had cooked up to benefit their mate and fellow rake, Emmett Fitchley.

"So they lived separate lives?"

"Largely," said Emilia. "I spent many years with my grandfather in Kent. My grandmother was rarely there. She died in London, and my grandfather said—" She stopped abruptly.

He lifted his brows in question, a faint smile on his face. It was hard not to smile back at him, and here in this quiet room, just the two of them in a golden pool of light, Emilia succumbed. "He said now she would have no choice but to spend eternity in Kent," she whispered. "In the family crypt."

Grandpapa had found that oddly amusing. Looking back, Emilia wondered if Grandmother hadn't done something scandalous or unpardonable, off in London by herself all those years, and Grandpapa had buried her in Kent to spite her long dislike of the place.

Dashwood grinned. "We all get our just desserts in the end, hmm?"

She grinned back. "Perhaps."

He stepped away from the table. "What happened today?"

Emilia came forward and studied the lie of the ball. He was right; she felt much calmer now. "I saw someone I knew," she said, keeping her eyes on her ball and away from him, standing with his hands clasped on his cue, his white shirtsleeves vivid in the shadows. "Years ago." She paused, then made a shot, pursing her lips when it also went wide. "It was not a cordial meeting, and I fear he may spread gossip about me, but worse than that, he saw Charlotte."

Silence.

"She behaved perfectly," Emilia assured him. "But he isn't a well-mannered person, and I fear . . . I fear he was too interested in her. I didn't introduce them, nor tell him her name, but he's a—"

"Scoundrel?" he suggested when she stopped.

Parker-Lloyd was a liar and a cheat who liked to make women feel small and powerless to resist whatever he wanted to inflict upon them, be it crude advances or petty slights. Even worse, he was wealthy and had aristocratic friends, so no one ever challenged him for it.

"Something like that," she answered.

Dashwood leaned down and made his own shot, potting her ball again. "Who is he?"

"Geoffrey Parker-Lloyd." Emilia was so relieved to have got the story out, she just told him.

He went still. Then he tilted his head back to look at her. "Who?"

She repeated the name.

Slowly Mr. Dashwood put down his cue and came around the table toward her. "How do you know him?"

Emilia blushed. "He was once friends with my father and uncle. And—and he knows Lord Fitchley." She tried not to think of his threat to tell Fitchley she was in London. She also tried not to think of how very alone she was with Mr. Dashwood, in his private, dimly lit billiard room. And he with his jacket off and his forearms bare, right in front of her.

He folded those arms and looked down at her for a long moment. "And was his only interest in Charlotte?"

Her face was on fire. "But that's terrible! He's not remotely respectable—"

"Of course he isn't," he cut in. "But your expression is more than outrage for Charlotte. He frightened you."

She took a deep breath—unfortunate, as she seemed to breathe him in, leather and brandy and man. "I would prefer to avoid Lord Fitchley, and I fear Mr. Parker-Lloyd will tell him where to find me, and Charlotte, and . . ."

"And Lucinda," he finished for her.

Emilia jerked her head in a nod. It was just layers upon layers of bad.

He was quiet for a moment. Emilia glanced up and caught him studying her, his amber eyes dark. He looked exhausted. No wonder, she thought, remembering that he'd not been home to sleep. Up close she could see the circles under his eyes. His jaw was covered with a shadow of whiskers, as if he'd not shaved today, either. She wondered if he'd even eaten.

"It was my fault," she said in a low voice. "If I'd thought more clearly, I would have sent for the dressmaker to come to us—"

"Don't be ridiculous." He held up one hand, his fingertips almost touching her lips, and Emilia was struck dumb. "You aren't to blame. Charlotte wanted nothing less than to visit Bond Street and see everything, and I agreed to it. Why should she, or you, have to hide away on the chance that a reprobate like Parker-Lloyd might happen past?"

"If he had no interest in me," she began.

This time he touched her lips, one fingertip to quiet her. "Then it might be Charlotte he fixed upon, which isn't any better. Don't blame yourself."

"No?" she said stupidly.

He shook his head, looking down at her.

His fingertip was barely in contact with her lower lip, but she thought she could feel that touch with every nerve in her body. It seemed to set off some kind of resonance within her, a faint hum that made her skin prickle.

He shifted his weight, fractionally closer to her. His head tipped to one side as he studied her with those turbulent, glowing eyes. His finger moved, slowly, gently, along her lower lip. For a moment the world seemed to pause around them, and Emilia forgot to breathe. If he didn't kiss her . . . if he *did* kiss her . . .

A tap at the door broke the spell. Dashwood looked away, his hand falling. "Come," he called, and Emilia retreated a step, her heart racing for a different reason now. She must be losing her mind.

The manager popped his head through the door. "More trouble in the kitchen, Dash. Guillaume caught one of the maids—" He caught sight of Emilia and closed his mouth.

"I'll be there in a moment." Dashwood was rolling down his sleeves. The manager glanced accusingly at Emilia again, and shut the door.

Blushing, she swung her cloak around her and crammed her bonnet back on her head as she searched for her gloves. One was on the table with her bonnet, but the other was missing. She turned in a circle, looking for it, only to find it in Mr. Dashwood's outstretched hand. Emilia took the glove with a murmured word of thanks.

"Miss Greene." A wry smile curved his mouth, which perversely only made Emilia's heart beat faster. Rumpled and tired and amused sat very well on him. "You did right, coming to tell me. I'll see to Parker-Lloyd."

She exhaled in relief. "Oh, thank you." He turned away and pulled on his jacket, then opened the door for her.

He led her through the corridor toward the entrance. The club had grown louder and livelier while Emilia had been there, and the click of faro boxes and chatter of roulette wheels competed with the dull throb of voices. As they turned into the main hall, the footman waiting there opened the door, admitting a throng of gentlemen, boisterous and well-dressed.

Suddenly Dashwood halted in front of her, spinning around. Unprepared, Emilia plowed into him, and he swept one arm around her as he flung out his other hand and dragged aside a drapery. Before she could protest, or even form a coherent one, he shoved her into the alcove behind it, stepping in with her and pulling the drape around them.

CHAPTER NINETEEN

She gave a muffled squeak as Nick crowded her into the service nook. They kept supplies for the main salon in here: cards, dice, counters, everything but markers, which were kept under lock and key in Forbes's office. It was a tiny space, carved out of an alcove that had once displayed a statue or a painting in the house's former days. There was barely enough room for one, let alone two.

Unless those two were pressed up tight against each other. Her hands were flat against his chest, the brim of her bonnet bumping his chin. Nick could feel every breath she took, and a shudder of lust tore through him.

He closed his eyes, even though it was pitch dark. He could see it all in his mind—how to hold the nape of her neck, how to angle his body so she fit perfectly against him, how to pull her closer and ravish her with kisses and make her quake with pleasure as he satisfied both of them.

His mouth went dry. Would her hands slide up around his neck? Would she cling to him? Kiss him back? Her longing gaze when they danced indicated she'd thought of all that . . .

Nick had not grown up in the ordered ways of the gentry. The women he'd known as a younger man hadn't been offended by direct inquiry, and the women who drifted up to him now *made* the direct inquiries. Perhaps that would change, with a viscounty, but . . . perhaps not. He'd seen for himself how titles disordered people's minds. Either way, he had no idea how to confront this thoroughly inappropriate desire for his new governess.

"Mr. Dashwood," she said breathlessly, "what—?"

"Shh." He squeezed her tighter and ducked his head. There was nothing but a velvet drape behind them; Nick could still hear the voices of the new arrivals, nattering at Frank. "Did you see who just arrived?" he breathed by her ear.

She shook her head, wisps of her hair brushing across his mouth. They were silky soft, and he finally identified the scent of her: honeysuckle. "Who?"

"Fitchley and his mates, including Parker-Lloyd."

She recoiled, turning her head as if to face him. Her cheek touched his, and then her mouth.

It was an accident. Nick was trying valiantly to cling to the shreds of whatever honor he had. When her lips brushed his, he froze—waiting, wanting, wishing—

She didn't retreat. Softly, tentatively, her mouth soft and light, she touched her lips to his again, and that was both enough and not nearly enough. Nick turned his head and something inside him growled in triumph as his lips covered hers. She inhaled, and her hand gripped his shoulder.

Not to repel, but to hold.

He gathered her to him and kissed her like a dying man striving for air. Her hands moved to his arms, clinging. He raised his free hand to cup her head and knocked her bonnet off. She moved against him, making a soft gasp of desire, and Nick's good intentions fled for good.

He licked the seam of her lips and she opened for him, moaning again as he tasted her. She pushed up on her toes, digging her fingers into his shoulders and gripping hard. His nerves lit up, crackling with desire and making him exquisitely aware of every little sound and movement she made as she kissed him back, just as hungrily and urgently as he devoured her.

He took a step, pressing her hard into the wall. Cards spilled around them, dice rattling out of trays to the carpet below. His hands were on her waist, lifting her and holding her with his weight. Her hands were in his hair, her voice in his ear, gasping "oh" over and over as he made love to her throat, as he shoved aside her cloak and licked the swell of her breast above her bodice. She bit his earlobe as Nick sucked lightly at the side of her neck, right below her ear. Her knees parted and he pushed his hips forward, against hers, and without thought his hand slid down her thigh, feeling for the hem of her dress.

And then he stopped, breathing like a racehorse after Epsom. *Bloody hell,* he though dazedly. With hands that trembled, he held her close for another moment, and then gingerly let her back down onto her feet. Sense seemed to return to her then, as she made a quiet sound of dismay and recoiled.

Only a few inches, because there wasn't room for more. But she retreated.

"I didn't mean," he began at the same moment she whispered, "I am so sorry—"

Silence reigned.

Nick cleared his throat. Outside it was quiet; Fitchley and his lot must have gone into the salon. Frank would be hanging up their coats before returning to his post. "It should be safe now," he said quietly. "To go out."

"Oh," she murmured. "Good. I—I ought to go."

He nodded—inane, given the darkness. "They didn't see you. They couldn't have." They had been facing Frank in the well-lit entry, and Emilia had been behind him in the dim corridor.

"Good," she said again. "I don't want to see them."

He breathed in—sweet, wild honeysuckle—and exhaled, willing his pulse to calm. His cock strained at the front of his trousers, and the mad, reckless part of his brain was still exploring the ways he could make love to her in this alcove.

"You're safe," he said again. Another deliberate breath in and out. "I would never . . ."

"Yes," she said when he fell silent. Her voice was higher than usual. "I would never . . . And we would never . . . It was a moment's madness. Understandable. A lapse. Neither of us to blame." She was also breathing hard and trying to hide it. "Nothing we need to speak of, later. Ever."

Nick was still thinking about the word *understandable*. "A lapse," he echoed. "Madness."

They stood in silence another moment, then Nick nodded curtly. "Right." He pulled back the drape.

She looked so beautifully mussed, he almost closed it again. Her eyes were dark, the blue almost eclipsed. Her hair was falling down, her bonnet was on the floor, and her bodice was askew, showing that delicate little ruffle again. He'd pulled it aside, when he put his mouth right there on her breast, which was still rosy from the rasp of his beard and the pull of his mouth. She tasted warm and rich, like fresh cream—

He turned on his heel and strode into the entry. Frank was leaning on his stool, talking with Forbes, but leapt to attention at Nick's approach. "Find James," he ordered. "Now."

Frank bolted toward the dining room.

"Hail a carriage," he told Forbes, who raised one brow but went out into the night. It shouldn't take long; the Vega Club paid a number of hackney drivers to loiter nearby when unengaged, for patrons' convenience.

Nick stayed where he was, slowly regaining mastery of himself. God. What had he done?

Emilia Greene—with her snapping blue eyes and determined chin and luscious figure—was his employee. A respectable lady, whom he had engaged to teach his impressionable younger sister how to be respectable. Pressing her up against the shelves of dice and cards and kissing her until neither of them could breathe was utterly unacceptable.

But . . . *understandable.*

A footstep made him look over his shoulder. Her bonnet was back on her head, and her gloved hands clutched her cloak tightly around her. The flush had faded from all but two scarlet spots in her cheeks, and she kept her eyes averted. "Mr. Dashwood," she began.

If she apologized, he would never forgive himself. "James is on his way," he said to forestall it. "He'll see you safely home."

She nodded, looking down.

They stood like that in silence until Frank came trotting back, James in his wake. James straightened when he saw Nick's expression. Nick knew the fellow fancied a girl in the kitchen, and had probably been there enjoying a bit of roast beef while he talked to his sweetheart.

"She told me," he told his man, before James could speak. "Take her home. If that man or any other scoundrel comes 'round the house, send someone to notify me immediately—and keep him away from my family."

"Yes, sir."

Forbes popped back in the door. "Carriage is waiting."

Nick jerked his head at James, who went right out. He turned to Emilia. Now he wouldn't even be able to think of her as Miss Greene, not when he had the taste of her in his mouth. *My family,* he'd said, meaning not just Charlotte and now Lucinda, but also Emilia. It felt right—even if it wasn't true. "Don't worry about Fitchley or Parker-Lloyd," he said quietly. "I won't let them hurt you—*any* of you."

She looked warily at him through her eyelashes. "Can you do that?"

Nick smiled coldly. "Watch me." He offered his hand, and she took it. He led her out and handed her into the waiting hackney. Then, unable to resist, he kept hold of her hand until she looked at him. "Don't worry," he said again. "You're safe with me."

He meant it in all ways. She seemed to know. She gave him a smile, uncertain at first but then growing. She leaned forward until they were face-to-face and Nick's heart leapt at the thought that she might kiss him good-bye. "Thank you," she whispered, and pulled the door closed.

Nick stood staring after the carriage until it reached the end of the short street. "So," boomed a voice beside him, making him start. "Shall I add that to the file on her?"

"What?" asked Nick evenly.

Forbes smirked. "You know what."

Nick turned and walked back inside. "Mind your business, Forbes," he said over his shoulder.

"That I will, Dash," came the jolly reply. "The entire time I'm tidying a closetful of cards and dice from the floor."

CHAPTER TWENTY

Emilia went to bed in a state of shock.

She had kissed Mr. Dashwood. He had grabbed her and pushed her into that alcove, but she was the one who'd kissed him, when he was trying to whisper an explanation in her ear and she somehow turned her head and found her mouth against his.

What had she done? Almost ten years of careful, proper behavior, never inviting or returning any man's interest, always mindful of her vulnerable place in the world . . . all gone in the touch of one man's lips on hers. She crawled into her bed and pulled the blankets over her head.

Although . . . oh, how *wonderful* it had felt. How alive she'd felt when he ran his hands over her. Her hand drifted over her right breast, her thumb smoothing over the spot where he'd sucked at her skin. Emilia closed her eyes, imagining her hand was his, pulling aside her shift, stroking over her nipple until it throbbed. She brushed her fingertips over her lips, picturing his face, and knew herself to be wicked and immoral.

But just this moment, she didn't care. Tomorrow, she would be calm and controlled again. Tonight . . . She undid the buttons on the front of her nightgown and slipped her hand inside, to cover her own breast, squeezing the nipple until it turned hard and aching. Her other hand slid down her belly, between her legs. Tonight, she gave in to the wicked urge and let her imagination run wild, imagining what might have happened in the billiard room if the manager hadn't interrupted them, and what Nick Dashwood would have done if she'd kissed him then. She imagined her hands were his, as she stroked herself; she pictured his face above her. She imagined his voice whispering in her ear—not words of love, but of passion, of desperate want. And it was his face she pictured when she found release.

She lay still, panting, her face damp with perspiration and embarrassment. It was *wrong* to pleasure herself while thinking of her employer. But with any luck, that had got it out of her system.

It had been a burst of madness, nothing more; she was recovered now. She had flown too near the flame but was carrying on, a little singed though otherwise unhurt. It would never happen again, and she would never speak of it.

Her resolve lasted almost two entire days. Mr. Dashwood had entirely disappeared, no longer joining them for breakfast, to Charlotte's disappointment—and Emilia's mingled shame and relief. Was he also horrified by that kiss? After all, she had told him he would be an eligible match, as a viscount. A quick tumble might suit the owner of a gambling club, but he could do so much better, in just a few weeks' time. Or perhaps he had realized it could hurt his sister if he carried on with her governess; Emilia knew he cared for Charlotte.

As had become her custom, she stretched their morning walks in the park as long as she could, to allow time for him to come home and retire in peace, if he were coming home at all. He had looked tired that night, she thought—up until he kissed her, when he hadn't seemed tired at all. He had lifted her against those shelves as if she weighed nothing, and managed to remove her bonnet and cloak with one impatient hand . . .

Distracted by thoughts she couldn't seem to banish, she was caught unprepared by a man stepping into her path, so close she stumbled to avoid bumping into him.

"There you are," said Baron Fitchley in a low voice.

Emilia's blood curdled. She lunged backward, only stopping when Fitchley said, "You can speak to me here like a civilized person, or I'll follow you night and day, telling everyone what you did. You didn't think you could hide forever, did you?"

Her chin came up. "I did nothing wrong," she said, her voice crackling with anger. "You are mistaken if you think I am hiding *anything*."

She had got a little ahead of Charlotte and Lucy, who were dawdling along, heads together over a bunch of leaves and flowers they had picked for a botany lesson. James was with them, as usual, and behind her back Emilia made an urgent motion, praying he saw it.

Fitchley's eyes skimmed over her face, then down her figure. "Parker said you'd aged well. Generous of him, if you ask me."

"No one did," said Emilia between her teeth.

He smiled. It was a poisonous smile, from a poisonous man. He looked a little older—his fair hair thinning, his middle beginning to spread—but he was very much the same as he'd been nine years ago. "Still as tart and saucy as ever. What a delight."

From the corner of her eye, Emilia caught a glimpse of James striding across the street, Charlotte on one arm and Lucy by the hand. Charlotte had her head ducked behind his shoulder, but Lucy was craning her neck, trying to see. She didn't know who he was. Emilia hadn't told her she had a guardian who might try to take her away.

Emilia started walking, dodging around Fitchley and striding away from Mr. Dashwood's house. It took her farther from safety, but also led Fitchley farther from Lucy. As expected, he fell in step beside her, unwilling to let a woman walk away from him without his permission.

"We have unfinished business, you and I," he said, walking close enough that their elbows bumped.

Emilia moved away, only for him to close the gap. "No, we don't. Everything between us was ended conclusively nine years ago."

He laughed. "You've been counting! So have I. Nine years is a long time to survive as a fallen woman. But there's more than enough time for you to change your mind."

Emilia prayed Arabella was staying at her father's house. She turned into Mortimer Street, refusing to reply to Fitchley.

"I *could* change your mind," he said, still wearing that vindictive smile. "I would probably enjoy it. You might even, as well."

Emilia crossed Edward Street, walking right out

into the traffic, ignoring the shout of a hackney driver who had to pull up his horse. She wished he'd drive over Lord Fitchley.

"Well, perhaps you wouldn't," mused Fitchley. "But then, a wife's duty is to submit, not to enjoy herself."

She kept her eyes forward to keep from striking him. "I am not your wife."

"No," he said, sounding amused. "But you should be. I've regretted your rash actions ever since you left, but I always believed that one day, we would meet again and I would persuade you to reconsider. Your dear uncle fosters the same fond hope. He's been frantic with worry about you these last years. It was very unkind of you not to write to him, letting him know you were well and wished to come home to your family."

She nearly leapt up the steps to the McCorquodale house and pounded the knocker.

Fitchley stopped at the pavement's edge. "I'm so pleased by our reunion, Emilia. I look forward to seeing you again soon. Until later, my dear." He tipped his hat, and strolled away as Arabella's butler opened the door.

Arabella was not at home, but the butler knew Emilia. He let her sit in the morning room until Fitchley was gone from sight, and then he had a footman escort her home. Emilia led the poor man on a winding route, finally slipping into Mr. Dashwood's house through the kitchen.

"There you are!" cried Mrs. Watson at her appearance. "Mr. Dashwood is ready to raise the constabulary!"

"Why?" Emilia tore off her pelisse and threw aside her bonnet. "What happened?"

"Why, you disappeared! James came back with the young ladies and said you'd been accosted by a man. Mr. Dashwood sent him straight out again—"

"Mr. Dashwood is home?" Emilia pressed trembling fingertips to her temples. She needed to collect herself, and shake off the creeping panic prickling along her spine. "Go on."

"Yes, he's home. Been here a full hour or more." Mrs. Watson glanced around and lowered her voice. "And there's something on his mind. Twice he sent Mr. Pearce out to watch for you and the young ladies returning, and all the while he was pacing the floor, not even touching his breakfast."

What else could have happened? Fitchley was bad enough, but he had stopped her after Mr. Dashwood was already home, impatiently waiting. Emilia nodded, not trusting her voice. She pressed Mrs. Watson's hand in mute gratitude and made her way into the house.

Mr. Pearce saw her first. "Miss Greene," he said in obvious relief as she came through the hall. He swept open the dining room door, and Nick Dashwood swung around as she stepped inside.

He was still in evening dress, although his jacket was gone and his cravat was pulled loose. His hair was rumpled, longer than usual, and the scruff of beard made him look wild and dangerous. Or perhaps that was his eyes, lit with unholy anger and fear. "Thank Christ," he growled, and took two strides forward and caught her in his arms.

Emilia couldn't help it; she threw herself into his embrace, inhaling deeply of his scent and clinging to him. So much for her resolve. Avoiding him had been her only chance, and now she realized it had never been a strong one. She had felt the first premonition the moment he'd given her a roguish wink that fraught morning in his office, and now she was lost.

He pushed back, holding her at arm's length as he scanned her face. "What happened? Where did you go?" His voice was eerily calm, almost deadly.

It took her a moment to form a coherent reply. She cleared her throat before she could speak. "We were at the park, the girls and I, with James. On the way back, I met Lord Fitchley." Mr. Dashwood's face darkened. "Or I should say, he met me," she corrected herself quickly. "I—I wasn't paying attention"—*again*—"and he surprised me. Did Charlotte and Lucy return safely? I signaled to James to leave me . . ."

"James saw. He brought them home." His gaze narrowed on her face. "What did Fitchley do to you?"

She exhaled a shaky breath. "He followed me. I didn't want to lead him here, so I went to a friend's house in Cavendish Square, where he wouldn't be able to follow. The butler recognized him and let me wait inside until Fitchley was gone."

Finally he released her and paced away, scrubbing his hands over his face. "Jesus, Mary and Joseph. I feared the worst. James and two other men are out right now, combing the streets for you."

"The McCorquodales' butler sent a footman to see me safely home. I knew Fitchley would never try to follow me into Arabella's home. She'd likely come at him with a fireplace poker."

He gave a bark of laughter before letting his head fall. In that moment he looked utterly exhausted; Emilia was at his side before she realized she was moving, her hand on his arm. "I'm well. I'm sorry to have worried you."

He caught her shoulders. "I *was* worried, damn it." He paused, as if struggling for words. "I . . . care . . . very much . . . about you. What happens to you. I promised to keep you and Lucinda safe, and I meant it, and when I thought I'd failed—" He gazed at her for a moment, until she began to think he was going to kiss her again, which made something inside her swell with anticipation—longing—

He let go of her. "We're leaving London. Pack for a fortnight, you and the girls."

"Why? Where are we going?"

For reply, he retrieved some papers from the top of the pianoforte. Emilia unfolded them and read, brow furrowed in confusion. It took her several minutes to understand. Then she gasped, looking up at him in speechless horror.

Fitchley had filed an appeal at the Court of Chancery as Lucy's guardian, requesting that she be given into his custody immediately.

CHAPTER TWENTY-ONE

"He won't have her," Dashwood said.

"That *monster!*" Emilia threw the papers aside and charged toward the door. *She* would take a poker to Fitchley before she let him touch Lucy, let alone handed Lucy over to him. Perhaps she'd take a poker to him anyway, just for her own satisfaction.

Dashwood caught her. "He won't have her," he said again. "I'll see to Lord Fitchley."

Emilia was breathing so hard, her whole body vibrated. "How?"

He only smiled, his cold, cutting smile.

"All right." She took a deep breath. He was still holding her, but she made no move to step away. "What shall we do?"

"We're leaving," he said. "I've had enough of Fitchley and his lot. He's been warned, and now he's about to reap some consequences."

She blinked. "What? Warned—when?"

Dashwood bent and collected the discarded papers. "He's a member of the Vega Club. I am not unfamiliar with Lord Fitchley. My warnings to him were on other subjects, and my patience was already worn thin. But I have no tolerance for assaults on my family." He studied the papers he held. "There's not been much family in my life. I take a protective stance over what I have."

Emilia thought of Lucy, and her throat felt tight. Lucy was all the family she had now; she knew what he meant. She nodded in agreement. "Where are we going?"

He smiled grimly. "Dorset."

GRANTHAM HAD BROUGHT the news of Fitchley's petition to the Vega Club that morning.

"I won't let him take Lucinda," Nick said even before his attorney finished speaking.

"You can't file a contesting petition until your title is granted. Until then, you're merely a distant cousin. Even as the head of her family, your chances aren't strong. Her father named Fitchley as her guardian, and the court will respect that."

"You mistake me, Grantham," said Nick evenly. "I don't mean to observe legal niceties this time."

Grantham paused. "Then you don't need me," he said carefully.

"No."

Fitchley's action hadn't been a complete surprise. It had always been a possibility, hovering at the edge of Nick's mind. The baron was spiteful and vindictive, and Nick had crossed him several times already. He'd never thought it would take long for Fitchley to recall his dear friend, the late Lord Sydenham, after Nick's petition for that title became known. He'd been expecting something like this, and preparing for it, ever since Emilia said the man's name, even before she ran into Parker-Lloyd, Fitchley's old mate who had some particular interest in her.

He was wild to know what that interest was. James had reported that Parker-Lloyd argued with her, holding her arm until James approached. He'd also overheard a few words of the conversation, which suggested Parker-Lloyd had had more than a passing acquaintance with Emilia, once, and that Emilia had been both infuriated and frightened by the man. *It was not a cordial meeting,* she'd said— but not why.

It was true Nick had worried more about Charlotte, after the way he'd had to search for her in the first place. His sister was young, beautiful, and alone, and Nick had been around wickedness and debauchery long enough to recognize how vulnerable that could make her.

But he'd never really thought the same about Emilia Greene. She was from a noble family, a lady despite her reduced circumstances. He'd thought her indomitable. She'd fought tenaciously for Lucinda's safety and welfare, but never mentioned her own. Nick was left to wonder why, and how on earth he could protect her.

"We're leaving London," he told Grantham. "A fortnight, perhaps. If you need me, send a message here to Forbes."

Grantham nodded. "Where will you go?"

"Brighton." Nick shrugged. "Perhaps Lyme." Brighton was more fashionable, but he'd enjoyed the school holidays he'd spent with a mate in Lyme.

Grantham eyed him thoughtfully. "If you haven't already made plans, you should consider Beaufort Hall in Dorset. The Sydenham estate."

It made sense. Grantham's arguments always did. Still, Nick hesitated. Charlotte had told him about Lucinda's nightmare. He didn't want to terrorize the girl again, if her fears were connected to the estate as much as they were to her late father.

"Be seen there as the new viscount," Grantham went on with growing certainty. "Stake your claim openly and obviously. And it can only help your cause if the people who knew Lucinda see her healthy and happy in your care."

"You told me it was a ruin," he retorted.

The attorney waved one hand, unruffled. "It can't be that bad. And you don't need to take up residence, merely inspect the place. Greet the neighbors. Let it be known you are taking possession soon, and intend to hire from the local village. It will create an air of . . . inevitability."

"That will sway the Committee for Privileges?"

Grantham smiled, looking very sly for a moment. "I've told you they have no legal grounds to reject the petition. Begin looking and acting the part of a viscount, and they won't see the point of resisting the inevitable."

Nick grunted. He'd thought of going somewhere more appealing, akin to a holiday. It would be his first one in years, after all, and he'd developed a tantalizing mental image of strolling on the seashore with Emilia on his arm. He had a feeling Beaufort Hall wouldn't offer that, even if it would help establish him as the next lord, as Grantham said.

Now, when he saw Emilia go pale at mention of the estate, he doubted again.

"Oh," she said faintly. "Why?"

"To avoid Fitchley and Parker-Lloyd and all

their sort."

"We can't stay away from London forever," she protested. "Not in Dorset!"

"Why not?"

She wet her lips, looking so anxious, he almost told her he only meant to stay long enough for his plans for Lord Fitchley to come to fruition. "It's not in good repair. Beaufort Hall, I mean."

He took her hand. "Is that the only reason?" She glanced at him, visibly tense. "Tell me, Emilia," he urged. "I know the house has been let go. I know the estate is mortgaged and neglected. Charlotte told me Lucinda had a nightmare about the place."

She shuddered. "Her father was cruel," she whispered. "He—he wanted a son, and he found his daughter a grave disappointment. The mark on her cheek . . ."

Nick frowned. He barely noticed Lucinda's birthmark anymore. Now that she wasn't pale and thin, but had some healthy color in her face, the mark was far less prominent. "He abused his daughter because of a mark on her skin?"

Emilia shook her head. "He abused her because he was a monster. He hated everything about her, the mark being only the focus of his cruelty. He drank, and he had a foul temper, and I truly believe no one liked him." She took a deep breath. "He's dead now, thank goodness, but I'm afraid the house will remind Lucy . . . I promised her she would never have to go back!"

Without thinking, he put his arm around her and pulled her close. She burrowed closer and rested her cheek on his chest, and Nick wondered if she could feel the thump his heart made in response. "I want her out of London, where Fitchley cannot get her. I would prefer to keep her where I can protect her, rather than send her to someone else." Emilia shook her head against his chest. Nick relaxed at that. "I only intend to stay a few days. She won't be alone there, not even for a moment, and if she wishes to leave, you and she can stay in the nearest village. I give you my word."

She stirred and Nick loosened his hold. "Why do you want to go?"

"It's the Sydenham estate. I am the new Lord Sydenham, or will be in a matter of months." Her eyes widened. He nodded. "Grantham says there's no fault in your work. It won't be denied."

"Oh!" Her face brightened, and she even smiled a little. "I'm glad to hear that."

He nodded again, inexplicably pleased himself. He shouldn't have been; it wasn't a surprise to him, but the expected, calculated result. But her smile always made him want to smile, too.

She seemed to realize the same moment he did that she was staring at him with warm affection. She blushed and bit her lip. "Sir—My lord—"

"Nick."

She blushed deeper. "I can't—"

"Please," he said. "After all, we are partners, are we not . . . Emilia?"

She rolled her lower lip between her teeth, and he watched, fascinated. "If you insist. But it's not—that is . . ."

"Is this about the other night?" he interrupted. "When you kissed me?"

She straightened so abruptly she seemed to grow a few inches taller. "What? You kissed me!"

A smile tugged at his mouth. "I kissed you back, I freely admit."

She gaped at him.

He leaned closer, gazing into her eyes. "What's more," he whispered, "I liked it. Very much. And I dream of doing it again."

She blinked rapidly and he wasn't sure she was breathing. He straightened and grew more serious. "But I am not a monster. I would never force my attentions upon a woman, especially not a woman in my employ. I would always wonder if she allowed me liberties because she felt she had no choice, and I would despise that, both for the woman and for myself." He turned away because she was still gazing at him in amazement, and the temptation to kiss her parted lips was threatening to make a mockery of his noble speech. "You are entirely safe from any unwanted attentions."

After a long moment of silence, he couldn't stop himself glancing back. She looked flustered, her eyes wide and unfocused. "I— Thank you. I understand. Yes. A few days, you say? We can manage. Lucy." She nodded. "Yes, Lucy. I—" She broke off. "You liked it very much?"

He gave one slow nod. She was thinking about that kiss. As was he. Nick had thought of little else, until Fitchley rudely interjected himself. For that alone, Nick had no regret about what he meant to do to the baron.

"Oh," she breathed. "Again? You would?" She raised one hand, delicately touching her lower lip as if in recollection.

"Yes," he said in a low voice. "Fair warning."

A rosy blush came into her cheeks, and she swallowed, glancing sideways at his mouth. Then she put back her shoulders and raised her chin. "When do you want to leave?"

CHAPTER TWENTY-TWO

E milia had no time to think about the
conversation, for which she was extremely
grateful.

Charlotte and Lucy were already alarmed, after
her encounter with Fitchley. Lucy, it turned out,
had protested when James seized her hand and
towed her across the street, but Charlotte had understood something was very wrong. Emilia found
them in the schoolroom, heads together and whispering furiously.

"Millie!" Lucy bolted across the room into her
arms. "Oh, Millie, you're alive!"

Emilia was surprised into a laugh at that. "Of
course I am! I see James did exactly as he ought, for
here you are, safe and sound."

Lucy looked at her anxiously. "Who was that
man? Was he a cock bawd?"

Emilia started. "What?"

Blushing, Charlotte hissed, "Lucy!"

Lucy bit her lip but didn't retreat. "Did he do
terrible things to you?"

"He was not a friend, but he did nothing to

me," said Emilia firmly. She gave Charlotte a wary
look; how on earth did Charlotte know that vulgar
term? And why had she taught it to Lucy? The girl
ducked her head and looked away. "Never mind
that now. We're to pack for a journey. Mr. Dashwood has decided we're leaving London."

Someone tapped at the door. Henry came in,
one small trunk on his shoulder and another in his
hand. "Here you are, miss." He winked at Lucy.
"Mrs. Watson's lamenting that she just baked a tray
of lavender cakes and now you're leaving. She won-
ders if you might like to take a basket with you."

Lucy's face brightened. "Oh, Millie, may we?"

Emilia smiled at Henry. "A marvelous idea!
Thank you, Henry, please ask her to do that." She
went to the wardrobe and opened it. "Come help
me, girls, or we'll end up forgetting something important."

Emilia had no idea when Nick had formed his
plan of leaving town, but she was mightily impressed when she led the girls downstairs an hour
later and found a travel coach waiting out front,
their trunks already being loaded into the back.
Pearce held a basket, covered with a cloth, which
Lucy bounded forward to take with a wide smile.
Charlotte hurried over to peer inside with her, and
Emilia guessed those cakes wouldn't last long.

"Everyone ready?" Nick came down the stairs
behind her. Emilia turned and forgot how to speak.

She had only seen him in evening clothes or
dressed for riding: polished, elegant, austere. It had
never sat quite right on him, handsome though it
was, and finally Emilia saw why. It had been a
disguise.

This was what he was. A ruffian, a rogue, a pirate lord. He might be on his way to rob stage-coaches on the turnpike. He was dressed all in black, save for the white shirt barely visible beneath a loosely knotted blue neckcloth. Battered leather boots came to his knees, and he held a broad brimmed hat. He hadn't shaved. His hair looked longer than ever, curling wildly around his neck. He was dark and dangerous and something inside Emilia seemed to catch fire and burn right through her bones.

At the bottom of the stairs he took his greatcoat from Pearce and replied to something Charlotte had asked. Finally he glanced her way, his golden eyes almost unearthly compared to the darkness that was the rest of him. "Ready?"

Dumbly she nodded, still transfixed by his appearance.

He put out his hand. "Then let's be off."

The first few hours passed comfortably enough. The cakes, as foreseen, were swiftly demolished, and to distract her charges Emilia brought out her copy of *Pride and Prejudice* and read aloud. Nick and two of his men rode beside the carriage for a while, but eventually Nick joined them inside.

"Won't you tell us where we're going?" Charlotte implored.

"Tonight we'll be in Farnham," he replied. "The Bush Inn was recommended."

She rolled her eyes. "And tomorrow?"

His eyes fell on Lucy, who had leaned her cheek upon one hand against the window. "We're going to Dorset," he said quietly.

Charlotte wrinkled her nose. "Dorset? Why?"

Lucy went pale. Emilia took her hand, and the

girl gripped it hard. "We shan't stay long," she murmured.

Lucy looked up at her with huge, frightened eyes. "You said we wouldn't have to go," she whispered, barely audibly.

Nick leaned forward. He and Charlotte sat opposite Emilia and Lucy. "It's important, or I wouldn't take you," he said gravely. "It's to protect Miss Greene."

Emilia jerked. Lucy peeked at him uncertainly. "From who?"

"The man who stopped her in the street this morning. He's a bad one, Lucinda."

"I know," she whispered, glancing at Emilia, who was thoroughly disconcerted now.

Nick paid her no mind, his attention on Lucy. Charlotte had gone quiet, listening hard as well. "Suppose someone tried to hurt me. I would not like that at all. I would probably want to fill a bucket from the privy and throw it on him." Lucy gave a surprised giggle. Nick grinned. "And if I were to do that, what do you think I would first tell my friends?"

"Don't tell anyone," said Lucy in a small voice.

Nick shook his head.

"Stand clear," murmured Charlotte.

"Exactly." Nick poked one finger in Charlotte's direction in agreement. "You and Charlotte are very dear to me. I would tell you and Charlotte, as well as Miss Greene and James and Henry and Mrs. Watson and Mr. Pearce and everyone else I like, to stand very, very far away, so you didn't get any muck on you. I want every disgusting drop of it to land on the bad man. And that's why we're going to Dorset for a few days. Can you bear it?"

Lucy's chin sank, but she gave a tentative nod. "I know what to be wary of," she told him. "I can try to help."

"Brilliant," said Nick fervently. "I was hoping you could. I'll rely on you." He leaned back, propping his shoulder against the corner.

"What—?" began Emilia, still reeling from the implication that they were leaving London to protect *her*. Surely he'd just said that to reassure Lucy.

But Nick gave a quick shake of his head, and then that roguish wink, before dropping his hat over his face and going to sleep.

NICK HAD SENT SOMEONE AHEAD, and the innkeeper at the Bush Inn was waiting for them, beaming. He had rooms prepared, plus quarters for the servants and a private parlor reserved for dinner. Nick sent off James and his other men to study the area, then gave them liberty for the evening.

They dined together. Emilia had been throwing him questioning looks all day, but she put aside her curiosity while the girls were with them. After dinner, Charlotte brought out a deck of cards, and suggested they play.

"Whist," said Nick lazily, watching Emilia. She blushed, but gave in when Lucy begged to learn the game.

Charlotte made Lucy laugh by sending the cards flying from one hand to the other.

"That's amazing," breathed Lucy, watching the cards seem to spring from Charlotte's grip.

"Oh! Nick can do ever so many more." Charlotte slapped the deck in front of Nick. "Show her how you make a two into a king."

Nick grinned. He'd learned any number of card tricks, and a great many cheats, too. He showed Lucy the trick, which was little more than sleight of hand, and then several others. Then they played whist, everyone helping Lucy. Nick, who partnered her, routinely dealt her good cards, and took unexpected pleasure in seeing her eyes grow wide.

"Oh, Millie, look!" she cried, wiggling on her chair in excitement. "I won!"

"Well done. A victor must have some spoils." Nick pulled a small bag from the pocket of his greatcoat and presented it to her.

Lucy gasped as she peered inside. "Lemon drops! Oh, thank you, sir!" She popped one into her mouth, then held out the bag to Charlotte.

Emilia shook her head with a smile, when offered the bag as well. "You won them! They're yours. But don't eat more than two or three, or you'll have a sick stomach tonight."

Lucy grinned, cradling the bag like a treasured prize. "I won't."

Emilia took the girls up to get ready for bed, and Nick sent for another bottle of wine. They were forty miles from London, had left with virtually no warning to anyone, and James had reported that he saw no one watching them with untoward interest. He judged it unlikely they'd been followed.

Perhaps such caution wasn't necessary, but when one set out to destroy a man like Fitchley, one didn't take chances.

For the better part of an hour Nick was left alone with his thoughts and the wine. It had been a very long time since that had happened, especially at this time of day. Night, he amended with a glance at the darkening sky outside the window. Normally he would be at Vega's, walking the salon, tending to problems, ever watchful for trouble.

And there was always trouble at a gaming hell, even one as sophisticated and discriminating as the Vega Club. Nick had seen all manner of cheating, lying, fighting, coercion, and cajolery. It was the life he'd chosen—and reveled in—but it was also . . . wearing. Playing cards tonight with Emilia and the girls had brought home to him how vigilant he had to be most of the time. Most people weren't that way; Emilia wasn't. She hadn't even suspected that he was deliberately dealing high cards to Lucy, just to see the child's eyes light up in shocked delight when she won a trick. It was the most enjoyable thing Nick had done since . . .

Well, since he'd fixed a game of loo the previous year, beggaring a ship owner who'd been violating the Slave Trade Act. Nick had taken *great* pleasure in that bit of cheating. Smiling at the memory, he got up and went to close the shutters at the windows.

The door behind him opened and closed. "They're in bed, but I doubt either will sleep, what with a bag of sweets and the excitement of the journey," said Emilia.

Nick grinned, closing up one window. "They can sleep in the carriage tomorrow."

"Yes." She was quiet for a moment. "What are we going to do at Beaufort Hall?"

He shrugged. "Walk around the grounds. See if the house is fit for habitation. Stop in the village and have a pint. Shake the vicar's hand. Whatever a lord of the realm would do upon inheriting his title and domain."

"Oh." Emilia pursed her lips, which fascinated

Nick to an unhealthy degree. "You didn't need to tell Lucy this was for my benefit. I know you were trying to reassure her, and I do appreciate that, but..."

He rested his shoulder against the side of the window embrasure. "Come here." She hesitated, and he motioned toward the window. "See the sky."

She came across the room and he stepped back to let her closer to the window. "Look there." He raised his arm and put his head near hers as he pointed. "That is Vega, one of the brightest stars in the sky. Sailors rely on it for that reason."

She looked at him in surprise, then moved to get a better view. Her shoulder brushed his chest, and he touched one hand lightly to her waist to guide her closer. She leaned into him, smelling of honeysuckle. Nick kept his gaze on the stars but felt surrounded by her, her scent, her warmth, her trusting presence nearly in his arms.

"I remember lying on deck, counting the stars, imagining the ancients doing much the same thing, thousands of years ago," he went on. "The navigator taught me the constellations and how to mark a journey by them. Without the stars to guide us, the seas would have remained as vast and mysterious as the heavens, because only a few people would ever have made it back to where they began. The stars, though, show the way.

"That constellation is called Lyra, after the lyre of Orpheus." He traced it with one outstretched finger. "Orpheus calmed the Sirens with his lyre, allowing the Argonauts to sail freely past, which was enough to make him a hero to sailors everywhere. But he also took his lyre into the Underworld to save his wife, who had died. Imagine the

nerve, to take such a gamble! But Hades actually
agreed to let her go, provided Orpheus didn't look
back at her. Eurydice would have to follow him out.
But at the very end, on the precipice of winning his
unthinkable prize—bringing his beloved back from
the dead!—Orpheus lost his nerve. He looked back.
She remained dead, and he was thrust back into the
world of the living, condemned to live with the
knowledge that he could have saved her, but failed."
Nick paused, remembering those nights at sea.
"Vega is the principal star in Lyra, the brightest one
at the top."

She tipped back her head, almost resting it on
his shoulder. "And that's why you named your club
Vega."

He smiled without humor. "My lucky star. A
reminder of where I came from, and a guidepost on
my way. A warning, never to try my luck too far."

She turned. She was almost in his arms. He
could feel her body brushing his. All he had to do
was lower his head to kiss her again . . .

Which he would not do. He flexed his arms to
keep from pulling her closer. In this private parlor,
away from the Vega Club, there was nothing to in-
terrupt, if he kissed her. If he put his hands on her.
If he pushed her against the nearest wall and—

Emilia looked up at him, her blue eyes soft and
inviting. Nick clenched his jaw and looked away.

"Nick," she said softly. He flinched at his name,
whispered as a lover might do. She put her hand on
his chest. "I have to tell you about Fitchley."

CHAPTER TWENTY-THREE

Emilia had been dreading this moment ever since he'd asked about Lucy's guardian.

She told herself that she'd never lied to Nick about Fitchley. She'd told him the baron was uncaring, unreasonable, and unfit to be Lucy's guardian, which was completely true. She'd merely left out exactly how she knew all that about him—and why she was so determined to avoid the man.

Nick didn't seem worried or startled by her words. He regarded her for a moment, then took her hand and led her back to the settee and poured wine.

Emilia took her glass but nervously set it down. "I might need that later."

"More can be ordered." He leaned back, legs stretched out and crossed at the ankle. He draped one arm across the back of the sofa. Even without the hat and greatcoat, he looked wicked and rough, and Emilia had to pinch the inside of her thumb to keep her wicked thoughts at bay. She'd thought he might kiss her, by the window, when she was all but leaning against him with her head on his shoulder.

She'd wished he would; he'd said he wanted to kiss her again . . .

But he hadn't. He'd said he wouldn't. He'd promised that she was safe from any unwanted attentions from him. Emilia wished he'd said something about *wanted* attentions. She truly might be going mad. She'd lain awake all that night, after the kiss, calculating exactly how many months until she would be free to do whatever she wanted.

Too many, was the answer. And in the meantime, Lucy needed her.

She took a deep breath. "I told you that Mr. Parker-Lloyd was once acquainted with my uncle and my father as well as with Lord Fitchley. The truth is that all four of them were great friends for many years. Perhaps they still are, save my father, who died several years ago."

Nick sipped his wine and waited, watching her with patient eyes.

"My father took after my grandmother, and was a creature of high society. He and my uncle were rather notorious in their youth, I believe, and fell in with Fitchley's crowd. The races were their passion, and Lord Fitchley's family owned a well-known racing stable. Naturally they wagered, and at one point my father suffered a large loss he couldn't pay. He was barely twenty-two. Grandpapa said he would pay the debt, but only if my father married and settled down. Papa had no choice—I believe it was a crushing amount—so he married my mother, who was a sensible girl from a good family."

She sighed. "You might guess that it wasn't the happiest marriage. Mama had a large dowry, but Papa's habits were well known, and both my grandfathers conspired to parcel it off in trust for her children. I was born a year later. Before I turned two, my mother died in childbed, along with the babe. It took Papa only two months to leave me at Grandpapa's estate and head back to London."

"I'm sorry you lost her," he said quietly.

Emilia nodded. "I don't even remember her," she confessed. "I have a portrait of her and some of her things, but no memories." She flashed a fleeting smile at him. "I'd rather have the memories."

His eyes were dark with compassion. "I understand."

"So." She straightened her shoulders. "I grew up at Grandpapa's estate, called the Willows, which was lovely. He was a bit gruff but really warm and kind. Whenever my father did come to visit, I was always glad to see him leave." She grimaced. "That sounds heartless, but he didn't care for me and I barely knew him. It was a great favor he did, leaving me with Grandpapa, whom I loved dearly." She paused, trying to think how best to explain the next part. "Grandpapa died when I was sixteen. I was away at school then, which was very fortunate for me. Uncle John became the new earl upon Grandpapa's death, and he was just as unlucky a gambler as my father. He was in debt when he inherited and he promptly set about trying to wring as much as he could from the estate.

"First he wrote to Mrs. Upton, the headmistress of my school, saying he wanted me sent home and my tuition returned. Grandpapa had paid it before he died, and Uncle tried to say those were estate funds. The headmistress was wonderful, and she protected me from my uncle's demands. She wrote back to him that she did not refund school fees, and that she would not send me back against my will."

Nick was frowning. "He wanted you tossed out of school for a few pounds?"

Emilia nodded. "His first choice, in every circumstance, was to preserve his own comfort. I believe he was eventually forced to sell some horses to cover his debts, which would have infuriated him. The stables were his passion, if not his fortune."

Still scowling, Nick drank and nodded for her to go on.

"At the time, Uncle and Papa were engaged in a very expensive enterprise. They intended to expand their stables, import several prized horses for breeding, and start a stud farm, but things didn't go to plan. One of the stallions died soon after arrival, and the property they bought wasn't as good for grazing as they had been told. They had gone into this with some friends as investors, and were now buried in debt, when it struck them that they could win some leeway with a betrothal.

"It took Uncle a few months to remember my trust. Not only did it hold half my mother's dowry, Grandpapa had added to it. Grandpapa had tied it up well, and there was no way my uncle could get at it. But the trust would become my husband's when I married, and eventually he hit upon a plan. He convinced Papa that the right marriage could benefit everyone—I would be tidied away, and my husband would be very grateful to my father for giving him a wealthy bride."

She closed her eyes. Nick made a faint noise, but when she looked at him, his expression was somber, no judgment or shock in it.

"My father told me I would marry Fitchley, who was nearly twenty years older than I. I was only seventeen. I argued and pleaded, but he was adamant." She cast a bitter look at Nick. "Later I discovered they owed Fitchley almost ten thousand pounds."

His face might have been carved from stone. He said nothing.

"This will sound terrible," she went on, "but fortunately my father passed away before he could force me to the altar. A carriage accident. He was drunk. He and his groom both died, and the horse had to be put down. It was dreadful. I was eighteen by then, and the day after I heard the news, I wrote to Lord Fitchley breaking our betrothal. My uncle was furious. Papa had named him my guardian, and he stopped my allowance, telling me to 'come to my senses.' I was too stubborn to give in, so I decided to support myself." She managed a smile. "After my expensive and excellent schooling, I was well-qualified to teach."

"Surely your mother's family would have helped you, or friends."

Emilia sighed. "My grandparents had died. My mother's sister married a stern man, who believed I should obey my uncle." She twisted her hands together. "I did inquire about withdrawing money from the trust, but Grandpapa had done too good a job, and the attorney wrote regretfully that he was unable to advance me any funds. My friends . . ."

She frowned at her fingers. Arabella had offered her sanctuary, more than once, and Emilia had been tempted, especially in the beginning. Her uncle had expected it; he'd sent a demanding letter to Arabella's father. The earl had thrown it on the fire, but Emilia had sensed danger in remaining where her uncle—and Fitchley—could easily find her. "I did not want to be a burden on friends," she said in a low voice. "And I thought it better to maintain some distance from my family."

"This was ten years ago?" he asked slowly, a faint frown on his brow.

Emilia nodded. "Nearly." She sipped more wine, feeling surprisingly at ease, now that the story was told. "I've tried to avoid my uncle and Lord Fitchley ever since, as they are somewhat . . . unforgiving. Fortunately a governess was nigh invisible to them, and I took care to choose positions away from London, in Bath, in Plymouth, in Dorset, which also helped." She turned to him earnestly. "Lord Sydenham told his solicitor to engage a governess for Lucy. I didn't even meet the viscount for several weeks. I had no idea he and Fitchley were friendly—indeed, I didn't think Lord Sydenham *had* any friends—and I certainly never guessed that Fitchley would be Lucy's guardian. It was a distinct shock to hear his name, after Sydenham died." She raised her glass as if in a toast. "And that was what set me off in desperate search of you."

He smiled wryly. "Never say I owe Fitchley a debt!"

She snorted bitterly. "No! Never! He's every bit as horrible now as he was then." She drank more wine. "How do you know him?"

Nick leaned forward and refilled her glass. Emilia made no protest. The wine had warmed her, and got her through a recitation of things she'd like to forget. She felt far better than she'd expected to.

It also made the conversation feel . . . congenial. Easy. Intimate. As if they were confidants, sharing secrets and advising each other. She really shouldn't feel this way about her employer. It just seemed to happen so effortlessly, over and over again. It hadn't happened with other employers, and she didn't know how to react to it.

"Fitchley has been a member of the Vega Club for close to a year." Nick refilled his own glass and sat back. "He's an ass, but that's not unexpected at a gaming club."

She studied her wine. "You told me you could prevent Lord Fitchley or Mr. Parker-Lloyd from hurting us. How do you plan to do that?"

"I have ways," he murmured over his glass.

"Yes, but . . ." She hesitated. "Can you really keep Lucy from him? I took such care to avoid him because I thought the courts would give her to him without question if he demanded it."

"There is that," he agreed. "Grantham said the same."

For a moment Emilia couldn't breathe. "I won't let him have her," she said, her voice low and fierce. "I *won't*. Even if it means I must take her and go into hiding—another country—anywhere he can't get her—Nick, he's *terrible*, he would never care for her the way she deserves—"

"I completely agree."

"But what can I *do*?" She gripped her shaking hands together. "The only reason I went looking for a Sydenham heir was to protect Lucy. Can't you petition for her as the head of her family, perhaps citing Fitchley's inattention since her father's death . . . ?"

"Oh, I have no intention of fighting Fitchley in court." He propped his foot on one of the extra chairs. "Answer me this: Why does Baron Fitchley want a little girl, whom he doesn't know, who is no relation of his, and who has no money? He's never paid her the slightest attention before now, and it would cost him a considerable sum to raise her for the next decade."

Emilia felt her face burn. "He wouldn't," she whispered. "Except . . ."

"Except that he's discovered how attached *you* are to that little girl." Nick tilted his glass, seemingly absorbed in how the lamplight shone on the liquid. "It struck me that he might believe that, by getting her, he would also get you. I sense you would not let her go to him alone."

"Of course I wouldn't!"

He finished his wine and set down the glass. "When does the trust become yours outright?"

Emilia wilted. "When I turn twenty-eight. Just over six months from now."

Nick nodded contemplatively. "I thought as much. Six months is a long time to resist the demands of a man who holds Lucinda like a hostage."

She dropped her head into her hands, feeling sick. He had spelled out the deepest, darkest fear in her heart. She could take Lucy and run, but she would have precious little to support them, let alone conceal them; if Fitchley found them, she would be at his mercy. If Fitchley took Lucy, though, Emilia would have no choice but to go with her.

When she'd broken their engagement, he had replied that she would change her mind. That he would be waiting. Her uncle had warned her that he considered the betrothal still binding, and that he wouldn't consent to any other. Emilia was old enough not to fear that any longer, but Fitchley's words the other day, in front of Arabella's house, *had* frightened her. He hadn't forgotten, nor changed his mind, and now he'd spotted the means to snare her once and for all.

"I make a point of knowing my patrons," Nick said, almost idly. "I need to know they can afford Vega's, and Fitchley can. He wagers heavily on the horses, and he wins."

So Fitchley was wealthy as well as titled and vindictive. There went her last hope, that he hadn't the means to carry through on his threats. Emilia thought she might be ill. Her stomach roiled and cramped. She shouldn't have drunk all that wine, she knew it—

"But he's certainly no saint, the Right Honorable Lord Fitchley," Nick went on. "He's got secrets, like all of us, and more than a few sins on his soul. I daresay he would strongly prefer they not become public knowledge."

She raised her head. "What? Are—do you have blackmail material on him?"

He had slid down on the cushions to rest his head on the back of the shabby settee. One leg was still outstretched, his heel propped on Lucy's chair from the card game. His hands were clasped on his belly. He looked like a panther lounging in the warmth of the fire, sleek and lethal despite his easy pose. At her dumbfounded question, he angled his head her way and winked.

Emilia gaped at him, her thoughts whirling.

"Don't fret over Fitchley," he said in the same lazy voice. "I suspect he'll withdraw his suit for Lucinda before we return to London."

"And if he doesn't?" she managed to ask.

Nick raised one shoulder, looking distinctly unconcerned. "Then we'll be there to witness his retreat. Huzzah."

Emilia stared at him. There was no doubt in his voice. He knew something. He'd *done* something.

I won't let them hurt you, whispered his voice in her memory.

Can you do that? she'd asked.

Watch me.

If anyone could protect them, he could.

What's more, he would.

Now the wine wasn't making her sick, it was making her bold. She got to her feet and faced him.

"Mr. Dashwood," she said. "I wish to resign my position as governess, effective immediately."

Nick jerked, shock on his face. Emilia leaned down, put her hands on his cheeks, and kissed him.

CHAPTER TWENTY-FOUR

Nick was so startled by her declaration that her mouth was on his before her meaning sank in.

She was no longer his employee. And she was kissing him.

Her hands were gentle on his face. Her kiss was sweet, but soft—too soft. Nick had started out of his seat at her announcement, but now he sank back, one hand slipping behind her neck to bring her with him. He'd told her he would never force his attentions on her, but if she wished to focus her attentions on him . . .

He was absolutely wild to receive them.

He pulled her toward him, and with a graceful twist she fell into his arms, sprawling across his lap. He never stopped kissing her, tilting her back over the arm of the settee, his hand drifting down her throat, fingers spread wide to absorb every inch of her skin. His thumb caught on the edge of her bodice. She gasped against his mouth and arched her back, pressing into his touch, and then her breast was in his hand, his thumb swirling around the taut nipple he could feel even through her dress and stays.

"I accept your resignation," he whispered, his mouth on her neck.

She nodded, shoving at his coat. Nick helpfully pulled one arm free, then the other. "I don't work for you . . . not now . . ."

She might well own him. She got his neckcloth loose and tore open the neck of his shirt. Nick heard the button pop off and land on the floor— but promptly forgot it, because Emilia pressed her mouth to the base of his throat and sucked at his skin until he shuddered.

She sat up, straddling his thighs, her hands on his shoulders. Nick's own hands spanned her ribs, his thumbs at the undersides of her breasts. She moved against him and he rolled his hips. Her breath came in little gasps, her knees widened, and his hand went to the buttons of his trouser fall, ready to tear it open and thrust hard inside her. He'd been fantasizing about this for weeks—almost since the moment she marched into his billiard room and said she had a proposition for him—and now she was here, in his arms, no need to wait any longer—

He stopped short, shaking. That's what Pa used to say: *No need to wait.* He would find any available woman and lead her away for a tumble against the nearest surface. Even as a boy, Nick had known what he was doing. The other sailors had mostly laughed, or muttered in envy. One or two had tried to shield his view, but everyone knew Sam Sidney did as he pleased.

He refused to be like that.

"Emilia." His voice sounded like a snarl even to

him. He caught her hands and gripped them. "This
— Tonight is not— Don't make a mistake," he
managed to get out.

What he thought was, *I don't want to make a
mistake.*

What he meant was, *I don't want to lose you.*

"It's not a mistake," she whispered. She twisted
her hands in his and linked their fingers. "Not
to me."

He could barely think above the throbbing beat
of his pulse. "I don't want you to resign your position as governess," he rasped.

She pulled her hands free and leaned down.
"Let's leave that for tomorrow." She rested her forehead against his, her eyes closed. "I will not regret
this."

He breathed hard. "You are certain."

Wordlessly she nodded.

His hands flexed on her waist. "Then come
with me."

EMILIA FELT giddy as they hurried through the
inn, clasped hands concealed in the sweeping folds
of his greatcoat.

She had heard his plea, and understood it. She
was twenty-seven years old, no green girl but a clear-
eyed woman who had seen something of the world
and who knew her own mind.

And what she knew . . . was that she
wanted him.

What's more, she trusted him.

It wasn't a mistake to follow her heart. It wasn't
a mistake to seize happiness when it appeared, unexpected and thrilling, in front of her. It wasn't a mis-

take to want love—she hadn't expected to find it with a ruthless, calculating gaming hell owner who was turning out to be one of the most honorable men she'd ever met, but she wasn't fool enough to shy away because of that.

At the top of the stairs, he paused. To one side lay her room, beside that shared by Charlotte and Lucy. Across the corridor was his room. He hadn't brought anyone like a valet, but had carried his own valise into that room when they arrived.

Nick held up the lamp, illuminating both doors. Emilia glanced at the closed door of the girls' room, then tugged him toward his. He gave her a slow, hungry smile, and followed.

Her nerves caught up to her as he closed the door and shot the bolt. In the morning, she would be amazed at her behavior tonight. Kissing him! Throwing herself into his arms! Telling him to make love to her!

Nick set down the lamp and faced her, and Emilia made a note to remind herself tomorrow that she was an independent woman, allowed to want things for herself. She had been so focused on Lucy and Lucy's needs, she'd done little for herself in two years.

Tonight she meant to make up for that, whatever tomorrow brought.

"Come here." Nick extended his hand. Emilia took it and went readily into his embrace.

For a moment he simply held her, his arms around her, tucking her into his chest. He rested his cheek against her temple, almost lovingly. Emilia breathed deeply, unprepared for how comforting it felt to be held this way, by him.

"Emilia," he murmured, his breath warm on

her cheek. His lips brushed her earlobe. "God above, how I want you."

She tilted her head, and his lips moved down her neck. "I know," she said unsteadily.

Nick gave a harsh bark of laughter. His hands slid down her back, from her shoulders to her waist to her hips, where they paused. He lifted his head and rested his forehead against hers. "But I also *like* you. If this will ruin—"

She put her fingers over his mouth. "You're no longer my employer, Mr. Dashwood. I do as I please now."

For a moment they stared into each other's eyes. "What does it please you to do, Miss Greene?" he asked in a deep voice.

Emilia's heart stuttered. With remarkably steady hands, she reached up and pulled away his undone neckcloth. "I want to make love to you," she whispered.

He gazed at her for a long moment, then kissed her. It began tenderly but grew hotter, more desperate. Emilia was so absorbed in kissing him that she didn't realize he had undone the buttons of her dress until he stepped back a pace and yanked the entire bodice down, shoving the dress to the floor as she pulled her arms free.

"This has been driving me mad." He ran his thumb along the narrow ruffle at the edge of her shift. "When we danced the quadrille, it was all I could think of."

She blushed, remembering that dance. "You never missed a step."

"If I'd missed a step, I would have lost sight of it." His arm went around her waist and he pulled her roughly against him. "Are all your undergarments covered in tiny ruffles?" he murmured, dragging his free hand through her hair and sending pins flying. "The question has tormented me."

She tugged at the top button of his waistcoat. "You'll have to find out."

His eyes flared, and a dangerous smile came over his mouth. "Let me make a thorough survey."

It should not have taken long. Emilia's clothing was simple, and he'd already stripped away the dress. But Nick took his time, turning her as he pleased and applying his mouth to every inch of skin as he uncovered it. By the time he dragged the shift over her head, leaving her in just stockings and shoes, Emilia could barely stand. He'd disrupted all her efforts to strip him, but his hair stood up in unruly spikes and his face was nearly as flushed as hers.

"Pink," he whispered reverently as he went down on his haunches. Emilia blushed furiously, but he was looking at her garter, the faded raspberry ribbon tied snugly around the top of her stocking. Nick raised her foot and rested it on his knee, one hand cupped under her thigh. He tugged the ribbon loose, and pressed a kiss to the spot as he drew off the stocking, his fingers stroking her leg, all the way down . . . and all the way back up.

Emilia wobbled, lightheaded. She clutched at his shoulders as he did the same thing to her other stocking. He rose suddenly, lifting her against him. She gasped, and then laughed a little as he carried her to the bed.

He lowered her to the mattress, looming over her. For a moment he just looked at her, his heavy-lidded gaze wandering over her body as if he meant to memorize it. And then, finally, he took off his own clothes.

Emilia had been to museums and seen the statues. Arabella was very fond of discussing, behind her fan, how well certain gentlemen's buckskin breeches fitted. And Lady Watney had had a private cabinet in her library, kept locked from the maids but which she'd opened to Emilia, filled with naughty poems and scandalous drawings. She was confident she knew what to expect.

Except . . . all those things were pale imitations of the reality that was Nicholas Dashwood.

She watched avidly as he tugged off his boots and shed his waistcoat. She inhaled a shivering breath as he stepped out of his trousers. But when he pulled his long shirt over his head and flung it aside, she almost stopped breathing.

In his usual evening wear, he looked lean and elegant—a dangerous gentleman, but a gentleman all the same. Without his clothes, it was clear he was no gentleman.

His shoulders looked broader; his arms looked thicker. Dark hair was scattered across his chest, but not so thickly she didn't see the image of a mermaid, marked into his skin. His stomach was flat with muscle, and his hips were lean. And at his groin, his male member rose rigid and strong, far larger than any ever seen on a statue.

"Oh," she said faintly.

He was magnificent.

He lowered himself over her. "Changing your mind?" he whispered, catching her nipple between his teeth.

She moaned as she clutched his head to her. *"No."*

"Good," he muttered, his tongue working enchantment on her skin. "I don't know what I'd do . . ." His arms closed around her, and she gasped again at the feel of his body covering hers, skin to skin.

He seemed content to kiss her all over, smiling when his whiskers tickled her and made her laugh, growling under his breath when his attentions made her arch and whimper beneath him. Emilia burned to touch him and explore him as well, but he kept distracting her until she finally gave it up and just clung to him, begging for more.

Nick reared back to sit on his knees. He spread her thighs wide, running his hands up and down her legs until she shuddered. "Let me make you scream," he said, watching her with burning eyes.

"No," she gasped, grabbing for his wrist. "The girls would hear—!"

"They won't." He caught her hand and leaned over her to pin both her arms to the bed. "The door is bolted," he said softly. "Don't think of the girls, Emilia."

She gulped, and nodded.

He laid one hand on her belly, lightly, brushing his fingertips in tantalizing little circles that made her muscles twitch. His thumb dipped lower, into the curls between her spread legs, and Emilia let out a high-pitched gasp. One corner of his mouth hitched wickedly; he did it again, and again, until she was trembling, writhing with desperate want, biting her lips to keep from screaming.

Then he took himself in his other hand and pressed the broad, smooth head of his cock against her. He dragged it up and down the folds of her intimate flesh, watching as if mesmerized. "I want to feel you around me when you come," he growled.

His voice was rough, guttural, and sent a flush of heat through her.

Slowly he pushed himself an inch deep. Emilia gasped but he distracted her with his fingers, sliding easily over her flesh, now wet and swollen.

With agonizing deliberation, he worked her into a fever, only to pause and let her catch her breath before beginning again. He was deep inside her now, his thighs like iron against her own quivering legs. When she arched and twisted, almost sobbing in search of release, he hooked his hands under her knees and pulled her tight against him again, and she felt him swell inside her, full and thick.

"Bloody Christ," he said, his voice shaking. Slowly, his forearms flexing as if it cost him all his strength, he spread her legs wide, flexing his spine and moving within her.

Emilia made a deranged sound, half pleasure, half agony. She reached for him, and he caught her hand, sucked her thumb hard into his mouth, then laid that hand on her breast.

"Touch yourself," his voice rumbled. "Imagine it's my hands on you. Show me how you like to be touched."

She tipped back her head and raked her fingernails down her throat before cupping both hands around her breasts. Every inch of skin felt scored and raw, her nerves jolting with every touch. *Imagine my hands . . .* She had already done that, pictured his big hands on her. She squeezed, pinching the nipples between two fingers.

This time he was the one to make an unearthly noise. And he continued to move, a slow, hard thrust of his hips against hers, in time with the maddening swirl of his thumb over that tender spot where all her nerves seemed to end.

Emilia pried open her eyes. She felt drunk, off-balance and short of breath. He watched her like a dark god, his eyes glowing like coals. When her eyes met his, he hiked her knee higher, looping his arm underneath so he could hold her hip as he moved, relentless, tearing her apart and making her feel like a new woman.

One who knew what pleasure was.

She arched under the climax with a soundless cry. Her knees drew back toward her chest and she flung out her arms, grasping for an anchor. Nick leaned over her, eyes closed, his hands planted beside her head. His shoulders rippled. As the waves of pleasure swamping Emilia began to ebb, he pulled back and thrust home, again and again. She quivered as her body responded, spiraling, plummeting, and then she felt him come undone. His hands fisted in the bedsheets, and he bared his teeth in a grimace as he thrust hard and deep one last time.

And as they lay still, wrapped around each other and breathing hard, Emilia realized how hopelessly in love with him she was.

CHAPTER TWENTY-FIVE

I n a dim and distant part of his brain, Nick knew
he had to let her go to her own room.

But not yet.

Maybe never, whispered a dangerous little voice
inside his head.

He ignored that and rolled over, taking her with
him. She sprawled limp and warm atop his chest,
her hair in his face and her head snuggled almost
affectionately under his chin. He felt her press a soft
kiss to the pulse at the base of his throat, and he
closed his eyes.

No one, aside from Charlotte, treated him with
affection. And Charlotte, his much younger sister,
could only provide a certain sort of affection.

He admired Emilia's nerve. He respected her
cleverness and resourcefulness. He adored her tart
wit. He lusted over her luscious curves and satiny
skin. And now he discovered that he craved her affection, too.

"What is this?" Emilia whispered, tracing one
finger over his tattoo.

Nick grimaced. "The scar of youthful foolishness."

She laughed, her shoulders shaking. "Why a mermaid?"

"Because I was nine years old," he said in amusement, "and I thought they were real. They *had* to be! Every sailor on board swore to me he'd seen at least one. Some convinced me I was too young to see them. 'Mermaids only show themselves to proper men, see,'" he said in imitation of the old tar's voice who'd told him tales of alluring women with fish tails who lived in the ocean. "'When you're a bit bigger, lad, they'll come to you.'"

Emilia laughed again. Nick grinned, remembering his indignation. Of course, what the tar had really said was that it was his cock that needed to grow before any females, human or aquatic, would want him.

"So why did you mark one on your skin?"

Nick snorted. "Because I was an idiot. I was a real sailor, and sailors have tattoos! So I got into the rum one night and a pair of them did it for me."

She lurched up on one elbow. "Into the rum—! At age nine? What did your father say?"

Nick said nothing. He started stroking her back, idly, and slowly she came back down onto his chest. "Did it hurt?" She touched the mermaid again.

"Like the devil." He tucked her closer. "I knew it would, which is why I stole the rum."

She shook her head. "But then you left the sea."

Nick's hand went still. "Not by my choice."

He felt the tension spring up in her back, and hated that he'd caused it. She said nothing.

There were two paths open to him here: he could say nothing, as he had done for so many years whenever everyone tried to learn anything about him, making clear to Emilia that the subject was closed and not to be discussed.

Or . . . he could tell her.

He could tell her something.

"My aunt," he said carefully, "felt a boy of ten should not be on a ship. She protested to my father, and in the end she took me in."

Emilia was quiet for a long minute. "You didn't like that," she said softly.

"I hated it." Nick ran his fingers up her spine again. "Not because I loved my father dearly, nor even because I longed to be a sailor, but because . . ." He smiled wryly. "Because she took me from the dangerous but thrilling adventure of the seagoing life, straight to one of solemn church services, cold baths, and strict rules. It was like caging a wild beast."

"Perhaps she feared for your safety," Emilia ventured. "Your father must have agreed, if he gave you into her care."

"She cared not to have a nephew who was a rude little heathen," he replied, amused. "My father cared for the money she offered him."

Emilia started, then jerked upright again. *"What?"*

He folded one arm behind his head and smiled at her expression. "Four hundred pounds, it cost Aunt Heloise, to pry me loose from my wicked sire. I've no idea if she ever thought it a good bargain, or simply refused to admit defeat by sending me back."

She stared at him in horror.

"Did you think your family tale shocked me?" Nick shrugged. "Mine is worse."

"Oh, Nick . . ." She sank back down to lie beside him, her expression troubled. "How dreadful."

"Don't," he said. "I suspect the challenge of trying to right my sinful nature gave her life for many years. She outlived everyone else in her family, and so left me her fortune. And that"—he waved one hand in the air as if revealing the solution to the mystery—"is how I funded the Vega Club."

"Oh," said Emilia. "Oh, my." Her voice quavered—with laughter, he thought.

Nick settled more comfortably against the pillows. "I sometimes wonder if she knows, from the heavenly hereafter, that I spent her money on a gaming hell, which was quite possibly the most concentrated expression of vice she could think of."

Emilia was silent, then— "Worse than a brothel?"

Nick paused, then chuckled. "Hard to say! Most gaming hells are both, to be fair. Heloise may not have seen much difference between the two."

"Do you . . . ?" She began hesitantly, but Nick interrupted.

"No," he said shortly. "There are no women for hire at the Vega Club, and never will be."

She must have sensed from his tone that it was not a topic for discussion. When she spoke again, she changed the subject. "Was it really so dangerous on board a ship?"

"Oh, yes. I'll never forget the time I fell overboard and had to climb the ropes back up."

"Overboard! A child of ten!"

"Eight," he said absently.

Emilia gasped. "I think I'm very glad your aunt took you, if that's what your father allowed to happen!"

He turned his head and looked at her. Her own father hadn't cared for her; he'd abandoned her to be raised by a relation, and he'd coldheartedly tried to barter her future for his benefit. Just as Nick's father had done. Her mother, who had presumably loved her, had died when she was very young. Just as Nick's mother had done. Perhaps they were more alike than he'd thought . . .

But her grandfather had loved her. She'd been raised as a lady, the granddaughter of an earl. Her low social position was by her own choice.

His was in his blood. Distantly related viscounts aside, Nick had never had any claim to being a gentleman. His aunt had tried to make him a virtuous man, but she'd been far too late.

He'd been told that he spent his first years being doted on by his mother, but he had no real memories of that time. After she died, his father had taken him to sea. In hindsight, Nick supposed that had been to avoid having to pay someone to raise him. He'd grown up scrubbing decks and hauling sails, living at sea except for visits to trading ports around the Atlantic.

With no one but other sailors for company for months on end, he'd learned virtually every vice known to man. By the time he was seven, he knew how to play cards and dice. By eight, he'd learned how to calculate odds and wager on anything. By nine, he'd learned how to cheat at all of it.

At ten, he started running the card games.

That, he knew, was what horrified his aunt most. The first time she'd set eyes on Nick, she'd harangued his father into marching him down to a church to have him baptized, though he'd been almost seven years old. Nick remembered cursing at the minister dripping cold water on him, and how horrified Heloise had been. The second time she saw him, she had scolded his father for letting him run wild, climbing the rigging dressed in nothing but worn-out breeches, as brown as a hazelnut from the sun.

But the third time they met, Heloise had caught him on the Liverpool docks dicing with—and mercilessly cheating—a group of young gents from Manchester. She'd raised a storm about wickedness and depravity, and it ended with Nick standing on the dock, raging impotently, while his father's ship sailed away without him.

His father hadn't hugged him good-bye. He'd cuffed Nick on the shoulder and told him to watch his mouth. His aunt had said much the same thing as she led him into her home: "You will learn to behave properly now, Nicholas."

He doubted he and Emilia were much the same.

"She wanted me to become a minister in her church," he replied lightly. "Can you imagine?" He rolled over, cupping her breast in one hand and taking the nipple into his mouth for a languid suckle.

"A minister!" She laughed breathlessly. Her fingers plowed into his hair. "I can't imagine anyone less likely . . ."

Nick made a noise of agreement, moving fully atop her and giving his attention to her other breast. Her knees rose alongside his hips and his stomach tensed in anticipation. He'd much rather do this than talk about his past.

So he pressed her into the mattress and had his wicked way with her again, relishing every excited gasp and ecstatic moan and pleading whisper she made, making love to her until she cried out in climax, then fell into exhausted slumber beside him in the rumpled linens.

Nick stretched in pure sated bliss, and got out of bed. He was still a creature of the night, and felt vividly awake. Emilia, on the other hand, was not; she slept soundly, one hand under her cheek and the other flung out toward him, as if inviting him to lie down next to her.

As if he should be next to her.

He stared at her for several minutes. What was he doing? This bold, clever, beautiful woman had upended his life and twisted him into knots. He'd burned to have her; now he had, and yet he still burned, even hotter than before. That would be bad enough, if she were simply a gentlewoman fallen on hard times and reduced to working for her keep. But Nick was finally putting some pieces together, after she told him her story, and it seemed the ground beneath his feet was crumbling.

As the owner of a gaming hell, Nick felt it prudent to know his patrons. When Lord Fitchley had applied for membership a year ago, Nick had, as usual, investigated him, and before he'd set his plan in motion for Fitchley's ruin, he'd reviewed that file.

Emmett Fitchley was nearly fifty years old, possessed of an old and respectable baronage, legendary for his good luck at the racetrack, and unmarried. But there were rumors, encouraged by the baron himself, of a longstanding betrothal to a wealthy heiress. Her name was never mentioned, but rumor held that she was young and unsophisticated. Fitchley hinted she'd been sent abroad to acquire some polish before their wedding, explaining why he continued to carry on as rakishly as ever.

Tonight, Nick felt a dark suspicion that heiress was Emilia Greeneborough.

The Earl of Harlow had never applied to the Vega Club. Nick had little knowledge of the man or his family, let alone their fortunes. But the Fitchley Nick knew would not have spent years waiting for a girl with only a few thousand pounds. He suspected there was a fortune waiting for Emilia.

Just over six months from now, echoed her voice in his head.

In half a year, she would be a wealthy woman, who would no longer need to teach French verbs and embroidery to young ladies like Charlotte. She would be able to take Lucinda and go anywhere in the world, forever free of Fitchley and her uncle—and uncouth cardsharps like Nicholas Dashwood.

What was he going to do about that?

Nothing, he decided; not yet. He had other business to tend to first.

Silently he pulled on his shirt and breeches, then cautiously opened the door. The inn was silent and dark. Three steps across the corridor, he opened the door of Emilia's room, then went back into his own room and carefully gathered her up, blanket and all. She barely woke; her eyelids fluttered open only when he laid her on her own bed.

"Shh," he breathed. "You're in your room, should Charlotte or Lucinda come looking for you."

She surprised him by looping an arm around his neck. "Thank you," she murmured, and kissed him once more before she drifted back to sleep.

It hadn't been a passionate kiss. It had been . . . sweet. Trusting. Given in gratitude and . . . affection. Nick stayed where he was for a moment, listening to her even breathing, and inhaling the scent of honeysuckle.

He could fall for this woman.

"Always," he whispered.

Gently he tucked the blanket around her. Nick retrieved her clothing and put it on the end of her bed, then closed her door quietly and went back into his own room, where he finished dressing. There was no way he could sleep now. Pulling on his greatcoat, he went out to patrol the inn property, no longer worried about being followed but far too restless and disquieted to sleep.

CHAPTER TWENTY-SIX

Emilia woke the next morning in her own bed, absolutely naked and wrapped in the blanket that smelled of Nick, her clothing from the day before neatly folded at her feet. A warm glow spread through her, and she closed her eyes and snuggled deeper into the blanket for a moment, inhaling the faint lingering scent of him, trying to cling to the memory before the bright light of day could dash it away.

She knew, in her heart, that she had crossed a critical line. She wasn't sorry—on the contrary, she imagined doing it again. Going to bed with Nick tonight. Waking up in his arms. Hearing his low voice wish her good morning, feeling his hands on her skin. Just thinking of it made her heart skip a beat and her toes curl.

But it was a fatal blow to her position. Part of her job—the *mainstay* of her job—was to teach her young ladies to be respectable. Seducing her employer was as far from respectable as a governess could stray. Resigning her post had been the right thing to do, but Emilia knew there was no way she could resume it. She would have to leave his household, for Charlotte's and Lucy's sakes—and Nick's, no matter what he said. Even viscounts had to observe some proprieties.

She lay staring at the ceiling. It would carve a hole in her heart to leave. The only comfort was that Lucy was in safe hands now; Nick would protect her from Fitchley, and she would have Charlotte for company. And Emilia . . . Perhaps, once she came into her inheritance, she could return and visit. She would miss Lucy dreadfully . . . and Charlotte . . . and Nick. Oh, Nick.

Throat tight, she threw off the blanket and got out of bed. *Think about that later,* she told herself. Lucy would need her more than ever while they were in Dorset; Emilia couldn't possibly abandon her now. When they returned to London, she promised herself, she would tell Nick—perhaps she could help him locate a new governess. She began dressing, pushing the melancholy thoughts from her mind. Until they returned to London, she meant to savor her stolen bit of happiness.

In Southampton, they stopped for another night. Nick took them down to the waterfront, where they watched the ships coming and going and ate fried oysters from a street vendor. That night she shared a room with Lucy and Charlotte, but Nick gave her a simmering glance as she shepherded the girls up to bed, and she almost fell on the stairs, light-headed with how much she yearned to go to him.

They reached Beaufort Hall the following morning. Knowing it was approaching, Emilia had made up games to occupy the girls, but as they drew near, Lucy became quieter and quieter, peeking out the window until she turned away from it with a little shiver. Emilia put an arm around her, and Lucy burrowed into her side.

From a distance, Beaufort Hall was an impressive sight. Three tall stories of pale stone rose above the grounds, chimneys bristling from the mansard roof. The house was nearly as deep as it was wide, with graceful stone stairs from the garden leading to a pair of French windows, visible from the elm-lined gravel drive that swept around to the grander main entrance. Today, the sun glittered off the tall sash windows and turned the façade the color of well-aged linen.

Only as one came closer did the vision of elegance fade away. Several of the windows had been boarded up; shutters shielded the rest, giving the house a blank, unfriendly look. Vines clogged the loggia, and the drive grew rutted and unkempt the closer they came. By the time they reached the entrance, Emilia had remembered in vivid detail why she had been so desperate to leave.

Nick had already ridden ahead and dismounted. He came to open the carriage door and help them down. Emilia noted he was especially gentle with Lucy, who clung to Emilia's hand and stared at the house with open anxiety.

"It's not the worst I've ever seen," Nick said.

"Not at all," exclaimed Charlotte, sounding awed as she tipped back her head to take it in.

Lucy gulped.

"You haven't been inside," replied Emilia.

He grinned. "Right you are. Shall we break a window and let ourselves in like a gang of thieves?" Without waiting for an answer he strode off, his boots barely crunching on the weed-infested drive.

"Is anyone still here, Millie?" whispered Lucy.

She took a deep breath. "Perhaps Mr. and Mrs. Stone." They'd been longtime Sidney family employees, rather dour and stern, but unquestionably devoted to the family.

But that had been several months ago. Only Mrs. Watson and her nephew Henry, who had come to Beaufort Hall with the late Lady Sydenham, had gone with them to London; the few remaining servants had left the day Emilia told them there was no money for salaries until she located the new viscount.

"Why don't you wait here?" she told the girls. She caught James's eye and he nodded. He began talking about climbing the stately elm trees that lined the drive, which made Charlotte giggle. Lucy even gave a hesitant smile.

Emilia picked up her skirts and ran after Nick.

She found him peering through a window on the terrace. Several of the panes were cracked, but none had fallen out; there was hope the interior hadn't been ruined by rain or pests. "A library?" he guessed, one hand shielding his eyes. "It could be, if there were any books on the shelves."

She shook her head. "Lord Sydenham didn't care for books. He sold whatever was here." He'd sold everything he could find a buyer for, until he began drinking too much. And then Emilia had sold the few bits left in pursuit of funds for food, each time saying a little prayer she wouldn't be sent to prison for it.

Nick nodded and moved to the French windows. They looked as if they hadn't been opened in months, with dead leaves stuck to the glass and grass growing tall through a fissure in the flagstones where they would swing. He tried the handle, and when it didn't move, to Emilia's shock, he turned and jabbed his elbow through the glass, breaking it neatly so he could reach inside and turn the lock to open the door.

"Oh my—!" She scrambled after him into the house.

He gave her a level look. "It's my house, isn't it?"

She flushed. "Well—yes—"

"I'll have it repaired." His gaze flitted around as he started forward.

They stood in the back of the hall, looking toward the front of the house. They passed the library door to the right, and the door to the left, which had been closed up by the time Emilia arrived. It had been a music room, she remembered hearing, but of course the instruments were gone.

They came to the central core of the house, the staircase hall, which rose three stories to the roof, where a glass dome let in light—or should have done. Emilia craned her neck, but the upper floors were shrouded in darkness. Nick, meanwhile, had continued onward, and pulled back the bolt on the tall, carved front door, shoving it open with a groan of hinges.

Outside, Charlotte whirled around, a smile on her lips. James was swinging his arms wildly in some comical pantomime, but stopped.

Lucy stood to the side, her face white and her wide eyes fixed on the door.

Nick coughed and waved one hand in front of his face. "I feel like a cave explorer. It's dark, dirty, and cold in here."

"Is no one home?" asked Charlotte.

"Just us," Nick told her. "And a legion of mice."

"If only we'd brought Sir Chester," Emilia said lightly. "He would be in alt!"

Charlotte laughed. Lucy's mouth trembled.

Nick flung the doors wide and left them open. He told the coachman and groom to put the horses to graze on the overgrown lawn and go examine the stables, whose roof was visible further along the drive, behind a wild scrub of shrubbery. Then he led the way from room to room, tossing aside draperies and shutters to illuminate them. Charlotte and James both picked up on his unspoken message to be cheerful, and soon the house was echoing with laughter and shouts of surprise as they discovered broken furniture, several nests of mice, and a pair of squirrels, who shot out from under a table draped in Holland covers chattering violently before racing out the open door.

Lucy stayed close to Emilia, holding tight to her hand. She said little as Charlotte peeked under furniture covers and James opened doors. It was a game to the two of them, but Lucy had terrible memories of this place.

Nick came and went down on one knee, a lit lantern in each hand. "Lucinda, will you guide me upstairs? I wouldn't want to fall down a concealed trap door and land in the coal cellar."

Lucy gave a small, hesitant, smile. She let go of Emilia's hand and took Nick's, accepting one of the lanterns from him as well.

Emilia followed them up the winding stairs. The lanterns grew more and more necessary as they climbed; she wondered what had happened to the glass dome above that used to illuminate the hall. The house had a deserted, hollow feel to it. It hadn't felt that way when they left six months ago, but the Stones must have shut it up and finally gone away, too.

A gallery ran around the staircase hall on each floor, with tall doors into each room. In the daylight it was impressive, all in cream with gold accents in the elaborately carved edges. In the dark it felt ghostly, as if all the light and life had faded from the place.

Emilia watched Nick and Lucy. She saw how the girl clung to his hand and stayed close to him, and how he held the lantern above her path so she could see better, though it left him more in the dark. He was offering obvious protection as he gently guided Lucy through the place she had feared. Her heart gave an unsteady thump; she was so head over heels for the man, it was somewhat frightening.

They peeked into the large drawing room, an antechamber, and a room Emilia had forgotten because it had never been used in her time here. It had been Lucy's mother's parlor, she remembered with a pang, as the lantern light fell on a pale rose carpet, mottled with dirt and eaten through in places. Lucy whispered to Nick something or other about each room, and he nodded gravely. Emilia was curious, but hung back, wanting Lucy to have someone else she could trust.

Only at the last door did Lucy halt. "That's a bad room," she told Nick, her voice faltering.

"Is it?" He nodded and raised his lantern. "I won't have that. We must reclaim it." He opened the door and walked inside.

Lucy ran to Emilia, who took the lantern and put her arm around the girl.

"I see what you mean, Lucinda," called Nick from inside the study. "This room is an abomination."

"A disgrace," whispered Emilia as Lucy looked to her in fearful question.

"It needs," went on Nick, "a large bucket of soapy water, applied with a mop." Light filtered out to them; he was throwing open the shutters on the tall windows. "And a broom." More light. "And a solid week's worth of dusting." Now Emilia could see into the room, the midnight blue carpet on the floor, the dark walnut paneling. Lucy crowded closer, her face pressed into Emilia's side.

"And most importantly," called Nick dramatically, "fresh air!"

She felt the whoosh of air, which felt like a pent-up breath being released. Behind them, Charlotte and James were coming up the stairs, wondering at how dark it was.

Emilia waited until Charlotte and James had gone into the room. "Shall we go in?" she whispered. Lucy's face was stark white in the lantern light, but after a moment she gave a tiny nod. Emilia held her close as they started forward.

This had been Lord Sydenham's study, where he sat smoking for hours, then drinking until he passed out on the chaise. It was where he summoned servants to shout at them and sack them. It was where he dragged his daughter when he was in his worst moods, slapping her until she cried and snarling that he'd never wanted a daughter and couldn't wait to be rid of her. It was where he'd been found dead one frosty morning last fall, crumpled on the hearthrug. As she passed through the tall doorway, Emilia saw the scar in the wood, left by a knife Lord Sydenham had once thrown at the butler.

She herself had been summoned here on a few occasions; the viscount had been furious about expenses for clothing and books, snarling that a girl child had no need to learn. She'd thought he might have wanted to throw something at her, too, but by then all his books and objets d'art had vanished, and he'd settled for shouting, calling her names and then roaring at her to get out of his sight.

In her memory the study was grim and gray, reeking of pipe smoke and the oppressive stench of the chamber pot Sydenham had kept under his desk. Today the stale smoky smell lingered, but the rest of it was far less ominous than she had feared it would be, with the windows open and a fresh, warm breeze wafting in.

Nick paced the room, hands on hips. "I take it this was Sydenham's private domain."

Emilia nodded, but Lucy spoke. "Yes," she said in a quavering voice. "It's my father's study." She paused. "It's a terrible room."

Nick nodded firmly. "There will be no terrible rooms as long as I own Beaufort Hall."

"No, none," said Charlotte gently, to Lucy. "Miss Greene, were there ever balls held here?"

"I—I don't know," she said in surprise.

"I ask because the room opposite this one looks rather like a ballroom, don't you think?" the girl went on. "Of course it's not fit now, but perhaps..."

Nick raised his brows. "Already planning fêtes and house parties?"

She smiled sheepishly and took Lucy's hand. "Why not? This house will be beautiful when it's properly fixed up, and I think a party would be just the thing to make it cheerier."

He looked around—at the room, at his sister, at Lucy bravely holding her hand, at Emilia standing with her hands unconsciously clasped in hope. "Yes," he said, gazing into her eyes so intently she felt it from across the room. "Yes, it might."

"What's this?" James lifted something from the mantel. Emilia barely had time to identify it before Lucy let out a low moan and bolted from the room. Emilia thrust her lantern at a startled Charlotte and flew after her.

She caught Lucy at the bottom of the stairs. "Come," she said, pulling the girl into a tight hug. "No one will hurt you," she whispered fiercely as Lucy's whole body shook. Emilia sank down onto the stair, Lucy sliding into her lap and clinging with all her might.

They sat there for several minutes, Emilia rocking gently back and forth, her heart throbbing. She'd worried about this.

Someone sat down beside her. It was James. "I'm sorry, Lucy," he said quietly.

She peeked at him through her hair. "I know," she whispered.

James lifted the offensive item. It was a short riding crop, the handle weighted with lead, the leather end split and frayed. Sydenham had carried it, liable to lash anyone or anything with it as he passed. Lucy shrank from the sight of it, but James took out his knife and with one hard crack, sliced the crop in two.

"No one will harm you here," said Nick from behind them. "I give you my word."

Lucy looked at Charlotte, who huddled beside her brother. "Promise?"

Charlotte nodded solemnly. "Nick keeps his promises, Lucy. Shall I tell you how he kept his promise to me, that I would always be safe?"

Lucy looked at Emilia, then climbed to her feet. "Yes." Charlotte held out a hand, and Lucy took it. The two girls went out the front door.

"Get rid of that," Nick said to James, who nodded and took the shattered crop away. "Her father struck her with it?"

Emilia nodded. "He struck everyone with it, sooner or later."

Nick put out a hand and helped her to her feet. "I'll send Rudy to take rooms in the nearest village. You and she don't need to stay here."

"But you will?"

"For one night. To prove it's mine." His face was grim.

Emilia rubbed her hands up and down her arms. Lucy had been doing well until the crop appeared. Perhaps she ought to scour the house, to find any other malicious reminders . . .

A door creaked, and footsteps sounded. Nick stepped forward, but Emilia recognized the intruder. "Mrs. Stone!"

The older woman pursed her lips, her back rigid and her face stony with disapproval. She had a basket over one arm. "Miss Greene. Come back, have you?"

"Yes." Emilia hesitated, looking at Nick. "Mr. Dashwood, this is Mrs. Stone, who was housekeeper here for many years."

Nick gave a polite nod. "How do you do, Mrs. Stone?"

The woman's eyes narrowed to slits as she looked him up and down. He still wore his dark and dangerous clothing, but he'd shaved that morning, and had discarded the sweeping greatcoat that made him look like the Angel of Death. He said nothing, merely returned her scrutiny. "Making very free of the place, aren't you, Miss Greene?"

"Yes," said Emilia evenly. "Miss Sidney is outside."

As if hearing her name, Lucy slipped around the door. She stopped short, but the housekeeper had seen her. "You look very well, Miss Sidney." Her expression thawed a fraction. "I'm glad to see it."

Lucy regarded her gravely. The Stones hadn't been unkind to her, but neither had they endeared themselves. Most of the servants hadn't, cowed by Sydenham's rages and threats. Only Emilia had defied the viscount to protect Lucy. "Thank you. I hope you and Mr. Stone are well."

The older woman's stern face softened more. "We are, miss, thank you kindly."

"We've come to see the house," said Lucy. Emilia blinked, surprised by her composure. "Mr. Dashwood is my cousin, the new viscount."

Mrs. Stone's eyes flared. "The new Lord Sydenham!" She shot a suspicious glance at Emilia. "Not a Sidney."

"No, ma'am," said Nick in the same pleasant but steely voice. "My aunt took me in as a child and changed my name. Miss Greene was quite the sleuth, making the connection."

"Hmph." She pursed her lips. "I hope your aunt left you a tidy fortune in exchange for the

name, young man. The Sydenham estate is
bankrupt."

He smiled—a predatory smile that Emilia had
seen before. "She did."

Mrs. Stone rocked on her heels. "Hmph. Well.
Fortunate for you."

"Yes." Nick looked up. "Why in God's name is
it pitch dark in here?"

"Mr. Stone boarded over the cupola," she told
him. "After the master died and Miss Greene run
off. It needed repair but there were no funds, so he
blocked it up."

"Ah," said Nick after a moment. "We'll have to
address that."

Mrs. Stone glanced around at all of them.
"You'll be taking up residence, then?"

Nick turned to face her with a cool stare. "Of
course. Beaufort Hall is the Sydenham seat, is it
not?"

"Yes, sir," she said after a moment's pause.
"It is."

Nick just smiled slightly, his point made.

The woman sniffed. Then, to Emilia's astonishment, she bent her knee and curtsied. "Welcome to
Beaufort Hall, my lord."

CHAPTER TWENTY-SEVEN

Beaufort Hall was not as terrible as Grantham had warned Nick to expect, but neither was it fit to live in.

It was clear that little maintenance had been done for years—possibly since Arthur Sidney inherited. The house had been stripped of most fittings that were worth anything, the cracked plaster in the dining room ceiling where chandeliers should have hung testifying eloquently to Sydenham's rapacity. The furnishings that remained were either worn or broken, and there wasn't a carpet or drapery without a scattering of holes.

He should be grateful Mr. Stone had boarded up the broken windows and the cupola light. That alone had prevented irreparable damage to the structure, not to mention the walls and floors. The house needed to be emptied and everything within sanded, painted, and polished, but the building itself seemed sound.

For the first time, Nick truly appreciated what Emilia had confronted. When he pictured her arriving, full of confidence and optimism, unaware of

the true nature of the post she'd taken, it made him
want to punch someone. Of course she couldn't
leave Lucinda here, with no one to protect the child
from an abusive father and indifferent servants.
And when the viscount died, no wonder she'd
launched her extraordinary crusade.

Under the exertion of a little charm, Mrs. Stone
thawed somewhat. She and her husband, who was
the head groom, had shut up the house after Emilia
took Lucy to London and removed to the small
coachman's cottage, from where she'd spied Nick's
coachman poking around the stables. The Stones
had been with the Sidney family for forty years, and
were loyal to all of its members, even the dissolute
Arthur—which the woman was now at pains to
explain.

"Not right, him," she confided primly, as she
led Nick on a tour of the servant's areas below-
stairs, while Emilia and the girls explored the gardens with James. "His mother's fault, I don't
doubt. A very cold woman, she was, very cold. It's
not right for a child to have such a mother. But
then, it's not my place. He was the master, and that
was that."

"Hmm." Nick kept his tone idle. "What of Lucinda? Was he a kind parent to her?"

Discomfort flitted across her face. "Well—fathers aren't meant to raise children. He had no no-
tion how it was to be done. His wife died," she
added witheringly, as if Lady Sydenham were to
blame for her own demise.

Nick thought that any decent man would know
it wasn't right to terrify his child, let alone strike
her. "Thank goodness for Miss Greene," he said, his
tone harder.

Mrs. Stone flushed. "Yes. Thank goodness," she muttered.

The woman should be ashamed. Sydenham had been her employer, true; but Emilia hadn't let that stop *her* from standing up for Lucinda. It wasn't as if Mrs. Stone's loyalty had been rewarded, either. Sydenham hadn't paid them a farthing in his last year—a fact Mrs. Stone had already managed to mention twice—and he'd left nothing in his will for the faithful retainers. They'd been reduced to scraping a living in the humble coachman's cottage, where they had no legal right to be.

It made Nick shake his head. Forbes had the right of it: *Think they're better than the lot of us,* his manager had said.

Later they went into the nearby village, where Nick did shake the vicar's hand after that gentleman came hurrying down the street from the church, coattails flapping in his haste. Word that the new Lord Sydenham had arrived got around at lightning speed, and by the time Nick stood a round at the Roaring Bull, it seemed the entire village was there to raise a glass to him.

After that it was easy to procure a wagonload of supplies to be sent to Beaufort Hall. Nick meant to spend the night at the estate. And to his surprise, Lucinda said she would, too.

"Are you certain it's a good idea?" Emilia asked softly.

Lucinda nodded, a film of fresh milk on her upper lip. She'd been rolling a hoop across the green with a pair of local children while Charlotte cried encouragement, holding a posy of flowers one little girl had given her. A few young men made periodic attempts to get her attention, though James's presence seemed to give them pause. "I'm brave, Millie. And James broke the switch."

Emilia bit her lip. "If you're certain . . ."

Lucinda glanced at Nick, who stood sipping his pint of beer. "Mr. Dashwood keeps his promises, and he promised nothing would hurt me."

"Well . . . Yes, he did . . ."

Lucinda nodded. "And he's going to stay there, so I will, too." She gulped the rest of her milk and ran back to the group of children with hoops.

"It will be an adventure," Nick said. It gave him an unfamiliar feeling to hear the child express such confidence in him. "Sleeping on camp beds, with lanterns for light and a picnic hamper providing dinner. Charlotte will adore the excitement of it. And I hope Lucinda won't be frightened if we're all nearby."

Emilia's expression eased. "Perhaps you're right."

He grinned, bumping her shoulder with his. "It does happen now and then."

She blushed. "Of course! I can't help but worry . . ."

"Lucinda showed courage today," Nick said quietly. "I wouldn't let her stay there tonight if she had dissolved in terror. I want her to know there's nothing there now for her to fear, and that she will always be safe in our care. I want her to see that it's just a house, where she can be happy and safe even after her terrible experiences."

"Of course," she said softly. "Thank you."

Between them, he caught her hand and gave it a squeeze. If she'd noted his use of the word *our,* she hadn't reacted. Nick admitted he was still testing it himself, but deep in his heart, it felt right.

She felt right—her hand in his, her presence beside him, her touch on his skin. He'd had associates, underlings, followers, and enemies his entire life. Not much family, and few friends. Emilia was his first true partner, and he liked it. He liked her. Nick wasn't sure what to call the feeling, but it was beginning to seem like destiny.

They headed back to Beaufort Hall in good spirits. Nick spoke to James, and the young man did an excellent job of keeping the two girls giggling with his antics and jokes. They arrived to find that Mrs. Stone, who'd been indignant that they meant to stay in the village, had thoroughly swept and dusted the drawing room. The draperies had been beaten and rehung, the ragged carpet pulled out, and the scuffed floor was still damp from scrubbing. Mr. Stone showed himself, a gruff older man who snatched off his cap when Nick approached. Leaving behind a cauldron of warm washing water, the Stones departed for their own cottage.

They ate a large picnic dinner on a blanket spread on the overgrown lawn, under a cloudless twilight sky. When the girls began to yawn, Emilia ushered them inside for bed while Nick, James, and his other men walked circuits around the house. Mr. Stone had kept the stables in good order, so there was a place to put the horses and quarters for the coachmen, groom, and Jock and Rudy, who were part of Nick's security team at the Vega Club. James would sleep in the house with the rest of them. Nick had seen with his own eyes how isolated Beaufort Hall was, and he didn't begrudge his men a decent bed for the night.

They returned to the drawing room to find Charlotte and Lucinda tucked into their camp beds with a pair of lanterns between them. Charlotte was reading aloud, and Lucinda was listening, snuggled into her blankets with her eyes closed but a faint smile on her face. James gave Nick a nod, settled by the door with his own lantern, and took out his penknife and a piece of wood half-carved into a woman's bangle. Nick smiled to think what Fanny from the Vega kitchen would say when James put it on her arm.

That, more than anything, told him he was growing a heart.

He was standing outside on the cracked and weedy terrace, surveying what had once been a formal garden before it went wild, when Emilia stepped up beside him. Her hair was damp; she must have been washing up after the girls. He closed his eyes and inhaled. She smelled fresh and honeysuckle sweet.

"You were right," she murmured. "Lucy's not frightened. I believe having Charlotte here has helped enormously."

He made a low noise of agreement in his throat.

"When Lucy had a nightmare, Charlotte was very understanding and comforting to her," Emilia went on. "She said she knew what it was like, to have nightmares."

Nick said nothing. Even his heartbeat seemed to have quieted.

"I've long wondered . . ." Her voice trailed off and she fell silent.

"What?" he asked after a long pause. "What have you wondered?"

Despite his efforts not to, it came out cool and clipped. The question rattled a door that he had long ago closed, locked, and boarded up in his memory. He knew what she wondered, and he felt the instinctive response rising in his throat: *No. It's not your place. Mind your business and stay out of mine.*

But she didn't say it. Instead she rested her cheek against his shoulder for a moment. "Nothing." She moved away, trailing her fingers along the balustrade. "What a beautiful night."

Nick followed as she went down the steps, hopping over the one that had cracked in half under the eruption of some prickly plant. He followed her lazy stroll across the grass to the picnic blanket, still spread on the west-facing lawn. She bent down to pick it up, and he stepped forward and caught her hand.

"Sit with me," he said. The sky was a deepening dark blue, beginning to glint with emerging stars. It was still warm from the day, and so outrageously quiet and peaceful—nothing at all like London would be at this time. Even the air was softer, sweeter.

Emilia glanced at him, then nodded. Nick sat down and stretched out his legs, propping himself up on his arms. She tucked her skirt beneath her and sank down, near but not near enough. She gave a startled exclamation when Nick swept an arm around her waist and hauled her right to his side.

"That's better," he murmured, nuzzling her temple.

"Yes," she answered breathlessly, "but Charlotte or Lucy—"

"They're on the other side of the house, half asleep," he returned, inhaling the scent of honeysuckle soap as he pulled the pins from her hair.

"James will raise a racket if one of them tries to come out."

Even in the dark he could see her blush. "Oh— Does he—?"

Nick pulled back to look at her. "Did I tell James to keep them away so I could make love to you without being disturbed? Absolutely not."

She gave a gasping laugh. "I never thought that!"

He caught her hand and kissed her palm. "James knows I don't like to be crept up on. And he knows both girls are supposed to go to sleep, so if either of them wants to come out, it will be for an urgent reason, and he will call out to find me as quickly as possible. Even if he stood outside the door, he wouldn't spot us from there." He ran his fingertips down her throat, over the bodice of her green dress, growling in satisfaction when she shivered as his thumb went over her nipple. "We're almost invisible," he added softly. "On this dark blanket, in this dark field. We might as well be marooned on a tiny island far at sea, just the two of us."

She made a breathy sound of longing, and he kissed her. Never before had he adored simply kissing a woman. A kiss had been a prelude, a signal of intent of other activities, like hoisting a flag as a signal before commencing the main action. He had put his mouth to other uses, with other lovers, but he found that kissing Emilia was more pleasurable than he'd ever guessed. She tasted like the treacle tart they'd had for dessert, and he felt dizzy, as if their blanket had begun to spin about as she turned into his arms and wound her fingers into his hair.

The soft crack of a stick breaking made him

raise his head, swiftly scanning the horizon. A shape stepped forward from the brush, creeping from the stable block. A deer, he thought in relief; a doe with fawns, judging by the two smaller shapes who followed.

Nick nudged Emilia, who turned her head and sighed with pleasure at the sight. "They can be terrible pests," she whispered, barely audibly, "eating the shrubbery and the garden. Grandpapa would rage about them. But they're so lovely."

He folded his arm around her. The interruption was both calming and frustrating; he watched the deer pick their way through the growing darkness until they melted into the shadows of a hedge.

He was still reluctant to do what needed doing, but Emilia had trusted him with her secrets. He wanted to be worthy of that trust. He wanted to show her it didn't flow in only one direction. He did trust her, and he wanted . . . He wanted . . .

There was the rub. He wanted, but he hadn't earned.

Everyone pays for his sins sooner or later, whispered Heloise's wispy voice in his memory.

If she really was the heiress Nick suspected her to be . . . If he wanted this new relationship to continue . . . If he wanted even more, for it grow into something he hardly dared think of . . . It would take extraordinary measures on his part. He'd had two days to think about it, and that had become clear to him.

He wanted her. He liked her. He was falling in love with her.

What was he going to do about it?

"I know what you meant to ask me earlier," he murmured.

She had settled against his side, her hand on his chest. At his words, she sat up a little straighter. "Oh—never mind it. I shouldn't have—"

He held her back when she started to move away from him. He pulled her down with him until they were lying together on the blanket, his arm around her as she rested against his side. She laid her cheek on his shoulder and Nick felt a surge of . . . not pleasure, not triumph, just overwhelming *contentment*. As if everything was right in his world, for the first time in ages. Certainly for as long as he could remember.

Perhaps it was, here on the still, secluded grounds of his very own estate, with his family safe and secure and Emilia next to him.

"You wonder," he said, "why Charlotte has a personal guard."

CHAPTER TWENTY-EIGHT

E milia went very still.

She barely remembered what she'd started to ask—a half-formed question that slipped out before she could stop it. Everything in her life now felt like a half-formed question, though. She no longer knew what their relationship was. She had resigned her position as governess, and he had accepted it, but she was still caring for Charlotte and Lucy and still hoping to spend her nights making love to Nick.

It was a risky plan, long term, but for now it made her ineffably happy in a way she couldn't remember being happy before, and it was so lovely to feel that way, she didn't care to contemplate how or when it would end.

But now that he brought it up, *yes,* she did wonder about Charlotte—though not as much as she wondered about Nick. His aunt took him in and changed his name, leaving him her fortune. He said he had no family other than Charlotte, who had been a stranger to him. Why had he not met his sister until she was old enough to have nightmares?

Why had he thought a pistol beside her bed was necessary?

So she lay perfectly still in the warmth of his arm, her head resting on his shoulder, and listened.

"To explain about Charlotte, I have to tell you about my father," he said. "Our father."

Emilia hadn't learned very much about Samuel, although it must be admitted that once she found out he was dead and had left a son, she hadn't cared. She'd been tracing a line, and cared only for the man at the end. But Charlotte had said Samuel Sidney was the reason Nick would never get married, and Emilia suddenly found herself deeply interested in his story.

"You found him through birth records and marriage registers, and Grantham says it's all correct. I never knew or cared much for my family history. I suppose we were much too far from the viscount's line to gain any benefit from it, and that's the only thing that would have motivated my father to speak of it. The truth is that by the time my grandfather came around, our branch of the Sidneys was rather humble." He glanced at her. "You know. You told me what their positions were. Vicar. Naval officer. Ship captain."

"Yes," she murmured, when he paused.

"My grandfather, whose naval career was less than glorious, realized his fortune did not lie in the navy. He married into a prosperous family in Liverpool and captained some of their ships."

Emilia nodded, searching her memory. "Yes, Mary Blake."

Nick exhaled. "The Blakes." He said nothing for several minutes. "They traded between England, the West Indies, and the American states. They had family connections in Bristol and Manchester, and a large percentage of their cargo was cotton and sugar from the plantations, which made them wealthy. I suppose that's what drew my grandfather, and why my father followed in his footsteps."

Emilia was beginning to wish she had found out more about the Blakes, but she'd been so frantic to find a living heir, she hadn't paused to investigate everyone she discovered along the way.

"My father ran into some trouble with the Royal Navy over his trading with the Americans—Horatio Nelson himself boarded his ship and threatened to impound the ship and its cargo. A merchant in Antigua, who desired a closer relationship with the Blakes, spotted an opportunity. My father was not a Blake, but a Blake cousin, which was apparently near enough for him to offer up his natural daughter as a prospective bride." Nick paused. "I understand that in the West Indies, society is a bit different. Illegitimate children are often accepted and acknowledged by their fathers. The merchant intervened with the governor, and my father married his daughter. That, and a dowry of two hundred pounds, were all it took to win Sam Sidney's cold heart. I was the result."

A faint smile touched his lips. "My mother and I lived in Antigua for my first few years. I've only faint memories of her," he said softly. "I've been told she was beautiful and merry, and that we had a small house on her father's plantation, where my father appeared only infrequently and never for long. I had a miniature of her, once, but it was lost in a storm at sea years later."

Emilia thought of the miniature of her own mother, safely tucked in her wooden box with her most prized possessions. She put her hand on Nick's chest without a word, and he clasped it.

"When I was five, my mother died of a fever. My father returned to Antigua a few months later and decided to take me with him. He had recently acquired an indentured servant, a girl called Sally. A Philadelphia merchant had been unable to pay his bill, and he traded the indenture contract for his goods. She was only twelve or so, but she was put in charge of me and we sailed with my father for the next five years."

"Only twelve!"

"Sally's father indentured her when she was ten years old, for no less than ten years."

Emilia gaped at him.

"That wasn't the worst for Sally," said Nick. "The worst was that my father purchased her indenture." He was gazing up at the stars again. "You would have liked Sally. She was put to work on the ship, just as I was, but she was clever, and witty, and unafraid of anything. She told me stories from mythology and sketched the fantastical creatures on the wall by my berth. She taught me how to read, from nautical almanacs. When I fell overboard, it was Sally who flung down a rope to me. She mended my clothes, until she showed me how to do it myself. She taught me how to sense my father's dark moods—I barely knew him—and she helped me find little crannies in the hold where I could hide."

That sounded dreadful to Emilia, but his voice had grown softer, even warm, with affection. "Why did you need to hide?"

His faint smile disappeared. "Because my father was not a good man, Emilia. He could be charming when necessary—in a contretemps with a merchant or a harbormaster—but generally he was cold-hearted and cruel. Discipline was strict aboard his ship." His fingers curled around hers tightly.

"You must have supposed, from my description of my aunt's taking me in, that I relished the seagoing life," he said quietly. "I suppose I did, on some level, because it was all I knew. It *could* be thrilling and adventurous. But it was also filled with terrible things. Sailors lashed raw with a cat-o'-nine-tails. Slave auctions, on the wharves of Charleston, South Carolina, where whole families of Africans were casually torn apart. Plantations in Antigua, where the poor souls enslaved there were forced to work harder than any animals, from dawn until night in the sweltering cane fields and sugar mills. I watched my father step over the body of a boy, no older than myself, and calmly conduct business with the man who had just whipped that boy insensible." His grip was like iron around her hand, but Emilia didn't move.

"Sally abhorred it—the brutality, the inhumanity. She refused to go ashore anywhere except Philadelphia. I suspect she had a family there, and she took any chance to search for them, but one time she didn't return. My father had her dragged back and the court added a year to her indenture. She never told me about her family, but that additional year of servitude was a blow. I remember hearing her weep quietly, repeating *Mama* over and over . . ." Nick paused. "She was still with my father when Heloise took me. I can still see her, standing and watching at the ship's rail as they cast off and left me behind. She was the only true friend I had, and I might have been her only friend. Neither my aunt nor my father cared."

For a moment he sounded angry all over again. Emilia's heart ached for the boy he had been, losing his mother and taken from that home, carelessly exposed to his father's wanton cruelty, then sent against his will, without his only friend, into the strict home of his aunt, who was another stranger to him.

"Did you ever see her again?" she asked softly.

"No." He turned his head to look at her. "Sally is Charlotte's mother."

CHAPTER TWENTY-NINE

"Oh," said Emilia, taken aback. "He— Your father married her?"

"No." He looked away. "No, he did not. I've no idea if she wanted to have a child with him, or if he coerced her."

"Oh," she whispered again, in horror.

"Charlotte knows," he said, as if she'd asked. "She was born the year our father died. Old Sam"— a note of viciousness entered his voice—"left Sally and Charlotte nothing but the clothes they owned and a few pounds. Sally was alone in Liverpool, a stranger in this country, with a babe and no money and not even the respectability of a marriage license."

His hand had gone completely still on her back. Emilia could feel the rock-hard tension in his arm beneath her, and wished there was something she could say to comfort him. Even her father, selfish and uncaring as he'd been, was not as bad as this.

"That is appalling. But . . . surely you don't blame yourself for it?" she asked hesitantly.

He gave a harsh bark of laughter. "I couldn't

have stopped him even if I'd known. Heloise
wrested me from my father's care when I was a boy
of ten, and I only saw him a handful of times after-
ward. Heloise urged me to write to him, encouraging him to repent his wicked ways before it was
too late, but he rarely wrote back." His mouth
twisted. "My aunt was right—I was better off with
her. But I despised her for leaving Sally behind.
Heloise knew what my father was. She could have
bought Sally's indenture and taken her as well, and
probably even more cheaply than she bought me,
but she didn't." He glanced at her. "I never forgave
her for that, despite all she did for me. Ungrateful,
she called me."

"No," she exclaimed. "Ungrateful, for wanting
something other than what she wanted! I ran away
from home to avoid the path my uncle wanted me
to take—a path many would call eminently respectable."

He cocked one brow. "You went on to an honorable, if difficult, line of employment."

She blushed. "I hadn't any other skills."

He laughed a little. "Too right you are. I learned
gambling on the ship, and I was good at it. The fact
that it horrified Heloise only made me more determined to pursue it."

Emilia wet her lips after a moment of silence.
"When did you learn about Charlotte?"

"After my father's death. A letter from one of
the Blakes informed Heloise that Sally had applied
to them for funds to support her child—my father's
child—which they refused." Nick's voice began to
crack, and he paused a moment before continuing
more evenly. "I had a *sister*. It was the first I'd heard
of it, and I flew into a frenzy, raging at Heloise to

send for them. She balked at that, but she did give Sally money. I was at school by then, but I threatened to run away and give myself to a press gang if she didn't. There was a very brief reply from Sally, thanking her for the funds, then nothing else." His face was grim again. "The moment I came of age, I went to Liverpool to find them, but it had been a few years, and I had no luck. When my aunt died, I hired investigators to search. I was in London by then, running the card games that became the Vega Club. Only five years ago did my search pay off, when the investigator found Charlotte in a workhouse in Manchester."

Emilia started. "*Where?* Why?"

"Sally was gone. She'd left Charlotte with a friendly family, but the man died and his widow couldn't feed her own children, let alone Charlotte. Charlotte told me her mother was going back to Philadelphia and meant to return for her, but I've not been able to locate Sally, here or there. It's a long and dangerous voyage."

"Oh, Nick," she whispered.

He turned to face her, deadly serious. "It took me years to find her, and I only did so in the nick of time. There are people, Emilia—evil men—who have a taste for children. A defenseless orphan, let alone a pretty female one, would be easy prey to them. By the grace of God, the matron at the workhouse tried to protect the children, and Charlotte was merely hungry and ragged. I took her out of there and installed her in a house of her own, where she had a warm bed and plenty to eat and pretty dresses to wear, and she will never be hungry or cold, ever again."

Mutely she seized his hand. He gripped it back,

hard, and she pressed her lips to his knuckles. *The most honorable man I know,* she thought with a throb of emotion.

"Is that how Charlotte knows what a cock bawd is?" she asked without thinking. She had been shocked to hear that term for a brothel keeper.

"Yes," said Nick flatly. "The matron at the workhouse used to tell the children not to dawdle, or the cock bawds would snatch them. She was right. I came through the gutters of London, building Vega's, and I know exactly how depraved some corners are. James is always two steps behind her when she's out of the house because I will not lose my sister again."

"And that's why you left a pistol by her bed at nights." Now she understood. A chill ran through her as she pictured Charlotte at Lucy's age, completely alone and vulnerable.

He grimaced. "I had no idea how to deal with a child's fears, and I was away all night. It seemed a good idea at the time."

She smiled. "It wasn't the worst idea. It comforted her, and that's what was important." Suddenly she gasped. "And *that's* why you agreed to my bargain!"

Nick smiled wryly. "Yes. Being the sister of a viscount would suit Charlotte, even if a coronet doesn't suit me."

"Stop!" She seized his shoulders. "It *does* suit you, Nicholas Dashwood," she declared in a low, fierce voice. "You're a better man than virtually everyone in the House of Lords. If titles were granted based on decency and kindness, you would be made a prince."

He laughed. "I've corrupted you completely, if you can say something so daft!"

She growled in outrage, and he laughed again, and she pulled him to her and kissed him, hard, insistently, with the full force of the love she felt for him.

"Now you know," he said a few minutes later, breathing hard. "My father was a monster, and I'm not much better." She opened her mouth to argue, and he touched his fingers to her lips to stay her. "But you're a lady and an heiress, granddaughter of an earl," he went on, his tone gentling. "In six months, you'll be a wealthy woman with no more need of being a governess. You'll be respectable and independent, and I don't want to be the shameful stain on your conscience."

She knocked his hand away. "Stain. You think this is a stain on my conscience?"

He gazed back somberly. "Even if you don't think so now, will you in a year? Five? Ten?"

Never, she thought. Lady Watney, who had reached the advanced age of seventy-four, had told her more than once that at the end of life, one's regrets were far more likely to involve the chances not taken, the opportunities not seized, the adventures not enjoyed. *What's a scandal or two?* she'd scoffed. *Make some memories that will keep you smug in your dotage.*

Emilia, at the less-advanced age of twenty-seven, had already missed many of the experiences she had anticipated as a girl. For her there had been no presentation at court; no giddy evenings at balls, no flirting with young men in the park, no stolen kisses in shadowed gardens. She had learned that, to her remaining family, she was little more than an asset to be traded away for their benefit. She had had to rely on herself, at the cost of more than girlish dreams. She'd worked hard for her keep, and could never forget that she was dependent on the grace of others for her living.

But when Nick had asked her to become Charlotte's governess, he had described it as a partnership. He had agreed to her terms, outrageous as they were from a governess. They hadn't always agreed, but he had always treated her as an equal, competent and respected.

If she was going to ruin herself over a man, she couldn't have chosen better than Nicholas Dashwood.

And she loved him.

"In five years," she said, "I will look back on this happily. My great gamble paid off beyond all expectations—I located the heir to the Sydenham viscounty, when even he had no idea who he was! I persuaded him to come to Lucy's aid, rather generously, and even cozened him into paying me a ridiculously high salary for governessing. And then I resigned the post, and he didn't rail at me or complain, he showed me paradise. No, Mr. Dashwood, I will not regret this, not in five years, nor in fifty."

His expression had been still as she spoke. At the end, something flitted over his face, too rapidly for her to identify, before he took her jaw in his hands and kissed her. Emilia's heart felt as if it would burst. She held him close and kissed him back. *I love you,* she told him inside her head.

"I stayed away last night," he said between kisses. "On the chance you might have changed your mind."

She laughed, suddenly giddy. She realized what

this strange new lightness was, that she had felt for the past two days. Not the thrill of becoming lovers, nor the elation of being in love. She had someone to trust. Someone who cared, who was on her side. Something had shifted when she unburdened herself of the true and complete story of her family and Lord Fitchley, as ugly and venal as it was. It had felt *good* to tell him those shameful secrets. They had been splinters wedged deep in her soul, ones she hadn't dared touch for years—but now she'd pulled them out, only to realize how great an effort it had been to keep them buried.

"I will not change my mind," she replied breathlessly. "Don't send me away tonight."

Even in the darkness, she saw the flash of his teeth in a dangerous smile. "No," he said in a dark, velvety voice, and then he turned over, pulling her atop him. "Never."

Emilia sat up, straddling his hips on her knees. "Nor tomorrow."

"Never," he said again, his voice lower. His hands were on her legs. "Don't leave."

She smiled, running her hands through her hair to remove the last of the pins. She had noticed that he was fascinated by her hair down. "Never."

His hands disappeared under her skirts and she felt his palms glide up her thighs, firm and purposeful. She shivered, not because his hands were cool from the night air, but because she was desperate for his touch. Tonight she didn't need to be seduced; tonight she was impatient, and she could feel him hard and thick beneath her, separated only by a few layers of clothing.

He knew it as soon as he touched her. She moaned, her head falling back and her hands spasming on his clothing. "You're as ready as I am," he breathed, and she managed to nod, moving in time with the strokes of his hand between her legs.

Without ceasing, he reached down and yanked loose the buttons on his trousers, shoving fabric out of the way until her bare skin met his. He groped for her hand and brought it to his straining erection, arching his spine to press against her palm. Emilia shivered again, marveling at how hot and hard he was.

"Take me," he whispered, nudging her, and Emilia wobbled on her knees for a moment as she tried to follow his lead. She hesitated a moment, with him poised at her entrance, then sank down.

Nick's fingers dug into the flesh of her thighs. "Mother of God," he said in a thin, rough voice.

"It feels bigger," she gasped.

"Yes." His voice sounded strained. *"Move . . ."*

She shifted, sitting upright, exquisitely aware of him deep inside her, and he ran his thumb over the spot that made her twitch and tense. His smile flashed pale and fierce in the moonlight, and Emilia moved again. She leaned forward and rocked her hips, and Nick responded with another swirl. Wanting more of that, she leaned back, and he began to stroke her in time with the roll and thrust of his own hips.

She let him guide her until she forgot to breathe and the stars above her seemed to shine bigger and brighter, blinding her as she came, and then Nick pulled her to his chest and held her tightly as he shuddered and gasped incoherently as his own climax took him.

Some time later she slid rather bonelessly off

him. Nick stirred, smoothing her hair from her face. "Are you cold?" he whispered.

"No," Emilia said with a smile. They were both still clothed, just a little disarranged, and she didn't think she'd be cold for hours.

He buttoned his trousers and dragged the edge of the blanket over her, tucking her close to his side and folding his arms around her.

I love you, she thought again.

"What do you think of the house now, seeing it again?" he asked.

Emilia blinked. "Beaufort Hall? It's a beautiful house. It just needs work." She smiled. "A great lot of work."

"You must see the potential more than I do, having grown up in fine houses."

"Hmm? Yes, it's got tremendous potential. And with a good gardener, so have the grounds. It's well situated."

Nick nodded. "It would be an enormous undertaking."

"Oh, not so enormous," she said, feeling nothing but bliss. "Mrs. Gregson—she was Lucy's nursemaid, and had been with the family since Lucy's father was a boy—she told me it was once renowned through Dorset for its elegance and beauty. Arthur's mother, I believe, was a great political hostess in her day."

"Mrs. Stone said she was a cold woman."

Emilia gave a tiny snort. "You should learn now, my lord, that the two often go hand in hand. A great society lady's balls may be the most sought-after invitation in England, but the woman herself will scarcely have a gentle word for any of her children. I daresay, to some of them, children are only a

means to dynasty and influence, and not small, defenseless people who need love and care and attention."

Nick was quiet for a moment. "Hence governesses like you."

She sighed. "I tried to take employment where
the parents were at least *fond* of their children. A
governess can only provide so much."

He said nothing, only continued stroking her
hair. Emilia thought she never wanted to move
from this spot, this position, this moment in time.

But that was impossible. The world outside
Beaufort Hall was still marching onward, the hours
of her stolen season ticking relentlessly past. She
couldn't be so fanciful as to pretend they weren't.

"What is happening in London, while we're
here?" she whispered.

Nick stretched, settling more comfortably
against her. "I don't want to spoil the surprise. I
promise it will be a good one."

She gazed at the stars, thinking of society host-
esses and invitations. "Nick. What are you
plotting?"

He tilted his head to meet her gaze, looking
vaguely amused. "Worried for Fitchley now?"

She couldn't stop a huff of outrage. "No!
But . . . you'll be part of that society. Fitchley has
friends, and they're likely to retaliate. You should
know they can be vicious. They can shut you out
and make things very difficult for you. You should
think carefully before antagonizing them." She hesitated. "I learned that the hard way."

The languid stroking on her hair slowed, then
with an abrupt movement he rolled over until she

was beneath him, and he was above her, braced on both arms.

"I know all about so-called good society," he said, meeting her gaze squarely. "I know who I am, and what I've done, and I make no apologies for any of it. I didn't grow up surrounded by dukes and earls, but trust me when I say to you, men are the same no matter their class. Fitchley is no different than the sharpers running games on the docks, luring in gullible marks to be cheated of everything they own. I don't give a bloody damn if not a single member of the *haute ton* ever looks me in the eye."

He touched her cheek and his voice grew softer. "But I do care, deeply, what *you* think of me. Tell me what worries you." His thumb stroked her lower lip. "I wouldn't hurt you for the world."

She looked up at him, torn. "Will your plan truly ruin him?"

Nick nodded. "Not only in the eyes of decent people but also in the opinion of everyone he cares about. That's what will bring him down. He cares nothing for the approbation of upright, honorable people. But among his own kind . . . He cares a great deal. He fancies himself a leader among them, and that's about to change. Not by my hand—by his own. The only thing I mean to do is make known certain acts."

Emilia thought about Fitchley being disavowed by the scoundrels and reprobates of his set. What could he possibly do that was intolerable even to them? But Nick was so certain . . . "Good," she said, quietly but fervently. "But . . . How?"

Nick grinned. He pressed a swift kiss on her mouth. And he told her.

CHAPTER THIRTY

They spent a few more days at Beaufort Hall. Charlotte and Lucy went exploring with James in the woods, and returned with breathless reports of a pond, excellent for wading and full of fish and, in Charlotte's telling, absolutely crying out for a boat to go punting. With Mr. Stone, Nick climbed onto the roof of the house and inspected the cupola light. It was a broad glass dome with a leaden figure of Aphrodite on top, and it must flood the staircase hall with light when it wasn't boarded up due to several broken panes of glass.

He was talking with Emilia about it when the first visitors came. "It likely needs to be re-leaded, too—who the devil is that?" Nick frowned at the slim young man hovering, cap in hand, just outside the front door.

"Oh, my." Emilia pressed his hand. "Of course." Without another word she went out and spoke to the fellow, who bowed and spoke earnestly for a few minutes. Emilia listened, nodding, and then spoke to him until a wide smile lit the man's face.

Nick strolled closer to the doorway, watching

but keeping his distance. There were actually three men and a young woman, who all looked nervous at the beginning but who were beaming when they finally turned and walked back down the drive.

Emilia came back inside. "They hope you'll be taking up residence, and wanted to know about positions."

Nick's brows went up. "So soon?"

"A great house like this is vital to the whole area," she replied. "Not only in what it produces, but the employment it offers and the things it buys. If you wish to restart the brewery, for instance, you'll need men who know how a brewery should be built, what equipment it should have, and how it should be run."

Nick grinned. He'd been surprised—and pleased—to learn there was an old brewery on the estate. But he grasped her larger point, that he had no idea how a country house ran. Heloise had had a fine house, but in the center of Birmingham. He'd never lived on a country estate, nor even had friends who invited him to stay at one. He'd imagined these big estates simply brought everything in from London or the nearest market town. "Fancy that. What would I do without you to inform me of these things?"

She laughed. "Oh, I'm only repeating what I learned from my grandpapa! Any estate manager will be able to tell you far more, in great detail."

But not so beautifully, thought Nick. Every day it hit him harder that he would be lost without her, for reasons small and large, some silly and some vitally important. No one had ever left him, smiling the way those villagers had done, after talking to him. Of course he could hire a man to explain to him how to run an estate; he trusted Emilia to tell him how it *ought* to be run, with respect for the people who lived there now and responsibility for the future.

And even, perhaps, how he ought to approach *his* future.

He had been away from the Vega Club for over a week now, and discovered to his surprise that he wasn't frantic to be back. He thought about his club frequently, but he'd left it in the capable hands of Forbes, who had been with him for years. If there were a problem, Forbes would handle it or send word to him. No word meant no problems.

Partly, Nick knew, he didn't miss Vega's because he was occupied with Charlotte and the house during the day and entranced by Emilia at night. Every evening after the girls went to bed, he and Emilia slipped off alone, with a blanket and perhaps a bottle of wine, and lay under the stars. The night it rained, they swept vines out of the loggia and huddled in there, keeping each other warm and making each other laugh. Nick told her about his patrons and the outrageous things they did and said. She responded with tales of the children she'd worked with, and *bon mots* from the elderly countess who had been her first employer. And when they heard shrieks from the drawing room that was their communal living quarters, Nick ran even faster than she did.

Lucy was sitting on her bed, blankets clutched to her chin, eyes wide. Charlotte was standing on a chair, holding the lamp with one hand and clutching her nightdress around her knees with the other. James stood by the fireplace, a club in his hand.

"I saw a rat," said Lucy in a tiny voice.

"I saw it, too!" cried Charlotte.

"It's gone now, Mr. Dashwood," said James quickly. He poked his club into the recess of the fireplace, and there was a scraping noise. "There's a hole here, some mortar will mend it."

Hand clapped to her heart, Emilia looked to Nick. "Why was there a rat in here? We cleaned this room thoroughly and removed anything that would attract them."

Lucy shrank into her blankets until only her eyes and forehead were visible. "I brought in some honey cakes," she whispered. It had turned out Mrs. Stone also knew the recipe, and she'd baked some as soon as the first load of supplies was delivered.

Emilia stared at her, then gave a gasp of laughter. Charlotte broke into giggles, and then Lucy did, and even James grinned sheepishly.

Nick folded his arms. "Are we taking such fine care of Beaufort Hall now that we feed our rats honey cakes?"

"No!" cried Lucy. "Not honey cakes!"

"Chester will expect roast beef and salmon patties," gasped Emilia, swiping at her eyes as she laughed.

"Eww!" Charlotte stepped down from the chair. "Better to stop up the holes in the walls instead."

Nick pointed at her. "Precisely. An excellent thought, though one that will be more difficult if that rat is off telling all his mates that there are honey cakes to be had in this room, right now."

Charlotte froze. Lucy stopped smiling.

"Goodness," said Emilia gravely. "We mustn't

allow that. We must . . . we must eat all the honey cakes at once, obviously."

Nick exaggerated his surprise as both girls goggled at them. "Eat the cakes! All of them! Right now! *Must* we, Miss Greene?"

She nodded, eyes twinkling. "Indeed, I see no other option, Mr. Dashwood. If we do not eat them, the rats will."

"Well, then." Nick turned toward the two open-mouthed girls. "Miss Greene says so, and Miss Greene is nearly always correct. Where are the honey cakes, Lucinda?"

Lucy looked at Charlotte in amazement, then drew a small plate with two squashed cakes from under her bed.

Nick heaved a sigh. "Only two! James, hand over that lantern. Any man who chases away a rat deserves a cake of his own."

He knew he was being ridiculous, but it felt good. The expressions on Charlotte's and Lucinda's faces made him want to laugh. Emilia came with him, and they walked through the dark house to the kitchens, where they discovered the honey cakes in the pantry. On the way back, she carried the plate and held his hand. Nick thought he'd never been happier than he had been these last few days in this dilapidated house.

When they reached the drawing room, the three young people broke apart from a whispered conference. Lucy looked guilty, but Charlotte gave a sunny smile and asked if Nick had brought any cider, too. They sat on the floor with all four lanterns wide open and demolished the cakes.

Nick was eating his second cake before realizing that the scent of lavender no longer bothered him.

Instead of Heloise's wheezing cough, now it made him think of Lucy's eager smile as she reached for another cake. Picturing joy rather than illness made lavender far more appealing.

Emilia brought out a broom when the plate was empty and swept up the crumbs, flinging them out the window into the softly falling rain. "Bon appétit, Monsieur le rat," she called.

Lucy giggled again, and Charlotte whirled on Nick. "Are you and Miss Greene sweet on each other?" she demanded in a whisper.

Nick raised his brows. "My cake was perfectly sweet, thank you." He waved her toward her camp bed.

"Because if you are, I think you should marry her," his sister added in a rush.

"Good night, Charlotte," he said evenly.

She flashed a brilliant smile. "Good night, Nicky!"

James returned to his bed. Emilia was tucking Lucy back into hers. Within a half hour, everyone was in their own bed, Emilia and the girls near the fireplace, where a rag was now securely wadded into the rat's escape hole, James and Nick on the far side of a sheet strung across some rope.

Nick did not fall asleep. He lay in the darkness, listening to the gentle sounds of his family sleeping, feeling the cool night breeze on his face. It was barely eleven o'clock. Normally he would be at the card tables now, making certain his dealers were stocked. In an hour he would stop by the kitchens, running full speed, for a plate of dinner. Around midnight most balls had passed their peak, and the noble gentlemen would arrive at Vega's. Around three in the morning was when things started to grow sharp, as players got deeper into their cups and the pots began to grow rapidly, sometimes to tens of thousands of pounds. Around four in the morning, he called a halt and began closing up the club for the morning.

He could restore Beaufort Hall from London. It appeared there were plenty of people looking for work nearby, and Nick expected he could staff the house in no time. He could hire a regiment of builders to repair the house and bring it back to glory. An estate manager would begin organizing the farms and other business. Some gardeners, to revive the garden and grounds. Grantham could handle most of it, only turning to Nick for thorny questions.

But Beaufort Hall was *his*. Like the Vega Club, which he had been building for fifteen years, from a shabby cellar room to the elegant establishment it was today. He hadn't delegated that; he'd inspected every property, approved every purchase, supervised every improvement. Clara Birtwhistle chose the actual furnishings and decorations, but only after Nick had told her exactly what he wanted.

Was he really going to leave Beaufort Hall to Grantham's care? Perhaps all he needed was the right partner . . .

Are you sweet on Miss Greene?

Beyond sweet, he silently answered. *Intoxicated.*

What was he going to do about that?

THE NEXT MORNING Louis arrived from London. He found Nick in the stables, surveying the rotted hay racks, and handed him two sealed letters. "Reports from Mr. Grantham and Mr. Forbes, Mr. Dashwood."

"Very good." Nick opened both. Grantham's included a note from his new newspaper partner, which was brief but very satisfying. "How fare things at the Vega Club?"

Louis grinned. "Well enough." He glanced around with interest. "Everyone's wild to know where you've gone off to."

"As you see." Nick eyed Louis. "What do you think of my stables?"

The younger man grimaced. His father had been a coachman at a large estate when Louis was a boy, and was now a stable master at Newmarket. Louis had grown up in stable blocks. "Absolute nightmare, sir."

Nick grinned. They hadn't been used in years, according to Stone, but once upon a time they had been magnificent—and could be again. The block was built of pale brick with a clock tower at the back side, forming three sides of a square with wrought iron gates closing in the fourth. Mr. Stone had kept the western side in order, while the rest had been neglected. But like the house, it was still sound, and would easily hold a household's horses, with space for guests. Perhaps Charlotte would get her wish, about a ball. "Not for long."

"Right, sir," said Louis, grinning back.

"How is your father?" Nick turned away and strolled out of the stable courtyard.

"Tip-top," replied Louis promptly. "He was pleased to hear from you, and hopes he can answer your question very soon."

Nick nodded. "That's very good of him. I'm greatly in his debt."

Louis muffled a snort. "Beg pardon, but he said he was happy to do it, *very* happy."

"And I am delighted he obliged me," he told Louis. "Tell me how things have been at Vega's."

Forbes's report contained the receipts and other business details. He would mention any problems as well, but Louis spent his evenings among the guests and saw things Forbes didn't. The young man did not disappoint.

Most of it was ordinary. One fellow, howling drunk, had thrown a punch at Forbes when Forbes told the waiters not to bring him more spirits. A widowed countess had accused a man of making indecent advances to her, and Forbes had suspended his membership until Nick returned. Guillaume, the chef, had been caught in the butler's pantry with one of the morning maids, who had become very flustered and broke into tears when Forbes asked her about it.

Nick frowned at the last one. The chef professed to have mended his ways, but his wife had indeed gone home to visit her family in Hertfordshire and not returned yet. Nick had enticed the man away from a wealthy banker's household with an outrageous salary, but he wasn't paying a chef who couldn't keep his hands off other women, no matter how delicious his pastries.

"And Lord Fitchley's been asking where you are," Louis added.

"What did you tell him?"

"That it weren't my place to say," replied Louis. "He pressed again and I said I didn't know—which I didn't, not until Mr. Forbes told me right before he sent me here."

Forbes and Grantham were the only people

who'd known where to find him. "How did Fitchley take it?"

Louis hesitated. "He laughed. But he asked Mr. Carter and Mr. Forbes and even Monsieur Guillaume in the kitchen as well, and he's been in every night since, as if he's keeping an eye out."

"Has he," said Nick without surprise. "Does he still seem eager to speak to me?"

Louis thought for a moment. "Impatient, I would say, or even angry about the delay."

"Has Forbes needed to speak to him about anything?"

"Not a once," said Louis, "and he's had me watching Fitchley every night. Mainly he sits and drinks in the parlor. Hasn't even placed a bet in the book, which is very unlike him."

A faint, satisfied smile crossed Nick's face. "Excellent. We're heading back to town tomorrow," he told Louis. "You're welcome to come with us or take yourself back now."

"Thank you, sir, I'll stay," said the young man with feeling. "It was a hard ride down, and I've no aversion to a more leisurely return."

"Very good."

"Nick? Nick!" called Emilia from around the rampaging shrubbery.

Beside him, Louis perked up. Then Emilia came around the corner, and Nick nearly missed a step at how beautiful she was with the sun full on her face. Her hair was coming loose and the wisps glinted like polished jet in the afternoon light. Her eyes had never looked so blue. She shaded her face with one hand and caught sight of the pair of them. "Oh!" She started to turn away.

"Miss Greene." He picked up his pace to catch

her. "Allow me to introduce Louis Darlington, who handles the turf book at the Vega Club. Mr. Darlington, this is Miss Greene."

She smiled and curtsied as Louis bowed, his eyes swinging so rapidly from Nick to Emilia and back that Nick wondered how the man didn't lose his balance.

"I've just told him we plan to return to London tomorrow," he told her. "Will we be ready to leave in the morning?"

"Er—yes," she said, recovering from her surprise quickly. "As early as you wish to leave, Mr. Dashwood."

Now Louis's head was turning back and forth.

Nick grinned. "Very good. I will tell you in confidence, Miss Greene, that he's just brought word things are proceeding as planned in London."

"Oh?" she said, still flustered, then comprehension dawned. "Oh!"

"Are they?" blurted Louis in astonishment.

Nick slapped his shoulder. "Indeed. It's going to be a grand show, lad. Like nothing you've ever seen before."

CHAPTER THIRTY-ONE

They stopped at the Bush Inn again on the way back to London. Emilia couldn't help but think how much everything had changed since then.

Lucy seemed to have grown up years. Going back to Beaufort Hall hadn't been the nightmare Emilia had feared. It was as if exploring the house with Charlotte and James, the rooms now filled with sunlight, had chased away some of the shadowy demons that had once haunted Lucy. The day before they left for London, Emilia discovered the three young people in the dusty, empty upstairs drawing room. James had located an ancient skittles set and they were whooping and cheering as they knocked over the pins and teased each other about errant throws.

Lucy had come running up to her. "Millie, I made a spare," she declared in breathless excitement. "Charlotte's made two, and James scored a strike!"

"Brilliant," she'd exclaimed, and even tried her hand at it.

Lucy's father would have roared at them in fury—for the noise, for the laughter, for the joy. Emilia had despised him for a long time, but now she was beginning to feel a little sorry for him as well, as she watched his daughter clap her hands in glee and run to set the pins upright again. He had been a deeply miserable man. The mark on Lucy's cheek, which Sydenham had cursed as a mark of the devil, was hardly visible when her cheeks were flushed with excitement.

This time they reached Farnham late in the evening. Lucy had fallen asleep in the carriage, slumped against Emilia's shoulder, and Nick carried her into the inn and deposited her right onto a bed. "Is Charlotte allowed to stay up?" she protested as Emilia took off her shoes and unbuttoned her dress.

"Charlotte is nearly as tired as you," answered Emilia, amused. The girl had been yawning behind her hand in the stable yard. "She's washing up and will be in bed soon."

"Good," mumbled Lucy, putting on her nightdress. "It's not fair if she gets to stay up."

"We're all tired," said Emilia firmly. "Wash your face and clean your teeth. Everyone is going to bed."

"Even y-y-you and Mr. Dashwood?" Lucy asked around a yawn, after cleaning her teeth. She swiped the damp cloth over her face and crawled into bed.

"Yes." Emilia tucked her in and kissed her temple. "Good night, my dear."

"G' night." Lucy yawned again, clutching Emilia's hand for a moment. "Millie, I love you."

Emilia's heart melted. "I love you, too, Lucy," she whispered.

Lucy gave a sleepy smile. "I was so afraid of going to Dorset, but it wasn't terrible at all, was it?"

"No. You were very brave, and I'm so proud of you."

The girl snuggled into her pillows. "Do you know what I did? I pretended inside my head that we were a family. Charlotte was my sister, and you were our mama and Mr. Dashwood was our papa, who would protect us from everything. And I liked it ever so much."

Emilia sat stricken.

Lucy yawned widely. "Is it all right if I keep pretending that? In London, I mean. I won't tell anyone. I don't think Charlotte would mind if I called her my sister. She hasn't got any sisters, either, or a mama."

"The two of you would make wonderful sisters." Emilia had to clear her throat to speak, and when it came, her voice was thin and unsteady.

Lucy nodded, her eyes closed now. "I wish you could really be my mama, Millie. You're just the kind of mama we'd like, Charlotte and I . . ."

Emilia couldn't move. *I wish I could be,* she thought as she watched Lucy sleep.

She hadn't forgotten her vow to leave when they returned to London; she just hadn't let herself think about it. She had talked with Nick about restoring Beaufort Hall, even though she wouldn't be there to see it. She had directed the Stones, and spoken to the hopefuls from the village, even though she wouldn't be the mistress. She had continued caring for Lucy and Charlotte, even though she couldn't be their governess much longer. And she had gone into Nick's arms every night, allowing herself to pretend their affair wasn't a stolen season, but a real future.

Now the bitter moment was all too near, and she was even less ready for it.

Charlotte came in, damp from washing up. Emilia helped her get ready for bed, and then, to her astonishment, Charlotte hugged her. "Thank you, Miss Greene," she whispered.

Emilia returned the embrace. "You're welcome, but for what?"

Charlotte smiled shyly as she climbed into her bed. "For making this journey so pleasant. I'd never been to the country. It's splendid, isn't it? I hope Nick repairs the house and wants to visit it often. You'll help him throw a ball, won't you?"

She tried to smile, but her face felt heavy and stiff. "I'm glad you enjoyed the visit."

"Oh yes," said Charlotte, smiling in memory. "I'm ever so grateful you agreed to be my governess, Miss Greene. Promise you'll never leave."

Her hands trembled on the blankets she was smoothing flat. "Oh, you won't want me forever . . ."

"Perhaps," said Charlotte sleepily. "But Nick will. You're so good for him, Miss Greene. I've never seen him happier than this week."

Emilia's face burned. Her heart was like lead. "Sleep well," she murmured. But Charlotte, like Lucy, was already fast asleep.

She had to tell Nick tonight. He would need time to find a new governess; the girls would need time to adjust to it. She let herself out of the girls' room, only to realize it was the same set of rooms they had had before. There was her same room, and across the corridor—

The room where Nick had made love to her.

The night he'd told her he meant to ruin Fitchley to protect Lucy—and her.

The night she'd resigned her post, because he had too many scruples to seduce a woman in his employ, but she was too deeply in love with him to miss her chance for a moment of wild happiness.

The night she took the biggest gamble of her life.

I will not regret this, not in five years nor in fifty, echoed her own voice in her head.

She still didn't regret it. For a moment her gaze lingered on the door, wondering if perhaps she could steal just one more night . . .

With an effort she looked away. Every bill came due, sooner or later. *Tell him now,* she commanded herself. *Before it gets harder.*

Before she gave in to the wicked part of her soul that whispered that Nick did what he wanted, and didn't care for the opinions of mysterious and nebulous "people" who meant nothing to him, and that perhaps she too could get away with indulging her wicked urges. She'd learned long ago that it didn't work that way, not for women.

She took a deep breath and went downstairs.

NICK STOOD OUTSIDE THE INN, watching the moon rise over the slate roof. It still felt novel to be outdoors after dark, and he was rediscovering his fascination with the night sky.

He was also, it must be admitted, hiding. Charlotte had been prodding him for days with little comments about Emilia, and how lovely it would be if the four of them became a real family. She teased him about wanting a baby niece for her and Lucy to spoil. She asked him if they would take a long wedding trip, and if she and Lucy could stay with Lady Arabella while Nick and Emilia were gone.

In aggravation he'd threatened to make her study geometry and Latin, and his sister had stopped teasing him. But she took one parting shot that found its mark.

"Just think how happy *you* would be, Nicky. It's clear Miss Greene makes you very happy, and I fear you'll be terribly sad if she leaves."

No, not sad. He would be devastated if Emilia left.

So what was he going to do to keep her?

"Good evening," came her quiet voice behind him.

Nick jerked around to face her. She wore the buttery yellow dress, glowing pale in the moonlight. Her hair was falling down, curls tumbling around her nape. She gave him a hesitant smile and his heart leapt with such joy, he knew what he was going to do.

"Fancy a stroll this fine evening?"

"Yes." She fell in step beside him. "I must speak to you about something."

"Oh?" His mind raced through probabilities, chances, how to better his odds. Should he go down on one knee? Was poetry required?

"Yes. I was going to wait until we reached London, but I think—I think it's better to do it now." She stopped walking, and a moment later Nick stopped, too. "I resigned my post," she said.

Still scrounging his memory for a romantic bit of verse, Nick nodded. "I remember."

She bowed her head. He could make her out

now, a pale figure in the night. "You must know . . . I cannot resume it, when we return to London."

That pulled him out of his thoughts. "What?"

"I can't continue as both your governess and your lover," she whispered. "Whatever you think about propriety, you must think of Charlotte and Lucy. It's for their sakes that I'm telling you now. You must find a new governess for them."

Nick looked at her for a long moment. He should have waited for her inside, so he would be able to see her expression. "Is that what you want?" he finally asked. Her head came up with a jerk. "You won't need to be a governess, in six months," he added. "Perhaps you're just as glad to be done now."

"No! I will miss them . . . so very much." Her voice shook. "I am *not* glad, I am—" She turned and started walking back toward the inn.

Nick took two long strides and caught her hand. "Then don't leave." He tugged gently, and she came easily into the curve of his arm, pressing close to his side. He rested his cheek against her temple, breathing in honeysuckle. "What if I offered you a different position?" he murmured.

"At your club?" She gave a weak laugh and raised one hand to disguise the swipe she gave her eyes with the other. "Look. There's Vega." She pointed at the sky. "I can find it now, thanks to you."

Nick glanced up. His lucky star. "No, not a position at Vega's."

She seemed to shrink against him. "What position, then?"

"Actually," he said slowly, "it's more of a proposition."

Emilia didn't move.

"That's what you said to me," he went on. "You barged into my office and told me you'd come with a proposition that only an idiot would refuse."

She made a smothered sound and tried to pull free. Nick clasped her hand.

"I can't say the same for this proposition. You might be an idiot to accept it. The proposition is . . ." He took another breath to keep from blurting it out in one unintelligible rush. No time for going down on one knee, and every line of poetry had vanished from his brain. Christ, he didn't think he'd ever been this nervous in his life. "That you marry me."

CHAPTER THIRTY-TWO

Emilia twitched, then tensed anxiously, certain she'd misheard.

Nick kept his gaze on the sky. "Not because it would put you out of Fitchley's reach. Not because it might strengthen my case for getting charge of Lucy, and not because you would finally get your own money, which you should have had all along." He wrapped both his hands around hers. "Marry me because we think alike. We make each other laugh. We suit each other perfectly in bed. You quit your post to seduce me, which is the most impractical thing I've ever seen you do," he added wryly. "I'm still prostrate with shock about that, even though I'm also wildly elated that you did."

She gave a shocked little laugh, then stopped.

He took a long, slow breath. "I know it's asking a great—"

"What else?" she blurted.

Nick went still. "What else?"

It felt like her stays had been winched tighter. The temperature seemed to have risen, and then plummeted, in the space of a few minutes. She was shaky, her skin damp with perspiration that now felt cold. Finally she knew what he meant about every decision being a gamble. Surely it would be easier to risk a fortune than to ask this question, which could break her heart. Not daring to move, she asked, quietly and evenly so her throat didn't close up, "Is there any other reason you want to marry me?"

Slowly he turned to look at her, even though it was so dark she could barely make out his face. "Yes," he said, quietly and precisely. "I've fallen in love with you and want you to stay with me for the rest of my life."

And that was how it felt to win the pot. Unable to speak, she went up on her toes and kissed him.

His arm around her flexed. "Is that yes?"

"Yes." She was still smiling in disbelief when his arms tightened around her as he lifted her off her feet. Emilia wound her arms around his neck and kissed him again, hardly believing this was happening to her.

When the kiss finally ended, she had to lean against him. "I've been in love with you since you told me to play my shot again at billiards."

His mouth was on her neck, but she felt him smile. "Do you know how tempting you looked, bent over my billiard table?"

She tried to choke back a shocked laugh. "No!"

"I imagined putting you on that table and having my wicked way with you—"

"Nick," she gasped.

"But I didn't, because it would have been my choice and not yours." He paused. "It must always be your desire, Emilia. I'm not above coaxing and begging, but I will only take what you want to give me."

"I know." She tugged at his neckcloth. "You're the most honorable man I know."

He scoffed. "That's only because you've had the misfortune to know men like Fitchley and Parker-Lloyd. Their lot would make anyone look good."

She smiled but didn't argue, and wet her lips. "How?"

"How what?"

"How would you make love to me on a billiard table?" she whispered.

Nick stared at her for a long moment, then took her hand and pulled her toward the inn. "Like this."

She almost had to run to keep up with him as he strode back inside. The innkeeper met them just inside the door. "Ah, Mr. Dashwood, I've left the wine in the parlor, as you asked—"

"Very good, sir, excellent." Nick fished a coin from his pocket and pressed it into the man's hand. "We're not to be disturbed. My wife and I." He'd been testing the words in his mind all evening. They sounded even sweeter when he said them aloud. From the corner of his eye he saw Emilia blush, but with an eager sparkle in her eyes.

"Of course," replied the innkeeper with a knowing wink. The guinea was already in his pocket. "Good evening."

Nick led Emilia to the same parlor they had had before. The coals were banked low, and the shutters closed. A decanter of wine and two glasses stood on the table, until Nick moved them to the mantel.

"You had a plan," said Emilia in surprise.

"No." He closed the door and turned the key. "I

had hope, and made plans in case an opportunity arose."

She watched him come back toward her. "So if I'd not gone outside . . . ?"

He caught one of the ladder-back chairs and swung it away from the table. "I'd have invited you down to have a glass of wine with me."

She tilted her head and smiled. "And now we shan't have wine?"

"Later," he said, and turned her around, to face the table. "After the demonstration."

She was trembling, and her laugh sounded slightly nervous. "That sounds very practical . . ."

"Hmm." He pressed his lips to the nape of her neck and fiddled with the top button. "In practice, I intend to ravish you on this table, Millie my darling. And then I might carry you up to my bed and do it again. You did say you'll marry me, didn't you?"

She twisted, her face glowing. "Yes."

He wrapped an arm around her waist, sliding his hand up over her breast. "And you love me?"

"I do," she answered breathlessly.

He kissed her. "Very good," he murmured. "Allow me to demonstrate what you can expect, as Mrs. Dashwood and then Lady Sydenham."

He bent her over the table as if she were playing billiards. She moved as he bid, laughing giddily as he told her to picture the two balls, then inhaling sharply as he raised the back of her skirt and folded it over her back. She gasped as he ran his hands up her thighs, urging her feet apart, and she moaned when he touched her where she was soft and already wet with desire.

Nick thought he'd lose his mind as he explored

her body—her stockinged legs, her rounded hips, the soft curve of her belly, now taut and quivering as he drove her wild. His own hands were shaking when he finally ripped open the buttons of his falls and guided his aching cock into her. He pressed deep, holding her hips as she arched her back, and then they were moving together, Nick with one hand fisted in her rucked-up skirts and the other between her legs, Emilia gripping the far edge of the table and meeting every thrust of his hips.

And then suddenly he had to see her face. He stepped back and lifted her from the table. None too gently he sat her on it, facing him, her legs dangling off the side. Her eyes were dilated and her face was flushed, and her breasts rose and fell rapidly. He tipped up her head and kissed her hard.

"I love you," she breathed, gripping his coat.

God. The blood roared in his ears. He pushed her back until she had to catch herself on her elbows. She melted against him, until he seized her knee and folded it back toward her chest and thrust home, again and again until the table rocked on its feet and Emilia looked at him with her lightning-bright eyes and gasped, "Nick—!"

When her back arched, her fingers spread wide, and her body clamped down on his in ecstasy, Nick felt a light-headedness that verged on euphoric. He went still, deep inside her, and climax roared through him, crackling through every muscle and sinew until he had to grab the table to stay upright.

Breathing hard, his face damp with sweat, he leaned over her, holding her close. He pressed his mouth to her breast, just above her still-buttoned bodice where that narrow, tantalizing ruffle was visible, and felt the rapid thrum of her heart.

He had never imagined himself in love, let alone wed. That was for other people—decent, *good* people. He wasn't the sort of man any reasonable woman would want for a husband, the son of a heartless beast, grown into a cold and calculating scoundrel. But here she was, in his arms, everything he hadn't even bothered to long for: a clever, resourceful, magnificent woman who looked at him with her heart in her eyes. He could hardly believe she was real. "I love you," he said dazedly, still astonished by how deeply he felt it, and shocked that she loved him back.

A dreamy laugh hummed through her body. She looped one arm around his neck, nuzzling little kisses on his temple. Nick shuddered at the tender intimacy. "Thank my lucky stars," she whispered.

CHAPTER THIRTY-THREE

The next night, Nick returned to the Vega Club.

He'd been gone almost a fortnight. It was like slipping into a familiar suit of clothes, but after such a long time, they didn't quite fit the same way. He was glad to be back, and at the same time, something was different.

He supposed it was him. The club looked exactly as it always had.

"How was your excursion?" Forbes looked wary as he fell in step beside Nick.

"Productive. How were things here?" Nick opened his office door and tossed aside his hat and gloves.

"Seven more member resignations, but also five more inquiries."

Nick nodded in satisfaction. As he'd thought, the pace had slowed.

Forbes handed him a small sheaf of papers plus a letter. "From the lads. And this, from Stewart Darlington."

Nick opened the letter and read it. "Excellent

news." He looked back up at Forbes. "I expect we'll have a fireworks display in the near future."

"Thought we might," muttered the manager.

Nick tapped Darlington's note on the desk. "It might cost us a few members, but I expect it will be much to our benefit."

Forbes's assessing gaze dipped from Nick's face to the letter and back up again. "Which members?"

Nick just grinned. He sat down and took out a few pieces of paper. "Send the lads out to deliver these at once." He wrote a few brief notes, all essentially the same, closed and sealed them, then wrote a direction on each. He handed them to his manager.

Forbes let out a low whistle as he read one name. "Are we risking Newgate?"

"Not us," said Nick in mild surprise. "Someone may, though. But if it sets your mind at ease . . ." He dashed off another message and wrote Grantham's name on it.

"What's afoot?" asked Forbes curiously. He'd been gathering information for weeks now at Nick's direction, but Nick had been deliberately vague about why.

Nick came around his desk and handed over Darlington's message. "We are about to be rid of Lord Fitchley."

Forbes's brows climbed higher and higher as he read. "Bloody saints," he muttered. "This is . . ."

Nick waited.

"Evil," finished Forbes. He looked up. "Dash, he won't make it to Newgate. Someone'll stretch his neck at the nearest lamppost."

Nick tugged his jacket into place. "I suppose some might feel inclined toward violence. I would, if it were my prize-winning colt he'd killed."

Forbes's jaw firmed. "It'll be a pleasure to toss him out."

Nick's smile was vicious. "Indeed it will."

He went out into the club and made his usual circuits. His appearance caused a small stir, people putting their heads together to whisper. Idly he wondered if it were his title petition, which had had its first hearing before the Committee for Privileges; his prolonged absence, which had been unusual; or some societal instinct that a storm of scandal was brewing.

Around ten o'clock, Forbes came to stand beside him. "Kinson and O'Malley are here," he murmured. "In the blue room."

"Very good. Send them dinner, would you?" A new arrival had caught his eye, and he headed to the front of the house.

Lord Westmorland appeared to be having an argument with his companion. Nick approached and bowed. "Good evening, my lords."

The marquess returned his bow. "Good evening, Dashwood. As requested, I've brought my brother, Lord William Churchill-Gray."

The other fellow nodded at Nick. He was as tall as the marquess, but much leaner, his brown hair bleached and his face tanned as if he spent all his days outdoors. "Mr. Dashwood. I understand you have some questions."

"I do, sir. Would you join me upstairs?"

He led the way to a private room. The two men there were eating, but leapt to their feet at the sound of the door. "Lord William Churchill-Gray," said Nick, "allow me to present to you Mr. Robert Kinson and Mr. Dickie O'Malley."

Lord William paused in the middle of his polite nod. "Bobby Kinson?"

"Aye, m'lord," said the man. He was young, slender, yet not very tall, and leaned on a crutch.

"You ride for Baron Fitchley," said Lord William with a flicker of his eyes toward Nick. "Nearly won the Oaks on a very middling horse."

"I *did* ride for Fitchley," said the man bitterly. "Turned me out, on account of my broken leg." He tapped his crutch on the floor next to his left foot, which was still splinted and wrapped. "The surgeon says it'll heal right, if I stay off it for three months, but Fitchley said that was too long and gave me the sack."

"Shortsighted of him," remarked Lord William.

Kinson glanced at the other man. "No, sir, to be truthful, I'm glad. After what Dickie told me, I'm well shot of the place."

O'Malley bobbed his head. "I was a training groom at Newmarket, sir. Bobby's got the right of it."

Lord William looked at him for a long moment, then turned to Nick. "Might I have a word, Mr. Dashwood?"

Outside the room, Lord William lowered his voice. "I have a suspicion what they're going to tell me. Are you certain I'm the right man for this?"

Lord William ran a renowned stud farm at Salmsbury Abbey, the principal seat of his father, the Duke of Rowland. He didn't breed racehorses, but splendid hunters and carriage horses.

Nick nodded. "I think you are. I need someone who's not at Newmarket." He'd already got a race-horse trainer's view of the matter from Stewart Darlington. "Will you hear them out? I only ask your considered opinion of their report of the horses' health, as an accomplished horse trainer."

"That I can give," Lord William replied, "thought I don't know what weight it will carry with anyone."

"For my own ears only," Nick assured him.

"All right, then." Lord William went back into the room, and Nick went downstairs.

Westmorland found him. "Is this about what happened at the Craven Meeting?"

The Craven Meeting was the first race of the season at Newmarket. This year, the odds-on favorite had run very well in his first match, but fallen ill before the next day's sweepstakes with a far larger purse, and a six-to-one horse had won. There had been grumbling against both jockeys and allegations of manipulation thrown at both stables.

Not Lord Fitchley. He owned neither horse and had placed no bet on the first race—but he'd placed an enormous wager on the second race, and won. It had only added to his reputation for possessing preternatural instincts about the turf.

Nick gazed blandly at the marquess. "How interesting you would think of that, my lord."

Westmorland eyed him. "I know what Fitchley's done, petitioning for the Sidney child. She's your relation, isn't she?"

"A distant cousin," agreed Nick. By now, everyone in London knew he was the Sydenham heir, not really a Dashwood but a Sidney by birth. "I've become quite fond of her."

Westmorland said nothing for a moment. "I owe you, Dashwood. I've not forgotten."

Last year, it had been Westmorland's plot that ruined Frederick Forester, the Liverpool merchant who ran a side business selling Africans into slavery in the West Indies. Forester had been a member of the Vega Club; Nick hadn't known of his illicit activities. Once he discovered them, though . . . That was the game Nick had fixed, deliberately throwing the largest pot in Vega's history and bankrupting Forester.

He didn't think Westmorland knew that last bit. The marquess had meant that his fiancée, now wife, had told Nick beforehand that several members of the club intended to ruin Forester. He wondered what Westmorland would say if he knew Nick had not only allowed it, he had personally ensured they succeeded.

"Think nothing of it," he told Westmorland courteously.

The marquess nodded. "Bear it in mind, if you ever need a favor." He strolled away.

Almost an hour later, Lord William reappeared. He met Nick's eyes and gave a nod before going to join his brother in the dining room.

So, it was true. An almost electrical charge shot through him. Nick had believed the tale would bear out, but now he had eyewitnesses, sitting upstairs in the private salon. He found Forbes by the hazard tables. "Show MacGregor upstairs the moment he arrives. If Lord Fitchley graces us with his presence tonight, let me know at once."

Forbes cocked his head. "Believe me, Dash, if he does, you'll know. He's not been quiet about his desire to speak to you."

Nick smiled lazily. "How convenient. I have something to say to him, too." He walked to the front and told Frank to fetch one of the boys. Jimmy popped out of the cloakroom and Nick handed him a sealed note and a sovereign. "Chop chop," he told the lad, and Jimmy nodded once before sprinting out the door.

Fitchley did not appear at the Vega Club that night, though some of his mates did. There was a mild confrontation between Westmorland and Geoffrey Parker-Lloyd, which ended when the marquess and his brother left. Nick gazed expressionlessly at Parker-Lloyd, who tilted his chin defiantly and slouched off to the faro tables.

It was almost six in the morning before the final confirmation came. He was playing billiards, as usual, too restless to go home. In London, he and Emilia couldn't sneak away as easily as they had done before, and he didn't want Lucy or Charlotte to spy Emilia leaving his bedroom. They had agreed to be discreet. Today he was going to obtain the marriage license; Grantham should have settlements prepared by the next day. Within a few weeks Emilia would be his wife, but until then . . . he was playing billiards.

The knock at the door interrupted his contemplation of the table, and consideration of whether he should have it removed to his house. Emilia liked to play. He liked to watch her lean over to play. They could make wagers on the outcome, and pay their forfeits right on the table.

"Come," he called.

The door opened to admit a tall, lanky fellow with rumpled dark hair and ink on his cuffs. He met Nick's gaze with piercing gray eyes as he laid down the large leather-bound turf book, where all the horseracing wagers at Vega's were recorded.

"Damn my eyes, but it's all here," he said in a Scottish lilt. "Your fellow Darlington made a good start of it, but Bobby Kinson fingered five more at Newmarket, and O'Malley kept receipts."

Nick put aside his cue. "I thought they would. What I want to know is, is it enough?"

Enough evidence, he meant, to persuade London that Fitchley had been poisoning horses to manipulate races. Nick had been struck by how uncanny the baron was in his wagering, and he'd put Stewart Darlington, who knew everyone at every track in southern England, to studying the baron's racing wagers. Fitchley won a staggering seventy percent of the time, and in half of those races, at least one horse had been withdrawn at the last minute. Bobby Kinson, who rode Fitchley's own horses, had been all too willing to talk about what he saw, as had Dickie O'Malley, who'd quit the Newmarket stables over what he suspected.

"Enough to have him hanged by half the sporting ton, if not brought before the assizes," answered Liam MacGregor.

MacGregor's newspaper, of which Nick was now part owner, was developing a reputation for being far more than a gossip rag—although their gossip columns were read avidly by all. Nick thought it best to fight on two fronts: hard news as well as the less-restrained scandal sheets. "Very good. When can you print it?"

Liam MacGregor gave a bark of laughter and ran one hand over his head. "I'll set someone to writing it this very morning. The afternoon edition, if all goes well. This will be the biggest story the *London Intelligencer* has ever published."

CHAPTER THIRTY-FOUR

Nick caught Emilia by surprise that morning. She was washing her face, bent over the basin, when his hands stole around her waist. She jumped, and he pressed his lips to the nape of her neck, still damp from scrubbing.

"How did you come in so quietly?" she asked in a whisper, tilting her head to let him continue. "I didn't hear the door at all."

"No," he murmured between kisses. "Took it off the hinges."

She started again, then spied the door to his private study, the one that had been disabled. As he said, it stood ajar, propped crookedly in the doorway. "How on earth—?"

He grinned, letting her turn in his arm to face him. "The bolts were on my side. I pulled them out, and voilà—the door opened."

She gave a surprised laugh, then clapped one hand over her mouth. "The girls will wake soon," she whispered.

He arched a brow. "How soon?"

"Too soon," she said with regret, glancing at the clock.

"Alas. I shall have to contain myself for another day." He kissed her again, and when he let her go at last, she almost swooned right back into his arms. "It will be in the newspaper this afternoon," he told her.

Emilia sobered. "All of it?"

Nick nodded.

She bit her lip. "He's going to be enraged."

"No doubt. Until further notice, James is armed." He nodded as she flinched. "So is Pearce, by the bye. And Jock and Rudy will be about the house, too." Jock and Rudy had gone with them to Dorset, though Emilia hadn't seen them much. They were much bigger and rougher looking than James, though very affable and polite when she spoke to them.

"What about the girls?"

He shot her a guarded look. "Shouldn't we tell them?"

Emilia thought about it. Her instinct was to say nothing, and protect them from any ugliness about Fitchley. But she knew that might not be possible; Fitchley had already frightened them when he way-laid Emilia. "Is there a way to do it gently?" she asked hesitantly. "I don't want to alarm them."

"Sometimes it's good to be a little alarmed. It keeps your guard up so you're not an easy mark. I would rather warn them, and let them know why Jock and Rudy are here."

Slowly Emilia nodded. "I suppose that's reasonable."

When they went down to breakfast, the girls were already there. Charlotte exclaimed in delight to see Nick so early, and he teased her about not lying abed too late. They sat down to eat, though the conversation to come never left Emilia's mind. She managed to eat a piece of toast before her appetite fled, and had drunk two cups of tea by the time Nick began.

"There is something I must tell you both." He leaned forward on the table, growing serious. "There's a fellow who's been hounding us lately—Miss Greene and I—and we're concerned he might come around here and stir up a fuss. I don't want him to bother either of you. Will you promise me to be very attentive to Miss Greene, and to James?"

Lucy had gone still, her eyes flitting rapidly from Emilia to Nick and back. "Is he after Millie?" she asked anxiously. "Is it the man who tried to snatch her off the street?"

Nick's expression grew somber as he turned to her. "It is."

The room went silent. Lucy seemed to shrink in her chair.

"I don't want you to be frightened," he went on gently. "I won't let him hurt either of you, or Miss Greene. Do you trust me?"

Slowly Lucy nodded.

"If he comes around here, or you spy him in the park, stay close to James. I've also asked Rudy and Jock, who went with us to Dorset, to spend some time here as well, and you can trust them as much as you trust me."

"Can't you stay here?" she whispered. "I trust you, Mr. Dashwood, better than anyone but Millie."

Something flickered over Nick's face. "I will be

here as much as I can," he replied. "I give you my word, Lucy."

Emilia tried to smile reassuringly at Charlotte, who was tense and silent. "We only want you to be aware. I feel dreadful that you were both so frightened when this man stopped me in the street. Mr. Dashwood has taken careful steps to protect us all."

"I give you my word, Lucy," repeated Nick.

Emilia realized it was the first time he'd said Lucy instead of Lucinda.

"What's his name?" asked Charlotte.

"Baron Fitchley." Nick said it without hesitation. Emilia tried to hide her flinch.

Lucy inhaled. "What?" asked Emilia quickly.

Lucy shook her head. Her eyes were so wide, Emilia could see white all around the brown, and her face was pale. "Is he going to come here?" she whispered.

"I doubt it," Nick told her. "And if he does, Pearce will be ready for him. I daresay he'll slice the man right to bits with that little silver tray of his."

Lucy's lips trembled. "Millie?" she appealed. "Are you afraid?"

"No," said Emilia firmly. "Mr. Dashwood has made every arrangement."

Charlotte sat up straight. "Will you leave me your pistol, Nick?"

"I will not," he said at once. "James has one, and that's enough. Neither of you will need to fight him off. I only want you to be wary. If James or Miss Greene says it's time to go home, or not a good day to walk in the park, you must listen, and not quarrel with them." He sat back, his tone lightening. "I expect in a few days he'll have worn himself out and gone away to sulk somewhere else. As Miss

Greene said, we don't want you to be frightened, only aware."

There was a very long silence. Emilia already regretted telling them; they should have made up another story to explain Jock and Rudy being around.

"I promise," said Lucy softly.

"I promise," echoed Charlotte.

Later, after Nick had gone to bed, Charlotte tugged Emilia aside. "Who is that man? Lucy went pale when she heard his name."

Emilia hesitated. Lucy had been in the room when Mr. Bennet read her father's will; she might have remembered his name. She wished she'd remembered that, and asked Nick not to mention it.

But what lie could Emilia tell? None. And she didn't want to lie to Charlotte at all. "Her father named him as Lucy's guardian," she said quietly. "But he's horribly unsuited. Nick and I will never let him take her."

Charlotte set her mouth and nodded once. "I understand. Thank you for telling me. I promise to help keep Lucy safe from him." She marched into the dining room without another word, and Emilia followed after a moment, barely able to focus on the music lesson.

CHAPTER THIRTY-FIVE

Pearce sent Henry out to get the first copies of the *London Intelligencer* that afternoon. Emilia paced the entry hall, waiting for it. Signor Giacomo was leading the girls in a giddy dance lesson in the dining room. Emilia had told him they were both to participate, and that he was to teach them the most boisterous dance he knew. He had brought an extra assistant, and the sounds of laughter rang over the tinkling of the pianoforte.

When Henry finally returned, she all but pounced on him, seizing the copy he handed her. It was right there on the front page: *Craven Murder at the Craven Meeting!*

Nick came down the stairs as she was reading, dressed in his usual evening wear. "MacGregor did his part well," he remarked, taking the other copy Henry offered him.

"When Lord F won a tidy fortune at the Craven Meeting this April last on Agamemnon, who placed well above the highly favored Etonian, it seemed naught but proof of that gentleman's infallible prescience in contests of the turf," Emilia read in a quiet rush. "But it has come to this columnist's attention that there is in truth a far more sinister explanation—that Lord F not only had prior awareness of a malady afflicting Etonian but in fact played a role in causing it. The *Intelligencer* has learned . . ." Her voice trailed off as her eyes scanned the page faster than she could speak.

"Mr. Kinson told several people he thought the horse had been tampered with." Nick turned the page of his own copy. "And the groom kept a receipt when he was asked to procure arsenic."

Emilia's breath caught in her throat. "Nick—this says he killed a racehorse!"

"It *is* so difficult to calculate the precise dose of arsenic that will sicken a horse, but not kill it," he mused. "I don't wonder that his man got it wrong a time or two."

"These are prime horseflesh." She pressed a hand to her forehead. Her father and uncle had been consumed by the stables; she'd grown up hearing about racehorses and the unchecked competition between rival horse owners. Training grooms would attempt to spy out information on opponents and gain any advantage they could. Fortunes were wagered, won and lost. Men had killed themselves over losses at the races. "Fitchley will be called out, if not simply attacked by a mob and shot through the heart."

Nick folded his newspaper and handed it to Pearce. "If he didn't want to risk that, he ought not to have poisoned horses all over Newmarket."

After a moment Emilia put aside her own newspaper. The reporter had done his job with enthusiasm; listed were several large, winning wagers by Fitchley, along with the particulars of the

odds and the horses running. There was a very
striking pattern of horses falling ill or being
physicked after their races. Only one horse had
died, but in violent agony. Fitchley had won over
four thousand pounds on the race that horse was
to have run.

The *Intelligencer* pondered suggestively how
many horses might have been tampered with, if one
valuable colt had been killed, and how many wagers
could have been upset by these machinations. The
Newmarket track was the domain of the wealthiest,
most powerful men in England. If Fitchley had any
sense at all, he would be on a packet to the Continent by tonight.

Pearce brought Nick's coat and held it for him.
He settled it with a jerk on his shoulders and Emilia
stepped up to him and gripped the front, heedless
of Pearce and Henry watching. "Be careful," she
pleaded. "Nick, he'll be crazed—"

He cupped her face in both hands and kissed
her. "Don't worry," he whispered. "I know what
I'm doing." He took his hat and gloves from Pearce.
"Bar the door until I return."

It was early yet, not even five. Too early for him
to go to the club. "Where are you going?" She followed him toward the door.

"The club," he said in mild surprise. "I antici-
pate a lively evening." And with a wink, he was
gone, striding out to the waiting carriage. Emilia
retreated to the window to watch him step inside,
the door closed with a snap by a large fellow she'd
never seen before. As the man stepped onto his
perch at the back of the carriage, Emilia saw the
butt of a pistol at his side beneath his smart coat.

She let the drape fall. At least Nick was taking a

carriage instead of walking as he often did, and with some strong fellows guarding his back.

The evening seemed to drag. Emilia ate dinner with the girls and tried to talk of pleasant things, but Nick's empty chair was a silent reminder of the less pleasant things. Nor could Emilia stop wondering what he expected to happen at the Vega Club. She wanted to go and see for herself, and she wanted to stand guard over Lucy and Charlotte, who were both subdued. She supposed they could sense that she wasn't as unafraid as she'd insisted at breakfast.

It only grew worse after she sent the girls to bed. She walked through the entire house with Pearce, checking every door and window, even though it felt slightly foolish. Fitchley would hardly bring a ladder into Portland Place and try to climb in the drawing room window.

No, he would go to the club to confront Nick if he hadn't fled town. She and the girls were perfectly safe here. James sat whittling in the entry hall, his pistol on a table beside him. Pearce showed her his own pistol, and assured her he knew how to use it. Emilia thanked him with a shiver. What dangerous people Nick surrounded himself with.

She was sitting in the drawing room, staring sightlessly at Lucy's dress in her lap, which she was meant to be mending, when the door creaked. Emilia jumped; she'd been lost in thought, but it was only Charlotte. "Miss Greene? May I come in?"

Emilia put aside the dress and smiled, not surprised. "Of course." She patted the sofa beside her. "Come sit with me."

Charlotte hurried across the room. "Will that terrible man really try to take Lucy away?"

Emilia sighed. "He didn't come for her when her father died, nor write to inquire about her. He doesn't even know her. He's just trying to stir up trouble." She clasped Charlotte's hand. "But it doesn't matter, because I will never give her over to him," she said firmly. "Not even if I have to steal away to America with her under a false name."

Charlotte bit her lip. "I don't want that to happen."

"I'm sure it won't come to that." Emilia silently hoped it was true. "Your brother has a plan."

"Yes, Nick often has plans . . ." Charlotte didn't look reassured. "But what if he plans to snatch Lucy?"

Emilia thought of the newspaper story, and of the gossip likely racing through London tonight. "He won't." She put her arm around the girl's shoulders. "He's done bad things to many other people, and I suspect they will hound him right out of England. Once he's gone, there will be no danger to any of us."

"How can you be sure?"

"Because I know the people he harmed," Emilia said. "They won't take it lightly. Some of them will be out for his blood, and he'll know that."

"Why would anyone do that?" Charlotte's trembling voice rose. "Why would he hurt people and try to take Lucy from us? What would he gain by any of it?"

Emilia thought of Emmett Fitchley's narrow, satisfied face. "Money," she said quietly. "He won a great deal of money through his evil actions. Money gives a man power, which he craves. He enjoys having sway over people. And I suppose he thought he'd never get caught. Men like him tend to think they will never be held to account for their sins."

"What would he do to Lucy, if he got her?"

Emilia didn't even want to think about that. "He won't," she said again. "Nick and I won't allow it."

Charlotte looked at her gravely. "But what if you can't stop him?"

Emilia never answered that disturbing query. From downstairs came a crash, a discordant jangling that sounded as if something had fallen on the pianoforte, and then shouts of alarm. Without stopping to think what it could be, she seized Charlotte's hand. "Come," she said urgently, and together they bolted up the stairs to the nursery. "Get dressed," she told Charlotte, who ran into her own room.

Lucy was dozing, but Chester was already on alert. He growled as Emilia threw open the door. "Lucy, get up," she whispered harshly, grabbing whatever clothes she could find.

Lucy sat up, blinking, but instantly frightened. "What's wrong?" she cried.

Emilia didn't know, but something told her to be ready to flee, to hide Lucy and make sure she was safe. "I don't know yet. Just come with me." Lucy scrambled to her, and they hurried out into the nursery to see Charlotte, a dress pulled haphazardly over her shift, shoes and stockings in her hand. Emilia pressed a finger to her lips, and they nodded.

She led the way quickly down the servants' stair to the kitchen, Chester running ahead of them with his tail bristling. Mrs. Watson spun around as they entered. "What's about?" she asked worriedly. "All the bells from the front have been ringing, and

Rudy shouted at me to stay away from the windows!"

Emilia dumped Lucy's things on the table. "I'm going to find out. Help Lucy get dressed. If you hear anything . . ." She hesitated. "Anything *alarming*, take the girls through the garden to the stable and tell Henry to saddle a horse. Stay there with them until Mr. Dashwood or I come back." She caught Lucy's terrified expression and squeezed the girl tightly, opening her arms to admit Charlotte into the fierce hug. "No one will hurt either of you," she whispered. "I promise. Nick promised. We mean it." She kissed both on the tops of their heads. "Stay with Mrs. Watson. I'll be back soon."

Lucy's quiet sobs followed her as she tore through the house, up the stairs through the baize door into the back of the hall. Emilia didn't know what she expected, but what she found was still a shock.

Fire.

Smoke billowed through the open dining room doors, where Pearce and other servants were beating the flames with their own jackets. Emilia recoiled in alarm, then ran after James when he bolted past her into the morning room. He tossed the chairs aside and Emilia helped him shove over the table, and together they dragged the heavy carpet into the dining room and heaved it atop the flames. Pearce had already ripped down the drapes at the window and flung them onto the fire, and the carpet snuffed all but a few flickers. By then someone had fetched the sand buckets from the kitchen, and Pearce quickly smothered everything.

"Check the rest of the house," said Emilia, breathing hard. "Mr. Pearce, will you and Henry go upstairs?" The butler nodded and rushed out, calling for Henry to follow him. Emilia and James ran from room to room on the ground floor, but the dining room was the only one affected.

When they were convinced the fire was completely out, twenty terrifying minutes later, Emilia was able to look at the mess. The front windows were smashed; the pianoforte, which had been near them, was in splinters. Beneath the ruined breakfast room carpet, the wooden floor would be scorched and charred. The fire had ignited the drapes, but Pearce's quick thinking had prevented more than some burns to the plasterwork and walls.

"What was it?" she asked at last, gazing in disbelief at the wreckage of Nick's elegant, empty dining room. Had it held a wool carpet and upholstered furnishings, wooden furniture and table linen, the fire might have gained more of a foothold. The whole room might be in flames, and soon the entire house. Her chest constricted as she said a fervent prayer of thanks for her instinct to pull Lucy and Charlotte out of the third-floor nursery, three flights of stairs from the safety of the street. If the house had caught fire—if no one had been able to put it out—the girls could have been trapped—

Pearce picked his way through the smoking rubble and poked around the pianoforte. "It struck the instrument first," he said, finally prodding a large chunk of stone from the tangle of wire and shattered rosewood that had once been a splendid pianoforte. "There was a second object, which must have ignited the fire."

"It was a bomb," said James.

"A bomb!"

"A sort of bomb," the young man said. "A

bottle of oil with a burning wick on top. The glass breaks on impact, spilling the oil, and the wick sets it off."

Now that the fire was out, he had his pistol in hand, and when Emilia started toward the windows to look, he hauled her back. "Stay away, Miss Greene," he said grimly. "Jock will have given chase, if there's anyone to chase. Until he returns, no one goes near the windows."

She swallowed hard. "Someone must go to Vega's," she said in a strained voice. "Mr. Dashwood needs to know at once—"

"I've sent Rudy already," said Pearce.

"I should go—"

"No," James interrupted. "You stay here. Mr. Dashwood's orders. We're not to leave you, and you're to be kept safe in the house."

She looked at the carpet, singed and smoking, and the black marks climbing the walls to the ceiling. "I don't feel particularly safe in the house."

"It's safer than you walking down the street, where anyone with a pistol could take a shot at you," he replied, and she closed her mouth to keep from bursting into tears. Surely even Fitchley wouldn't take a shot at her . . .

I'll follow you night and day, he'd threatened. She herself had told Nick he would be enraged by the newspaper report.

Emilia shivered and rubbed her hands over her arms. "Can we board up the windows?"

Pearce nodded. "Henry's already gone to the mews for some boards."

The stables. She turned toward the back of the house. "Very good. Thank you, Mr. Pearce.

James . . ." She touched his arm, and he nodded. "Thank you all. I should go . . ."

Still dazed, she made her way back to the kitchen. She must reassure the girls and try to calm them enough to go back to sleep. She wouldn't say no to a cup of hot tea laced with brandy, either.

As Mr. Pearce had said, Henry was on his way back into the house with several boards under his arm. Mrs. Watson was hustling behind him, holding a bucket of nails and a hammer.

"Where are the girls?" Emilia asked.

Mrs. Watson paused to wipe her face. "Right in the sitting room, Miss Greene. I tucked them in there when I carried up the sand buckets. The poor things were tired, Miss Charlotte holding Miss Lucy in her arms."

Emilia smiled gratefully. "Of course. Thank you so much, Mrs. Watson." The woman nodded and hurried off. Feeling drained, Emilia turned toward the tiny sitting room that Mrs. Watson shared with the cook. She would have to apologize to Charlotte and Lucy. She wasn't sorry she had brought them down here, where they could have made an easier escape if one had been necessary, but she *was* sorry that she had frightened them so terribly. Perhaps they would all just pile into Emilia's bed tonight.

She opened the sitting room door. "Charlotte?" She stepped inside. "Lucy?" There was a rocking chair, a settee by the fire, and a small table. A pair of lamps burned on the table and the mantel, illuminating the room. Chester the cat was there, hissing from his position under the settee.

But Charlotte and Lucy were not.

CHAPTER THIRTY-SIX

I t began as a deceptively normal evening at the Vega Club.

Nick arrived early. He sent the carriage away and told his men to take turns in patrol around the outside of the club. Inside the club he gathered his staff and put them all on guard. If Fitchley wanted to confront him face-to-face, Nick meant to be ready.

Emilia had said he would flee to the Continent. Nick agreed that would be the wisest course for Fitchley, but there was a vengeful streak in the baron that would probably make the man do something stupid and much riskier.

To tell the truth, Nick wanted a confrontation. Fitchley had hounded and frightened Emilia, and then he had tried to take Lucy. Nick wanted to gut the man, and to twist the knife as he did it.

But several hours rolled by without any sign of him. Even his companions were absent, and Nick began to wonder if Fitchley had been more sensible than he'd thought. It was certain that he wouldn't have found many friends in the Vega Club tonight.

Word had gone round faster than rumors of a high stakes table setting up. Nick overheard more than one heated discussion about Fitchley. He avoided joining any conversation, but received the strong impression that every race in the previous year at Newmarket and Epsom was undergoing some serious study.

Excellent.

It was ten before the Marquess of Westmorland snared him. "Might I have a word, Dashwood?"

Nick bowed his head. "Of course, sir." He followed the marquess to a secluded corner of the salon, where a handful of other men were waiting. "Good evening, gentlemen."

"Is it true?" asked Viscount Heathercote directly.

Nick gazed back calmly. "Of what do you speak, my lord?"

"This business about Fitchley," asked another fellow named Marlowe. He glanced swiftly toward Westmorland as he spoke, and Nick guessed Lord William had told his brother all.

"Ah. The report in the *Intelligencer*," he replied calmly. "It is very shocking, of course."

"Do you doubt it?"

Nick returned Westmorland's probing stare mildly. "I have no reason to, my lord."

"So you're ejecting Fitchley?"

Nick drew out his watch and checked the time. "Naturally I cannot discuss one member with another. If the report is true, however, it would be . . . inconsistent with the standards of this club."

Heathercote frowned. "How do you intend to judge the truth?"

Ah. Now Nick remembered. Lord Heathercote's father, the Earl of Masham, owned Etonian, the horse who had been favored in the Craven Meeting. The horse who'd taken ill and been withdrawn before the sweepstakes race.

Nick smiled slightly. "I have my ways. And to be blunt, it does not matter whether the reports are proven true or not. My word is the last word, the *only* word, on who shall belong to this club. Rest assured, I have the Vega Club's interests at heart at all times."

It sounded fair-minded. It was even true. And Nick knew perfectly well that if he expelled Fitchley, everyone in London would view it as confirmation of the *London Intelligencer*'s report.

"Of course." Westmorland's shoulders eased.

"Right, then." Heathercote stood up. "Dinner?"

Westmorland shook his head. "I've promised to join Georgiana at her friend's rout. Another time." He glanced at Nick. "Thank you, Dashwood."

Nick bowed his head and walked away. He turned toward the dining room and caught sight of Forbes coming toward him—not at his usual purposeful walk but virtually at a full-out run, dodging patrons and footmen left and right. Instantly alert, Nick met him by the small pantry. "Rudy wants you," said Forbes, breathing hard. "Urgently. He's at the kitchen door."

This time Nick ran, ducking into the service hall and bolting past startled servants with platters. Rudy leaned against the wall, red-faced and winded. "Someone threw a brick through the window," he told Nick. "And then a fire-bomb."

His heart almost stopped. "Is the house on

fire?" he demanded. "Did everyone get out? Was the fire brigade summoned?"

Rudy shook his head. "I was around by the kitchen but ran inside, quick as a blink, and helped Pearce put out some of it. It was in the dining room, where there weren't much to burn, so Pearce sent me here. Young Henry was standing by to go for the fire brigade if needed, but the fire was out. Jock took off after a fellow who might've done it. They were long gone by the time I went back outside."

"Miss Greene?" demanded Nick.

"She came down as I was going out, alarmed but unhurt. She must have been upstairs with the young ladies."

Nick stood still, every breath rippling through him like the first stirrings of a hurricane. Fitchley had attacked his home—his family. His servants and retainers. His cousin. His sister. His beloved.

He'd been right—and terribly wrong. If Emmett Fitchley wasn't on a ship to France already, he'd soon wish he was.

"Go back," Nick told Rudy, his voice sounding oddly distant. "Take William and Ned. No one goes near the house, do you hear me?"

Rudy nodded. "Aye, sir." He ducked back out into the service area, where he would find the two men on their patrol of the premises.

Nick turned and strode back into the club. He had to go home. He'd miscalculated, thinking Fitchley would focus his rage here, on him. He'd armed his servants at home only as a precaution. Instead the villain had attacked an innocent woman and children. His thoughts raced through London ahead of him, to Emilia. She'd been worried, and he had dismissed her fear. *Don't worry. I know what I'm doing.*

Idiot.

He ought to have left them in Dorset. Hidden them away in Queen's Court, or even sent them to the McCorquodale family, who would take them in for Emilia's sake. It was his fault, because he hadn't wanted to be parted from any of them, and in his arrogance, he had left them vulnerable.

Deep in self-censure, he didn't catch the change in atmosphere until he reached the main salon.

"Dashwood!"

He stopped. Lord Fitchley stood in the middle of the main salon. He'd lost his hat but still wore his greatcoat; he must have charged past Frank. His pale hair stood up around his head, and his face was dark with hatred. "You insufferable bastard," he snarled.

Like the recession of a mighty wave, Nick's fear drained away, leaving exposed the implacable rock that was fury. He started forward again, hands loose at his sides, gaze never wavering from Fitchley. Dimly he heard a few people scurry toward the doors, but not many. They wanted to see the fight.

Nick was going to oblige them.

"Lord Fitchley." He spoke quietly as he walked, one purposeful step at a time. "I've warned you about insulting people in this club, sir."

Fitchley flung out a shaking finger pointed in accusation. "This man," he spat, his voice raised—though it wasn't necessary, as the entire club had fallen silent. "This contemptible *charlatan* has slandered my good name, accusing me of unspeakable dishonor! I never harmed a horse in my life. I wouldn't doubt it if this club, even Dashwood personally, committed the appalling acts they accuse me of! Who else is so eager to take our money?" His red-rimmed eyes swept the room in search of support. "Who else imposes such ridiculous odds and refuses to adjust them? I daresay it suited this club, and its conniving proprietor, when that horse died!"

Nick raised one brow. "Odd, how eagerly you yourself placed wagers here, if the Vega Club is conniving to cheat people."

Fitchley's eyes glowed like coals in his mean, sallow face. "You put Kinson up to this, didn't you? How much did you pay the lying little weasel to blacken my name?"

"Mr. Bobby Kinson?" Nick affected astonishment. "The man who rode your own horses to several magnificent wins, securing fame and good fortune for your own racing stable . . . is a lying little weasel?"

"He's behind that rubbish in the bloody papers," snarled Fitchley. He glanced around the room and raised his voice. A ripple of whispers had gone around at the jockey's name. Bobby Kinson was famous. "A pack of lies, which you got that gossip-mongering Scot to print. It's not true! I sacked Kinson because he's lost his touch, and he'd begun drinking. Ask him how he broke his leg! Admit you conspired to defame me and I'll not summon the constables."

Nick bared his teeth in a nasty smile. "By all means summon the constables. I wish to report an arson. Someone attempted to burn down my house tonight." He lingered on the word *someone* until Fitchley flushed. Another ripple of whispers. Louis started forward, but Nick gave a hard flick of one hand, staying him.

"So you don't deny your role in this libelous action." The baron's face twisted with rage. "I'll sue you for slander."

"Indeed," said Nick in a bored tone.

"And for damages!" Fitchley's voice rose to a near-scream. "For alienating my betrothed wife!"

Nick let one corner of his mouth curl up at that. So, Emilia *was* the heiress whose fortune Fitchley had been borrowing against. Grantham had turned up that interesting morsel of information: Fitchley won a lot of money, but he spent even more, and he had taken loans against his expectations.

As expected, the smirk was too much for Fitchley. With a roar, he charged.

Nick let the first punch connect. Half the aristocracy in London was here in this room, watching, and he wanted them to see Fitchley attack him. He'd have fifty witnesses that his defense was justified. He'd already shifted his weight and recoiled just before Fitchley's fist met his jaw, dampening the blow.

But he stepped into his counterpunch, driving Fitchley's chin up. A hard right to the man's ribs, and Fitchley reeled backward. Nick turned his fist sideways and clubbed the center of Fitchley's chest, driving the air from his lungs, and the baron gave a loud wheeze. He seemed to realize he had erred, and he staggered sideways, the spite and anger in his face giving way to shock.

Nick shoved his shoulder, forcing the man further off-balance again. Fitchley stumbled, his coat trailing on the floor. Nick stepped on it and hooked his other foot around the man's ankle to sweep his feet from beneath him, sending the baron crashing face-first to the floor. In a flash Nick was on his back, one hand fisted in the baron's hair, yanking back Fitchley's head to expose his throat to the wicked little knife Nick held in his other hand. Blood streamed down the baron's face from his nose.

"How dare you come into my club," he said for the audience, "and threaten my patrons and employees. If you have a disagreement with me, approach me like a man, not a coward." He leaned more of his weight onto his knee, on the man's lower spine. Fitchley cried out in pain and enraged terror, scrabbling with his hands as he tried to retreat from the knife. Nick let the tip of the blade prick Fitchley's skin, just below his chin.

"Did you attempt to burn down my house tonight?" Nick whispered. The baron jerked, trying to twist away, and Nick dug the tip of the knife a little deeper. A scarlet rivulet of blood trickled down Fitchley's throat, and he went still, except for the violent shudders of his breathing. His eyes were wild, rolling from side to side. "If you make the slightest move toward my family ever again, I'll dissect your innards into bait for the sharks, while you watch." He put his full weight on Fitchley's spine, ignoring the high-pitched sound the man made, and added in a quieter-still whisper, so that only Fitchley could hear him, "Emilia Greeneborough is not yours, and never will be—and neither is Lucinda Sidney."

He released the baron with a shove and rose to his feet. "Lord Fitchley, your membership has been revoked, and you are banned from the Vega Club." Expression composed once more, he turned to face the room, cleaning his blade on his handkerchief before replacing it in his jacket.

Dozens of pale, stunned faces stared back at him. The room was utterly silent. "Ladies and gentlemen, I apologize for the disruption. Mr. Forbes, open the cellar and see that everyone present has a glass of wine, with my compliments. Louis, if you please?"

Furious whispers began as he and Louis heaved up Lord Fitchley and dragged him into the Cold Hold. Nick left Louis guarding the man, crumpled in a chair, and sent for one of Forbes's boys to fetch a constable.

Lord Heathercote intercepted him as he left the Cold Hold. "Allow me to escort Lord Fitchley."

Nick hesitated. He'd meant to send Fitchley to the prison, which would prevent him from fleeing England until any charges could be brought. However, Heathercote's family had been one of the victims of Fitchley's actions. He had an interest. If Heathercote took the man, no one could blame Nick for whatever befell the baron. He would be blameless, or near enough.

Before he could reply, the front door opened. Frank must not have barred it again after—inexplicably—allowing Fitchley entry. Nick tensed, but his apprehension swiftly turned to alarm. It was Emilia, streaked with grime, her hair falling down and her face flushed, with James hard on her heels.

"Oh Nick," she gasped, out of breath, "the girls —the girls have gone missing."

CHAPTER THIRTY-SEVEN

Nick stared at her. Emilia, her chest heaving after the exertion of running all the way here, could only nod. "Someone threw a stone—there was a fire-bomb—"

He jerked, as if roused from a trance. "I know about the fire. Were the girls hurt?"

She shook her head. "No, we managed to put it out. I left them in the kitchen with Mrs. Watson, but when I went back for them, they were gone."

"Gone? Where?" he demanded.

She put up her hands helplessly. "I don't know! No one saw them leave, but they aren't there. We searched the entire house."

Nick stepped backward, his face blank. "Charlotte? Is gone?" Moving jerkily, he turned and opened a heavy wooden door behind him, disappearing inside.

I will not lose my sister again. She could still hear his words, spoken low and fiercely in a quiet Dorset night. The thing Nick feared most, and she had allowed it to happen. Emilia's stomach plunged.

As she stood paralyzed with shame and fear, a gentleman standing nearby craned his neck, peering into the room after Nick, then sidled toward the doorway. She didn't know who he was, but nervously she followed.

The room within was small and spare, all in shades of gray. The tall young man named Louis, who had come to them in Dorset, stood with arms folded in front of a bricked-up fireplace. There were two large leather armchairs, and Nick knelt in front of one.

"Do you know?" he was asking, his voice flat and emotionless, as Emilia slipped into the room.

To her surprise, it was Emmett Fitchley huddled in the chair. He looked nothing like he had that day in Portland Place; his face was ashen and bloody, his hair stood out in all directions, and his clothes were a mess. Fitchley prided himself on his appearance. Emilia glanced sideways at Nick, wondering if he had done that.

"Sod off," said Fitchley thickly. Blood had clotted around his nose and was smeared over his left cheek, as if he'd tried to wipe it away.

Nick tilted his head. "If you know, and don't tell me . . ."

"You'll do what? Ruin me?" Fitchley sneered. He caught sight of Emilia and a spark of hatred flared in his eyes. "You've already done that."

"There's quite a lot I could still do," replied Nick in a terrifyingly quiet voice.

"Don't trouble yourself," interjected the stranger. "Allow me."

"If you've taken those girls, you'll prefer his company to mine," Nick said, still staring at Fitchley.

Fitchley twitched before turning away. "I don't have them. Keep the brat, and welcome to her."

Nick said nothing for a minute, then rose to his feet. "If you have nothing to tell me, Lord Fitchley, then I have nothing more to do with you." Fitchley hunched his shoulders. "He's yours," Nick told the unknown man, and he strode out of the room without looking at anyone.

The stranger turned to Emilia and gave her a charming smile. He was a handsome fellow, expensively dressed. "Your pardon, Madame. Lord Fitchley and I—"

She nodded, distracted. "Yes." She ran after Nick, all the way to his office.

She found him leaning over his desk, hands braced wide on the polished surface, head bowed. "Tell me what happened," he said without looking up as she burst in behind him.

Emilia told him—how Charlotte had been unable to sleep and had come to her, how she and Charlotte had heard the crash, how she had gathered both girls and hurried them to the kitchen, the devastation in the dining room, how Pearce and James had put out the fire. "The girls were both in the kitchen with Mrs. Watson," she finished. "Safe in her sitting room with Chester! Mrs. Watson left them only to bring the sand buckets to the front of the house, and by the time I went for them, they were gone."

"No one could have slipped in the back?"

"I don't know," she said, her voice beginning to crack. "Henry opened the gate to go to the mews for wood to board up the broken windows. He and Mrs. Watson were out of sight of it for no more than a few moments, and they saw no one lurking to slip in. There hardly seems time enough for someone to have gone in and carried away the girls without being seen or heard by anyone, and there were no signs of struggle."

Slowly Nick straightened, his gaze distant. "What were you discussing with Charlotte before the crash, that she was unable to sleep?"

Emilia pressed a hand to her brow. "She wanted to know if Fitchley would really take Lucy," she said, fighting back tears. "She wanted to know if he could, and I admitted Fitchley is Lucy's legal guardian. I told her we would never allow it, though, and that Fitchley would likely leave England. I was doing my best to comfort her—"

"I know." He touched her shoulder absently. "I have an idea where they are."

She froze, then seized his arm. "Where? How do you know?"

He moved away, turning toward the door. "Did you come in a carriage?"

"No, I wouldn't wait for one—we ran all the way here, James and I . . ."

"I see." He opened the door and whistled. A moment later an earnest-looking boy loped into the corridor. "Tell Mr. Forbes I want a hackney." The boy nodded and disappeared. Nick picked up his greatcoat. "Do you have a cloak?"

Emilia flushed. She'd run from the house without pausing for anything. James had only caught up to her a few streets later. "No."

He draped his coat over her shoulders and went out. Emilia followed, through the concealed door and toward the black-and-white tiled entrance hall. They met Mr. Forbes by the alcove where Nick had kissed her so passionately, and the enormity of her failure hit Emilia.

Her job had been to protect Lucy and Charlotte, and both had disappeared while in her care. Nick thought he knew where they were, but he might be wrong, and nothing changed the fact that Emilia had failed to keep them safe in their own home, even with armed men on the property and the servants on alert. Nick had trusted her to do one thing, and she had failed.

She didn't hear what he said to his club manager. The man gave her a sympathetic look as Nick led her out, and Emilia's eye blurred with tears. She couldn't bear sympathy now.

James was waiting by the hackney, and Nick paused to speak to him. Emilia clambered into the hackney by herself, holding Nick's coat around her. Alone in the carriage, she wiped her streaming eyes. Nothing mattered until they found Charlotte and Lucy. If they were safe, she would fall on her knees and thank God, even if Nick never forgave her.

If they weren't safe . . .

Nick stepped in and the carriage lurched forward.

"I'm sorry," she whispered. "Oh, Nick, I'm so sorry—"

"It's not your fault." He was peering out the window, watching their progress.

"It is." Her throat felt rough, and she thought she might be sick. "I spoke too freely to Charlotte. I ought not to have frightened her. Lucy was already scared enough. I should have stayed with them! I should have ordered Mrs. Watson not to leave them! I should have—"

Nick took her hand. "Shh," he murmured. "If I'm right—"

"What if you're not?" she all but sobbed.

"If I'm right," Nick repeated, "I think I understand what happened. Do you trust me?"

She hesitated, still heartsick and terrified but slightly reassured by his hand around hers. "Yes," she whispered.

He turned toward her, even though the carriage was too dark to see each other. "Charlotte once feared someone coming for her, too. She was about Lucy's age when I found her, and she'd been on her own for a few years. She'd learned to be frightened of a great many people who would take advantage of a helpless child alone. I imagine Lucy appears just as vulnerable to her."

Emilia didn't see how that explained anything. "Where do you think they've gone, then?"

"I told you I brought Charlotte to a house where she would be safe. I couldn't bring her to live with me because I was never home, and it wasn't unknown for men who lost heavily at Vega's to turn up on my doorstep, pleading for leniency—sometimes threatening terrible things if they didn't get it. I didn't want them anywhere near my sister, so I set her up in a quiet little house between the club and my home, with a kind staff and friendly neighbors. You've seen it. We took tea with Charlotte there."

Emilia began to calm down, remembering the snug little house in the flower-filled courtyard. "She would feel safe there?"

"She would, because there's a bolt-hole." Emilia started, and Nick's grip tightened on her hand. "It's merely a concealed cupboard, but Charlotte told me she found it comforting, to have a place where she could hide if she grew frightened. You already know I left her a disabled pistol. The hiding place was another thing I didn't know how to refuse. I understand she kept a toy animal in there when she was younger, with a blanket and a pillow, her own safe refuge."

Emilia let out her breath. "Do you really think that's where they are?"

"I do." He put his arm around her, and Emilia let herself be gathered to his side. "I own that court, and the house that was hers has been empty since she came to live with us. I wouldn't be surprised if she has a key."

The carriage slowed and turned. When it stopped, James jumped down to open the door.

It was the same courtyard she remembered. The house to the left was dark, but Nick walked up to the door and tried it. It opened under his hand, and he pushed it all the way open and gestured for Emilia. James jogged over with a pair of lit lanterns. Nick took one and sent him to scout the courtyard. "Let's go," he told Emilia, and led the way.

The little house was very dark; all the shutters were closed, so no moonlight crept in. Emilia instinctively kept close to Nick, who raised the lantern high. "Charlotte?" he called.

They went up the stairs, peeking into the rooms on each floor and calling the girls' names. When they reached the bedrooms, a faint creak sounded. Nick walked into one room and went around the bed frame, holding the lantern higher, and Emilia saw the thin opening of a cupboard door.

"Charlotte?" she cried. "Lucy? Are you here? It's us."

The door opened all the way. Lucy's pale face peered out. "Millie?"

"Yes," she said, collapsing to her knees and opening her arms. Lucy scrambled out of the cupboard and into her lap, and Emilia bent over her.

"I didn't want that man to get Lucy." Charlotte crawled out, too, and Nick put his arms around her. "I heard the cries of fire, and I thought he'd set the house on fire to chase us out where he could snatch her."

"That was very brave," murmured Nick. He pressed a kiss to his sister's temple. "But you gave Miss Greene a dreadful fright."

Charlotte looked anxiously at Emilia.

"No," said Emilia before Charlotte could speak. "*I* am sorry that I frightened *you*. I'm so, so sorry . . ." Her voice broke and she hugged Lucy tighter in speechless relief.

"Is he gone?" Lucy had her arms around Emilia's neck, but she didn't sound quite as frightened now.

Emilia smoothed back her hair. "Yes, dear, he is. You don't have anything to fear from him any longer."

Lucy's apprehensive eyes studied her. "Never? Charlotte said he is my guardian and that he would cause soldiers to come and take me away from you."

Her heart twisted. "Never," she swore.

"Never, Lucy," added Nick. "I give you my word."

After a long moment, Lucy nodded and tightened her arms around Emilia's neck. "Good."

Emilia buried her face in Lucy's hair. How she loved this child.

Nick cleared his throat. "There is something

else I want to tell you, and this seems an opportune moment. I have persuaded Miss Greene to marry me."

Charlotte gasped. Lucy lurched upright. Emilia raised her head and gaped at Nick.

He gave her a wink, that faint, mischievous smile on his lips. There was no trace of the terrifying blankness he had showed when she told him his sister had disappeared; it was as if that moment had never happened.

"Truly?" Charlotte clapped her hands together. "Oh, Nicky! How brilliant!" She flung her arms around him before whirling to Emilia. "Now we will be sisters!"

"Really, Millie?" asked Lucy hopefully. Emilia knew the rest of her question: *Will you be my new mama?*

Will you always protect me and love me?
Will we be a family?

Throat tight, she nodded.

Lucy beamed up at her with shining eyes. "I'm so happy!" She turned to look at Charlotte. "But I will *not* call you Aunt."

Someone laughed. Charlotte rolled her eyes and Lucy hugged Emilia once more before climbing to her feet, looking much happier.

"Gather your things, young ladies," said Nick. "Let's go home to celebrate."

"Is everyone all right at home?" asked Charlotte hesitantly.

Nick heaved a sigh. "No. I'm afraid the pianoforte suffered a terrible injury and did not survive."

"The piano—? Oh!" Charlotte exhaled in relief, looking at Lucy.

"No more scales," whispered Lucy, almost happily.

Charlotte gave a surprised snort of laughter, then another. She caught Emilia's eye and shrugged sheepishly. "At least there is *some* good news."

"As if the news that I'm to be married wasn't happy enough for you," said Nick with a trace of indignation.

"Oh! Yes, that is very happy news," his sister replied.

"That almost sounds like approval." Nick raised his brows in amusement.

"It is," declared Charlotte, giving both of them a firm nod. "I'm so glad you listened to me, Nick."

Even Emilia smiled at that.

The girls gathered their cloaks from the cupboard, and Emilia saw Lucy cuddle a threadbare stuffed lion under one arm. The two girls went down the stairs, holding hands as if they were sisters, and Emilia heard them call out to James.

Nick stopped her in the doorway. "Don't blame yourself for any of this."

She looked down. "I failed them. I failed you—I gave you my word I would keep them safe. Instead they were so frightened and felt so vulnerable in my care that they fled—"

He kissed her. "You didn't fail me," he said. "You didn't fail them. I'm the one who said we must tell the girls, which frightened them, and I'm the one who miscalculated about Fitchley's intentions, leaving all of you vulnerable." He cupped his hands around her face. "You brought them to safety when the fire broke out. You made certain the flames were put out. You came running to alert me the instant you realized they were missing, so we could search for them together. We each of us made mistakes, yes; but together, we made it come out right."

She looked at him, her eyes wet.

"We are partners," he said softly. "Partners don't need to be perfect individually, they just need to work together perfectly as a pair."

She sniffled. "Do we?"

He nodded thoughtfully. "We do. I had no idea what to do with my sister, but under your guidance she's becoming courageous and capable as well as well-behaved and educated. You were apprehensive about Fitchley taking Lucy, but I've handed him over to some very vengeful people who will amply distract him from that. And if you marry me . . ." He paused. "It would fill my cold, dark heart to overflowing with joy and love."

She frowned at him through her tears. "Your heart is not cold or dark, nor empty of joy and love."

"I thought it was, until I met you," he countered. "Just as I never would have guessed I was heir to a viscounty until you told me. There's no end to the amazing things you've taught me, Miss Greene."

She pursed her lips, trying not to laugh.

"I realize you don't need me the way I need you—"

Emilia gasped in indignation. "No! Never say that!" She bit her lip. "I *do* need you. I want you. I love you." She paused again. "I love you more than I can say."

He smiled. "Another way we're equals. Because I love you madly, Millie." He cupped her face in his hands and kissed her again.

CHAPTER THIRTY-EIGHT

Three months later

"What do you think?"

Emilia looked out at the glittering room. The Marchioness of Westmorland had said the party would be small and intimate, but it was not. For one thing, it was in the Duke of Rowland's Berkeley Square mansion, which was neither small nor intimate. That should have been her first warning, she reflected, when Lady Westmorland mentioned her "little gathering" would be held at the home of her father-in-law, the duke. To Emilia's eyes, it was far too much.

But one could hardly say that to the hostess.

"It's beautiful beyond words," she said honestly.

Lady Westmorland beamed. Tall and slender with golden curls, the marchioness was a few years younger than Emilia, but vivacious and welcoming. "I'm so pleased you think so! This will be my first London party. We spent last summer at Salmsbury, and then the King died." Her husband was in the Home Office, and so had observed mourning for His Majesty a bit more carefully than most of London.

But she and Emilia had become friends, after the events with Fitchley. Nick had said something vague about Westmorland feeling he owed Nick a favor, but then the marchioness had come to call, and before Emilia knew it, she and the lady were laughing like old friends, calling each other by their Christian names. They discovered they had gone to the same school, only a few years apart, and both had many fond memories of Mrs. Upton's Academy.

"It's too kind of you to do this for us," Emilia began, but Georgiana waved it away.

"Rob and I are delighted to do it," she said. "We're both indebted to Mr. Dashwood—that is, Lord Sydenham!" She shook her head. "It will take me some time to think of him that way."

Emilia smiled ruefully. "I understand." She still barely remembered to respond when people said "Mrs. Dashwood," and soon she'd have to re-member "Lady Sydenham."

"I hope you don't mind," said Georgiana, "but I've invited two of my dearest friends tonight. They were with me at Mrs. Upton's, and are eager to make your acquaintance."

"Of course I don't mind, it *is* your party . . ."

Georgiana laughed. "No, no, it's for you and your husband! But Eliza and Hastings have only just returned to town—they've got a baby boy, and I thought they would never come back from Corn-wall—and Sophie and Ware are leaving soon to spend the winter in Somerset. We used to have tea together regularly, but now we're all married, and seeing each other is so much harder with husbands."

"I heard that." Lord Westmorland came up behind his wife and gave her a wicked little smile. "Confiding in Mrs. Dashwood how much trouble I cause you?"

"No one would believe me if I told them all the trouble you've caused me," she replied with a speaking look. She turned to Nick. "Has he recruited you to support his favored bills?"

Nick bowed his head. "He's tried, my lady."

Westmorland—who had told her and Nick to call him West—clasped his hands behind him and smiled. There was something a little dangerous in that smile, and Emilia remembered that Arabella had said the marquess used to be a terrible rogue and a rake, before he married. "I think I've got him, for Mr. Brougham's campaign."

Mr. Brougham was one of the leading campaigners of the abolitionist movement. Emilia knew Nick had given money to support it.

Nick just smiled.

The Westmorlands excused themselves to see to last-minute preparations. Nick drew Emilia to his side, his hand settling at the small of her back. Together they looked again at the decorated room.

It *was* glorious, with walls of robin's-egg blue, a soaring coffered ceiling edged by a frieze of peacocks and apple trees, and woodwork shining with golden gilt. Large planters had been grouped around the four marble pillars and a few trellises against the walls, with flowering vines trained to climb toward the ceiling. In the light of four crystal chandeliers, the room was stunning.

Small, intimate gathering, indeed.

"I believe Lady Westmorland hunted us quite deftly."

Emilia smiled. She knew "hunted" meant they'd been tricked, lured into a game they were meant to lose. "She's not a gambler."

"You'd be surprised," he murmured.

Charlotte hurried up to join them. She had been in the retiring room, fixing some drooping curls with the help of one of Georgiana's maids. "Oh, isn't it *beautiful*?" she said on a happy sigh, gazing at the trellised plants. "I've never seen anything lovelier!"

"Is it?" Nick affected surprise. "I've been too busy admiring the ladies to notice anything about the room."

Charlotte beamed. "You should be! We *are* splendid tonight." She certainly was, with her hair arranged in shining black curls and dressed high on her head. Her yellow silk dress was embroidered with gold spangles that sparked every time she moved, and around her neck she wore a strand of pearls. She was fifteen now, and they had told her she could stay for the first two hours of the party.

Nick gave his sister an approving look, then surveyed Emilia until she blushed. She did feel beautiful in her gown of aquamarine silk with a delicately embroidered gauze overlay. It floated when she moved and made her eyes look like the ocean—or so Nick had said. "Indeed you are," he murmured. "Magnificent, both of you."

Charlotte bobbed eagerly on her toes. "Oh, if

only Lucy could see this! May I go examine the flowers?"

Lucy had not come; she was at home with her babies. Two months previously, a little tortoiseshell cat had begun visiting the kitchen and mewing for scraps. Lucy and Charlotte had christened her Fleur, and last week Fleur had birthed four kittens under the scullery sink, three of whom bore a suspicious resemblance to Sir Chester. Lucy was in love. In exchange for promising she would practice her French by reading to the kittens every day, Nick had let her bring Fleur and the kittens up to the schoolroom, where they now resided in a large box Henry had built for them.

Emilia had worried Lucy would feel slighted, left out of the party, but she hadn't even wanted to come. "I think the kittens are about to open their eyes, and I must be there," she'd declared. "I'll tell you about it when you get home."

"Yes, you may. But guests will arrive soon," Emilia told Charlotte.

Charlotte grinned. "I'm watching for Lady Arabella. We have plans to make." She darted off.

Nick sighed. "Between Beaufort Hall and Lady Arabella, we'll be skint before Candlemas."

"Oh dear." Emilia pretended to frown. "Perhaps I've gone too far, buying gowns like this."

He growled next to her ear, his hand stealing around her waist. "No, no, I insist you buy more gowns like this. Tell me what you're wearing under it, so I have something pleasurable to tide me through this ordeal of proper behavior."

Emilia laughed. He only spent five nights a week at the Vega Club now, and was sometimes home at midnight; he claimed he was trying it on, being a respectable man with a family. He had made Tom Forbes a partner with a twenty percent stake, and he'd agreed to attend society events like this one on occasion, but Emilia couldn't forget the dark, dangerous scoundrel he really was. "You want to hear about my petticoat? It has no ruffles but there *is* a bit of lace . . ."

He made an approving sound. Emilia tapped her chin. "Perhaps I should mention the corset. It's very snug, but Arabella insisted it's the latest fashion for holding one's bosom appropriately. What do you think?" She turned toward Nick, whose gaze dropped straight to her low-cut bodice.

"It looks just right to me," he murmured.

"And then there's not much else to speak of," she said with an airy sigh. "Merely my shift, though it's not much at all, made of that fine lawn you can see right through"—Nick inhaled—"and my stockings, tied with green ribbons."

"Everything else is coming off, but those can stay on," he said under his breath. "How you do torment a man, Mrs. Dashwood."

"How you do provoke me, Mr. Dashwood," she replied with a saucy smile.

"Who could blame me?" He raised her hand to his lips, his eyes glittering with the promise of more.

"Carriages are arriving!" Georgiana called, and Emilia blushed scarlet. She and Nick had been married for eight weeks, and he delighted in leaving her hot and breathless at the most inopportune moments.

The evening was a whirlwind. Georgiana had invited several of her own friends, since Emilia had lost touch with everyone except Arabella; and some of West's, although Georgiana whispered that she ought to ignore most of them. "Particularly that one," she told Emilia as Viscount Heathercote sauntered away, giving Arabella an intense study as he passed her, while Arabella eyed him thoughtfully in turn. "He's a terrible rake."

"Yes, I see," murmured Emilia. Lord Heathercote was the man who'd offered to take away Lord Fitchley. Nick wouldn't tell her what Heathercote had done with the baron, but the *London Intelligencer* reported that Fitchley's racing stable was for sale, with offers to be submitted to a solicitor in Holborn. Fitchley himself had not been seen since that night.

Georgiana gave a little cry. "And here is Sophie! And Eliza!" She darted forward and embraced a dark-haired woman who'd just come in with a tall blond man. Another couple was behind them, shedding their cloaks.

"Who is that?" whispered Charlotte.

"I believe it is the Duke and Duchess of Ware. Very best manners, now."

Charlotte gave her an amused look. "You're not my governess still, Emilia."

Emilia sighed, but with a smile. "I keep forgetting that I cannot tell you what to do any longer! If only I had the same sway over a sister." Charlotte giggled.

Georgiana came back, arms linked with the new arrivals. "Mrs. Dashwood, Miss Dashwood, may I present to you the Duchess of Ware?"

"Sophie to my friends, please," said the dark-haired woman with an amused glance at Georgiana.

"And this is Lady Hastings," Georgiana added. "Otherwise known as Eliza."

The other woman, petite and curvy with

honey-blonde hair, smiled shyly. "It's a pleasure to make your acquaintance. Georgiana's told us so much about you both."

"Oh, what did she tell?" asked Charlotte, too eagerly. Emilia touched her arm. They hadn't rehearsed meeting a duchess or a countess.

"She said you are good-hearted and brave, and we admire that tremendously," said Sophie. "Mrs. Upton would be proud."

Emilia smiled. "I hope so. Mrs. Upton meant a great deal to me."

"And to all of us," put in Georgiana.

"We wanted you to know that you have our support—and friendship, if you wish—as the new Lady Sydenham," said Eliza. "It's always helpful to have friends in this society."

"Yes," said Emilia ruefully. "Thank you. It's lovely to have friends."

"I should warn you, our husbands are off cornering Mr. Dashwood right now," said Sophie.

"Why?" Charlotte had restrained herself, avidly studying Lady Hastings's gorgeous sapphire gown and the duchess's hairstyle, but now she looked intrigued by the conversation. "Everyone we've met tonight says they owe Nick a favor. Did he teach them all how to cheat?"

"No," said Lady Hastings at once, and Georgiana laughed.

"Perhaps," murmured the duchess with a smile and a wink at Charlotte.

"Is he very good at cheating?" asked Georgiana with interest.

"So good no one can ever catch him at it." Charlotte grinned. "Not that he would cheat Lord Westmorland!"

Georgiana laughed merrily. "Oh my, West would be very intrigued to see him try . . ."

"He's not teaching anyone how to cheat," said Emilia, flushing. "No one is cheating. Stop speaking of cheating, Charlotte."

"Until later, that is," whispered Georgiana. "Then you must tell me all about it. But you may trust me when I say we all owe Mr. Dashwood a great deal."

Emilia looked at them, three beautiful, elegant women married to wealthy, powerful men. "What sort of debt?" she asked nervously.

The three of them exchanged glances. "We all met our husbands because of the Vega Club," said Eliza.

"There may have been some scandalous wagers involved," murmured Sophie.

Emilia thought back to the night she'd drunk too much wine and brandy and brazenly dared Nick to make a wager. She said nothing.

"But Mr. Dashwood was tremendously forbearing and helpful when we needed it most," put in Georgiana hastily. "And voilà! We all ended up married, partly thanks to him."

"Oh, I see! Then they are *desperately* indebted to him," declared Charlotte.

Sophie laughed. Eliza blushed. Georgiana linked her arm through Charlotte's. "Have they talked to you of schools yet?"

Charlotte's eyes grew round. "No."

Georgiana lowered her voice confidentially. "If you want to go to the best school for young ladies in England, you shall have three references from us."

"And Lucy?" asked Charlotte eagerly. "My little sister?"

"Of course," declared Georgiana. "We are always expanding our sisterhood."

The four others fell into an easy conversation—Charlotte was asking more questions than was polite, but Emilia didn't have to heart to stop her. Sophie, Eliza, and Georgiana were openly encouraging the girl, and it couldn't hurt for Charlotte to make friends of them.

She looked across the room to where Nick was, indeed, cornered by the duke, the marquess, and the earl. He was listening intently to whatever they were saying, but he caught her eye. Lord Hastings said something that made the rest of them laugh, and in that moment Nick gave her a sly wink.

Emilia couldn't keep from smiling in reply. How she loved that man. He captivated her, heart and soul.

She told him so when he found her a short time later. He grinned. "The most valuable thing I've ever won in my life!"

She faced him, somber for a moment. "You have," she said in a low voice. "When I think how we began—"

He nodded. "With you telling me I would be an idiot not to agree to your proposition."

"And how cold-hearted I thought you were—"

"An uncouth cardsharp, yes."

"Which was all *wrong*—let me finish," she protested, laughing in spite of herself. "I was entirely wrong about you!"

He slid one arm around her waist as he drew her behind one of the planters, into the cover of the climbing vines. "I was entirely *right* about you," he murmured, touching one fingertip to her chin. "I knew the moment I laid eyes on you, I was in trouble. 'Nick old man,' I told myself, 'that woman is too intelligent and determined for you to resist, and so beautiful and passionate that you're going to make a damned fool of yourself over her.'"

"You did not," she exclaimed.

He raised his brows in a sly, knowing look.

She blushed. "Did you cheat, when you made me play cards?" she asked on impulse.

Nick blinked. "What—?"

"Charlotte says you're very good at cheating," she told him, "so good no one can ever catch you at it. And I wondered if perhaps you didn't take more of a role in that card game, that night I came to the club, than I thought."

He looked at her for a moment. "The one where you thrashed me as a reckless gambler, refusing to take responsibility for my actions but blaming all my choices on cards and dice?"

"You mentioned the dice," she pointed out.

Nick grinned. "Of course I cheated."

Emilia's mouth dropped open, but then she laughed. "You scoundrel!"

"I told you I was, the night we met." His grin faded. "You're right—I did want you to win that wager, because I couldn't let you walk away."

"*How?*" she demanded, both appalled and delighted. "I dealt the cards!"

He winked at her. "I didn't believe in luck—or in scruples." He touched her lip as she drew breath. "But . . . I was wrong. Nothing I ever did in my life should have earned me this much happiness. Luck is the only explanation for how I ended up here, with you. With Charlotte, and Lucy, and even all this." He glanced dubiously around the elegant room.

She gripped his wrist. "It wasn't luck."

He leaned his forehead against hers, clasping her hand to his heart. "Whatever it was, I'm damned fortunate."

Emilia's heart gave another sigh. "It was fate."

THE WAGERS OF SIN

What happens at the infamous Vega Club . . .

MY ONCE AND FUTURE DUKE
The Duke of Ware does not gamble—ever. But to
separate his younger brother from the tempting
Sophie Campbell, the duke makes a breathtakingly
scandalous wager. When it comes to love, though,
all bets are off.

AN EARL LIKE YOU
Heiress Eliza Cross has given up hope of true love
and marriage. When the handsome Earl of Hastings
sweeps her off her feet and proposes, it seems too
good to be true . . . and it just might be. Gambling
with love means risking your heart.

WHEN THE MARQUESS WAS MINE
Lady Georgiana Lucas hates the Marquess of
Westmorland--no, *despises* him. But when he turns
up beaten unconscious with no memory of who he
is, Georgiana calls him her fiancé to help him—only

for the marquess to wake up, and make Georgiana
wish it were true.

THANK YOU FOR READING!

If you enjoyed this story, I hope you'll consider leaving a review or rating online to help other readers.

If you would like access to special previews, exclusive giveaways, and my very latest news, join my VIP Readers list at www.CarolineLinden.com. New members get a free exclusive short story as a welcome gift.

ABOUT THE AUTHOR

Caroline Linden was born a reader, not a writer. She earned a math degree from Harvard University and wrote computer software before turning to writing fiction. Since then the Boston Red Sox have won the World Series four times, which is not related but still worth mentioning. Her books have won the NEC Reader's Choice Award, the Daphne du Maurier Award, the NJRW Golden Leaf Award, and RWA's RITA Award, and have been translated into seventeen languages. She lives in New England.